KAYAK

KRISTAL STITTLE

Cover art by Kerisson Wemerson
Interior Illustrations by Blacky Shepherd
Edited by Alex Woodroe

Published by Tenebrous Press.
Visit our website at www.tenebrouspress.com.

First Printing, February 2026.

Print ISBN: 978-1-959790-57-0
eBook ISBN: 978-1-959790-58-7

Cover art by Kerisson Wemerson.

Interior illustrations by Blacky Shepherd.

Edited by Alex Woodroe.

Formatting by Lori Michelle Booth.

All creators in this publication have signed an AI-free agreement. To the best of our knowledge, this publication is free from machine-generated content.

Selected Works from Tenebrous Press:

Dear Stupid Penpal—Rascal Hartley

Clairviolence: Tales of Tarot and Torment—Mo Moshaty

Reef Life—Hazel Zorn

Puppet's Banquet—Valkyrie Loughcrewe

Casual—Koji A. Dae

All Your Friends are Here—M.Shaw

TRVE CVLT—Michael Bettendorf

A Spectre is Haunting Greentree—Carson Winter

From the Belly—Emmett Nahil

Mouth—Joshua Hull

Lumberjack—Anthony Engebretson

Posthaste Manor—Jolie Toomajan & Carson Winter

The Black Lord—Colin Hinckley

Dehiscent—Ashley Deng

More titles at www.TenebrousPress.com

For Patty
and our time on the water

1:
NOW

WHEN HE FINALLY stopped paddling, the only sounds Keith could hear were the rushing pound of his own heartbeat, and the screaming of the cicadas. He could no longer scream with them. Exertion had stolen his voice over an hour ago. He'd been paddling for so long that his tears had dried on his face.

He was in a bay, an unfamiliar one. Just how far had he come? His arms ached, hanging from his shoulders like leaden weights. His hands were cramped, and patches of skin had been rubbed raw. Balancing the paddle across the kayak, he dipped his fingers into the water on either side. It was blessedly cool, and he relished the feeling as it crawled up to his wrists.

There was no one else around. In the lull of the cicada songs, there were only birds. No voices, no splashing. Had *no one* else escaped? Or had they just gone another way?

Keith had no idea where he was. He hadn't been paying attention; all he'd been able to do was flee. His memories were a wash of white noise, his body having driven itself onward entirely on instinct.

I'm alone, Keith realized. It didn't shock him, he was too drained for such a strong reaction, he merely accepted the fact.

For months, he'd expected to find himself on his own. Despite his supposed mental preparations, he now stalled, unsure what to do next.

Take an inventory, he decided. Before figuring out his next step, he should see what he had to work with.

The kayak was the most important thing. About eight and a

half feet long, maybe two feet wide, the bright green plastic boat had saved his life. On either end were black plastic pull handles attached by short ropes, and, closer, a stretchy sort of bungee rope for holding items down; the length of this at the rear was over a depression for holding larger items, but that was currently empty. Behind the rear pull handle was a black plug for draining, which Keith hoped he'd never have to use. Inside the nose of the kayak, two rails ran along either side for the adjustable footrests. The backrest of his otherwise moulded seat was also adjustable: a flexible bit of black plastic wrapped in a padded fabric. He could change the amount of give by using the straps that threaded through the buckles just ahead of his body on either side. The only other thing built into the kayak was the seat's moulded cup holder between his legs.

The second most important item he possessed was his paddle. The fifty-inch body was aluminum with a black coating, and at either end was a nineteen-inch white plastic paddle. There were little rubber rings near the paddle heads, but no one had ever told Keith what they were for. In the middle of the paddle, the aluminum could be taken apart using a simple button connector to make two pieces. The six holes the button could latch into would allow him to change the overall length by about two inches, or the angle of the paddle blades to one another. The fact that the paddle could come apart made nighttime storage easier.

Night. That was still hours away. Based on the height of the sun, it was around noon. Keith hadn't noticed it until then, but his skin was feeling rather warm. He needed to find some shade, but first he wanted to finish his inventory.

Tucked into the nose of the kayak was a blue and yellow lifejacket. As a strong swimmer, Keith thought it wouldn't be very useful, but he might be able to hold it above his head to keep some of the sun off.

Reaching his hands under the seat, he found two plastic pillars supporting the front edge. He pushed deeper under the seat between them, where the tips of his fingers brushed against an unexpected obstacle. He thought he'd find nothing, but there was something made of a hard, smooth plastic, different from the boat. He couldn't get a grip on it.

"I need to be in a better position," he told himself. His voice rasped, still sore from his earlier screaming.

After balancing the paddle behind him, Keith pulled his legs up out of the kayak and hung them over the side. He twisted sideways, crunching his body as he attempted to get his arm farther under the seat. With his face mashed into the plastic rim of the seat opening, Keith was able to grab the object. When he pulled, however, it snagged against the pillars. The kayak rocked precariously from his efforts, one of his feet dipping into the lake.

"Fuck!" Keith cried out, trying to steady himself.

He abandoned the object, as keeping the kayak from tilting so much that it filled with water was far more important. There was a rumble through the plastic as the paddle slid off the back into the lake.

"No, no, no, no, no!" Keith nearly threw himself into the water as he lunged to grab his only means of propulsion. The kayak wobbled again, but this time he could see it happen. The craft was more stable than it felt, the water not getting nearly as close to the lip as he had thought.

Clutching the paddle to his chest and taking several deep breaths, Keith attempted to calm himself. If the kayak sank, he would almost certainly die. He needed to be more careful.

This time, he tucked the paddle under the bungee cords on the nose. Before twisting about again, he checked to see if he could reach the object from a normal sitting position, since he had managed to pull it forward. Turned out he could, and he was grateful. The thing wasn't meant to go under the seat, and he couldn't get it to squeeze between the pillars. Probing with his fingers, he determined it was a small bucket with a lid. He untwisted the solid lid, which was lined with finger deep ridges and was at least an inch wider than the bucket. Once that was off, he could squish the bucket a little and finally pry the thing free.

A boat safety kit. The bright orange, eight inch long plastic container could be used as a bailing bucket, and inside the lid was a reflective surface for flashing signals. That would probably be more useful than the waterproof flashlight: Keith discovered that no one had bothered to put any batteries in it. There was also a pea-less whistle, and a fifty-foot length of yellow tow rope that had a clip on one end and a plastic floater on the other.

Worth the struggle, Keith thought as he panted.

That was it for the kayak. Everything else he had was on his person: a grey T-shirt, now sweat-stained, and a pair of blue swim trunks. On his wrist, he wore his dad's watch. It couldn't tell the time anymore, but it was all he had left of the man. He shoved those thoughts away, just as he did that morning's memories. He had gotten good at hiding things from himself.

While taking this inventory, Keith had drifted. He was still at least twenty feet from shore, but that was more than close enough to hear the low, rumbling growl.

He whipped his head around toward the source of the sound, and there it was. A fucking dirt devil. The reason Keith, and everyone else, hadn't been able to safely set foot on dry land for the past year.

2:
THEN

"**B**EDTIME," DAD TOLD KEITH, his head stuck in through the open bedroom door.

"What? I thought I got to stay up to watch."

Dad snorted when he laughed. "You thought that, did you? Not on a school night."

"*Everyone* I know is going to watch."

"Yeah, on YouTube in the morning, just like you will be. Watching it live will only make you tired, and it's a school night. Maybe if it were the weekend I'd help you win over Mom, but it's not, so bed."

Keith grumbled and moaned. He was sixteen, why did he even still have a bedtime?

"Turn that off," Dad gestured to his laptop. "Teeth, pajamas, under the covers. You get caught trying to watch, and it'll be no more electronics in your bedroom."

"*Dad.*"

"Hey, I didn't make the rule. Take it up with your mother if you disagree. Now let's go, into bed, hustle, hustle, hustle." He clapped like he was still coaching Keith's Timbits Soccer team.

Keith just rolled his eyes. He knew he still had an hour before lights out, there was no reason to rush. Mom always insisted he spend his time before sleeping reading an actual paper book. She constantly complained that he was straining his eyes by looking at screens all day, and that it was bad for his sleep patterns not to keep his distance from them before bed. Because of her job, she spent more time in front of a screen than he did.

He went through the routine of getting ready for bed,

including shouting a goodnight from the top of the stairs. Both his parents replied simultaneously with their own goodnights. It had taken awhile, but Keith was glad he had taught his parents early on that they didn't have to come say goodnight in person. Even as a little kid, he hadn't been keen on the forehead kisses, and the overly tucked blankets. As quickly as he could, he had claimed the night for himself. Unlike his best friend, Russell, whose mom still saw him to bed every night she was there, and sat on the foot of his mattress for a couple of minutes, asking him about his day.

Two books currently occupied Keith's nightstand. One was a book his mom wanted him to read, the other was the next in an epic fantasy series he'd been making his way through for the better part of two years. He read one chapter of the former before plunging into the latter. The time when he was supposed to stop reading slipped by. When he noticed, he debated whether he could get away with starting the next chapter, but since he had expressed his desire to watch the meteorite, he knew his parents would be on alert for him trying to stay up late. Instead, he set a new alarm on his phone before switching off the light.

Like most other teenage males he knew, Keith was a heavy sleeper. Even when he knew he'd be waking up earlier than usual, he was almost completely out by the time his mom cracked open his door. He knew this, and had made sure to set his alarm for fifteen minutes before the event, giving him plenty of time to rouse himself. He didn't really need that much time, as his excitement leapt into his brain the moment he heard his alarm.

Texting Russell, he learned he had done the same thing as Keith, and when they got invited to a group chat, it seemed like most of their year was there, along with a few others from ahead of them and others from behind. Some had permission to watch but most didn't. When he and Russell joined, people were making jokes about three guys who had been crashing at one house, and had tried to stay awake the whole time. They might have made it, had they not gotten drunk and passed out. The meteorite would strike shortly after three a.m.

In the list of members who were a part of the chat, Keith spotted Aisling's name, and found himself sitting up straighter. She wasn't the prettiest girl in school, but she was smart as a whip, with a tongue that could lash just as painfully. Best to be on guard with her listening in. He sent a private message to Russell, just in case he hadn't noticed.

Mandy wasn't on the list, which was both disappointing and a relief. Keith wouldn't have to worry about saying anything that made him look stupid, and he'd *want* to say something, anything, if he knew she might read it.

A creak out in the hallway had Keith laying his phone flat on his mattress, jammed under the covers. He closed his eyes, pretending to sleep, hoping whatever parent it was didn't notice that he was propped up on his pillows more than usual. At least he'd had the wherewithal to keep his phone on silent.

The sound didn't come toward his room. Instead, Keith heard a creaking on the stairs. His parents were sneaking down to watch the meteorite on the big TV. Keith shook his head, wishing he had thought to grab his laptop earlier.

With less than a minute to go, Keith switched over to the live feed. The chat had started to go pretty silent anyway. The talking heads had stopped, so there was nothing easy to make fun of. Now, NASA was just showing a view of the island from a camera placed on a second, nearby island. A countdown ticked away in the corner. It was a wholly unexciting shot. Dark blue ocean, early morning sky, and a big mound of rock and dirt wedged between the two. It was an uninhabited island that some sea birds used as a breeding colony. Luckily for the birds, their nesting season didn't begin until next month, although where they were going to go after this was anyone's guess. Scientists had already crawled all over the island, making sure no rare forms of life were hiding in any crevices, and placing instruments that had low odds of survival.

It happened fast. So very, very fast. Keith barely saw the streak that appeared only for a couple of frames. Not long enough for him to even realize it was anything before *WHAM!* A blinding light, and the feed jumped to another camera on a ship that was even farther away.

The Atlantic had been relatively calm before, but now it was surging, the view rocking with the ship it was attached to. Within the swinging, Keith saw dirt and steam being hurled into the air.

Another feed, this time an aerial shot from an extreme distance. The ships below were tiny specks as they fought the sudden tides. First the waves were pushed outward by the blast, and then there was a sucking inward as the ocean rushed back to fill the void left behind. Debris towered into the sky, spreading as it struck the upper atmosphere. And then the plane shuddered as the blast wave hit it. Miles and miles away, and the roaring air pressure was still enough to shake the craft.

The feed stayed with the airplane for a minute. Two minutes. Three minutes. Keith simply stared. A chunk of the Earth had just been vaporized. It was really only by chance that NASA had spotted the rock coming before it reached them, that they had had enough time to alert people and set up all these cameras. Keith shivered in his warm bed. How easy it would be for another rock, a bigger one, to catch them completely unawares and wipe them out. That was how the dinosaurs had died.

As the feed returned to the talking heads, Keith was fearing the wrong thing.

3:
NOW

BY THE TIME Keith had paddled out to the middle of the bay, the dirt devil had retreated out of sight. It had been an unnecessary reminder of why Keith needed to take care of his kayak. He could only swim for so long, even with the lifejacket.

The sun was hot. In an attempt to keep it off his back, he held the lifejacket up for some shade.

Now that he had inventoried everything, he needed a plan. The winter house was gone, there was no going back there, but he could turn around and search for other survivors. He doubted he'd find anyone. His memory was admittedly scattered, but he'd been alone by the boats. He had been right beside them when the attack occurred, and had immediately taken off.

"Coward," he chastised himself. He'd been taught to do just as he had done, but he was still a coward, nevertheless. He hadn't stopped to help anyone. Thinking about it now, he hadn't needed to paddle as far as he had. He could've waited nearby and still been perfectly safe. Instead he had run, he'd fled, just paddling and paddling until he'd ended up here. Wherever here was. He had no clue; he was completely lost.

Guilt, like a great and winding worm, shifted inside him.

Keith wanted to go back. To go looking for others who surely must have gotten away just as he had. He should have stopped and turned around long ago, but there was nothing to prevent him from doing it now. This was a mistake that he could correct. Others he couldn't—he couldn't even think of them right now—but this one he could.

His shoulders still ached, forcing him to take it easy. He paddled slowly back toward the channel he'd taken to reach this small bay, grateful that the current and wind were with him. The lifejacket refused to stay balanced on his head, so he eventually tucked it in behind him as extra padding for the backrest. Hopefully, whoever he found first had some sunscreen, or maybe an umbrella. This was the worst time of the day to be out, when the only shade clung to the shoreline, closer to dry land than Keith could safely get.

It wasn't very far down the channel when Keith came to his first conundrum. The thing forked. He looked left, and he looked right, and neither direction was any more familiar than the other.

"Shit," he muttered. He didn't normally talk to himself this much, but even just cursing made him feel less alone.

He turned the kayak around, hoping he'd see the land around him the way he would have seen it while travelling that way. He paddled to one side, and then over to the other. Again, there was no recognition.

"Remember!" he commanded himself, but could not. There was just a black hole there, flanked by the guilt worm. When he thought of his escape, all he could see was the nose of the kayak in front of him. His body remembered the journey as pain, while his eyes had retained nothing.

He was going to have to guess. Keith chose the right, figuring he might have been able to remember the big rock along the left if he had come from that direction. He was kidding himself, of course, it was just a ruse to make himself feel more confident about his decision. The fact that he knew that this was what he was trying to do, meant that it didn't work.

Because the current and the wind continued to be with him, Keith didn't paddle much. Most of the time, he just made sure he kept to the middle, pointed the right way, and allowed nature to bear him along. He spent most of the time studying the land, hoping for something, anything, that would spark a sense of familiarity.

Another dirt devil appeared. Or maybe it was the same one, because it was on the same shore as before. Keith glared at the beast. This one was six feet at the shoulder. Jan called the big ones adults, although no one had ever proven whether the smaller ones were younger. No parenting had ever been noticed by anyone Keith had ever talked to, and it wasn't like the little ones were any less vicious. Besides, how could there be adults and children already? They'd only been here a year.

The dirt devil followed Keith. Its scissored claws, not quite talons, clattered and scraped whenever it crossed bare rock. When there was soil beneath, the beast was silent. No growling this time, just an intense watchfulness. That was the physical part Keith hated most about the things: the intelligence in their gaze. Even with their strange eyes—bright blue sclera, white irises, and cross-shaped pupils—you could tell when they were watching. When they were studying. Those alien things *thought*.

Keith kept to the middle of the channel. He wanted to move to the far side, but worried there might be another dirt devil in hiding over there, that the one watching him was trying to drive him in that direction. To push him into a trap.

Maybe it was. Maybe it was trapping him, but not in the way Keith had imagined. He became so focused on the dirt devil that he stopped paying attention to what was right in front of him.

Keith was moving faster. Even when he didn't paddle at all, the kayak was borne along at a greater speed than before. When he finally noticed, he tore his gaze away from the dirt devil to face a very different kind of horror.

He definitely hadn't come this way before. He was headed for some rapids.

4: THEN

"**ARE YOU _STILL_** talking about the meteorite?" Keith wanted to slap his hand over Russell's mouth before his friend could answer, but it was too late.

"Yeah. Did you know that there's still dust from the impact up in the atmosphere? Every continent will have at least a little bit on it by the time it settles." Russell had always been interested in space, to the point that he hadn't caught Aisling's sneer as she walked up to them, and had answered her honestly.

"Not Antarctica." It was an unexpected reply from her. "The experts aren't sure if any will land there."

"I read a report this morning that claims a bunch of scientists down there found some foreign particles on the Antarctic peninsula."

Aisling's severe brows pinched together. "Show me."

"Sure." Russell brought out his phone and started searching for the article he'd mentioned.

Keith could only stand there, trying to keep his mouth from falling open as he felt more befuddled than he ever had in his life. The Athenian goddess of horror stood six feet tall, putting her a full head above the much softer formed Russell. She leaned down to peer at his phone over his shoulder, her eyes of judgement darting back and forth as she read.

"Huh," she eventually said, straightening back up. "Can you send that to me? I want to check their sources."

"Sure! I don't think I have your number though."

Aisling took his phone from him and did it herself, a chime from her pocket alerting them to her success. Then she strode away, other kids in the hall swiftly stepping to either side as she approached.

"Dude!" Keith hissed at his friend.

"What?"

"Dude! That was fucking Aisling O'Connor, are you fucking kidding me?"

Russell just shrugged like it was no big deal, but his face was smeared with a shit-eating grin. "I guess she's still interested in meteorite stuff."

Most people they knew had lost interest pretty quickly. For a whole sleep-deprived day, it had been all anyone could talk about, especially with all the new videos from various angles being released on the internet. The day after that, it was more subdued, having to compete with the latest crop of must-see TikToks. Then a celebrity couple broke up, the one playing a couple on the show every girl seemed to be watching, and there was intense speculation about what that would mean for the series. By the time the week had ended and Monday rolled around, no one but the space nerds still cared. And Keith, since he was best friends with a space nerd. Frankly, thinking about space too much left him feeling small and terrified. Russell had dreamed of becoming an astronaut since he could say the word star, but Keith would much rather stay where the air didn't come out of a can, and a broken window wasn't going to kill you. Still, he admired his friend's sense of purpose and dedication. Keith was only just now learning to drive a car, and his friend already knew how to pilot a small airplane.

The bell rang.

"See you at lunch," Russell called out, hurrying off to his first period of the day, an advanced level math class. Keith had English, much more his speed. He spent most of his time in first period admiring the back of Mandy's head, where she sat one row over and three seats ahead of him. In his daydreams Mandy would struggle with the reading and come to him for help with the assignments. Then he'd show her the comic he was working on, and she'd be impressed.

Second period was marketing, and by the end of it, everyone was on their phones, the teacher included. The first reports of monsters had hit the internet.

5:
NOW

E TRIED TO paddle the other way, but his arms and shoulders were just so sore, and the current was already too strong. Keith swung his little plastic boat back around to face the rapids again, knowing he had no choice but to ride them out. Grabbing the lifejacket, he strapped it around his body and made sure all the buckles were tight.

Ahead wasn't the kind of white water rapids extreme kayakers liked to tackle, but they were more than anything Keith had ever attempted before. He didn't even know what kind of water his kayak could handle. From his understanding, this thing had been built for beginners to paddle around in calm waters, exploring swamps and stuff. Well, it was time to see what both he and the boat were capable of.

The first challenge was easy. Keith didn't have to do much to avoid a boulder sticking up out of the water. The channel was still wide, and the current did most of the work. Or was it now a river? Without a map, Keith would never know. The specificity of waterway nomenclature was not one of his strong suits.

The water got faster, and the way got narrower. Maybe these were white waters after all. Keith had to focus, barely able to look more than a few feet in front of him as he searched for shallow rocks. The kayak rode high, he could glide over most obstacles, but one sharp point could sink him. He fought to stay in the deeper water as swirls and eddies attempted to pull him elsewhere.

A small dip shot his kayak's nose into a hump of rushing water, spraying him in the face, and leaving a small puddle inside his boat. He tried to avoid those after that, not wanting to get flooded, but this was easier said than done. The river had a mind of its own. Several times, Keith found himself rolling dangerously to one side or the other, even slopping in more water on occasion. He heard the scrape of rocks as they brushed against his hull, but his heart rate couldn't climb any higher than it already had. His mind was on fire as he battled the water, his muscles screaming in the distance where he had no choice but to ignore them.

A sluice caught him, briefly blinding Keith when its spray slapped him in the face. By the time he shook the water free, he found himself spinning out of control, turning sideways to the current and headed for a rock.

With a scream, he lashed out with his paddle, striking the rock. He pushed himself back around, and then found a bit of reprieve. A tiny swirling whirlpool was off to one side. Keith drifted into the middle of it, the water turning him in place as he attempted to steady himself.

There were more rapids ahead. He took a breather, trying to give himself time to think. He grabbed the emergency kit, dumped the contents into his lap, and started to bail while he thought.

It would be so easy to get onto the shore. The little whirlpool swirled about an alcove of flat rock. Keith could probably stand in the shallow water if he wanted to. It would be so easy just to climb out and drag his kayak ashore. He imagined other people had done the same once upon a time.

There were no dirt devils in sight, but that didn't mean they weren't lingering nearby. His choices were to risk them, or to risk the rough water some more. For Keith, that wasn't a choice at all. Against the river, he stood a chance.

When he had bailed out as much of the water as he could, Keith returned everything to the container except the tow rope. Balancing carefully, he clipped one end to the pull handle on the back of the kayak. After a generous length, he tied a crude knot around himself, and then to the paddle. He might fall out, or the boat might sink, but at least he wouldn't lose it. He figured losing the kayak was more deadly than any dangers the rope connecting him to it might present.

He couldn't see much of the water ahead. Not far beyond his little whirlpool, it took a hard bend around a spit of cliff. The water moved fast into the bend, but he couldn't see any rocks from where he sat. What he could see, was the way the water climbed the far side, riding part way up another cliff before crashing back down again. He'd have to avoid that if he could, try to stay along the inner corner.

There was no sense in waiting around. Keith found the stream of water that left the whirlpool and pushed himself into it, rejoining the current.

He tried to tell himself that it was like a water slide, but that idea was only able to survive for a couple of seconds. Luckily, Keith found himself capable of outliving it.

Despite his efforts to hug the inner wall of the corner, he was drawn away by the force of the current. It was either go with the flow or get rolled. At least he managed to avoid climbing the wall.

There was barely any time to think. Keith was forced to trust his instincts as he barrelled along down the river, doing his best to dodge rocks both hidden and visible. A few times he lurched through what he thought of as pits, believing for a moment that he was going to be buried in water. The kayak took a couple of hard knocks, each one making Keith grit his teeth, but his craft held together. If that had been his body, he'd have been shattered.

A brief pool of calm appeared, giving Keith just enough time to look a little farther forward. A smooth edge. Some sort of waterfall lay ahead. Not a big one, but enough to cause Keith to grab either side of his kayak with his paddle pinned under his arms, and tilt his body backward in the hopes that he could keep the nose up. And then he went over. The drop lasted only a second, maybe two, but Keith had no idea what he was going to land on. Would he be caught by deep water? Or were there pointed rocks stretching up to break him? A second or two, just long enough to consider his mortality.

Then *slap*, he impacted on water. The kayak's nose bumped into a rock immediately afterward, spinning Keith around. He felt his tail dip, but instead of another sheer waterfall, this was just a quick slide down an angled rock face. Backwards and out of control he shot down the river for a few harrowing seconds, and then it was over.

The river spit him out into the side of a wide channel. The current weakened, leaving him slowly drifting. Sodden, but alive.

6:
THEN

IT'S RUSSIA, it's gotta be fake." By the end of the school day, this was the general consensus. To believe otherwise was to believe in literal monsters.

"They have a lot of wild dogs there," Renly spouted off to anyone who would listen, as if he were some sort of authority on the matter. "It's like Bigfoot."

"Some of these videos are a lot clearer than Bigfoot," Keith pointed out. "And that thing was way too big to be a dog."

"They film the fucking dogs, and then digitally alter them, duh." Renly rolled his eyes.

The two of them were walking home with Russell.

"You've been quiet," Keith mentioned to his best friend.

"Huh?" Russell looked up from his phone, not having listened to anything Keith and Renly had been discussing.

"What are you looking at?" Keith asked. Russell had had his nose glued to his phone the entire way.

"Russian news."

"You can read Russian?" Renly scoffed.

"No." Russell was peering at his phone again. "I'm trying to see if it exists."

"If what exists? The monster things?" Keith wondered.

Russell shook his head. "Russian news. New Russian news."

"I don't follow," Keith admitted.

"Yeah, man, speak normally," Renly added.

Russell took a breath. "Ever since those videos started hitting YouTube, I can't seem to find any Russian news. Like, their official channels went dark."

"So?" Renly shrugged. "It's Russia. They're always as dark as your asshole."

"No," Russell huffed, becoming exasperated. "There's always news. Even here, even if it's just propaganda, there's news. But right now there's nothing."

"Take it easy, buddy." Keith patted his shoulder. "If something were actually happening in Russia, wouldn't our own media be covering it?"

"They are."

That made both Keith and Renly pause.

"That's why I started looking," Russell elaborated. "They were the ones who mentioned the lack of news, so I decided to see for myself. They're right, there's nothing."

"Wouldn't, like, CNN or whoever-the-fuck have embedded reporters in Russia?" Renly asked.

"I think so," Russell agreed. "Nothing on CNN has mentioned a loss of contact with one of their own, but they also haven't mentioned receiving any word from them either."

Keith couldn't help it; he took out his phone and started skimming headlines. Most of them were about the videos, but a few had cropped up about the Russian silence. His eye caught a headline from the BBC, about another of these videos coming out of Brazil, but he didn't have time to click on it.

"Russell! Russell!"

All three boys turned as Aisling rushed toward them on her bike.

"Russell, did you see?" She screeched to a halt beside him.

"See what?"

"Look." She handed over her phone.

Keith attempted to peek over his shoulder, but a glare from Aisling made him take a step back instead.

"Do you see it?" she asked Russell.

"How old is this?" Russell asked in return.

"What are they talking about?" Renly whispered rather loudly to Keith.

Keith shrugged as Aisling continued speaking to Russell. "Since it happened."

"Are they friends?" Renly then asked, although another shrug was the only response Keith could give him.

"Holy cheese!" Russell cried out. Unlike Renly, he was hard-wired not to swear.

"You see it now?"

"Yeah! Holy fudge! Does NASA know?"

"Of course they know, but you think they're going to say anything right now? Not a chance."

"How did you find this?"

"The timing was suspicious, so I went looking for it."

"Can someone please fill us in?" Keith asked as politely as he could.

"The winds," Aisling put bluntly, as if that explained anything.

"Russell?" Keith hoped his friend would be a little clearer.

"So, the meteorite, right?"

"I remember."

"Yeah. Remember how we talked about the winds before? How some particles from the impact could end up settling on every continent?"

"Jury's still out on Antarctica," Aisling interrupted.

"Right. Anyway, based on the impact site and the winds at the time, the first place a bunch of that stuff would settle on is Russia."

"You think the meteorite is connected to those videos from Russia?"

"You don't?" Aisling scoffed.

"You think they're *aliens*?" Renly started howling with laughter. He didn't even notice the way Aisling tensed up, her right hand curling into a fist.

"Could be aliens," Russell said, the insult rolling right off his back. "They'd have to be seriously fast growing if that were the case. Might be something smaller, too. Like a microbe that causes a mutation. They could still be dogs, just messed up ones."

Renly had almost interrupted, but Aisling's threatening step toward him had him clicking his teeth back together before a word got out.

Keith thought of the headline then, the one about Brazil. He was about to ask about that when the explosion happened.

7:
NOW

IF KEITH THOUGHT his muscles had been sore before, then this was them in revolt. There was no position in which his shoulders didn't feel like they were going to pop free of his sockets, at least not one he could find in the kayak. Every time he tried to move them, he had to grit his teeth against the waves of agony. The feeling from his hips told him they'd been bruised by the times he'd been thrown into the sides of the kayak, and if that weren't enough, he also felt dizzy. His stomach was prepared to eject its contents at a moment's notice. Keith had felt this way once before, during gym class. He'd been determined to outdistance Renly during the twelve-minute run. He'd succeeded, and promptly puked on the grass afterward. He wanted to puke now, but couldn't risk it, not knowing when his next meal would be.

He had to get out of the kayak. If he could find a place to lie down, that would be perfect. There was no way he could paddle any farther, though.

Fighting the pain, and being as careful as he could, Keith climbed out of the boat and slipped into the lake. The chill was refreshing, and the life jacket made him comfortably buoyant. He needed to use only his legs to move around, which, while tired from bracing against the inside of the kayak, weren't nearly as whipped as his arms. With the rope still connecting him to both boat and paddle, he didn't worry about being separated, and took a moment to enjoy floating there.

Eventually, he had to move. He needed to bail out the kayak again, and come up with a new plan. There was no way he was going to be able to get back up through the rapids.

After making sure the paddle was secure inside the body of the boat, Keith unclipped the rope from the rear pull handle and moved it to the front. Then he started swimming. He didn't use his arms, he just floated on his back and kicked with his legs. Progress was slow, with the kayak moving in jerks, but it was progress. Every few minutes, Keith rolled over to search for tiny islands or rocks near the surface. When he didn't spot one, he'd flip onto his back again and keep kicking, following the current while paying a lot more attention to its speed.

It took long enough that Keith started feeling chilly by the time he found a rock. He climbed up on top of it, but couldn't get completely out of the water. It was a long wedge, slippery with algae, and he hoped he didn't encounter any zebra mussels as he balanced himself on top. The rock was submerged enough for more than half his hipbones to remain underwater while sitting upright.

The iliac crest, Keith thought, remembering the anatomy lessons he'd gotten from the internet while trying to improve his character artwork. *My iliac crests are above the water.* And they hurt equally on both sides.

The rock stretched away to the shore, where it eventually broke the surface, but Keith wasn't going to risk getting any closer to dry land than he was already.

Sitting on his perch, he dragged over the kayak and began bailing it out. He did his best, even tilting the kayak forward and back as much as he could in an attempt to get the water out from under the seat.

This was all just a distraction. Focusing on the water in his boat allowed him to delay tackling the larger problem: what was he supposed to do? He had taken a wrong turn, and now had no way of getting back to the winter house. He had no way of finding out if anyone else had survived. What he wanted to do was just sit there, like a lost little kid, and hope that someone would find him.

Selfish, stupid, coward.

Angry at himself, Keith threw down the bailing bucket into his kayak. The hollow plastic bin bounced off the hollow plastic seat, flipped up into the air, and landed in the water. Keith scrambled to grab it, not certain it would float. He slid off his perch, his feet scraping along the rock as he tried to keep upright. The bucket was retrieved, but now Keith was even angrier at himself. He huffed his way back up onto the rock, and although he wanted to throw something again, he wisely did not. Instead, he put his meagre supplies back into the safety kit, and then tucked it under the bungee cords on the back of the boat.

He took several deep breaths to calm himself. His mother had taught him to do that whenever he started wailing as a little kid, but he hadn't tried it in a long time.

When that didn't work, Keith resorted to screaming. His voice echoed long and loud over the lake. It reverberated off the rocks, and rose beyond the trees. A bird was startled into flight.

When he stopped, when his lungs had no more air to force through his vocal cords, the silence that followed was oppressive. The birds returned to singing, and the cicadas buzzed, but that was all. No distant engines. No far-off planes. No voices calling back to his, assuring him that everything was okay, and that they were coming to get him, he just needed to stay put. He felt like the last human on Earth.

8: THEN

"**H**OLY FUCKING CROW CRACKERS!**"** Renly shouted. "What in Blackbeard's name was that? Did you guys fucking see that? The sky just fucking exploded!"

"That wasn't the sky, you moron," Aisling barked at him. "It was just a transformer."

Renly started laughing so hard he looked ready to fall over. "So not only do you believe in aliens, but you think the Transformers are real, too?" He started walking about like a stiff robot. "I am Megatron, take me to your leader, puny human, or I will turn into a truck and crush you."

"Megatron was a jet," Keith quietly, and somewhat unconsciously, corrected.

"You know what? Morons would be insulted that I called you one," Aisling fired back. "I knew your grades were low, Renly, but I always thought it was because you're lazy. Turns out, it's because most people's pubic hair has more intelligence than you."

"Fuck you, Aisling." Renly's hands balled up into fists. He was considerably smaller than Aisling, but that hadn't stopped him from fighting bigger guys before. Maybe he'd hold back though since Aisling was a girl.

"Okay, calm down." Russell actually placed himself between the two of them. "Renly, a transformer is part of the electrical grid. You know those big grey things attached to the tops of some poles? It's one of those. When they blow up, they can create one heck of a light show. That one must have been close. I'm thinking maybe on Hillcrest."

"Yeah," Aisling agreed, no longer looking like she was going to murder Renly that instant, but was still considering it for later on. "Yeah, it probably was. I'm going to go check it out." She snatched her phone back out of Russell's hand and remounted her bike. "Power's probably out in the whole neighbourhood, now." She left as abruptly as she had arrived.

"Fucking bitch," Renly muttered after she had gone. "Who does she think she is, anyway? Acting like she's above everyone all the time."

"Well, in a way, she sort of is." Keith gestured with his hand to indicate her height. He wanted to defuse Renly's anger. Knowing him, he'd go and do something stupid because of it. It worked somewhat: Renly laughed.

"Do you guys want to go see what happened?" Russell asked.

"You mean follow her?" Renly scoffed. "Yeah, no thanks. But by all means, you go ahead. Just bring a footstool with you, it's the only way your dick'll reach her pussy."

Russell sighed. "Keith?"

"I think I should get home." *Shit, was that too much?* Keith worried. Would they realize that he was afraid? His palms had gotten sweaty even before the transformer blew.

"Why?" Renly questioned him. "Not like you can do anything. As stuck up as Aisling is, she's probably right about the power being out if that flash came from something on the electrical grid."

"I have a laptop and data on my phone, not to mention a pile of homework to get to."

"Ugh," Renly sighed. "Don't remind me. I was hoping we could play some *Call of Duty*."

"No power," Russell mentioned again.

"Yeah, I know, I said I was *hoping*. But you're right, I should get home too. My mom can get a little wiggy when the power goes out. I should make sure she doesn't start giving away all the meat out of our freezer."

They walked another block before Renly broke away from them.

"See you turds later!" he called out as he disappeared down his street.

"Hey, mind if I come over?" Russell asked the moment Renly was out of earshot.

"Yeah, sure."

"I can help you with your homework."

"I don't actually have that much homework."

"Why did you say you did?"

"Because I want to get home. And to lose Renly, frankly. Like, I'm trying to be understanding because his dad left and all, but he keeps getting weirder."

"Yeah, the cursing *has* gotten a bit excessive. He can still kick my ass in *Call of Duty* though."

"Yeah."

"So why do you want to get home?"

"I don't know. Something feels wrong."

"Wrong?"

"Yeah, like . . . " Keith didn't know how to explain his sense of foreboding. If it were anyone other than Russell, he would never admit to it. "I'm just worried something is going to happen."

"Like what?"

"Like those things in Russia showing up over here. I think I saw a headline about there being one in Brazil."

Russell took out his phone to check. He was silent for a suspiciously long time.

"Long article?" Keith eventually asked.

"I didn't see anything about Brazil," he answered distractedly, his focus still on his phone.

"What are you reading then?"

"Reports about the same things popping up in Spain. And New Zealand. I don't know any of these news organizations though, so I don't know if they can be trusted."

"It might be the whole thing is becoming a viral scam. Like, people keep finding out how to fake their own stuff, and are piling on. Like Slender Man." That's what Keith desperately wanted it to be.

"Yeah." Russell put his phone away, but his thoughts clearly remained elsewhere.

The boys had always lived on the same street, just two houses down from one other. Only old Mrs. Phelps' place separated their homes, and she didn't care if they climbed over the fences or played in her yard, just so long as they didn't touch either her flower or herb gardens.

"Looks like my parents aren't home," Russell commented on

his empty driveway. His dad was never home this early, but his mom worked as a trauma surgeon, and sometimes was rotated onto unusual shifts.

"Well you said you wanted to come over. We'll see what my dad's up to." Keith's dad was a small-time carpenter who made custom furniture in their garage. Mom was the steady breadwinner in their house, holding down an important administration job with the government that Keith had never been interested in asking more about. Dad's job was definitely cooler.

The garage door was wide open, Keith's dad using the sunlight to see by. He was carefully running sandpaper along the edges of an intricate design he'd been carving into a table.

"Is it done?" Keith asked excitedly, briefly forgetting about his concerns.

"No, but I can't use my Dremel without power. Almost though, I just need to finish that corner over there."

"Wow, this is amazing, Doug." Not only had Russell grown up with Keith's dad acting like a second father, but Keith's parents were both the kind of people who would rather have his friends call them by their first names.

"Thanks, Russell."

"Who's it for?"

"A company in the States that wants it for their meeting room. They do a lot of green initiative stuff, hence the leaf motif. Once the carving is done, I'm going to fill it with this shiny green resin I figured out how to make. There's a test sample over there if you want to see it."

Russell immediately scurried over to the corner of the garage to look at the sample.

"You heard me say that the power is out, right?" Dad mentioned to Keith.

"Yeah, and we already figured out that it was. We saw the transformer explode."

"A transformer exploded? How close were you?"

"A few streets over, not close."

"Wow. I wonder what made it explode?"

"I couldn't find anything about it in the news," Russell said, rejoining them beside the big tabletop.

"Probably too recent. The power's only been out for a few

minutes now, although if a transformer exploded, it could be pretty serious. Might take them a while to get it back up and running."

"Think Mom'll come home early?" Keith wondered. He really liked the idea of his whole family being together.

"I doubt it. The outage would have to reach pretty far, and besides, her office probably has a backup generator. What about your dad's place, Russell? Might he be home early?"

Russell shook his head. "No, they have a back-up generator there, too." His dad was a loan officer.

"Well, you know you're always welcome to hang out here until he gets back. Depending on what's going on, though, your mom might be late."

"Yeah, thanks, Doug."

"You know, if it's going to be a while until the power's back on, I might as well call it a day. Why don't you boys help me clean up, and then we can gather the flashlights and candles in case this lasts until nightfall."

"We should also check the landline," Keith suggested.

"Good thinking," Dad agreed.

"I can't believe you guys still have a landline," Russell groaned as he started to pull out the shop vac.

"Hey, if it's working right now, then maybe it was worth all those telemarketing calls," Dad chuckled. "Also, you're going to need this." He then handed Russell a broom, just as Keith's friend was rediscovering the power outage via the vacuum. Certain habits were hard to break.

With the three of them working together, it didn't take long for them to clean up the workshop.

"Now you get why we don't have an automatic garage door," Dad commented as he grabbed the handle and pulled it shut.

"Still pretty sure it's because you're cheap," Keith responded as he set the lock in place, using his phone as a flashlight. This was the usual banter between them, and while Keith found some comfort in it, there was still a chord of concern vibrating deep inside. He wanted his mom to be home, for the whole family to be together.

At the same time, he rejected his unease. He felt stupid for feeling this way. It was just a power outage, he'd been through plenty of them before. His concern—he refused to admit that it was fear—made him feel like a kid, and he *hated* feeling like a kid. He had turned sixteen last month, he had already gotten his G1 driver's license and had spent some time behind the wheel of his mom's car. He was not a child. He'd even been thinking about getting a summer job after school let out.

Inside the house, Keith and Russell dropped their backpacks and started to gather up flashlights and candles. The whole time, Keith kept telling himself that it was a pointless task, that the stuff on the news would all turn out to be a hoax, and that the power outage was not only unrelated, but was also not a big deal. It would come back on within the hour. He was worrying about nothing.

9:
NOW

KEITH WANTED TO curl up and dissolve into the lake. He wanted the pain to go away, both the physical and the emotional.

What am I going to do? kept repeating in his head, over and over and over again.

His despair also made him angry, and he slapped at the water. He couldn't keep that up very long, his shoulders protested too much.

It was like his thoughts were trapped on a circular track, spiralling around and down, ever deeper and ever darker. The guilt worm bore a tunnel through his being.

"Stop it," he said, as if it were that easy to command his emotions. "You can't afford to be any more stupid than you already have been. Pull yourself together. What would Russell do?"

Thinking of his friend produced a pain like a stab, but he was going to hurt no matter what. Besides, Russell would have known what to do. He was smarter than Keith. Russell wouldn't have gotten into this mess to begin with, but if he had, he would know what to do. So what would he do?

"He'd whip out some sort of GPS, and find a safe way back," Keith sneered, berating himself in a roundabout way. "Or wait until nightfall and navigate by the stars."

But where would he navigate to? This rock was good for a pit stop, but Keith couldn't remain here forever. For one thing, he'd need food.

Keith's stomach grumbled at the thought. When had he last eaten? Not long before the winter house got attacked, but hours had slipped by since then, and Keith had expended a lot of energy within that window. Water wasn't a problem, he had plenty to drink so long as he was willing to risk a waterborne contagion or parasite, but in terms of food, he had nothing.

"Okay," Keith sighed. "Okay."

It was difficult to accept that he was going to be alone for an indeterminate length of time, but he could push that aside for now. Feed it to the guilt worm. He needed to take the one step in front of him. Deal with the immediate problem, which at the moment was food. Where could he find food? And how could he get it?

Breaking that down into smaller steps meant climbing into his kayak first. He peeled off his sodden life jacket, squeezed out as much water as he could, and flopped it over the nose where he hoped the sun would dry it out.

Standing up on the rock was somewhat precarious. Keith had thought he might be able to wring out his shirt, and maybe even his swimsuit a little, but there was no way he could balance without holding onto the kayak. He hunched there awkwardly, trying to wait for the worst of the water to drip off of him. His toes gripped the rock as best they could, but he could feel that one foot was sliding, ever so slightly.

He didn't so much as climb into the kayak, as fall into it. His intention was to pull it to him, twist sideways, and sit. He sort of did this, after a fashion, but it wasn't anywhere near as graceful as he had imagined. With the rocking of the boat, and his unstable footing, he just sort of went from standing, to sprawling awkwardly. His torso made it into the opening, but his limbs definitely had not. He clung to the far side of the kayak, his legs bent ridiculously as he tried to keep them from flipping the whole thing over. With much fumbling and cursing, he struggled to keep his weight balanced while shifting around into a properly seated position. He managed, but grace was nowhere to be found.

It was unfortunate that fishing was not an option. Having attempted to catch fish with his hands before, he knew not to bother trying now. It was not a skill he possessed. That left him with one option for food: cottages.

Just the thought of it made him queasy, offsetting his hunger.

There were no cottages in the area, so he had some time to

warm up to the idea. Because it was easier, he continued to follow the flow of water.

A swampy area sat off to one side. Keith approached the lily pads, hoping to spot some frogs, or ducks, or maybe even a Canada goose. How he would catch any of these with what he had on him, he had no idea, but he would have liked the opportunity to try. Maybe he could lasso one of the birds and strangle it. If he got lucky, he could possibly sneak up on a frog or turtle, and snatch it with his hands. But he had to know where to sneak first. The only life Keith could spot from the edge of the lily pads, were insects. They were more likely to make a meal out of him, than he would out of them. He moved on.

The channel slowly expanded until Keith was no longer sure it was still a channel. Cottages lined both shores, but he didn't know which one to pick. How was he supposed to decide? How was he supposed to know which one had food inside? He'd have to get closer to start with.

He took his time. Each place was scrutinized as he drifted ten feet off the dock. There were requirements he wished to have filled. The places along a cliff, he quickly decided against. They had long staircases down to the water, and he didn't want to have to climb them. Some cottages were scratched off because they were set too far back. A place was given a positive mark when Keith spotted a car nearby. That suggested someone had come here last year. When the dirt devils arrived, some cottages had been opened for the summer and some hadn't, meaning not all of them would contain food, but a vehicle was a positive sign. Fully intact structures were also a good sign. There was one place right at the edge of the water, but it had clearly been attacked. All the windows were broken, and there were deep gouges in the wood. Not only could critters easily get inside and ravage whatever was left, but Keith also didn't trust the place to stay standing.

If the channel was now a bay, it was a triangular one. It widened more on one side than the other in a sort of arc. Keith wondered if it kept opening around that bend, leading into a much wider portion of whatever lake he was in, but as he passed some cottages, he saw he was wrong. The land swooped back around to the far side. At the farthest point, however, he saw a place he was very much interested in.

The cottage was larger, with two storeys and plenty of windows. Its most appealing feature was that it sat in the middle of a huge, flat rock. While the back of it appeared fairly close to the trees, there was at least twenty feet of clearing on either side, and nothing between the building and the water.

Keith got closer and could see a car poking out from around one end. It used to be a shiny black luxury sedan, but wasn't any longer. Something had put a hefty dent in the roof. The windows were either a spiderweb of cracks or missing all together, and every tire was completely flat.

Despite the state of the car, the cottage itself looked intact. All the windows Keith could see were shut, and contained no cracks. The same could be said for the doors. Whether those doors were unlocked or not was a completely different question, but Keith had no way of telling from where he floated. Most people here kept their doors unlocked even before the dirt devils showed up, but glancing at the car again, Keith wondered if the owners had even made it inside. If they hadn't, the doors could still be locked from the previous winter.

There was only one way to find out. Keith used the tow rope to loosely tie his kayak to the dock. A ski boat hid beneath a cover on the far side, sitting just above the water on a boat lift. Keith briefly debated with himself about taking it. The gas would be no good if it even had any, and it would be difficult to paddle, but it would also be more spacious.

Food first, he reminded himself. He could take a look at the boatlift later.

He'd tied up near the shore, where the massive rock sloped into the water like a beach without sand. Keith was able to slip out of his kayak, standing in water that reached only to his knees, which were knocking together. He was already within grabbing range.

Trying to keep his breathing steady, he stepped out of the water.

10:
THEN

"**K**EITH, WAKE UP!" Dreams still fogged his mind so much that not even Keith knew what he mumbled.

"Keith!"

His whole body was shaken, and rather violently. "I'm up, I'm up," he grumbled, wiping at his sleep-encrusted eyes. It was still dark out. "What's going on?"

"Come on, get up!"

He finally noticed the urgency in his mom's voice. The panic. He let her haul him out of bed and onto his feet, even though he was only wearing his boxer shorts.

"Where's Dad? What's happening?"

"He's getting Mrs. Phelps." Mom was still holding on to his hand and dragging him toward his door.

"Mrs. Phelps?" Despite the dark, Keith managed to snag a T-shirt off the back of his desk chair, and his phone from off his desk. He tried to check the device before remembering that he'd turned it off due to the power outage.

The day before, the power had never come back on. Dad had insisted that Keith and Russell stop checking their phones for news, saying it was probably all misinformation anyway. They decided to believe him because they wanted to, and the three of them spent the afternoon playing board games on the back porch. When Russell's dad got home, he joined them, and Keith's mom picked up takeout for everyone, including Mrs. Phelps, who had been invited over. It had been a nice evening out back, one Russell's mom really appreciated when she returned from the hospital; power outages always caused an uptick in accidents. Keith had turned off his phone at some point, acknowledging the fact that he was unlikely to be able to charge it, and wanted to save its battery.

"Where are we going?" Keith now followed his mom downstairs, no longer holding her hand so that he could pull on his shirt.

"We're going to the Blattys'." She grabbed a baseball bat from beside the front door before opening it.

"Why? Mom, what is happening?" He stressed each word as she ushered him outside. Instinctively, he scanned the street, hoping that no one would see him in his boxers. The street wasn't empty like it should have been. He spotted two separate families bundling half-asleep children into their cars. A third was walking at a brisk pace down the street. Elsewhere, flashlights darted about within houses, windows blinking as they caught the glare. Somewhere a generator was humming, but Keith couldn't tell where.

"Just go." Mom locked the door behind them. Keith didn't have his keys with him, so it was either head to Russell's, or remain outside in his underwear.

It was only then, by the light of a bright waxing gibbous moon, that Keith noticed his mom was in her pajamas. This was just as alarming as the baseball bat, since Keith *never* saw his mom in her pajamas. She was fastidious about getting dressed first thing in the morning, even on her birthday and Christmas. The last time Keith had seen his mom in her matching flannel pajama set, had been when he was little enough to want to climb into his parents' bed after a nightmare. That must have been more than a decade ago by now.

As they passed Mrs. Phelps' door, Dad emerged with the elderly woman.

"I'm much too old for a sleepover," Mrs. Phelps was complaining. She wore a nightgown that hung just past her knees, and a pair of slippers. Her crown of unbrushed, swirling white hair shone in the moonlight.

"I know, Mrs. Phelps, but this is an emergency," Dad told her as they turned toward Russell's. Dad, wearing pajama pants and a T-shirt, tossed his keys to Mom so that she could lock Mrs. Phelps' door. The woman had no family within the whole province, and so both Keith's and Russell's families had sort of adopted her into each of theirs. The three households had keys to one another's places in case of an emergency, but this was the first time Keith had seen any of them used.

Keith finally held down the button to turn on his phone. It wasn't even on for a full minute before the emergency broadcast had it screaming and buzzing into the night air.

"Oh!" Mrs. Phelps startled from the sudden blast of noise. Keith had startled as well, even though he had been kind of expecting it. What else could get everyone in the neighbourhood up and rushing about like this in the middle of the night?

It was an alert from the government. Keith didn't know what he had expected the message to say, but it wasn't what he read. Get to a large water source? What did they mean by an attack?

Keith didn't have a chance to dig for more information, as Mom's hand locked around his arm and pulled him sideways. He'd been heading to Russell's front door, but she quickly redirected him to the side of the house. They passed through the gate and into the Blattys' backyard.

"Hey!" Russell waved.

"Hurry up!" Mr. Blatty added.

All three family members were in their pool. Glow sticks bobbed about like some sort of rave, while Mr. Blatty held a flashlight above the water to light their way.

"Oh, I can't go in there," Mrs. Phelps insisted. "I'm not wearing a bathing suit."

"None of us are," Dad reminded her, still guiding the woman to the steps. Mrs. Phelps was old enough to have never gotten a cell phone, so she wouldn't have received the emergency message. It must have been terrifying to be woken up by Keith's dad.

"I'm not going in," she put her foot down.

"I've got this." Mom took over care of Mrs. Phelps, while Dad made sure Keith kept moving.

"Warning, the water is *not* warm," Russell said just as Keith started to step in.

Keith gasped as he reached the floor of the shallow end, the water up to his waist. Not wanting to accidentally kill his phone, he placed it just beyond the curved cement lip of the pool, beside the Blatty family's phones.

"Just be thankful we had it filled earlier this week," Mr. Blatty commented. "I don't know where we would go if we hadn't."

"Probably down to the lake," Dad replied, holding both his arms up above the water, his phone clutched in one of them. "I'm betting a lot of people are headed that way."

"There are rivers that are closer," Mom corrected him. "Come on, Mrs. Phelps."

Mom had grabbed a large towel from a nearby stack and wrapped it around the old woman. She was still reluctant to get into the pool, especially when her toes touched the water, but Mom managed to guide her in. She remained standing on the bottom step, refusing to go deeper.

"They just said water, they didn't say how deep," she insisted.

Mom reluctantly agreed. "Keith? I still want you to stay deeper. Just in case."

"Mom, it's cold," he complained.

"Just a little deeper. Please."

"Keith, listen to your mother," Dad added.

Groaning, Keith waded away from the edge. He hissed as the water climbed up his belly, past his navel. He was practically up to his armpits.

"Any farther and I'm swimming," he insisted. He was at the edge of the drop, where the shallow end took a sudden, sloping plunge into the deep end.

"That's fine there." Although Mom sounded like maybe it wasn't. "Keep away from the sides, though."

"Here." Russell waded over and passed Keith a pool noodle. He had another one for himself, on which he rested his arms. Keith followed suit.

"What do you think this is all about?" Keith whispered to his friend. Their parents were clustered near the steps, whispering among themselves in the same manner.

"I think it's a hoax. Okay, not a hoax, but like, an accident? Remember that story I told you about, that I heard in my programming class? The one about people in Hawaii all receiving an alert that a missile strike was inbound? People started putting their kids down in sewers, thinking they were all about to die. Turned out it was just bad UI, and the guy who did it had only meant to run a test."

"I remember. You showed me a screenshot of the UI. The missile thing was prepared ahead of time, though. It was an option to choose from. You really think the one we received would be part of such a list? Besides, there was a typo in it."

"There was?"

Keith nodded. Russell got great marks in math, but his essays were only ever average.

"I suppose you're right. I don't know why they'd have something like that prepared ahead of time. But why wouldn't they tell us why we needed to get to water? You know a bunch of people are just going to ignore the alert."

Keith shrugged. He knew no more than Russell about the why of it all. He wished it was just what Russell thought, that some bad UI had sent everyone into a panic, but he couldn't. It was just too weird a message. And that typo . . . To Keith, it looked like the kind of mistake someone would make when typing in a rush. Say, like, someone trying to get a message out in a hurry. He wished he hadn't left his phone by the side of the pool, because then he'd be able to Google what was happening like his Dad was.

No one saw the dirt devil arrive. Dr. Blatty spotted it first, and her scream drew everyone's attention to it. It stood in the shadows over by Mrs. Phelps' fence, but it didn't stay there long. It stepped forward as Mr. Blatty's flashlight found it, and they all got to see those eerie eyes for the first time. Eyes on either side of a fleshy bat-like nose, and above a maw that they would soon learn opened far too wide, and was full of shark teeth.

11:
NOW

KEITH DIDN'T KNOW if he should run or tiptoe up to the cottage. What he wanted to do was wheel around and dive back into the water, where it was safe. He couldn't do that though. Although the danger had banished his hunger, that wouldn't last. Food was required. What had his Dad taught him? Humans needed air first, water second, and food third. The first two were already taken care of, there was just number three now.

He ended up neither running nor tiptoeing, but a strange hybrid of the two. In a half crouch, he scuttled across the rock toward the cottage. The jury was still out on how well dirt devils could hear. Their lack of visible ears made some people think it wasn't great, while others thought they made up for it by being sensitive to vibrations in the ground. Either way, being quiet and fleet of foot seemed like the best way to avoid them.

Crossing that void seemed to take both an eternity and a second. Keith's head was on a swivel, his eyes darting in all directions as he anticipated an appearance by one of the creatures at any moment. He was actually surprised when he made it to the narrow deck without an encounter.

Huddled up against a set of glass doors, he cupped his hands to cut out the glare. He didn't like having his back so vulnerable, his eyes no longer on the forest, but he had to check. Even before trying the handle, he had to make sure there wasn't anything waiting for him inside.

It was a nice cottage. The pair of sliding glass doors he peered through led into a vast living space, the centre of which stretched up into the second story. A balcony up there gave a partial view, where a few doors stood open. He guessed they were bedrooms, maybe a bathroom. To his left was the kitchen, the only place he should need to go. The living room covered pretty much the rest of the ground floor, reaching a few windows at the back, with a staircase tucked into the far right corner. All the glass was intact, but there was at least one closed-off room, behind the kitchen, that he couldn't tell anything about. None of the furniture had been toppled, or even appeared to have been jostled. If he didn't know any better, he'd expect to see someone emerge from one of those upper rooms at any second, yawning and stretching as they awoke from a nice afternoon nap.

The hairs on Keith's neck stood up. He wheeled around, fully expecting to spy a dirt devil staring him down, but there was nothing. The rock remained clear. If a devil came for him, he would have heard the telltale clicking of its claws on the stone, and yet he continued to expect an ambush.

The doors weren't locked. Keith slipped inside, then pulled them almost, but not quite, shut behind him. He didn't want to latch them in case he needed a hasty exit, but he also couldn't leave them wide open, allowing anything to just saunter in.

Right beside the door, he found his first treasure. A large, rubber, waterproof sack was slumped on the floor. Keith snatched it up as he made his way to the kitchen. His bare feet made padded sticking sounds each time they lifted from the linoleum.

The kitchen was a sort of alcove. Along all three walls were counters and appliances; a small island kept it separated from the rest of the cottage. Keith placed his new bag on the island and started rummaging through the cupboards. There was no point checking the fridge, anything that needed to be kept cool would have spoiled long ago, but he hoped to find some canned goods. He didn't care what was in them, so long as he had them.

His luck was poor. The first several cupboards he checked were full of dishes. When he found food, they were cereal boxes that some mice had discovered first, and then some spices that were no good on their own. He actually located a manual can opener before he found any cans, which was probably fortunate, since he likely would have forgotten to grab one otherwise.

The tins finally revealed themselves. Keith's elation lasted about a second. Before he could even grab one, there was a crash from the back of the cottage.

Dropping to all fours, Keith pressed up against the back of the island. Where had that come from? It had been loud, and was definitely glass shattering. Most likely a window. Was it in the room he hadn't been able to see inside of? Had it been upstairs? Or was it one of the windows at the back of the cottage? The sound had been so startling, and so abrupt, that Keith had gone straight into hiding without bothering to better determine the source.

His ears strained. He tried to hear over his hammering heart, his hands clamped over his mouth to quiet his breathing. There was no clicking. There was no anything, not from inside at least.

On shaking legs, hands still over his mouth, Keith slowly stood up. He peered over the island, his gaze sweeping back and forth across the room. The space remained as untouched as before. There were no shadows sliding around what he could make out of the balcony railing. No teeth were rushing toward him.

Gently picking up the sack, Keith lowered it to the floor with him. As silently as he could, he plucked tinned food from the cupboard and placed each one in the waterproof bag. There were a little over a dozen cans in all. If Keith had felt he had more time, he would have continued to search the kitchen more thoroughly—there was probably some dry pasta he had missed—but not knowing if danger was near meant that it was time to get out. The top of the bag rolled down to seal out any water, and then the two ends were bent around and clipped together with a buckle so it couldn't unroll. The stiff, folded rubber caused the top to form a sort of ring, which made for an excellent handle.

Keith stood carefully, eyes and ears attuned to even the slightest change. He was a little over halfway to the door when an explosion of sound came from upstairs. Wood cracking and splintering was punctuated by the sharp shattering of glass. Something was definitely in a room up there, and it wasn't small, and it wasn't happy.

Figuring his own sounds would be hidden beneath the ruckus, Keith bolted. He flew out the doors, his feet barely touching the deck before he was throwing himself off of it. His flight hadn't gone unnoticed. Behind him, the destruction of wood burst out of the room, through the balcony railing, and thumped heavily onto the living room floor. Keith didn't need to check over his shoulder for what it was, he already knew. If he had been unsure, the clicking of claws as the devil righted itself was all he needed.

As he neared the water, Keith swung his arm and hurled his sack on ahead of him. Just as his fingers released, the doors burst outward in a rain of glass. A dirt devil was after him, its claws clicking on the stone, approaching rapidly. They were fast, so goddamn fast. It was practically on top of him already.

Keith's toes touched the water. Not knowing how deep it got, he threw himself bodily at the lapping waves. One last gasp of breath, and his face was under. With hands and feet, he gripped the rock, kicking and pulling, following the bottom of the lake, trying to submerge every part of him.

It was cold down there, but the chill was actually a relief. It meant he wasn't spilling hot blood back on the rock. His body continued to swim outward, still in a panic, but he was safe. Underwater was the safest place in the world.

12:
THEN

KEITH DIDN'T KNOW what to make of that first dirt devil. It didn't seem real. Those hunched shoulders and long neck were sort of like a bear, but the skinny legs were that of a dog, and its stubby, bloated tail he could only compare to a dinosaur. The fur made it especially difficult to accept as being real. It wasn't so much like fur, as it was thick, brown wires, or maybe branches. Even the finer hairs on its legs and face were crinkled and stiff, looking like they might hurt to touch. With its lack of ears, it was difficult to tell where the neck ended and the head began. Around those horrible eyes, the fur fell away, leaving them ringed in clay coloured flesh. The only other place where its skin could be seen, was that wrinkled nose on the end of a short muzzle.

As the dirt devil reached the cement patio that surrounded the pool, its claws made a clicking that Keith would come to learn well. When he first saw it, he thought that maybe the creature was mutated. Each long toe had two talon-like claws: one that curved down like normal, and a second that curved up alongside it. It was the second claw that was always clicking, the underside tapping against whatever surface it walked on.

Everyone in the pool gaped at the creature. Other than Dr. Blatty's initial scream, they were silent. No one knew what to make of this thing. Only a few seconds passed in this manner, but time had warped, stretching out to feel longer. Probably because what came next happened so fast.

The dirt devil lunged toward Mrs. Phelps. Its legs were skinny, but powerful. The claws on its front feet opened, its toes spreading.

Mrs. Phelps screamed as they punched through her flesh. She was yanked from the water, her towel falling away to reveal that her nightgown had turned transparent where it had gotten wet. The old woman was thrown to the ground, her shriek of pain rising in pitch as something in her snapped. The devil was back on her in an instant, and its mouth—a mouth that opened too much, too wide, longer than its muzzle, stretching past its eyes—clamped down on her hip. One second Mrs. Phelps had two legs, and the next she did not.

Everyone was shouting. Keith stumbled backward, over the drop, dunking his head so that he came up spluttering. Russell grabbed onto him as if he'd nearly drowned, and then wouldn't let go.

Mr. Blatty charged to the pool steps, snatching the baseball bat out of Mom's hands as he passed her.

The devil tossed its head, getting all of Mrs. Phelps' leg into its mouth and swallowing it whole. She lay perfectly still on the ground under it, her silence more disturbing than her screams. The beast lowered its maw once more to take the other leg off. Keith wished he couldn't see, but he also couldn't tear his eyes away.

Mr. Blatty was a strong man. He swung that bat with all his might, the roar bursting from him more at home in a zoo than a suburban neighbourhood. Had he been swinging at another man, even Dr. Blatty wouldn't have been able to save him. But the dirt devil took the blow like an elephant smacked by a fly swatter: it got annoyed. The beast's back leg kicked out at Mr. Blatty with perfect aim. It was so casual that it didn't seem right the way Mr. Blatty's body flew through the air. He landed in the pool with a great splash.

He landed in the pool. He should be fine. Keith kept thinking this over and over again, as though this were a movie. When the good guys landed in water they were always okay.

"Dad!" Russell shouted, releasing Keith and surging through the water to be beside him.

Keith's dad was already there; he had almost been hit by Mr. Blatty's return to the pool. Dr. Blatty joined them in a heartbeat, her face expressionless as she sank into her profession.

"Keep Russell back," she ordered Mom. Mr. Blatty was wheezing terribly. He struggled to breathe, even though Dad was holding his head up out of the water.

Keith turned his attention back to the dirt devil. It ripped another piece off Mrs. Phelps and swallowed it whole. Two more bites, and then there was only bloody offal remaining. The dirt devil licked at the sodden grass, its tongue stumpy so that it had to bend down low.

"Come on, Charles!" Dr. Blatty shouted. "Stay with me!"

"Dad!" Russell called to him, his voice wavering despite trying to sound strong. "You'll be okay, Dad! Just hold on!"

"We need to get him out of the water and onto his back. I can't do much like this. I need supplies, damn it!"

Keith had never heard Dr. Blatty curse before, not even a small one like that. He looked over just as she and his dad hoisted Mr. Blatty up onto the pool's edge. Dad then ran over to the cell phones near the steps, his own having been dropped into the water during the chaos.

"Dad, look out!" Keith screamed.

The dirt devil had wheeled around and was rushing at him. Dad stumbled, slipped, and sank under the water. With extreme strength, the devil balanced on its back legs, its scissor-claws reaching out, trying to grab Dad. When its front paws touched the water, it shrieked. At least, Keith interpreted the warbling bellow as a shriek, based on the way it suddenly withdrew. It scrambled awkwardly backward on its rear paws, shaking the front ones furiously. When it put its feet down on the grass beyond the cement patio, it was suddenly fine. But angry. The level of expression in its eyes made Keith feel queasy.

When the devil rushed the side of the pool again, Dad was out of reach, but it stretched for him anyway. Claws raked through the air, startlingly close to Dad's face. It caused everyone to flinch, to retreat even farther from the sides of the pool. As if that were its plan, the devil turned on a dime. It grabbed Mr. Blatty and leaped back to the grass with him.

And then it was gone. The dirt devil, with Mr. Blatty gripped in its claws, disappeared. It . . . dissolved into the soil, somehow pulling a full-grown man down with it.

"Charles!" Dr. Blatty screamed, scrambling to get out of the pool.

"No!" Dad lunged and grabbed her waist, pulling her back into deeper water.

"Charles!" she kept shouting as if Dad weren't there. She kept trying to get to the side of the pool, but did nothing to bat him off.

"Mom?" Russell cried.

Dr. Blatty wheeled around. She rushed through the water, half swimming, half walking, and wrapped herself around Russell when Mom let him go. Just as quickly, Mom came to Keith's side and grabbed hold of him, as if she needed to have a child in her arms.

"Where'd he go, Mom?" Keith whispered, unable to find a louder voice. Unable to add to the noise that had already assaulted them. "Where did Mr. Blatty go?"

"I don't know, baby. I don't know."

13:
NOW

WITH KEITH'S LUNGS screaming for air, he was forced to rise to the surface of the lake. Emerging with a mighty gasp, he continued to keep his eyes closed. If he was somehow near the shore, he didn't want to see his death coming at him. But there was no pain. No claws grabbed his shoulders and hauled him free of the lake. He was safe. Water was safe.

When Keith turned around, the dirt devil was nowhere in sight. He assumed it must have left the rock while he'd been underwater. The thought of it merging into the stone made him shudder, but he knew that wasn't possible. They could disappear into dirt, and sand, and even gravel, but solid rock stopped them.

Doggy paddling his way back toward the dock, Keith searched for the bag he had grabbed. It was bright blue, so the fact that he didn't spot it right away alarmed him. He had trapped quite a lot of air in there when he had closed it and figured it would float, but maybe he was wrong. Maybe there was a hole in the bag, and it sank, and the risk he had taken was for nothing.

The bag was floating, it was just under the dock. Keith fished it out in shallow enough water that he could walk. He brought the bag to his kayak and put it in the rear hold. Because the hold was shallow, he briefly unclipped the bag, and secured it to the rear pull handle. With the stretchy string over top, it wouldn't be going anywhere.

As he untied the kayak from the dock, Keith considered climbing up onto the wood. He had begun to shiver from the cold water, and he knew it would be warm up there. It should also be fairly safe, since any dirt devils would have to cross the big stone to reach the dock, giving him plenty of time to leap back into the water.

Instead, he got into his boat. He took his shirt off and wrung it out, but the water from his swim trunks puddled on the seat. After putting his shirt back on, he paddled away from the cottage. He didn't want to be anywhere near a place where he had encountered a dirt devil.

Out in the middle of the triangular bay, it was time to eat. When Keith had clipped the bag to the rear handle, he hadn't been thinking about this part. Twisted around, he frowned over his shoulder at the bag, with its opening so far away from him. Frowning, of course, didn't help. It didn't magically turn the bag around, or allow him to correct his previous mistake.

"Just do it," he told himself.

Moving slowly to keep his balance, Keith rolled over so that he could kneel on the seat. The back of the kayak sank lower into the water as he placed a hand to one side of the bag and leaned over.

"Shit," he muttered, trying to keep his weight shifted back over his legs.

Stretching his other arm to its limit, he reached the buckle and unclipped it. With a tight grip on the rolled top, he tugged the bag free of the bungee string. The kayak rocked precariously, and Keith clenched his hand around the rubber sack for all he was worth. Based on the way the rest of his day had gone, he felt certain that he would drop his food now, and with the buckle undone, the bag top would unroll and all his supplies would sink. He saw this clearly in his mind's eye, even as he pulled the bag to him and twisted back around into a proper seated position.

"Lesson learned," Keith sighed, plunking the bag down between his knees. That's where it was going to stay from now on.

The first tin he withdrew was tuna.

"Great." Keith was sick of fish. It seemed like every day he ate fish, and he never really liked it to begin with. Still, he'd have to eat the tuna sometime, so it might as well be now.

Digging beneath the cans for the can opener, Keith startled when his fingers touched a soft fabric. He hadn't looked inside the bag before using it, and it seemed it wasn't as empty as he had thought. Can by can, he took everything out of the sack, placing it all on his lap. He counted as he went, and discovered that he had fifteen cans in total, and thankfully they weren't all tuna. Underneath them, alongside the can opener, he discovered a beach towel and a swim mask.

The cans went back into the bag, counted again to make sure he hadn't missed one. He placed the swim mask and can opener on top, and rolled up the bag again, just in case what he planned to do tipped him over.

Keith was alone in the bay. Cottages watched him with blank windows, but he knew that they were all empty. No one could see him. Still, a cord of nervousness thrummed in his chest as he carefully stripped out of his shirt and his swim trunks, and then wrapped the dry towel around himself. He shifted the damp lifejacket into the back, and laid out his clothing on the nose for the sun to dry. No longer was the celestial orb overhead, but off to one side, seeking the west. Shadows stretched out from the trees on the shore, long enough that he could hide in the shade if he wanted. For now, he'd continue to risk burning his skin in order to warm himself.

Finally, he ate. Reaching into the bag, he once again grabbed a tin of fish. Salmon this time, not much better, but it was an improvement on the lake fish he had gotten used to. He ate with his fingers, picking out every flake, and even drinking the juices afterward. He kept the empty tin, figuring he could use it as a cup when he got thirsty, although he'd have to be mindful of the sharp edges left behind by the can opener. He also kept the lid, tucking it inside the emergency kit should he need something to cut with at some point.

"What's the next step?" The words came out of Keith's mouth, but they carried the inflection of his father. It's what he would say when they worked on a project together, whether it be furniture, Lego, or math homework. *What's the next step, Keith?*

The kayak had been drifting through the bay the whole time Keith had been eating. He was at the edge of the shadows now, and would have to start paying attention to how close he got to the shoreline. But the shadows actually told him what he needed to do.

Night was coming, and if he wanted to see the sun rise the next morning, he needed to find a safe place to sleep.

14:
THEN

"**KEITH, COME OVER** here a minute," Dad called.

Keith glanced at his mom, but she was now busy comforting Dr. Blatty and Russell. He had wanted to help his friend too, but he hadn't the first idea about how. All he could do was stand nearby and mope.

His dad was closer to the edge of the pool than he probably should have been, but he knew even less about what to do in the face of such grief. For the past hour, he had been trying to get a cell phone to work. When the thing had charged at Dad, it had kicked half the phones into the pool, and crushed the other half.

"What's up?" Keith whispered. It didn't seem right to make noise.

"I'm going to lift you up on my shoulders."

"Why?"

"I want you to look over there." He pointed to where Mr. Blatty had disappeared. "We need to see if it's still in its hole."

Keith didn't get the impression that there *was* a hole, but then where else could it have gone?

"You know I'm not a little kid anymore. Maybe I should lift you?"

Dad gave him a look like that was the silliest idea he'd heard all week. The truth was that Keith was scared. What if there *was* a hole, and he saw Mr. Blatty being eaten one tiny piece at a time? What if his friend's dad was still alive, breathing in that terrible way, moaning in pain, and what if he saw Keith and reached out for him and . . .

Dad crouched down in the water, and Keith scrambled up onto

his shoulders. It had been a long time since he'd perched atop another person like this, and it took him a bit to find his balance. A couple of times Dad tried to stand, only to end up squatting back down as they started to topple. Finally, they managed to get Keith up in the air. It was cold in the pool, but Keith didn't find any warmth outside of the water. In fact, there was a small breeze up there that chilled him even more.

"What do you see?" Dad asked through gritted teeth. He was strong, but like Keith had said, he wasn't a little kid anymore.

"Nothing."

"The hole?"

"No, there's no hole. There's nothing." Keith could see only grass.

"Maybe it's too dark."

"My night vision is fine, Dad." The cheap glowsticks were almost entirely out, and the flashlight had met the same watery fate as the cell phones, but the moon was still bright, and Keith could see quite clearly.

"Do you see a depression? Anywhere the soil's been churned?"

"No, nothing. It looks normal."

"Is the grass torn up anywhere?"

"No!" Keith was getting exasperated.

"Maybe you're not looking in the right spot."

"I know where it happened. Dad, stop!"

But Dad kept turning this way and that, trying to get Keith to look in different places.

"Dad!"

Instead of seeing signs of Mr. Blatty's disappearance, his eyes landed on the scene of Mrs. Phelps' dismemberment. The blood-soaked grass shone black in the night, but what Keith hadn't been able to see from the pool, was a hand. Just a hand, severed neatly at the wrist, lying palm up near the edge of the dark circle.

"*Dad!*" Keith lurched, throwing himself backward and his dad off balance. They splashed into the water, where Keith freed his legs from his dad's shoulders and kicked himself away.

"What is going on over here?" Mom hissed, charging through the water just as Keith managed to stand again. He didn't know how to answer, the image of that hand burned into his mind. There was no reason for the thing not to have eaten it. It was like it had left it there on purpose.

"We needed to check out the thing's hole," Dad explained.

"There's no hole!" Keith shouted, his voice cracking. He wondered how many people had heard him. A few times since their own encounter, they had heard distant screams and shouts. "There's no hole! I told you there's nothing there!"

"But that's not possible!" Dad shouted back. "There has to be *something*, it can't have just disappeared."

"Why not?"

All three members of Keith's family wheeled around to face Russell, who had left the far side of the shallow end to join them near the steps. His mom followed, her hands on his shoulders.

"What's that, Russell?" Mom asked him in a gentle voice.

"Why isn't it possible for it to have just disappeared? That's how it appeared in the first place, isn't it?" His voice was detached, like he was talking about his homework instead of the monster that had killed his father. "That thing is an alien. Like, a real alien, from outer space. We have no idea if it's bound by the same laws of physics and biology that we are."

"What makes you think it's from outer space, sweetie?" Dr. Blatty asked. Her eyes appeared raw, even in the dark.

"Because it came on the meteor. It was dust, and now it's that thing, so it definitely doesn't adhere to life as we understand it. The first one appeared in Russia. Remember, Keith? When I was talking to Aisling? She found out that that was where the wind would have first carried the dust from the meteor. From there, it kept going. It will have landed everywhere by now, except maybe Antarctica. It's made of the dust."

"That doesn't make sense," Dad muttered.

"Of course it doesn't," Russell agreed. "Why should alien life make sense to us? The fact that it has any recognizable parts at all is crazy. Just because it looks predominantly mammalian to us, doesn't mean that it is. For all we know, it can change its shape, and that's just the one it chose this time. We don't know anything about it." His voice had climbed with every sentence, his eyes widening as they stared out into nothing.

"Shh," his mom soothed him. "Take a breath."

"We do know one thing." Everyone turned their attention to Dad. "They don't like water. Remember that sound it made when it touched the surface of the pool?"

Mom nodded. "And *someone* figured it out in time to send us that warning."

"But then why would they eat us?" Keith asked. "Aren't we made up of water?"

The blood on the grass. The hand.

"Alien," Russell shrugged.

"You can't just say *alien* to explain everything," Keith groused. "There has to be *some* rules it follows."

"Maybe it's the chlorine in the pool it doesn't like," Dr. Blatty suggested.

Mom shook her head. "Then why would the alert just say water?"

"They might not have known it was that specific at the time. Or, it could have to do with the purity of the water. There could be something in our blood that counters their negative reaction to it, allowing them to eat us." Dr. Blatty suddenly paled as she remembered that her husband was one of those who'd been killed. They didn't know if he had been eaten like Mrs. Phelps, but he was gone just the same.

"Mom?"

"Yes, Keith?"

"I'm cold." He hadn't wanted to say anything, but the shivering was getting pretty bad. He was also tired of what they were talking about. Really, he was just tired, period. He had no idea what time it was, only that he should still be asleep in his bed at home.

"I'm cold, too." Mom walked over and wrapped her arms around him. Keith could feel her shivering like he was, but at least her upper body was mostly dry. Falling off of Dad's shoulders had resulted in his whole being receiving a thorough soaking.

"We need to get out of the pool," Dad sighed.

"That creature . . . alien . . . when it touched the water it reacted like it was burned." Dr. Blatty gazed toward her house. "If only we had a way to carry the water with us. Then we could splash it on the thing if it appears again."

Keith could see that his dad was psyching himself up, and knew what he was planning even before he told anyone.

"I'm going to go get us some pots," he announced.

"Doug, no!" Mom left Keith's side in order to grab Dad's arm, although he hadn't yet made a move to exit the pool.

"We can't stay in here. The boys are freezing."

"But what if it's just waiting for you to try something like this?"

"Dad, here." Keith pulled off his sodden shirt. "You can throw it at the thing." Did he want his dad to go? Not at all. But he also knew that look on his face, the one that said no one was going to be able to change his mind.

"Here." Russell also took off his shirt.

"Thanks." Dad accepted them and dunked them under the surface to make sure they were properly drenched. "The door's unlocked, right?"

"Yes," Dr. Blatty nodded. "Do you know where the pots are?"

"In the cupboard beside the oven."

"Yes, good. That thing appeared and disappeared over the grass. We don't know what it's doing, but hopefully that means it can't come out of more solid surfaces. You shouldn't have to cross any grass." There was the stone patio and then a large wooden deck between the pool and the back door. "But we've seen how fast it can move. We should try to splash water outside of the pool before you go. Maybe a wet surface would slow it down."

Dad agreed.

Both Russell and Keith worked in a frenzy at this task. It was something useful to do. While Russell swept his arms, trying to create waves big enough to wash out of the pool, Keith cupped his hands and threw frankly pitiful amounts of water as far as he could. A few droplets barely reached the deck, let alone the door. Neither mother liked having their sons so close to the edge, but then they were there too, also helping out.

"Here, hold onto this for me." Dad pressed his watch into Keith's hands. When Keith was little and afraid to go to school, his dad would give him the watch. It was a promise that Keith was safe, and that Dad would come back for him.

"Good luck, Dad."

He grinned with confidence. "Thank you, although you know I don't need it." And he dashed out of the pool.

15:
NOW

K EITH TRAVELLED IN SPURTS. He paddled for a bit, then rode the current, then paddled for a bit again. While his goal was to find a place to sleep, he didn't really know what he was searching for. Somewhere safe, but what did that look like? All he saw was dirt.

Maybe he should be trying to travel faster. He didn't need to see much before deciding an area wasn't safe. He was just so tired, though. Physically, mentally, emotionally, he was completely wiped out. Just sleeping there in the kayak would have been fine, if it weren't for the fact that he'd drift up against the shore eventually. Too bad he didn't have an anchor, then he'd be able to stop anywhere he wanted to.

His hopes soared as he entered a long bay and spotted a raft off someone's dock. He paddled hard for it, excited for the simple act of stretching out. With the idea of resting so close, he didn't care if he over exerted himself. He could lie down and sleep.

A sour twist of his stomach accompanied his dashed plans. The raft was wooden, and very old. So old, that things had begun to grow on it. Dirt. It was possible that this dirt was perfectly safe, that it wasn't housing a monster, but Keith couldn't be certain. He could search through it, he could check and pray that nothing snapped him up, but what if there was a hollow between the boards and the floats? It looked like there might be, but there was so much dirt filling the cracks, that Keith couldn't be certain. If there *was* a hollow, and if that hollow were completely filled with dirt, then it was more than he could safely sift through. He checked for an anchor line he could detach and clip to his kayak, but couldn't find one. It was probably under the middle. Defeated, Keith paddled away.

I want to go home, his thoughts kept repeating, as if that would suddenly make it possible. He wasn't even sure what he meant by home. The winter house? Or did he want to go back to last year? If he had the power to change anything, he'd divert the meteor, stop it from ever striking Earth. If that was too much, then he'd go back to yesterday. He'd stop himself from making the mistake that may have killed everyone he knew. Everyone who'd been left.

Keith shook his head. Those thoughts were too dark. He tried to convince himself that what had happened wasn't his fault, but who else was there to blame? Maybe it was for the best that he was alone. If someone had survived, if he were with them, they'd hate him. For now, he could escape his guilt, hide from it in a cloak of loneliness, panic, and despair. While these weren't great feelings, they were better than that terrible worm boring through his mind.

He believed all this as if he had any control over what he was feeling at any given time.

Keith felt terrible both inside and out as he resumed his search for a place to spend the night. On top of everything else, he now had to pee, but the shadows were getting long, and it would be a lot harder to find a safe spot in the dark. The discomfort helped him focus.

Eventually, it got to the point where Keith couldn't ignore his bladder any longer. He spotted a small hump of a rock and made his way toward it. While he could probably just pee over the side of the kayak, he wasn't confident enough to try that just yet. He'd probably end up tipping over, or somehow getting piss in his boat.

The small rock turned out to be exactly what he was looking for. Well, maybe not exactly, but it was good enough. It was larger than he thought, as the initial hump hid a lower flat spot behind it. Scrambling awkwardly out, Keith stood naked on the rock and relieved himself in the lake. His clothes were still damp, but he put them back on. The sun no longer reached the water anyway, and without any wind, he couldn't imagine them getting much dryer until tomorrow.

The sky was a fiery orange as Keith prepared for the coming night. The flat part of the rock wasn't large enough for him to stretch out on, but he didn't imagine that it would be very comfortable even if it were. After checking all his supplies again, and making sure that they were secure in either the waterproof sack or the emergency kit, Keith placed them in the center of the rock. He disconnected the paddle into two pieces and placed those with them. The only things he didn't put there, that he kept on the raised portion with him, were the life jacket and the towel. While the flat part wasn't large enough for Keith, it was a little bigger than the opening of the kayak. Keith carefully dragged it out of the water, and flipped it upside down, his supplies nestled in the seat opening. He hoped it would drain some of the water that he hadn't been able to bail out. In the dying light, he searched the bottom of the kayak for leeches. Just the idea of having one of those latch onto him while he slept made him shudder.

It was still too early to sleep. Keith was tired, but not in a way that he thought he'd lose consciousness. Instead, he sat on the raised section of the rock and squeezed as much water out of the life jacket as he could.

The bugs were merciless. He had always been one of those lucky people who wasn't favoured by mosquitoes, but that didn't mean they ignored him completely. He slapped his skin whenever he even thought he felt one, and waved them away from his ears until the stars came out. While they'd be a nuisance all night, their numbers reduced with the full dark.

The constellations overhead shone brightly. There was no moon that night, nothing but those distant flaming orbs. Keith found all the stars Russell had taught him and tried not to cry. A satellite drifted by, its motion separating it from the stars. Was there anyone left to make use of that satellite? Were there astronauts trapped aboard the ISS? Keith imagined what it would be like up there, just drifting around and around the planet. There'd be no dirt devils, but of course, by now, anyone who'd been left up there would have run out of food. The garden they grew wasn't likely to be enough to sustain them for very long. Of all the ways to die in space, starvation had probably been pretty low on their list. But maybe they hadn't starved. Maybe they had jumped into their Soyuz and returned to Earth to deal with the dirt devils alongside everybody else. Keith wasn't sure which of those two options he'd choose.

Eventually he climbed onto the hull of the kayak. It wasn't

really dry, but then neither was he. Using the lifejacket as a pillow, and the beach towel as a blanket, he tried to sleep. This was as difficult a task as just about everything else he'd done that day. While the plastic kayak had a bit of give, making it better than the rock, it wasn't exactly comfortable. Whenever he stretched out, he was made aware of the gentle curve to the bottom of the boat, and anytime he rolled, he felt like he was going to fall off or break through it. And, of course, there were the dark thoughts, the gravity of which strengthened whenever the sun went down.

"Fucking mosquitoes," Keith grumbled, swatting another one away from his ear.

16: THEN

DAD MADE IT inside the Blatty residence, but Keith still struggled to breathe, taking only short, shallow gasps. He kept expecting one of those things to show up at any moment. His whole body seemed to thrum, as he waited helplessly for his dad to return.

"Close the door, Doug," Mom muttered, her fear emerging as intense irritation.

Dad had left the sliding glass door open behind him. It was a heavy door, so he probably hadn't shut it in the name of haste, but Keith agreed with his mom. Dad had left himself exposed by doing that. Because of the open door, however, they could hear him clattering around as he gathered the pots.

Keith's heart skipped a beat when his dad reappeared. He wanted to lunge out of the water and grab him, but managed to restrain himself. Dad's bare feet thumped across the deck, and then slapped along the patio. At the edge of the pool, he leaped, clearing the steps and splashing down into the water where it was safe. The stacked pots he had clutched in each arm popped free, some of them sinking to the bottom before Dad could catch them. They weren't difficult to retrieve.

"I didn't know whether to go for volume or handle type," Dad said as they sorted through his stash. "I grabbed a bit of both."

"This one is no good." Dr. Blatty took hold of the largest pot. "You *have* to use two hands to carry it when full, and even then it can be a challenge."

"We can use it to slosh more water out of the pool though," Russell pointed out.

"That's a good idea, honey, but before we go draining the pool, we have to decide why. Where are we going?" There was steel in Dr. Blatty's eyes as she turned to Keith's parents, visible even in the dark.

"I think we should go down to the lake," Mom suggested. "People there have sailing yachts, and house boats. Maybe we could get a ride on one. It'll keep us on the water without having to be in it while the government deals with this."

"The lake is what, thirty minutes away?" Dad pointed out. "That's a long time for a maybe."

"Do you have a better suggestion?"

Dad did not.

"The plan's not perfect, but then neither is staying in the pool," Dr. Blatty said. "I suggest we go inside our houses, change into dry things, maybe grab a few supplies we think we might need. Cash. We should bring any cash we have, in case we have to pay our way onto a boat." The steel wasn't just in her eyes. Dr. Blatty had mourned her husband for a bit, and had now put that aside in order to deal with the problem at hand.

"I don't think we should split up. We'll get things from your house, and then go over to ours," Mom decided, and Dad and Dr. Blatty agreed.

Neither Keith nor Russell had been given a say, but then what could either of them have said? Keith didn't want to leave the safety of the pool, but his teeth were chattering out a Morse code, telling him that he must.

After experimenting with the pots, it was decided that the ones with a long handle worked best. They tended to be smaller and couldn't hold as much water as the pots with a stubby handle on either side, but they made it easy to fling the water, which seemed important. Keith and Russell used the really big pot, lifting it between them and dumping its contents out across the stone patio. They made a mighty puddle between the pool and the deck. Using the small pots, they flung more water onto the deck itself. Somewhere a car alarm started wailing into the night.

"Okay, we're going to do this quick," Dad took charge. "I'll go first, but Kimiko, I want you right behind me. Boys, you follow next. Sigrid, are you okay bringing up the rear?"

Mom nodded that she was.

Keith wasn't sure what was making his legs shake more: cold, exhaustion, or fear? As they rushed up the steps out of the pool, he thought his knees were going to buckle on him. They almost did when he reached the highest level of the multi-tiered deck, and some of the water sloshed out of his pot. Russell gave him a look like he had dropped an expensive new phone, as if Keith had done it on purpose.

Once they were through the door, Dad pushed it shut, and they all took a second to confirm that they had really made it. Dr. Blatty was the first to move. She went over to the sink and started the water running. She not only plugged up the sink, but began filling bowls and glasses as well.

"Boys, I want you to stay in here," she instructed them. "Russell, is there anything you *need* that I might not think to pack?"

"All I need is my laptop."

Dr. Blatty flashed him a smile, but it was quick and pained, and in the dim light of the kitchen, it was almost a grimace.

"I raided your linen closest," Mom said as she returned to the kitchen. Keith had only just noticed that she and Dad had left. "Doug's filling up the tub, and the bathroom sinks in case we need a retreat."

Mom wrapped a big towel around Keith and held him tight, after handing another to Dr. Blatty so that she could do the same for Russell.

"Thanks, Mom."

"Hey, this is also for me," she joked half-heartedly. "I'm cold, too." Another towel was draped across her shoulders.

"Place the glasses and bowls across the entrances," Dr. Blatty instructed Russell. "You might be tempted to let the sink overflow, but please don't let it. We don't want to deal with water damage when we come home."

"Okay, Mom."

"Sigrid? Could you help me pack?"

"Of course." The two mothers left extra towels on the small kitchen table and went to gather supplies.

Keith scrubbed himself with the first towel he had been given and then wrapped it around his waist like a skirt. Before helping Russell with the bowls, he grabbed a second towel for his upper body.

"Are you okay?" Keith risked asking as they lined up water glasses between the kitchen and the dining room.

"No."

"Yeah, me neither."

"I bet I feel worse."

"Yeah. Do you want to talk about it?"

"No."

Keith hoped his best friend didn't notice just how relieved he was by that answer. Even though Mr. Blatty had simply disappeared, Keith kept picturing Mrs. Phelps' hand every time his thoughts approached anywhere near the subject.

"Well . . . if you need anything, you know I'm here for you, right?" Keith said awkwardly.

"I know, man. Do you think we should fill up the plates? They're kind of shallow."

"Yeah, we can use them like puddles, and place them around on the floor."

Anything that could hold water in the kitchen soon was, forcing them to be very careful where they stepped. Russell had surrounded the table on three sides, a wall making up the fourth. Once they knew they couldn't do any more, both boys climbed underneath with the rest of the towels and huddled there.

"I'm so fucking tired," Keith whispered.

"Me, too," Russell whispered back.

"I keep thinking I'll wake up."

"Same."

"Hey, do you remember when we used to build forts in your basement?"

"Yeah."

"I think this is our first fort with a moat."

Russell actually managed a chuckle. "If we had tried this before, my mom would've murdered us." His choice of words spoiled his mood.

"We definitely would have spilled something," Keith tried to keep things light. "*Especially* if we had played defend the castle."

"Yeah." Russell responded, but the earlier connection felt like it had gone. He was retreating into himself again.

The sweeping beam of a flashlight announced the arrival of an adult.

"Keith? Russell?" Dad hissed from the hallway entrance. It seemed that no one wanted to raise their voice above a whisper. Even when Dr. Blatty had been fussing about by the sink, she had done it as quietly as she could.

Keith stuck his arm out and waved so that he'd be seen.

"You guys made a minefield," Dad commented as he picked his way over to the table. "Russell, your mom wanted me to bring you this change of clothes."

"Thanks."

Both Keith and his dad turned their backs, giving Russell some privacy to change. Based on what he could hear, Keith imagined Russell struggled a bit given the confined space under the table, but it was better than standing among the dishes elsewhere on the floor. It wasn't long after Russell had gotten dressed that they heard the gentle sobbing from elsewhere in the house.

"That's my mom." There was no inflection in Russell's voice as he said this.

"Do you want to go see her?" Dad asked.

Russell shook his head. "She doesn't like crying in front of me. Sigrid's with her though?"

"Yeah."

"Okay."

"Hey, do you boys want to help me pick out some food? I figure we should make sure we have something to eat while we're out on the lake."

Russell and Keith climbed out from under the table. Now that Russell was dressed, it made Keith feel even more awkward to be in just his boxers.

Keith ended up making sandwiches for everyone at his dad's suggestion. If they couldn't sleep, they might as well eat. He liked to think he was good at making sandwiches. Sometimes he imagined opening a sandwich shop. It would be a little place, near a park, where people could pick up a bite to eat for an impromptu picnic. His wrappers would be made of a recycled material, and he'd encourage all of his patrons to dispose of them properly. His own art would adorn the walls, and he'd be a part of the community, the kind of place with regulars who could count on their names being remembered.

Mrs. Phelps' hand.

Keith paused, the knife only partway through quartering Russell's favourite, peanut butter, pickles, and bologna. The image had cut sharply through his daydream. Instead of a well-lit shop that allowed in plenty of sunlight, he'd been plunged back out into the night, with its blood-soaked grass.

"Keith? You all right?"

"Yeah, I'm fine." He wasn't, but it seemed easier to lie to his dad than to explain. He finished with the sandwiches, and handed them around when Mom and Dr. Blatty came back to the kitchen. It was crowded with all of them in there, and the dishes scattered across the floor added an extra challenge, but they all found a place to stand and eat. Keith watched everyone eat mechanically, looking like they didn't even taste what he had made. He cursed himself, wishing he was at home where he had more ingredients to work with, and if the power had been on, he could have toasted the bread properly. His contribution sucked.

"So, our house next," Mom said when they had finished.

"That's a lot more ground to cover than from the pool to the back door." Based on their tones, Mom and Dr. Blatty had been thinking about the same thing.

"A lot of grass," Dad agreed.

"We know the water works," Keith mentioned, wanting to be helpful. "You guys have a sprinkler, right? We can point that toward our house and soak the ground." He thought it was a brilliant idea.

"Why don't we just drive?" Russell said instead.

"I never thought of the car," Dr. Blatty brightened at her son's idea.

"Yeah," Mom agreed. "Our house is so close, driving would normally just be a waste of gas. Great idea, Russell."

Keith sulked in the corner.

17:
NOW

THERE WAS NO hiding from the sun. Keith tried pulling his beach towel over his head to little effect. Maybe he could have used the life jacket, but he gave up before even moving it. It wasn't like the rising sun was the only thing making it difficult to sleep.

"Arrrg," he grumbled, shoving the towel aside. With another groan, he sat up, feeling the plastic of the kayak shift disconcertingly beneath him. He scrambled off onto the raised hump of rock and studied the hull of his boat. It popped back to normal, but he worried that if he slept on it too many times, there'd come a day when it wouldn't. He'd have to find a better location for tonight.

Sitting on the rock, Keith rubbed his face and looked up at the glowing sky. The sun hadn't actually risen above the treetops, yet it was still too bright to consider sleeping. Instead, he sat there and tried to come up with a plan, one that was better than just finding the next place to sleep. He needed a long-term goal.

"I have to find a winter house." It was as simple as that. He had all summer to locate one, so that could definitely be construed as long-term.

Keith didn't like this plan for one simple reason: luck. Finding a winter house would come down to luck, something he didn't have a lot of. Time was on his side for the moment, but that was a finite resource.

"Then I guess I'll just have to cover more ground," he told himself. The more places he saw, the better his odds of finding shelter.

After taking a moment to wake up a little more, Keith reluctantly got to work. He flipped the kayak upright and placed it on the water, but kept hold of the front pull handle. He reassembled the paddle, and then retrieved his empty tin from his supplies and used it to take a drink. The water was calm, so he let go of the kayak for just a moment to pee off the other side of the island. The boat floated away a little, but was still close enough for him to easily pull back with the paddle.

Everything hurt. His muscles were stiff, and he'd slept uncomfortably whenever he'd slept at all. A chill had settled deep into his bones from wearing damp clothes for so long. While he wasn't fond of being woken up by it, he knew he'd appreciate the sun once its warmth reached him.

Keith sorted through his food. Fourteen cans left. If he ate two a day, that gave him food for a week, but could he survive on two a day? The cans were of varying sizes, with some of their contents sounding more filling than others. There was more fish, but also beans and soup. He wished he had more variety than that, but unless he raided another cottage, that's all there was. For breakfast, he selected a can of baked beans. Maybe if they had been heated, he'd have found them less repulsive. Still, he choked down most of the can, and saved the rest for when he next got hungry. The can just fit in the kayak's cup holder, so after carefully placing the lid back on, that's where Keith stored it.

To prepare for departure, he clipped the tow rope to the front pull handle, and then wrapped the other end around the handle of the waterproof sack, which would sit in the bottom of the boat. The lid of the emergency kit had a small loop of string attached to it, so Keith took the time to undo one of his seat straps so that it could be threaded through the string. This allowed him to hang the kit somewhat awkwardly over the side, where it'd be out of the way. His lifejacket he tucked under the rear bungee string, and the towel was carefully folded and pinched under the front string. He made himself a mental reminder to refold it later, to make sure all of it got some direct sunlight. A dry towel was more useful than a damp one.

With that, all of his gear was ready to go. It was time to get into the boat, and start paddling again. Keith just sat there on the rock, holding the kayak steady with his feet. He wasn't looking forward to paddling again. He didn't *want* to. The rock might have been small and hard, but it was also safe. He didn't have to do anything while on that tiny island. Then again, there wasn't anything *to* do. Sure, he could sit there all he wanted, but that wasn't going to change anything. Only the weather would change, and it would be a shame to waste what looked to be a clear day.

Sighing, Keith climbed into the kayak, nearly spilling his remaining beans in the process.

Because he'd undone the seat strap, Keith took a moment to readjust it to what he thought might be the most comfortable position, and then punted off the rock. He was on his way again.

Progress was slow, but at least it was progress. Because it was easier, Keith continued to follow the slow current, keeping the wind at his back whenever possible. He ended up heading down a wide channel that expanded at the end into a massive bay. Not far was a floating marker to warn boaters of shallow rocks, so Keith paddled up to it as a place to decide what to do.

This was truly a lake he found himself in now. The far shore would take him the whole day to reach at the pace he'd been paddling. But was that where he even wanted to go? His eyes swept the jagged shoreline. Sometimes it bent back on itself, hiding what was there beyond a spit of land. Another channel, or just an alcove? Were those scraggily trees on an island or a peninsula? He hoped to see someone alive moving about, or even a distant trail of smoke that he could follow, but there was nothing. Birds flitting through the sky were the only signs of life.

It was tempting to paddle straight across. If there *was* someone around here, they would likely see him. He also had to admit that the idea of being surrounded by so much water was alluring. Unfortunately, it went against his goal. He had the best odds of finding the things he needed by staying closer to the shoreline. Also, the sun would be merciless out there. His bug bites were starting to get itchy; he didn't need a sunburn on top of them.

The thought of the sun decided his course. He picked the shoreline casting the most shade and began to follow it. Despite wanting the rays' warmth, he told himself that he had to be smart about it. Not that he ever imagined living long enough to have to worry about getting skin cancer. Not these days.

18: THEN

IN THE END, they used both Russell's and Keith's ideas. In the garage with his dad, Keith held the flashlight while Dad tried to open the large door without any power.

"Too bad their door isn't like our cheap one," Dad joked to Keith, but Keith could only offer a weak smile at the attempt.

"Just use a crowbar," Dr. Blatty eventually huffed. "If my garage door has to be broken for us to get out of here, then so be it." She was at the back of the garage with Mom and Russell, poking through the junk they stored in there, checking if there was anything they should bring.

Keith noticed the way Russell kept eyeing the trio of bikes hanging from a rack along one wall. He and his parents would sometimes take family rides together. While it had become less of a thing these days, Russell was probably thinking about how there'd never be another. If Keith ever lost his parents, he didn't know what he would do. He had no idea how Russell managed to keep from curling up into a ball on the floor right now.

A loud bang made everyone jump.

"Wasn't me," Dad said, the crowbar in his hand but not yet used.

"That was a gunshot," Dr. Blatty explained, just as a second one went off. "Close, too."

"I didn't think anyone on our street owned a gun," Dad commented.

"Well that's just naive." The eye roll could be heard in Mom's voice. "You'd think having grown up in the U.S., you'd know better."

"Maybe I just believed that here was better," Dad huffed.

"You two sound like you're about to make a mountain out of a mole hill," Dr. Blatty interjected. "We have much bigger things than gun control to worry about right now."

"Maybe they shot it," Keith hoped. Everyone knew what *it* he was referring to.

Three more rapid shots followed by a sharp scream put that idea out of their heads.

"How close was that?" Mom asked quietly.

No one could say for certain, but any degree of close was too close.

"Keith? Help me out here." Dad waved him over. He'd jammed one end of the crowbar under the bottom of the garage door and then shoved a winter tire up against it for further leverage. "Grab hold, and lean all your weight on it. Ready? One, two, three."

Keith and his dad pushed down on the end of the crowbar. The garage door resisted, but eventually the bottom panel buckled and bent. It wasn't a huge hole they had created.

"Whew," Dad huffed when they gave up trying to make it larger. "We're going to need to exit through the front door, but at least we can get the hose out."

"Can you see anything out there?" Mom asked.

Keith dropped to his belly to take a look while Dad put the tire back. "Not really," he reported. "I think the sun is going to come up soon, though."

Russell had unspooled the hose and dragged the end over. Keith got out of the way as his friend shoved it through the opening and Dad turned on the water.

"Sorry, Dr. Blatty, I got your towel dirty." Keith shouldn't have lain down with it wrapped around his waist.

"It's okay, Keith. Also, I think it's time you start calling me Kimiko."

"Really?" Keith hoped he didn't sound as surprised as he felt. Russell's parents had always been really formal about things with Russell's friends, Keith included.

Dr. Blatty—Kimiko—seemed to take a moment to think about it, and then nodded sharply. Decision made. *Why* she'd made that decision, now, Keith couldn't understand. He didn't want to. He was also unsure whether he liked the decision. Russell's mom had *always* been Dr. Blatty. Too much had changed tonight already. Why couldn't he just wake up?

"I soaked as much of the driveway as I could from here," Russell reported. "I also tried to spray the walkway, but I couldn't get much."

"You did great, Russell." Dad patted him on the shoulder. "The pots should get us the rest of the way."

As they worked their way back through the house to the front door, Mom asked, "Why can't we just stay here? Seems perfectly safe inside."

"The alert said to get to water," Dad reminded her. "If it were safe inside, they would have told us to shelter in place."

"Maybe they overreacted."

"I don't think they did."

When they reached the door, Keith noticed his mom hanging back. "Mom?"

"I don't want to go out there," she admitted.

"Come on, honey, we agreed on this plan," Dad reminded her.

"I'm afraid."

Keith had *never* heard his mom say she was afraid of anything. She enjoyed watching horror films, even when no one else wanted to watch them with her. She picked up spiders and other creepy crawlies with her bare hands to release them outside. When they went to Canada's Wonderland, she rode on all the rides with no hesitation, even the ones that made Keith's stomach feel fluttery just by looking at them.

Dad stepped over to her and took her hands in his. "We'll be all right," he said in a quiet voice, his eyes on hers. "We have a plan. We know how to defend ourselves. Most importantly, we're together. We're going to stay that way."

Mom's eyes flicked over to Keith, then to Russell and his mom, before returning to Dad.

Mrs. Phelps' hand.

Keith turned away from his parents and grabbed one of the bags Dr. Blatty—Kimiko—had packed. It was Russell's old backpack, the one he'd used before they started high school. It was stylized to look like the back of an astronaut's EVA suit. The one he used these days was like Keith's: as uninteresting as possible. All the bags Kimiko had packed were of a kind that could be slung over a shoulder, except for one. Keith knew they had put canned goods—along with some other food—into the wheeled suitcase, making it the heaviest of them all. Dad, of course, volunteered to be the one who'd drag it.

"Do you have the keys?" he asked Kimiko—Dr. Kimiko.

She nodded. "The car's unlocked." They watched as she pushed the button on the fob again, and the headlights outside blinked. They were going to take Mr. Blatty's car because it was the closer of the two on their driveway. "Remember, don't bother with the trunk. We'll just jam in everything around the seats. It'll be a short trip."

"I know, Mom." Russell's knuckles were white around the handle of his pot of water.

"Are we ready?" Dad asked, turning specifically to Mom.

She stepped up next to Keith and squeezed his hand. It was crowded in the entryway. "We're ready."

Dr. Kimiko opened the door and they all scurried out. Movement had Russell flinging his water out over the lawn, but it was only a robin, it's startled flight making them all jump.

Keith focused on the rear door of the sedan. With his long legs and his panic, he quickly pulled ahead of Mom and Russell and even Dr. Kimiko. He ripped open the door and leapt inside, crawling across the seat to leave room behind him for the others. As Dr. Kimiko got behind the wheel, Russell threw himself in after Keith.

"Doug!" Mom hissed at Dad.

"One second." Dad had stopped in front of the car. With the big bag standing beside him, he scooped up the hose and began to soak the sedan. In his sodden pajamas, he looked like a crazy man.

"Dad!" Keith shouted, wanting him to get into the car just as badly as Mom did.

Still, he spent a full minute or more spraying the car.

Dr. Kimiko lowered her window a crack. "Get in!" she barked, her order allowing no room for disobedience.

Dad dropped the hose and scuttled over to the passenger seat. He shoved the bag in first, down into the foot well, before hopping in and perching on the seat like a bird. As he was swinging the door shut, it suddenly slammed, a body striking the outside of it.

Everyone in the vehicle screamed as one of those monsters leapt up at the glass, its teeth clacking.

Keith hurled his water, succeeding only in soaking the interior of the car and the back of Dad's head.

Dr. Kimiko slammed the car into reverse and stomped on the gas pedal. Everyone got thrown forward, not a single body secured by a seatbelt.

There was a squeal of metal, and then the upper half of the monster appeared on the nose of the car, its claws punching through the hood like paper.

The car was thrown into drive, and again the pedal was hammered. Dr. Kimiko reacted in a split second, yanking the wheel to one side. Mr. Blatty's sedan slammed into Dr. Kimiko's car on the other side of the driveway, momentarily crushing the creature between the two. The sound it made was phenomenal, like a cat had been given the vocal cords of an elephant. It thrashed in clear pain, its claws slicing through the car as though it weren't made of metal, but butter.

"Reverse!" Dad screamed. "Before it kills the engine!"

Dr. Kimiko growled as she released the beast. They watched it hobble off the pavement and quickly sink into Mrs. Phelps' lawn.

"Let's get out of here before another one shows up," Russell insisted. "Please, Mom, let's go. That was a different one. That one was smaller. It was smaller, Mom, there's more than one of them. Hurry up before the big one comes back." He was blathering, not even paying attention to the fact that his mom *was* getting them out of there as fast as possible. The car made weird noises; something from the front end was dragging.

"Mom, you okay?" Keith asked when he noticed she was holding her face.

"Yeah, I'm okay, just a bloody nose," she told him, briefly pulling her hands away. When Keith saw the blood, his insides turned to liquid. "I hit my face on the back of the seat."

"Sorry," Dr. Kimiko called over her shoulder.

"It's fine."

When they stopped the car, they were in Keith's driveway, parked behind Mom's tiny sedan. The plan had been to leap out, throw the bags into the van, and then rush inside, but no one moved. They all eyed the lawn warily.

"We can't stay here," Dad broke the silence.

"We can just take my car to the lake," Dr. Kimiko replied, her eyes never leaving the grass.

"No, we can't." Dad directed everyone's attention to the hood. Something in the car had broken, and now steam was coming out.

"Shit." Dr. Kimiko turned off the engine.

Russell was taken aback even more than Keith. Hearing his mom swear was like having a dog walk up to you and ask for directions.

"Van's unlocked," Mom reported, pressing her fob to blink the lights. Her voice sounded funny as she kept a hand over her face.

"What about the front door?" Dad asked.

"That's locked," Keith told him, remembering watching his mom do it.

"Here." Mom tossed her keys over to Keith. "You'll have to do it. It'll be easier for you."

Dr. Kimiko huffed. "I spilled the water from my pot."

"Mine too," Dad reported. "You did the right thing though. Sigrid?"

"Also empty," Russell reported for her, since Mom was now keeping her head tilted back.

"We have this." Dr. Kimiko pulled a half empty water bottle from a cup holder. "Russell, I want you to carry it. You stay right beside, Keith, okay?"

"Okay." His hands shook as he accepted the water. Was he thinking what Keith was? That it wasn't enough? The water on the car hadn't stopped the thing from slamming into the door or grabbing hold of the bumper so that it could climb up onto the hood.

"Keith, Russell, hand me your bags," Dad told them. "I'll move them into the van while you go unlock the front door."

He did as he was told, but, other than that, Keith couldn't respond. His throat felt squeezed, and he knew the moment he tried to talk, he'd probably start crying. He didn't want to do this. Unlock the door? It was such a simple task, one he had completed a thousand times, but now it felt like too much responsibility. He didn't want to do it.

"You boys ready?" Dr. Kimiko asked, her hand gripping her door handle.

"Yeah," Russell answered for both of them, before Keith could say that he wasn't.

"All right, let's go!"

19:
NOW

THE BEANS WERE polished off sometime around noon. Keith guessed it was noon based on the lack of shadows for him to hide in. He floated off shore with his life jacket balanced on his head, and the towel draped over that to block the armholes. If this was what the start of June was like, he couldn't imagine how high the temperature would get in the middle of July. How was he going to survive those days when the temperature soared up to thirty degrees Celsius?

That was thinking too far ahead.

"You'll find people before then, an established winter house," he urged himself on. "All you have to do is paddle."

Put that way, it sounded so simple, so why was he struggling?

Exhaustion, hunger, despair. He answered only in his mind, as if that would make them less real. *Guilt.*

"Boredom," he added. Because it was true, he was also bored. He wanted someone to talk to, he wanted to get out of the boat and stretch, he wanted to do something more with his hands. "I want to get rid of this stupid ear worm!" he shouted. All day long, the same snatch of song played in his head. He had no idea what the title of the song was, and he *knew* he had the lyrics wrong because he had made them up to go with the tune.

Hey, hey, Mr. J! You hit Harley, that's not okay. Batman related lyrics, because why not? Maybe if he could think up more it would be less infuriating, but that was all his mind would produce. In the hopes of distracting himself from the music behind his made up words, he dug into those lyrics. Who would be saying that? Only Harley Quinn called the Joker, Mr. J, as far as he knew, but he also couldn't picture her speaking in the third person like that. So who'd chastise the Joker for hitting Harley, and also call him Mr. J?

"Poison Ivy!" Keith told no one.

He could see the two-page comic now. Two small panels at the top of the page. The first has the Joker working on something, probably a bomb. In the second panel, Harley gloms onto his back.

"Puddin'!" Keith shouts for her.

A larger panel as the Joker socks her in the face, *pow!* Then he's facing the rear of the next panel, scowling down at an unseen Harley, while from behind him comes a *Hey*. In the next matching panel, there's a bigger *HEY, MR. J!* as he wheels around, still angry. Wait, might people think Harley is saying that? No, she'll be sitting up now, small in the background, holding her head with stars around it.

Her nose would be so bloody. Keith pushed away the thought, not liking where it had come from.

The last panel on the page would be the Joker looking unusually afraid, while a speech bubble points out, *You hit Harley*.

"That's not okay," Keith said aloud as he imagined the second page. It would be a splash page, one big panel with only those three words for text. Poison Ivy, front and center as a great and terrible beauty. Her face would display the fury of a goddess, with her thorny vines filling the space around her, ready to lash out.

Yeah, that would be cool, Keith thought.

He wished he could draw it. For that he would need paper, blue pencils, and a ruler to throw down his sketch lines. Once those were done, he'd take to his pens and ink his lines. A scanner would be needed next to get the image onto a computer. There, he'd separate the blacks onto their own layer, and clean up his lines using his tablet. Colour would come after that. First the flats, then the highlights and shadows. Once it was done, he'd post it online, and hope that people whose opinions mattered both saw it and liked it. He could just jump straight to the computer, and do his sketching there, which is what a lot of other online artists he followed did, but he liked his pencils. Besides, it was the way some of his favourite professionals did it, and he wanted to be a professional.

Well, he used to. Back before. Back when such a dream was

possible. But now he had no internet for posting, no tablet for colouring, no computer or scanner, not even a pencil or a single sheet of paper.

"Fuck!" Keith shouted at the nearest thicket of trees.

A sharp bark answered him.

Keith jumped, his sunshield sliding off his head and nearly landing in the water before he caught both lifejacket and towel. He jammed them down on his lap as he wheeled himself around, using the paddle one handed.

"Hello?" he called toward the trees. "What's there?"

He wanted it to be a dog. If it was dog, then there had to be a human with it. Without anyone to take care of them, large land animals tended to get chomped pretty fast. Creatures of the water stood the best chance on their own, followed by those of the air, but land dwellers? Only the ones so small they went ignored, really had much of a hope. They, and any squirrels or chipmunks smart enough to spend as little time on the ground as possible. Dogs needed a person to keep them on the water.

"Hello?" Keith called again, and was ashamed when his voice wavered. He didn't call out a third time.

Sitting in his boat, Keith strained his ears for another bark, wishing he could silence the gentle lapping of the water against his plastic hull. His eyes raked the terrain for movement. Had he been tricked? Had the sound come from a dirt devil attempting to lure him to shore? They could be tricky like that sometimes.

It also could have been some other animal that hadn't really barked, and Keith had just mistaken the sound for one.

What if I made it up? Keith shuddered at the thought. He could be going mad. After everything else that had happened, it seemed par for the course. Maybe losing his mind wouldn't be so bad.

Unless he went so crazy he went for a walk on the land. That would be pretty bad. Still, at least it would be over.

"No," Keith hissed at himself. "Don't think that way."

He pictured his thoughts like a city, populated by everyone he knew, and all the fictional characters he loved. In the middle of that city was a huge hole, that was pitch black only a couple of feet down from the edges. Those were the thoughts he didn't want. He had to throw them in the hole and then try to ignore that they were there. He had to not fall into it. Not get grabbed by the guilt worm that had bored it, and lived among the shadows.

Seeing no dog, no anything, Keith moved on. He had taken a long enough rest and it was time to paddle again.

His hands hurt. Near the webbing between his thumbs and index fingers, calluses were forming. Was he paddling wrong? Or did this happen to everyone who spent a lot of time kayaking?

"A fellow kayaker," someone would say when they shook hands and noticed the calluses.

Great, you're already speaking for someone who doesn't exist, Keith thought.

The shoreline always changed, and yet it was all the same anyway. The details varied, but it was always the same kinds of trees, bushes, grass, rocks. Cottages dotted the landscape, their docks spearing out into the water. Most of these places probably hadn't been occupied in going on two years. It depended on how early people opened up in the spring, although even the early birds would have been gone for over a year now. Boats were pulled out of the water, floating docks were disconnected and tied to the shore, deck furniture was hidden away, and curtains were drawn tight—that last one was probably pretty popular with inhabited places as well. Nowhere was there anything appealing enough to make Keith want to approach. He just kept gliding past, often making up stories about the people who used to own such places.

That cottage was owned by a CEO who underpaid his employees. He had a rivalry going with the owner next door, who *didn't* underpay his employees. They were both trying to make their retreat seem more appealing than the other, which didn't just mean big and grand, but to capture the essence of a cottage. The next place along beat them both in that regard, as it had been built by the original owners' hands, and then passed on to their children. No high-priced designers there. A different cottage was the secret retreat of an A-list movie starlet, whose neighbours were hunters who had no idea who she was. That satellite dish marked a hacker hideout. That hot tub had seen several steamy affairs. This little unassuming shack was actually owned by foreign royalty.

The odds of any of that being true were astronomically low, but at least it was something to keep Keith's mind occupied and away from the hole. And hey, spacefaring dirt devils crashing into Earth had even lower odds, yet that had happened, so maybe Keith wasn't always totally off the mark.

Dinner consisted of tomato soup. He slurped from the can while standing on a flat but submerged rock, pacing tiny, careful circles to stretch his legs. There was a short cliff nearby that had a tree growing from the top of it at a severe angle. A few of its branches hung just shy of the water. Keith planned to spend the night beneath them, having found nothing better. It wasn't going to be comfortable sleeping in the kayak, but it wasn't like sleeping on the hull had been comfortable either.

Pushing the nose of his boat between some of the branches, he found one with a convenient handhold.

"Ugh, spider webs!" Keith slapped at his face to get them off. He then used the paddle to sweep between other branches, hoping to remove any webs his face had missed. There could now be a spider in his boat and he'd have no idea. What a cozy bedmate.

Keith used the tow rope to secure himself to the tree. He had to be careful about it though. A dirt devil couldn't reach him from shore, but it might be able to if it climbed the tree. Keith couldn't be certain. The branches within range were thin and over the water, so it didn't seem like any dirt devil would risk it, but if one did, Keith wanted to be able to disconnect and push out into deeper water in a hurry. That meant connecting the tow rope in such a way that it could hold him in place, but could also come free if he gave it a sharp tug. He experimented a number of times until he was satisfied.

Sleep was fretful. He shifted about in the kayak, always hoping to find a more comfortable position. Sometimes this rocked the boat, startling him into a higher level of wakefulness, and causing him to check the tree branches for any movement that might indicate a dirt devil. When he did sleep, it was full of dreams. He got to talk to his dad, and hang out with Russell. His mom baked him . . . something, it seemed to keep changing between a pie, and brownies, and his favourite muffins. He was at school, trying to find his history teacher in order to hand in an assignment. Towards morning, he dreamt that he was on a date with Mandy. They sat outside a surreal café, watching some sort of water horse thing move up and down a river-street. Keith wanted to talk to Mandy, but she couldn't hear him. There was singing coming from somewhere. It wasn't loud, and yet it was loud enough to drown out anything he said. It made him angry, not being able to get Mandy's attention. It was his anger that eventually woke him up.

And he discovered that the singing wasn't just in his dream.

20: THEN

K EITH BOLTED FOR the door of his house. He didn't wait to see if Russell was able to get out of the car fast enough to keep up with him, he just ran. His desire for haste almost carried him across the lawn, like it would have done on any normal day. At the last moment, he pivoted to follow the side of the driveway up to the front patio.

At the door, he tried to jam the key in upside down. He surprised himself with how quickly he registered what his mistake had been instead of repeatedly trying the wrong thing. It was like he was of two minds, the one that was in extreme panic, and the one that was calmly telling him the correct thing to do.

When the door opened, he threw himself inside, with Russell literally pushing on his back. Mom and Dr. Kimiko piled in right behind them, then grabbed the door to close it.

"What about Dad?" Keith shouted, torn between stopping them and not.

"He'll be here in a minute." Mom shoved Keith deeper into the house. "Start filling everything in the kitchen."

The kitchen was very similar to Russell's, but more spacious because his family didn't have a table in theirs; they always ate in the adjacent dining room. Keith gathered up all the glasses, bowls, pots and pans, and piled them up beside the sink where Russell began filling them. He was relieved when he heard the door open and his dad call out that it was just him.

"I'm going to go get some clothes," Keith told Russell, grabbing a pot that had already been filled and then heading for the stairs.

"Doug?" Mom called out as Keith reached the top.

"Just me, Mom!" he responded. "I'm changing my clothes. Dad's downstairs and I have a pot of water."

"Turn on the faucets in the bathroom!"

"Okay!"

Before reaching his room, he detoured into the bathroom. Keith put the stopper in the sink and turned on the water. He figured the overflow drain would prevent it from spilling if left unattended. For the tub, he put in the stopper as well, but turned on the showerhead to fill it. He imagined jumping beneath the spray in the event of an emergency, although the pressure was down with so many taps open, and he wasn't sure it would actually stop anything from snatching him.

We need rain, Keith thought as he entered his room. Once it rained, the things should drown. Shouldn't they?

Keith closed his door to change, but he found the barrier made him anxious. Not because he didn't feel safe in his room—it was the safest he'd felt since being woken up—but because he didn't like the idea of there being an obstacle between him and everyone else, should they need him. He changed quickly, opening the door as soon as he was decent.

Picking up his backpack, he upended it onto the floor. Books and papers and gym clothes fell out in a heap. He snatched only two things back up from the pile: his sketchbook and his pencil case. Rushing around his room, he stuffed into his bag things he thought he'd need, like his laptop along with its charger. For a few seconds, he searched for his phone before remembering that it was toast. After his clothing was jammed inside, he returned to the bathroom for his toothbrush, toothpaste, and deodorant.

Somewhere glass shattered, and someone started screaming. Keith didn't have time to identify who, before a terrible, unearthly squeal rippled through the whole house. He froze in the doorway, torn between rushing to help, and jumping into the shower to save himself. More glass was shattered and the terrible sound retreated into the night where it abruptly ceased. It was replaced by the pounding of feet on the stairs, with a second set coming to the bathroom. Keith was swept up into his mother's arms, and it was a good thing she was moving so fast, or else he might have brained her with his pot, the way she had come swooping out of the dark like that.

"Dad!" Keith shouted, trying to prevent his mom from shoving him into the shower. He'd *just* changed.

"It's all right!" Dad called back. "We're all okay!"

Keith wriggled his way free of his disquietingly silent mother and headed for the stairs. When some light reached her, he saw the paleness of her face, like a corpse, and so he went back to her and took her hand in his. She had been terrified in ways he couldn't begin to understand.

Downstairs, the rear door was a mess of glass on the floor, the framing around it bent and sliced. Broken dishes also littered the tile, and Dad sat on a counter with red drops of blood all around him. Dr. Kimiko was wearing a small headlamp, disinfecting a long gash on his arm; the kitchen's first aid kit stood open beside her.

"Mom, I don't think you need to use that much," Russell was telling her.

"We don't know what kind of diseases that thing could be carrying," she answered him.

"It's an alien. If it's carrying a bacteria or virus, that would also be alien. Stuff like that evolves to attack what it knows, it wouldn't know us."

"And yet invasive species happen all the time," Dr. Kimiko grumbled.

"Just let her do what she feels she needs to," Dad told Russell, his face constantly wincing from the stinging.

"What happened?" Keith asked.

"One of those things smashed through the back door like it was nothing," Russell reported.

"It came after me," Dad continued the tale. "Got a piece of me, too. If it wasn't for Russell's quick actions, I don't want to think about what could have happened."

"I just started throwing the water glasses at it," Russell shrugged.

"It really didn't like that. Went back out the way it came."

"Mom, where are you going?" Keith turned as she slipped away from his side.

"Back upstairs to get the bags I packed. We're leaving *right now.*"

Help his mom or stay down here? Keith didn't know what he should do. His dad had nearly died, *again*, and he hadn't even been there. But what could he have done if he had been? He'd frozen in the bathroom doorway, so what made him think he could have done any good down here? Not like Russell, who could act decisively, and then even be humble about it afterward. He would make a hell of an astronaut.

As for Keith, he followed his mom upstairs to be a pack mule.

"Did we forget anything?" she asked as they lugged the bags to the top of the stairs.

It was such a common place question that it was jarring in the dark, and took Keith a moment to answer.

"Probably." They often forgot something small and pointless when they went on vacation, so it was pretty much guaranteed that they would forget something now, as they had packed in a panic.

"You have your toothbrush, deodorant?" Mom continued.

"Yeah."

"Change of clothes, pajamas?"

"Yes, Mom. Do you have any medications you or Dad might need?"

"Yes, I packed them first."

Everyone gathered in the front hall, just like they had at Russell's house. Bags were divided among them, and pots of water were handed out.

"Which of us should drive?" Dad asked Mom.

"You should. You drive the van more than I do. Also, the seat will already be set up for you."

"Okay." He turned to everyone. "I flipped up the back seat, but Keith, only your usual seat in the middle is up. All the bags from the Blattys' are in the other side, so watch out for it when you open the door. We'll just toss this stuff on top. Is everyone ready?"

"I have to pee," Russell admitted, his face turning red beneath the beams of their flashlights.

"Right. We should all go," Dad said.

"You should also change out of your pajama pants," Mom told him.

Dad hadn't been upstairs yet. While he went to change and use the bathroom off his bedroom, Russell and Dr. Kimiko used the main floor bathroom, and Keith and Mom returned upstairs to use what Keith liked to consider as his own bathroom.

"Do you think we should turn the water back off?" Mom asked

about the taps when Keith was done, and Dad joined them in the upstairs hallway.

"You're the one who wanted to leave immediately," Dad pointed out. "This now feels like stalling. What's going on?"

"I know. It's just . . . " Mom turned in place, gazing at all the walls. "This is our house. Our *home*. We *have* to go, I just . . . . don't like the idea of abandoning it. I don't know what to do. Every thought I have is conflicted."

"We're not abandoning our home," Dad told her, sweeping Mom into an embrace. "We'll turn off the water if it makes you feel better." He guided her into their room.

Keith ran to his bathroom and turned the taps off in there. He knew how his mother felt. Every decision felt wrong, somehow.

"We'll be back soon," Keith told his mom as they returned to the main floor. "As soon as it rains, those things are toast."

"In the meantime, we have to *go*," Dr. Kimiko spoke impatiently from the front door. "What is she doing?" She huffed as Mom headed for the kitchen.

"Turning off the taps. Just give her a minute," Dad answered.

"She's the one who freaked out about us needing to leave the moment she saw your injury."

"I know. And she knows. She just needs to do this."

"Guys?" Mom called from the kitchen. "You're going to want to come see this."

21:
NOW

WHERE WAS THE singing coming from? Keith paddled away from the tree branches and short cliff, his head swivelling in all directions as he attempted to locate the source.

"Helloooo!" he shouted at the top of his lungs. When his echo died away, he could still hear the singing. It didn't stop, it didn't call back. "HEEEEY!" he screamed.

He was pretty sure there were multiple voices singing, but he couldn't be certain because of how distant they were. When the wind was just right, he realized that the thumping he heard wasn't his heart, but the much more steady beat of a drum. Somewhere, people were singing and playing music. After all he'd been through, somehow this simple fact managed to shock Keith. Or maybe it shocked him *because* of all he'd been through. When was the last time he had sung in a group like that?

Keith's stomach rumbled, and the pressure on his bladder was becoming untenable. He hadn't wasted a second since waking to take care of himself. He had just paddled, trying to find the source of the song.

"NO!" he shrieked as it grew quieter. "STOP!"

He couldn't head in the direction he thought the sound was coming from, because the land was in the way. He travelled at an angle, but the music grew quieter, more distant. They were singing as they moved, and currently they were moving away from Keith.

This time when he screamed, he didn't have words to go with it. He screamed and screamed and screamed some more. By the time he stopped, his throat was raw and the singing was completely gone. He couldn't even hear the drum.

His loneliness came crashing down again. Just as he was getting used to the idea of being on his own, he was reminded of how badly he wanted to be near people. It was a need, as much as food was, and he'd risked leaving the water for that. He thought he'd risk leaving the water now if there was any hope it'd lead him to people. But there wasn't. They were gone.

Keith didn't know what to do. It was like his body was too small. Everything inside was pressing outward, needing to go *somewhere* but there was nowhere to go. No obvious direction to take. He was a migrating bird whose compass had started spinning.

"Stop it, stop it, stop it, STOP IT!" he shouted at himself. This panic wasn't doing any good. He needed something to do, something to focus on. Something more than just his hunt for a winter house.

I have to pee. His bladder was a good enough distraction. In his attempt to find the singers, he had paddled away from the previous night's low spot, and so needed to locate another rock.

He ended up near the shoreline. Since he was thinking about his bladder in order to not think of anything else, it became way too urgent to keep searching. He paddled toward the land until it was shallow enough, and climbed out into knee-deep water. The mud sucked at his toes, seaweed brushed his ankles. He had never liked the feeling of either, but would have to suck it up. Hopefully he didn't get a leech attached to him.

Releasing the pressure of his bladder helped a little with the overall stress-pressure he was feeling inside. He no longer wanted to claw at his skin or scream until he passed out, but he could sense that he was on the edge. That hole in his thought city was pulling at him, having gained its own gravity. He needed a rope, a lifeline, to keep from toppling in.

The kayak was going to be that lifeline.

Keith was frustrated with always being afraid of tipping. He had made it down a set of rapids without flipping over, but that was definitely more luck than skill. If he was going to live in this boat for even another day, he needed to become a lot more familiar with what it was capable of.

After eating breakfast while standing in the muck—refried

beans this time—he peeled off his shirt so that it wouldn't get wet, and went for a swim. It was the closest he could get to a shower, but that wasn't his reason for it. Towing the kayak behind him, he headed for a dock. The water was fairly shallow for a good distance out along most of this area, as evidenced by the long docks. Keith picked one at random. Upon reaching it, he waited a couple of minutes to see if a dirt devil would show up. When none did, he emptied his kayak of his findings, placing them all on the end of the dock, with the towel on top in case he took long enough for the sun to reach the little pile.

As he moved the emergency kit, his heart squeezed. There was a whistle inside. He had completely forgotten about it until now. The whistle was probably louder than he could scream. Keith clenched his teeth to keep from screaming again. It was too late now to change what had happened. Besides, they might not have heard the whistle either.

Once again towing the kayak, now with only the paddle poking up out of it, Keith moved away from the dock, along the shore. He found a spot where he was deep enough to swim, but shallow enough that he could put his legs down in an emergency. He was also far enough from shore to not have to worry about the dirt devils. Or at least, not have to actively worry. There was a part of his subconscious that was solely dedicated to thinking about the dirt devils at all times. They roamed the outer edges of his thought city, and dwelled in the bottom of the pit.

Now that his stuff was safe, and he shouldn't be at too much of a risk, Keith got to work. The first thing he needed to figure out was how to get into the kayak when he didn't have anything to push off of. That seemed like the sort of skill that could save his life one day.

He very quickly learned to not try going over the sides by simply hauling himself up. Even just one attempt came very close to flooding his boat. He almost hadn't stopped himself in time.

So if he couldn't climb up the sides, that left the nose and the tail. The nose felt like a good idea in terms of having most of the kayak's own weight on the opposite end from him, but he quickly found fault with that plan. The nose was pointed, there was no way to keep it from tipping to one side or the other. This left the tail.

The very back of the boat was flat, and roughly as wide as

Keith's torso. With a few tests, he could see that climbing over the back wasn't going to be easy. The draining plug and pull handle would likely scrape him up, and the shallow back bin would flood, but, with care, he might be able to prevent the main compartment from flooding, which was the point.

"Fucking weakling," Keith cursed himself, even though he was a lot stronger than he had been just a year ago. There wasn't really anything to grip along the sides of the kayak, so he had to deliberately push down the tail in order to slide on like a seal. Once he grabbed the opening around the seat, he could pull. With his legs dangling to either side, he kept their weight off and balanced the kayak better, but his nuts sure didn't appreciate the position, and his thighs weren't the most flexible. He'd never even gotten close to being able to do the splits.

"Arrrrrggg," he grunted as he pulled himself forward. His butt eventually hovered over the seat opening, allowing him to push himself upright while swinging his legs forward. He plopped down inside and quickly curled into a ball as his lower body protested its treatment. He might have stayed that way for a while had his guts not reminded him of what happens to food that's been eaten. Getting out of the kayak without flooding it was much easier than getting in had been.

Keith followed the current away from his training ground before doing his business. This wasn't his first time having to deal with a number two while squatting in a lake closer to shore than he would have liked. What he wouldn't give for some toilet paper. Or even just some soap would be nice.

Having learned he *could* get into the kayak without flooding it while swimming, this time Keith opted for the easier method of standing in the shallows. Still not graceful, but less painful.

Keith rocked the kayak every which way, testing its limits. He ended up slopping some water inside, but not enough to flood it. Scrambling all around, he found various positions in which he could sit. He leaned over the front and back, he curled up with his head inside, he knelt on the bottom of the boat and the seat, and once he even stood. That last one nearly had him taking a header over the side. Standing was possible, but precarious until he worked on his balance. This wasn't just about what the kayak could handle, but what Keith could.

KAYAK

Tired of twisting and stretching and crunching, Keith decided it was time to move on. As he gathered his things from the end of the dock, he noticed how he hadn't needed to shelter them from the sun. Clouds had rolled in. Dark ones.

Thunder rumbled off in the distance and Keith's head shot up. Lightning could prove deadly if he moved away from the shore: being the lone boat out on open water could be a tempting target for a storm. But that wasn't why Keith went on high alert.

A storm meant rain.

22: THEN

THEY HAD ALL made it safely into the van and were on their way, but Keith couldn't stop reliving his memories of what his mom had called them all over to see before they'd left.

One of the monsters was in the backyard. It was pacing in circles, and swinging its head around. At random moments, it would plunge its head down against the ground. No, not against, *into*. Its head would disappear beneath the grass. When it reared back up again, the earth looked untouched. Some grass was flattened by its feet as it circled, but that was it. The silence as it did this was disturbing.

"Honey, we should go." Dad grabbed Mom's shoulders and pulled her a little farther away.

"Russell, did you hit it in the face with the water?" Mom asked him.

"Uh, I don't know. Maybe? I wasn't exactly aiming."

"I think you might have blinded it," she said.

"That makes no sense," Dr. Kimiko huffed. "How is it doing that? How is it disappearing into the ground like that, and then just . . . reforming? And if it can reform itself, how can it be hurt? Shouldn't it just be able to put its eyes back together in a way that works?"

"Maybe that's what it's trying to do," Russell suggested.

"I want to go," Keith admitted. "Mom? Dad? I don't want to be here if it *does* heal itself. I want to go."

"Yeah," Dad agreed.

"Wait," Mom hissed. "It's gone."

Her words were unneeded as they'd all watched it sink into the ground like a diving submarine.

"Nothing we've seen suggests it can't move underground just as fast as it can above ground. Let's go before it comes up near enough to the door to pounce." Dr. Kimiko pulled Russell toward the front door. It was a good thing she had.

Dad was shepherding both Keith and his mom when she gasped. Even while being guided away, she'd been watching over her shoulder. Keith whipped his head around to see what had happened. His dad had too, which meant that a split second later, both of Keith's parents were pushing him away, and trying to prevent him from seeing. But Keith saw. The monster was back, but it hadn't come alone. It had brought something with it. Or rather, someone.

Mr. Blatty. As the creature emerged from the ground, it was holding his head between its teeth.

That was all Keith managed to glimpse. After that, everyone hustled out the front door and jumped into the van. No one tripped, no one threw their water in a panic, and no monsters slammed into any doors. Keith had had to scramble over the bags already in the van to reach his seat, but he hardly acknowledged that. He didn't even comment when Russell accidentally kicked him on his way into the back. Dad didn't wait. Mom barely had time to get around the front of the car and jump into the passenger seat before he had started the engine and got them moving. Dr. Kimiko was still throwing the sliding door shut, crouched awkwardly among the bags, when they exited the driveway.

Had Mr. Blatty still been alive? Keith couldn't get the idea out of his head. There was no way. Was there? He couldn't have been alive.

What Keith wanted to do was ask his much smarter friend. Russell would have been able to easily convince him that no, Mr. Blatty couldn't have been alive. But Keith couldn't ask, because to Russell he wasn't Mr. Blatty, he was Dad. He knew it was fortunate that neither Russell nor Dr. Kimiko had seen, but that also meant he couldn't talk about it. In the driver's seat, his dad had a white-knuckled grip on the steering wheel, his face set grimly and his eyes locked forward. Because he was seated behind her, Keith couldn't see how his mom was reacting.

"Keith, put your seatbelt on." Dr. Kimiko tapped his shoulder and nearly had him jumping out of his skin.

Keith fumbled with the restraint, both as he tried to grab it, and then when he tried to click it in place. Dad's eyes met his in the rearview mirror, and Keith didn't like what he saw there: raw fear.

He was probably thinking of Mr. Blatty as well. It was *Mr. Blatty*. While shocking all by itself to see someone they knew—someone they thought dead and gone—just be unearthed like that within the jaws of a monster, it was even more sinister than Keith had initially thought upon seeing it. Now that he had time to think, he was deeply unsettled. The creature had chosen to bring up Mr. Blatty, someone it had snatched from two houses over. Did it know? Did it know that they knew him? Did it know they had travelled from one house to the other? It felt deliberate. Surely other people had been sucked into the ground that night, but this one . . . This thing got hurt by Russell, pretty badly based on the way it had been acting in the yard, and then it had gone and grabbed his father. Keith couldn't help thinking that it knew. It knew exactly what it was doing, that bringing up that person would hurt them the most. It *knew*.

"Hey!" Russell suddenly shouted, startling everyone out of their thoughts. "That's Aisling!"

Keith instantly spotted her. "And Mandy!" he added. He'd know the back of her head anywhere.

Aisling was pedalling a bike. Not her bike, not the one he had seen her on before—God, had that been just yesterday?—but one that didn't suit her. It was baby pink, for one thing, and had rainbow streamers flapping off the ends of the handlebars for another. But it also had a banana seat, which allowed Mandy to sit behind her. She had one arm wrapped around the much taller girl, while her free hand held a Super Soaker at the ready. They both glanced over their shoulders at the approaching van.

"Doug, stop the car!" Mom's tone was just shy of a scream.

Dad hadn't even pulled the van over before Dr. Kimiko was moving. She was of a mind with Mom, and was out of her seat and opening the sliding door before they could stop.

"Get in!" several voices rang out as one, including Keith's.

The girls didn't hesitate. The van paused only for a few

seconds. The bike was abandoned, and they leapt inside. Dr. Kimiko swung the door shut behind them, having to fight the van's acceleration since Dad didn't wait.

"Russell?" Aisling was surprised to see him. She probably hadn't even seen who was in the van before accepting the ride.

"I'm so glad you're okay!" he cried out.

"Seat belt stays on!" Dr. Kimiko barked at him when it looked like he might unbuckle it to hug Aisling. Keith had the compulsion to do the same, except with Mandy, and not just because he had always dreamed of holding her. There was something uplifting about seeing people they knew alive and well, to know that they weren't the only ones to have survived.

Dr. Kimiko ordered the girls to strap in beside Russell. Aisling folded herself up in the middle. Once Mandy was buckled in, she curled up against the taller girl, clutching her Super Soaker to her chest.

"I wish we had thought of those," Keith said, needing something to say. He then wished anything else had come out of his mouth, feeling that that was dumb the moment it left his lips.

"We don't have any," Russell reminded him. "We were only ever allowed dinky squirt pistols."

"I've seen too many eye injuries," Dr. Kimiko said out of habit. "Although . . . I suppose they have a use in our present situation." She was crouched awkwardly among the bags.

Aisling also had a Super Soaker, which she placed between her feet. "Let me help you," she offered Dr. Kimiko. "Hand me those bags and I'll place them in the trunk. We won't be able to get the seat up, but at least you'll have more space."

"Thank you." Dr. Kimiko started handing her things. "I'm Dr. Blatty, Russell's mom."

"Aisling. And this is Mandy." So far Mandy hadn't said a word.

"That's Mr. and Mrs. Benchley, Keith's parents."

"Please, call me Doug," Dad called over his shoulder.

"Sigrid," Mom added.

Keith should have made introductions. He felt so stupid. He always felt stupid when he was in close proximity to Mandy, as if he could do nothing right.

"Cool. So where are we going?" Aisling asked.

"The lake," Russell and Keith answered as one.

23:
NOW

RAIN WAS COMING. Keith could smell it. He had chosen his target, and now he just needed to wait. He needed the water from the sky to reach him.

A few feet off a dock, he floated in his kayak, hoping that the lightning wouldn't get him. He had chosen this place because of the boat in the water. The little aluminum boat had been rained on so much that it had sunk, but it meant someone had been here. Someone had opened this cottage sometime last year, which meant they might have brought food with them. Even if they hadn't, Keith hoped to find other supplies, other things he could use. A raincoat would be nice. A tarp he could use to keep the rain out of his kayak would be even better.

It started to spit. The raindrops were chilly landing on Keith's face and arms, but they were wonderful as well. He never felt truly safe on any land that held dirt, but it was a lot better when it was raining.

The dozens of droplets were suddenly joined by hundreds, thousands, millions of others. A downpour soaked everything in an instant. Keith paddled to the dock, and hauled himself up onto the boards. Earlier, he had secured the tow rope to the kayak, and now tied it to the dock. His towel, already getting heavy with rain, he draped over the opening in a feeble attempt to prevent flooding. He would have thrown the lifejacket overtop as well, but the wind had picked up, and he was afraid it would get blown away. Had he taken a second, he might have been able to secure it, but there was no time to waste. Storms like this could fade away as abruptly as they appeared.

During his wait, Keith had laid out his plan. He ran for the farthest structure first. The shed was off to one side and fairly run down. Even at a distance, he had been able to spy the lock on the doors. The hope was that it had been left hanging there, open. It wasn't, so time for plan B. Keith had seen this kind of prefab shed before. Mrs. Phelps had had one in her backyard for her gardening tools. The pair of sliding doors ran on a track. Without hesitation, Keith braced his shoulder and rammed it low into the thin metal. This would have been better if he could kick the door, but without shoes, that sounded like a shortcut to a broken toe.

After a couple of frantic strikes, the door bent out of its track. Had there been anything directly on the other side, his plan would have failed utterly, and he could have badly hurt himself, but now was the time for taking chances. With the door free of the bottom track, Keith switched from ramming into it, to a steady, constant push. The track at the top groaned, and the doors buckled, but eventually enough of a gap formed that he was able to get a good grip with his hands. Lifting up, he managed to rip the doors free of their upper tracks. Although still in the way, Keith could now batter the metal sheets to the side, crashing them into who knows what, while they tried to twist around each other, the lock acting as a crappy omnidirectional hinge.

There was a light switch, but, of course, it didn't work. Keith was forced to work in the dim storm light, his bare feet stepping carefully along the plywood floor. Thunder roared outside, the little shed practically shaking with it. The lightning was never at the right angle though, never giving him a flash bulb look of what lay in the dark. The shed was cluttered with stuff stacked up along all the walls. Racks of tools took up most of the space, which was exactly what Keith had been hoping for. Two stacks of outdoor plastic chairs blocked his way in. Grabbing one, he dragged it outside, tossing it away.

There were so many things he wanted to take from inside the shed. He wanted the power drill, and the chain saw, and even whatever that big metal bar was. But he only had a single kayak, and he needed to be picky. The first things he collected were a bundled-up ski rope, and a short length of boat rope. He also grabbed a boat bumper, even though he couldn't think of an immediate use for it. As for tools, he took only two: a hammer and a small pry bar. The handsaws were tempting simply because they were sharp, but if that's all that stood between him and a dirt devil, then Keith was dead. In a corner were several tightly rolled tarps. Keith scooped up a paint-stained fabric one, and a crinkled blue plastic one. He was ready to hit his next target when he thought to check behind the shed doors. A table saw filled most of the space, but he was glad he had thought to look. While the shovels wouldn't be of any use, and the log splitting axe and sledgehammer were too big, there was a small hatchet among them. Keith fumbled with everything in his arms, briefly dropping the hammer and nearly crushing his foot, but he grabbed the small axe.

The ground squished between Keith's toes as he ran back toward the dock. He knew he was safe while it was raining, but the feeling of grass beneath his soles spurred him onward.

He piled everything on the dock except for the hammer and hatchet. Those he took with him to his next target, a tiny plastic shed near the end of the dock. It was actually more of a bin than a shed, and Keith wanted to know what was stored in it. Just like the tool shed, it was also locked. Using the sharp edge of the hatchet as a chisel, he hammered the flat back to chip at the plastic part that held the lock. He really wished he had found a pair of bolt cutters in the tool shed. It was very possible that some were in there and that he had just overlooked them. He was beginning to think he should go check again, that this was a waste of time, when the plastic finally broke.

Ignoring his sore hands, he threw the lock aside, and lifted the lid. The first thing he saw was a bundle of pool noodles. He grabbed one for himself—the green one, like his kayak—and tossed the rest aside. A bucket of swim gear had his attention next. He already had a mask, so he ignored those, but from among the flippers, he snatched up a stubby pair that appeared to be his size. Even better, were the jumbled water shoes. Those he tried on until he found the best fit, and then kept them on. It was nice to have his feet off the ground. Also in the bin were some red jugs of gas for which he had no use, and a small stack of lifejackets. Deciding he didn't need a second lifejacket, Keith abandoned the bin to add his new finds to his pile at the end of the dock.

Was it raining less? Keith turned his face to the sky. Thunder still crashed, but not as close. The wind had also slackened. He was less afraid of his kayak being battered against the dock or of his things being blown off.

There was still the cottage to check. The thought of a greater supply of food and maybe even a change of clothes encouraged him to continue. Bringing only the hammer this time, he sprinted for the largest target, no longer needing to worry about hurting his feet now that he wore the simple shoes of mesh and rubber.

Unlike the last cottage, this one's door was locked. The hammer made short work of the glass, creating a hole more than large enough for him to reach in and turn the latch. Had he not found the shoes, he had no idea what he would have done. Shoes were wonderful.

Crunching the glass he'd broken, Keith entered a screened-in porch that had boards over the windows. Was it something to do with how this place was closed up in the winter, or had someone stayed here long enough to cover them? Whatever the case, it made the room extremely dark. The only light source was what came in from behind Keith, and with the storm, that wasn't much. He waited until his eyes adjusted to the gloom.

The door was situated near the corner of the building. To his right, there was only a shallow wooden counter with a small sink at one end. There were no shelves or cupboards around the counter, just a pair of stools tucked up underneath. Keith might have just swept his eyes over it and moved on, had it not been such a curious set up. Instead, he gave it a little more attention, which was when he noticed the leather bundle rolled up and tucked behind the tap. With a quick glance at the rest of the room to make sure there was nothing that would stab him in the back, he approached the sink. Unrolling the bundle, he found several razor sharp knives. He knew the look of them immediately, since he had been using them for the better part of a year. This was a knife set for preparing fish. If Keith had found nothing else here, just this find alone was worth it.

The rest of the porch didn't appear to hold anything of use, just a sitting area and a dead freezer that was empty. There were windows in the wall leading to the rest of the cottage, but some curtains had been drawn tight on the other side. The glass door was equally covered, only this time by cardboard. Not something someone would do for the winter. Thinking of the sunken boat outside, Keith gripped his hammer tightly as he tried the doorknob. Locked. He would have to smash out some glass again.

It was unlikely that there was anyone inside. If someone had managed to live here still, then there would have been a strong smell of fish in the porch. Fish had become a very important staple in everyone's diet; Keith was overly familiar with the stink. Yet still he hesitated. This felt more like an invasion than anything else he had done. He didn't know why that was, it just was. All because someone had survived here long enough to put up some cardboard?

He tapped out the rectangle of glass nearest the lock far more gently than his crash through the front door had been. The cardboard then needed to be punched in, but that was easy and he had the lock snapped open in seconds. He pushed the door in, but remained standing on the porch. It was even darker in the next room. There was also a smell that wasn't as familiar as fish, and he couldn't immediately place it. He guessed mice.

Once his eyes adjusted to the deeper gloom, Keith knew he was in a kitchen. While he didn't like having the dark at his back, he immediately began searching the cupboards and drawers. It was difficult to tell what he was looking at. The faint light managed to outline the edges of pots, dishes, and drinking glasses, but anything without a reflective surface or of an unfamiliar shape, required Keith to use his hands to figure out what it was. In one such shadowy cupboard, he felt the thin cardboard of a cereal or cracker box, but as he made to snatch it, something moved inside. A blur burst out of the top of the box with a skittering of claws. A second of screaming escaped Keith's mouth as he threw the box away from him and then slapped his hands over his mouth.

Mice! He had curled up into a tight, squatted position on the floor, where his limbs faintly trembled. *Just a mouse. It was just a mouse.* He reminded himself that the last cottage had also had mice get into the cereal.

His head whipped around to face the darkness. He expected something to have been drawn by his cry, but there was only a pitch black nothingness. That side of the space was a cave. His eyes strained, but there was no crashing, no clicking along the unseen floor.

He had to keep searching. Turning his back to the nothingness, he resumed his investigation. Whenever he took a step, his feet crunched on cereal, making him wince. How he'd love to eat that cereal, but there was no way that the mouse hadn't ruined it. Although he wanted cereal so badly he didn't care what kind it was, he had no interest in little turdy surprises or urine spices.

Junk drawer, Keith identified with some dismay. He'd been able to search most cupboards and drawers fairly quickly, because once he identified what one item was, he essentially knew what the rest should be. A pair of utensil drawers had slowed him down, but even then he had an idea of what to expect. A junk drawer could easily contain something of worth to him, so he was going to have to go through each item individually.

A bundle of rubber bands and a ball of string he kept. The alligator clips and paper clips, he took a pass on. A kitschy bottle opener took him awhile to identify, and then he spent another chunk of time trying to decide if he could use it. He eventually put the thing aside. If he ended up with any bottles, he'd find his own way to open them. The pens and the pad of paper gave him pause. He couldn't think of a use for them, but he felt a strong desire to take them. With them, he could draw. Rather bitterly, he put them aside.

Jackpot! he thought, pulling out an item from the back. He held it closer to the light to be sure. It was a headlamp flashlight, just like the one Dr. Kimiko had had so long ago.

"Please work," he hissed as his fingers hunted for the power button.

The beam of light shot directly into his face. Rays of pain briefly blinded him, blunting Keith's elation, but he was still excited as he pulled the straps on over his head and began adjusting their size. Precious, beautiful light.

He turned to shine his new prize into the dark, still listening closely for sounds of a threat. What he saw was a dining set, and then a jumble of living room furniture farther along. The curtains covering the windows to the screened-in porch had duct tape holding down all the sides. Two hallways led off in different directions.

The hairs on the back of his neck stood up. Why? Keith turned his head every which way, thinking his subconscious must have seen something, but there was nothing unusual, other than the taped curtains. Maybe he had heard something?

No, Keith realized with horror. It wasn't that he heard something, it was that he was *no longer* hearing something. The rain had stopped.

24:
THEN

TRAFFIC WAS BAD. Traffic here was always bad, but this was horrid. People had been making their way south to the lake ever since the alert had gone out. Not all of them had made it, leaving wrecks to cork up lanes that forced those still moving to creep around them. Keith was fairly certain that his dad had no idea where they were actually going, that none of these streets were familiar to him. It didn't matter though, as anything south eventually hit the lake.

As they passed by another abandoned car, Keith stared out at it, just like he had all the others. Most of them were regular accidents, people who had lost control in their haste and slammed into light poles, mailboxes, buildings, and each other. There was evidence of people who had had accidents and kept driving. Some accidents weren't accidents at all. In this instance, the claw marks torn through the metal spoke of what had happened to those people.

"What now?" Mom sighed as they slowed to stop. This had happened a few times.

"Probably another accident," Dad huffed.

"Or maybe someone's picking someone up," Russell offered a more hopeful outlook.

There were a lot of people on foot. A few would be the owners of the abandoned vehicles, but more were those who hadn't tried driving at all. Maybe they didn't own a car, or maybe one of those things had ruined it before they could even reach it. Keith bet that in a different emergency situation, more cars would have been abandoned even when they ran perfectly fine, but not this morning.

No one wanted to leave even the modicum of safety their vehicles provided. Those on foot were often on the road, weaving between the crawling traffic. Several of them had discovered that they should carry water, and had either pots or drinking glasses in their hands, a few lucky enough to be toting water guns. There were groups with luggage, while others hadn't even had time to change out of their pajamas. Keith shuddered whenever he saw someone staggering along on their own, their expression distant and lost. He didn't want to know what they had seen.

Mrs. Phelps' hand. He shuddered.

"Well, we're not stopping for anyone," Mom stated for what felt like the dozenth time, as if she hadn't been the one to shriek about stopping for Mandy and Aisling.

Mandy still hadn't said a word about what had happened, but she wasn't so withdrawn anymore. She sat upright, no longer clinging to Aisling, and watched what was going on outside. Keith was still trying to come up with something appropriate to say, but everything he thought up was wrong. Not knowing what she had been through, he couldn't even guess what she might need to hear. He wondered if she even noticed the times he opened his mouth to speak to her, and then closed it again as the words died without ever getting past his tongue. Aisling certainly had, based on the weird looks she kept giving him. It was like she didn't know whether to be amused or angry.

"Why haven't we started moving again?" Dr. Kimiko complained. She stood up and leaned between the front seats, trying to see what the holdup was. This was taking longer than usual. People both ahead and behind had begun beeping their horns, as if that would make any difference.

"I wish they'd stop honking," Aisling groused. "It's like announcing to those things that we're all just sitting here."

"Devils," Mandy said, drawing everyone's attention to her. "They're devils."

Aisling snorted, but also agreed. "Yeah, dirt devils because they suck."

"Isn't that a vacuum company?" Keith blurted out.

"You. Joke." Aisling passed one hand over the other, indicating that it had gone over his head.

Keith faced forward before anyone could see him flush.

"I like that name," Russell said. "Dirt devils. It's accurate. Mom!" His attitude changed on a dime as Dr. Kimiko opened the side door.

"I'm just seeing what's going on." She didn't even get out of the van, she just stood in the opening, holding on to the roof rack for balance.

"Well?" Dad asked when she came back inside and shut the door.

"I think this is the end of the line. I think we've reached the back of the parking lot."

"Did you see the lake?"

"No, there's a bend up ahead with some townhouses blocking my view. I *think* I saw a mast poking up over that building over there, but I can't be certain."

"Do either of you have your phones?" Russell asked Mandy and Aisling. "Can you check where we are?"

"Yeah, I'm on it." Aisling dug her cell out.

"I lost mine," Mandy sighed.

"Yeah, ours got broken," Keith empathized.

"That sucks."

It was the longest conversation Keith had ever had with her, and while a part of him knew this was not the time, he felt a little euphoric about it. He wanted to ask her more, about how she'd lost her phone, but was able to clamp down on that impulse. Mandy probably didn't want to think about last night, just like he didn't.

Mrs. Phelps' hand. What carnage had Mandy seen? What had caused her to become separated from her parents?

"We're not super close, but we're not exactly far either," Aisling announced.

"Let me see." Dr. Kimiko took her phone and held it where Keith's parents could see the screen as well.

"Are the cars really stopped all the way to here?" Mom spoke in a hushed tone that probably wasn't meant to be heard by Keith.

"I think so," Dr. Kimiko answered, although she didn't sound totally positive. Not as positive as anyone who heard her wanted her to be.

A scream sliced through everyone's thoughts. The close proximity had them all ducking for cover beneath the windows. Even Dad, whose foot slipped off the brake, making them roll gently into the car ahead of them. He wasn't the only one, as they were soon bumped from behind. A few more screams followed the first, then running feet pounded along the pavement past the van. A dozen car doors slammed, one squeal of tires was closely followed by a crunch, and then there was silence. Keith could only hear the thundering of his heart and the panicked breathing of those in the van with him.

"Keith, are you alright?" Mom whispered, breaking the stalemate.

"I'm fine." He had twisted awkwardly in his seat in order to slouch down, the seatbelt digging into unexpected places. Mandy didn't have that problem. Quick as a jackrabbit, she had unclipped her seatbelt and slid down onto the van floor, where she now crouched with her Super Soaker at the ready. Aisling was sprawled across the abandoned seat, where her own seatbelt looked like it was biting painfully into her belly.

"We have to get going," Dr. Kimiko hissed. Her hand rested on Mandy's shoulder, but her eyes were locked on Russell.

"Get the bags," Mom instructed as she unbuckled and climbed into the back.

Keith released himself but only to crunch down in front of his seat. He wasn't in a good position to help with the bags, so he raised his head instead to peer out through his window. There wasn't much to see. They were stopped on a street of shops and restaurants. There was no grass, which was a positive, but the way the buildings were butted up against one another, they formed a funnel. No place to go but forward. As he spied, Keith watched a small family scuttle past, keeping low. Another man showed up about a minute behind them. He ducked into an alcove formed by the door to a beauty shop, clearly exhausted. Plastic water bottles had been duct taped around his limbs and torso. If he were attacked by one of those things—a dirt devil—he'd wound it as it wounded him, but the weight slowed him down, and made movement awkward. The man spotted Keith watching and gave him a nod. Keith nodded back, and then the man was gone, sweating profusely as he continued toward the lake.

"Do we really need all this stuff?" Aisling wondered as the last of the bags was hauled out of the trunk. It had gotten rather crowded in the passenger compartment, especially since Dad had followed Mom's lead in climbing back there.

"Yes," Dad said.

"It's not just useful to us," Dr. Kimiko elaborated. "We can use some of it to bargain with if we have to."

"You believe you have anything worth more than the rest of these people?" Mandy said rather despairingly with a flick of her head toward the other cars.

"I have to believe," Dr. Kimiko answered grimly.

They had two bags a person before picking up Mandy and Aisling, so all four teenagers were given backpacks and allowed to keep their hands free.

"You guys lead the way," Dad told them.

"Maybe someone with a water gun should bring up the rear," Russell suggested, but it was shot down.

"This isn't like one of your war games," Dr. Kimiko told him. "The four of you go first. You run if you have to. You leave us behind if you have to."

"Mom—"

"You'll do it."

Russell's mouth flattened into a sharp line. Keith knew him well enough to know that he was hiding fury. Whether it was aimed at his mom for telling him that, or at the dirt devils for taking his dad, he was less certain about. It was probably both.

"Okay, let's go." Dad hauled opened the sliding door on the driver's side and they all spilled out onto the pavement. There wasn't a lot of space between the stopped vehicles, and none where others had left their doors open. At least those could be closed. Some cars were parked crooked, forcing them to squeeze through, or even climb over the hoods. Not all of the cars they passed were empty, and Keith found his eyes meeting those within. His own fear was reflected back at him.

"Help! Help!" came a voice from inside one of the cars.

Aisling and Mandy had been leading the way and found it first.

"Help me!" an old woman shouted from the back seat. The rest of the car was empty. "The child locks are on! I can't get the door open!"

"Just climb through the front," Aisling told her, eager to keep moving.

"With my hip?" the woman thumped her cane on the car floor.

She reminded Keith of Mrs. Phelps. She had the same kindly,

maternal face. He couldn't believe someone would have just left her behind like this.

"Move." He pushed Aisling out of the way and grabbed the door handle. The woman was sitting right up against the side, eager to get out.

"Thank you, dear," the woman sighed with relief when Keith opened the door and held out his hand to assist her. "Now you're going to give me one of those fancy water guns of yours." The muzzle of a very real pistol was jammed into Keith's gut.

25: NOW

THE RAIN HAD stopped, but the ground would stay wet for a while longer. Keith still had time.

With his newly found headlamp, he finished sweeping the kitchen at a rapid pace. He startled more mice, and a number of large beetles he'd rather have not known about. There was food, but all of it had either gone bad, or been ravaged by the critters, including a cupboard completely stuffed with Kraft Dinner. That one was particularly upsetting, as it had always been one of Keith's favourite meals. In the end, all he found that wasn't ruined were some spices, a few packs of taco mix, a box of salt, three more tins of soup, and a small bag of flour. The tins were good, and the spices, salt, and taco mix could at least be used for flavouring, but he wasn't sure about the flour. He grabbed it anyway, figuring if he got desperate he could mix it with water and drink it.

"Shit," he hissed, realizing he didn't have a way to carry all that stuff. He hadn't found any bags in the kitchen, so he selected a big pasta pot and placed them in it for the time being. Maybe the pot would also be useful, if he ever found a way to start a fire on a rock.

Leaving the pot of food on the table, he went to explore the rest of the place with his hammer leading the way. He still kept thinking he was going to come across something terrible in here. The little hairs on the back of his neck were standing on end, and the beetles skittering off into corners kept making him jump.

The first hallway he tried had two doors on either side. The window at the end matched those in the kitchen, in that it was covered up by an unbroken layer of cardboard and duct tape. Not even a sliver of light could get through. None of the doors were latched, but none of them hung wide open either. Keith approached the first one and gently pushed the door inward with the head of his hammer.

A bedroom. Nothing spooky here. Well, the covered windows might have been a little spooky, but the queen-sized bed was neatly made, and there were no occupants. Keith made a quick raid around the room, searching the shallow closet, the dresser, and the nightstands. All were empty except for a few coat hangers in the closet, and a bundle of spare blankets on its shelf. Tempting, but with the two tarps he'd already snatched, he was probably good on that front for the time being.

The second door he tried was the same: an empty bedroom. It was a slightly different layout with different art on the walls and different, yet equally useless, knickknacks on the dresser and nightstands, but to Keith it was the same. There was nothing here for him. He did begin to debate about grabbing a pillow or two, though. He'd think about it while he searched the remaining two rooms.

He found where someone had lived, at least for a little while. The bed wasn't made, and the closet door stood half open, revealing clothing hung neatly inside. Still fearing a corpse, Keith checked the far side of the bed before opening the closet the rest of the way.

"Poncho!" he almost shouted, managing to strangle the word at the last second so that it was more of a hushed croak. He grabbed the bright blue slick fabric and pulled it on over his head. He now had something to protect him from the rain.

Unfortunately, none of the other clothes he found was one-size-fits-all like the rain poncho. It must have been a woman staying here. Keith blushed when he opened her underwear drawer. Holding up shirts and pants to his body, revealed that everything was much too small for him. He didn't even have to try it on to know.

"Come on, lady, don't you have, like, a boyfriend sweater or something?" Keith whispered to himself. "A loose pair of drawstring yoga pants? Anything?" If she had owned such an article of clothing, she was wearing it wherever she was.

The fourth bedroom wasn't like the other three. It was larger, and instead of a queen-sized bed taking up the middle of the room, there were a pair of bunk beds pushed up against opposite walls. The woman hadn't been staying here alone. One of the lower bunks was rumpled, and based on the toys and the size of the clothes left on the floor, its occupant hadn't been very old.

Keith found himself drifting over to the bed; he couldn't help it. He lay down in the dark, with only his headlamp for company. What must it have been like for the child who had stayed here? He clicked off the headlamp and wondered if the kid was afraid of the dark. He would have been. He still was, and clicked his light back on after a few seconds. The other bunks were empty. Who had once occupied them? Siblings? Cousins? Friends was a good bet, whether they were related or not. But they hadn't made it here. There was only evidence of one child. Alone in a room meant for many.

Wiping absently at his tears, Keith got off the bed before he could get comfortable. He took the pillow from it—the pillowcase depicted a cartoon version of The Hulk—and added it to the small collection on the kitchen table. He hoped it wasn't full of mouse leavings.

The second hallway was much shorter, more of an annex. There was a bathroom he rooted around in without much luck. The toilet paper had been turned into a rodent nest, and he wasn't comfortable with the idea of putting a previously used toothbrush in his mouth. Maybe down the line he would be, but for now, he just pocketed the tube of toothpaste.

Across from the bathroom was a shelving unit full of linens, boardgames, and some miscellaneous junk. He didn't think he'd have a use for an extension cord, but a white plastic cube-shaped container about the size of his hand was full of batteries, so that was definitely coming. He'd test whether the batteries worked later. Also, he took a second beach towel, figuring that with it, he could always have a dry one when he needed it.

To one side of the shelves was an opening. There was a little laundry section, but also a small home office. Keith wandered over to the desk and gazed down at the papers scattered about, expecting something boring like tax forms.

Art. The person who used this office was an artist. Little cubbies above the desk were stuffed with pencils and markers. Poking out from under the paper to one side was a ruler, and various angle devices. Keith sat heavily on the swivel stool and sifted through the images. They were magnificent. If Keith had to guess, he'd say the artist worked as a freelance concept artist, with a specialty in fantastical landscapes. These were likely just roughs or sketches, the final product probably being produced on a computer at the artist's house, but even they were better than anything Keith could do. In one drawing was a dirt devil, and so he figured they were made by the missing woman. Her line work was so skilful, so confident, and she had an amazing grasp of lighting and colour values. This woman had honed her craft to a fine point.

Under the startling depiction of the dirt devil, Keith found a different drawing, by a different hand. It was also a dirt devil, but much cruder. The woman—the kid's mom most likely—had written in a neat hand in the corner: Drew, age 5. So the kid had only been five years old. As Keith sifted through more of the drawings, he found more of Drew's artwork, but there was only the one of the dirt devil.

He couldn't resist. Pushing the drawings aside, Keith found a clean sheet of paper in a desk drawer and set to work. There was no blue pencil so his construction lines were going to be more obvious, but that didn't matter. The odds of anyone seeing this were slim. He drew his own dirt devil. It was better than Drew's but far less real than the woman's. It wasn't even as good as he could normally draw one, having fallen a bit out of practice and not having done any warm-up sketches first. Still, it wasn't bad. Underneath his sketch, he wrote down all the things he was taking with his apologies. It felt good to do, like somewhere, someone who owned this place was still alive, and that one day things would be normal again and that they'd come back here.

When he turned to leave, Keith spotted a fishing rod next to the entrance. He searched frantically for a nearby tackle box, but there was none. Still, even just the fishing rod with its one hook and sinker was better than no fishing rod at all. Keith suspected he now knew where the woman had been when she disappeared: fishing. Somewhere out there she had the tackle box and another rod. Had Drew been with her? Or had he been ordered to wait here, alone? No, Keith liked to picture them together. And not dead. They had been picked up by someone in a boat, that's what happened. They hadn't been able to return for their stuff, but had been borne away to safety. One day, *they* would be the ones to come here and find Keith's drawing added to their own.

Keith had taken a lot of stuff and was thinking about how he'd stash it all in the kayak as he headed for the door. It was awkward carrying the pot with the pillow and towel balanced on top, the battery case dangling from his fingers, and the fishing rod tucked tightly under one arm. Because of his distraction, he was only a step away from crunching on the broken glass of the shattered front door, when he saw it.

A dirt devil was outside, squatting on the path between the cottage and the lake.

26:
THEN

A COLD SWEAT broke out all over Keith's body like a bad rash. There was a *gun* jammed into his ribs. Not some water pistol or a cap gun. There were no Nerf bullets here. Keith froze in both body and mind. His eyes were locked on the old woman's hand, the one holding the revolver. One of his own hands rested on the car roof, the other still partly held out, stopped on its way to offering aid.

"Stay back!" the lady shouted, not looking at Keith.

He managed to flick his eyes away from the gun, and in that split second he saw his parents and Dr. Kimiko approaching. Their faces displayed only confusion and concern. They had been too far back to have properly seen what happened and were having trouble processing what they now saw.

"Keith?" Dad asked, loading a whole series of questions into just his name.

"I got this, Mr. Benchley, don't worry," Mandy told him with a surreal amount of confidence. She stepped between Keith and the adults, using her body to hide what was happening.

The woman's eyes were bright and alert as she watched Mandy. Keith felt the gun press harder against him, and saw a slight tightening of her finger around the trigger.

"There's no need for that," Mandy spoke in a soothing tone. "You can have my water gun, it's fine. There's no need for violence."

The woman didn't move as Mandy held out the Super Soaker, apparently expecting a trick.

"Toss it toward the front seat. You hit me with it, and your friend here won't have to worry about those creatures anymore."

"I understand. I'm complying. I'm going to toss it now."

"Keith?" Mom's sharper tone loaded his name with different questions. He still couldn't bring himself to move, not even to raise a reassuring hand.

Mandy casually tossed the water gun into the car. Her aim was good, and it landed on the front passenger seat.

"Now back up!" the woman ordered.

Mandy took one big step backward.

"You too!" she barked at Keith. "Clear the door."

Keith wished he could step back like Mandy had, all calm and smooth like. Instead, he took a series of tiny, stumbling steps that nearly had him falling on his ass. The only reason he didn't was that he bumped into another car behind him, and somehow managed to brace against the side mirror.

The woman lunged at the door, able to reach without getting out of the car, and swiftly shut it.

Mandy stormed toward the lake while Keith's parents rushed over to him.

"Is that a gun?" Mom practically shrieked as she looked in at the old lady through the car window. "You pointed a gun at my son?" She stepped forward as if ready to yank the woman out of her vehicle, but the muzzle of the revolver placed against the glass stopped her.

"Go! Go!" Dr. Kimiko urged, pushing Russell ahead of her.

"Are you okay? Keith, are you okay?" Dad asked, dragging him along by his shoulders on one side and Mom on the other. Mom was full of fury.

"I'm fine. I'm okay." Although his voice shook. "Mandy took care of it."

"How did you do that?" Russell asked her, completely awed.

"I don't want to talk about it!" Mandy wheeled around to shriek at them. She then primly turned to one side, pulled back her long hair, and vomited between two vehicles.

Without a word, Aisling stepped up alongside Mandy and handed her the remaining Super Soaker. She accepted it before she had even finished wiping off her mouth. As they continued to move forward, Mandy tucked herself up under Aisling's arm like a frightened child, as if she hadn't just been a total badass a minute ago.

"Keith, are you sure you're okay?" Mom asked, still throwing furious glances over her shoulder.

"I'm fine. Really."

"None of us are fine," Dr. Kimiko grumbled.

There were no arguments there.

"No more stopping," Dad decreed. "Understood? We don't stop until we reach the lake."

Keith nodded. His parents reluctantly allowed him to leave their sides so that he could go walk near Mandy, and the water gun. Russell stayed close on his hip.

"Thank you, Mandy," Keith managed to squeak out, still trying to process what had just happened.

"Don't mention it." She didn't turn when she answered.

"I don't know what would have happened if you—"

"I said don't mention it!" she snapped at him, giving him a brief look at her red-rimmed eyes and the tears still drying on her cheeks.

"It's okay, Keith," Aisling told him, much more calmly. "She knows. Just . . . We're not going to talk about it, okay?"

"Okay." Keith sensed there was something deeper. The way Aisling spoke suggested she knew what.

As they headed toward the lake, they saw other people still sitting in their vehicles, too afraid to get out, but they didn't try to convince any of them to walk. In fact, if they noticed in time, they scrambled over to a different alley between the parked cars. They saw other people on foot as well, but everyone tended to avoid one another. At least until they couldn't anymore.

"Whoa." Russell spoke for all of them with that one word.

Dr. Kimiko had indeed spotted a mast above the rooftops. It belonged to a boat that was still on the shore, but a horde of people were working to change that. The big yacht was sitting on some sort of frame and being moved by a huge collective. They pushed and pulled, straining to shift the thing. There was a road and a small parking lot between them and the water, both stuffed with vehicles. Other people were working to get them out of the way, smashing windows so that they could throw the cars into neutral, or even drive them if the keys were still inside. But there was nowhere for the cars to go, and so they had to move more and more of them, getting a few inches wherever they could.

"I should help," Dad muttered, stepping toward the scene.

"No!" Mom grabbed the back of his shirt. "You could get hurt." They could hear the cries of those already injured, those who had been in the wrong place at the wrong time.

"But we could get on it," Dad argued.

"Look at them," Mom insisted. "*Look*. There are already way more people trying to help than could fit on that thing. There's going to be a fight about who gets on, and I don't think it's a fight we could win."

"Keep moving toward the lake," Dr. Kimiko insisted with a nudge to Russell's back.

So they kept moving.

"Mom?" Russell said uncertainly.

Past the road and parking lot, the beach was packed. People were jammed in shoulder to shoulder. Large groups gazed about, lost and confused.

"Link arms," Aisling suggested, reaching for Russell.

They formed a human chain, and Keith ended up between Russell and Dr. Kimiko.

"Push for the water!" Dad shouted over the din toward Mandy.

"I don't know where it is!" she shouted back, angry and frustrated. She was leading the way, driving her body into any opening she could find. It was easy to get turned around. Keith was taller than she was, and he couldn't see beyond the masses either. Everywhere he turned, his eyes met panicked, frightened, angry faces. Some of them held small children in their arms, their grips fiercely tight. They made Keith worry about the objects he sometimes stumbled over. It wasn't always sand he was walking on.

"Head left!" Russell shouted. "That way's south!"

"How do you know?" Mandy tried to head that way despite questioning him.

"The shadows! The sun!" Russell answered.

Of course. It was still early, so they knew the sun must be in the east, meaning everyone's shadows would fall to the west. If they kept the sunlight on the left side of their faces, they would head south. Even if the water wasn't perfectly south of their location, they'd hit it eventually.

"I think we're close!" Mandy shouted down the line.

And then the attack began.

27:
NOW

KEITH NEARLY DROPPED his pilfered supplies. He stood there, frozen, wondering if the dirt devil had seen him. It wasn't charging, so it most likely hadn't. It just sat there on the pathway, occasionally flinching as a drop of water fell from a tree overhead.

The sun was out. Keith felt betrayed by it. After the storm had stopped, it must have cut through the clouds. It dried up the earth faster than he had anticipated. Fast enough for this beast to have emerged. There were theories about where they went when it rained. No one knew for sure, but Keith believed they found a patch of dirt that remained dry by hiding under a rock or something similar. Maybe this devil's shelter hadn't been very effective and that was why it emerged so soon. It was sitting on the path after all, the paving stones having dried much more rapidly than anywhere else.

Was the ground still wet? Could Keith make a break for it? No, he didn't think so. Not from where he stood, at any rate. The paved path led straight up to the door. The moment Keith opened it, the devil would know he was there and be on top of him before his feet found the grass.

Carefully stepping back out of sight, Keith retreated to the kitchen. He gently placed his items down on the table and closed the door to the screened-in porch. There had to be another way out.

He had seen a second exit beside the bathroom, across from the office, but hadn't really thought about it at the time. It was obviously a door that led outside, and he hadn't needed one until now.

Shining his headlamp around the rear exit, he frowned. Not only was the glass covered in cardboard like everywhere else, but a significant amount of tape had been used to make sure the door stayed shut. Briefly returning to the kitchen, Keith grabbed a butcher knife. The blade was sharp, making short work of the old tape. He even sliced away part of what was holding the cardboard in place, making himself a spy hole. Unfortunately, there wasn't much to see. To his left was the outer wall of the bathroom. Across a shallow porch was a long covered shelter that had failed to keep the woodpile within from rotting. To his right, a barbecue obstructed part of his view, leaving only a small patch of forest visible beyond it. He couldn't tell if there was a way off the porch around the side, or even say for certain how long the porch was. He was going to have to stick his head out.

Keith pushed on the door and had it open less than a hand span before learning why it had been thoroughly taped shut. The hinges screamed, sharp and grating in the quiet, post-storm air. Simply reacting, Keith let go of the door and backed away, which only made matters worse. It squalled again as it swung shut with a slap.

Going with his gut, Keith ducked into the office. Maybe he should have gone for the bathroom where there was a door, but he had failed to think things through. Along the inner wall, Keith crammed himself up against a stacked washer and dryer. Just as he did, he heard a sharp twisting of tortured metal come from across the cottage. The dirt devil had entered the building, taking the shortest route between it and the sound.

Just as Keith thought to turn off his headlamp, the door between the screened-in porch and the kitchen went with a mighty crash. He managed to inhale one last time, and then stopped breathing altogether. Considering his heart had climbed up into his throat and was wailing away in there, he wasn't sure he'd be able to breathe even if he wanted to.

Furniture broke with lightning cracks, and was shoved aside with a clatter and scrape. Keith ignored those destructive sounds, instead listening to the clicking that drove it. Seconds was all it took for the dirt devil to cross the cottage, but for Keith it seemed like it must have been minutes. However much time had passed, it wasn't enough before the dirt devil was right beside him. There was never enough time before one got so close, no amount of mental preparation made anyone ready for it. Keith's fight or flight was at a standstill; there was now only the prey's hope of going unnoticed.

The backdoor shrieked in a completely different way than it had before. Keith squeezed his eyes shut, and wanted to bury his face in his hands, but couldn't bring himself to make even that small move, the poncho too crinkly to risk anything. All he could do was listen as the dirt devil sliced the door to ribbons. When it was done, in which direction would it search? Did it think the sound was someone leaving or entering the building?

Leave. Leave. Leave. Leave. It was the only thought Keith was capable of possessing. Just one word, a prayer, a desperate attempt at psychic suggestion.

There was silence as the beast stood still. As far as anyone knew, they didn't breathe, at least not in the traditional way. They only made sound when they moved.

Finally, that awful tapping started up again. It was accompanied by a gentle sort of rustling, like thin branches just barely touching the side of a house. It was going outside through the hole it had torn. Keith still didn't dare move, fearing a trap of some sort. His lungs were desperate for air, but he wouldn't risk even an exhalation. He waited in agony until he could no longer hear the dirt devil.

Keith let the air out of him slowly, still fearing a trick, still believing it would somehow hear him, or smell him, or sense the change in the flow of air. He opened his eyes a crack, thinking there was going to be some terrible visage before him. Even if it had gone, it could have left something behind. Someone.

The office appeared undisturbed, so he opened his eyes a little more. It didn't look the same now that there was sunlight streaming in through the broken door, but everything was untouched. Keith leaned forward onto his hands, careful not to bump the washer and dryer beside him in case he made even the faintest sound of crumpling metal. Every whisper from the poncho had him wincing. He kept his eyes locked on the opening beside him, studying the shape of the shadows. The lack of movement gave him the confidence to slowly stick his head around the corner.

The door was a tortured wreck. Dirt devils were probably smart enough to figure out latches, but why bother when they could just slice and dice their way through anything? It would be obvious to anyone who saw this what had happened here.

Keith stepped lightly back toward the kitchen and living room, mindful of the debris on the floor—which included the abandoned butcher knife—not wanting it to crack or rattle. He wanted absolute silence, and while he thought going barefoot would make that easier, he kept his shoes on in case he took a wrong step.

With the entrances smashed at either end of the cottage, he didn't need his headlamp to see the flurry of destruction within. There was a clear path from the screened-in porch door to the back hallway. A couch had nearly been split in half, while the coffee table actually had been, its pieces spread to either side. A rocking chair was now a loose collection of sticks, the kitchen chairs were everywhere, and the kitchen table was smashed up against the fridge with two of its legs collapsed. Keith made his way to where his supplies had been left.

The flour bag hadn't survived, but he had already known that from the smudges of white powder the dirt devil had left in its wake. Turning his headlamp back on to see better, Keith assessed the damage. The tinned food was okay, and the pot hadn't taken a direct hit from the devil's claws, so it remained intact. The battery caddy had popped open, scattering its contents. Keith returned what he could to the case, hoping the flour hadn't ruined them—if they had even worked to begin with. The towel escaped harm, but the pillow was slashed open. He had taken that on a whim anyway, so decided not to grab a fresh one. The toothpaste and fish knives were jammed in his swimsuit pockets, so they were totally fine, and his hammer had to be located beneath some debris. The string was a shredded mess, and the rubber band ball had vanished, likely having bounced away. Finding the fishing rod would have broken his heart if he weren't so hopped up on panic. The thing was in pieces. A closer inspection revealed that the fishing line appeared intact. He didn't want to spend the time separating the reel from the broken bits, so he gathered up the whole thing. His supplies were easier to carry this time.

Stepping through the screened-in porch, Keith's head kept darting from side to side like a bird's, searching for predators. The opening that had been the front door was larger now. He saw nothing on the path to the dock, but that didn't mean there wasn't something out there, waiting for him.

A hat hung on a hook to one side of the shattered opening. Keith grabbed it absentmindedly and placed it on his head. It wasn't the kind of hat he'd want to be seen in by a beautiful girl—an old person's hat, with a wide floppy brim all the way around—but it would help protect his head and ears from the sun. He had almost forgotten that problem during the storm, but because the traitorous sun had unhelpfully emerged, it had reminded him.

In the shade beneath the trees, the ground was still dark with moisture. If Keith was going to go, he had to go now before that changed.

Darting through the opening, he leapt off the small deck. He ignored the path and instead aimed for the soil. It was the opposite of what he would normally do, but right now, that's where the moisture was.

As he hit the ground and stumbled he felt a breeze on the back his neck. The hairs there stood up straight, and he tripped from sudden fear. He dropped his supplies as he tried to keep to his feet, needing to get farther, to put distance between himself and the dry ground.

Once his balance was steady, he pivoted to confirm what he had felt. A dirt devil was on the path, eyeing him. It had nearly gotten him. There was a boulder on the far side of the path, not right against it, but close enough that Keith figured the thing had been sheltering underneath. He watched as the beast took a tentative step onto the wet grass, then growled and shook its paw. Still too wet for it to want to pursue Keith for any distance, but that wasn't going to last.

Keeping as far back as he could, Keith squatted and shot out a hand to grab the pot, which luckily still held just about everything. The dirt devil mirrored him with a claw, but it was too distant to snatch anything. The battery caddy lay separate, however. It had bounced when it had hit the ground, and unfortunately was nearer to the creature. Too near. Disappointed, Keith abandoned the batteries. He tried to convince himself that they probably wouldn't have worked, anyway.

The ground along the shoreline was more exposed to the sun. It could be dry enough for the dirt devil. Not wanting to give it time to check, Keith bolted. A shrub grew, untended, right at the water's edge. Keith leapt over it, but wasn't expecting just how wide the thing was. He crashed through the backside, scraping his legs and back before hitting the water. But he did hit the water, and that was all that mattered to him.

As he waded deeper, he noticed the rocks heaped around the shore. He could have easily broken his ankle, and had gotten extremely lucky that he'd landed where there was mud.

What wasn't lucky, was that the dirt devil had moved. It was on the dock now, beside Keith's other pile of supplies, as well as the rope keeping his kayak in place. The beast's eyes were on Keith, but it had lain down in what was likely a comfortable position for it. The dirt devil looked content and ready to wait for him.

28:
THEN

THERE WAS SO much screaming. Keith's ears filled with the sound. Perhaps there were words in there, but he couldn't make out any. The only punctuation came in the form of gunshots, which were few and far between, but also dangerously close.

Keith thought of the gun that had been jammed into his gut. The thought was fleeting, there and gone in an instant, but it didn't help the way his body was reacting to this new development. His heart seemed to fill his chest as he was flooded with panic. People were surging toward the water, and Keith had no choice but to go with them. In the mad scramble, he felt his arms slip free of first Dr. Kimiko and then Russell. He couldn't see anyone he knew anymore, just a blur of terrified strangers.

His shoes sloshed into the lake, but he couldn't stop there. Too many people were still pushing and shoving from behind. An elbow struck his stomach, hard enough to knock the wind out of him. Gasping for air, he continued to wade deeper. As he stepped over and even onto the fallen, he knew what would happen if he stopped. Those poor people were being drowned in the crush.

Deeper and deeper he was forced to go. The water rose above his hips, the biting cold taking his breath away again, but this time he fought to keep it. Sometimes his feet fell upon sand, and other times on something he'd rather not consciously identify. He came close to tripping again and again, forcing him to grab whoever he could to stay upright. People snatched at him just as often, almost bringing him down at times. He couldn't recall exactly when he had lost his backpack. It had been ripped off his shoulders when someone had fallen into him, and while he'd caught the straps with his elbows, he ended up having to abandon the bag a second later because it pinned his arms.

First his ribcage, and then his shoulders entered the water. He was swimming, or trying to. His legs kicked furiously, trying to make up for the limited motion of his arms. He had put on his shoes when he'd left his home, figuring they would be better for running than his sandals, but now they were weights strapped to his feet. Others struggled as well, sinking and spluttering beneath the surface of the water. These people were dangerous. They grabbed onto those nearest them, tried to climb on top, and pushed their would-be rescuer under. Every tug, every bump, every hand that touched Keith had him ready to hold his breath. A part of him *wanted* to dive underwater. He wanted to sink below the pack and swim beneath their feet. To clear this mad plan from his mind, he thought of a frozen lake. If he went underwater, there was no guarantee he'd be able to find an opening back to the surface.

Just as he was about to give up and try anyway, the pack loosened. He wasn't being shoved in the back anymore, and people began to spread out a little. Keith could finally sweep his arms properly to keep himself on the surface. Some people stopped at that point, but most continued deeper, relieving the pressure behind them. Keith followed suit. He wanted to get out of range of anybody who thought to grab him.

I never want to be touched again, he thought as he finally found a bit of space to himself.

Even farther from where he swam was a flotilla of boats. Yachts, both motorized and of the sailing sort, drifted alongside much smaller ski boats. There were personal fishing vessels of all sorts, and a variety of human-powered craft. Keith could make out some of the faces of the people aboard these vessels, their looks of horror as they watched what was happening on the beach. The screaming finally started to die down, but Keith didn't know if that was because the attack had stopped, or because he had managed to get far enough away. He could make out words now, and that was worse. People shouting names, searching for those they had been separated from. People begging, pleading for help, crying that they weren't strong swimmers. Keith tried not to listen. Instead, he focused on the much more comforting sound of engines. Not all of the people on boats were sitting back and watching. Some of them were coming to rescue whoever they could. Small boats mostly, with the bigger ships acting as stations where the loads of rescued swimmers could be dropped off. One of the big yachts was heading away from the scene, already crowded with people pressed against its railings. Beyond the line of personal craft were much larger industrial ships.

Keith headed for where the boats were picking up people. He focused solely on getting to them. He even managed to kick his shoes off along the way.

"Kid! Hey, kid! Over here!"

Keith had been so focused on a particular sport fishing boat that was loading up, that he didn't realize it was he who was being shouted at. Not until he was splashed in the face.

"Hey!"

"Come with me," said the guy who'd swum up beside him, a lifejacket keeping him buoyant. "We got a windsurfer board over there that a bunch of us are holding on to. We figure if we stay together in a clump, one of the boats is more likely to come over to us."

The plan didn't sound terrible, and Keith was growing increasingly exhausted. The idea of having something to hold on to had him instantly agreeing.

The windsurfing board still had its sail attached and lying off to one side. People who didn't look nearly as tired as Keith felt, held on to it lightly, whereas a crowd lined the sides of the board itself.

"Make room. Got a kid here," said the man who'd come to get him.

A man old enough to be retired shifted to one side, opening up a space for Keith to grab hold. He didn't realize just how exhausted he was until he was given the chance to stop.

"You all right?" the retiree asked him.

"Better now," he panted, his arms tangling with all the others draped across the board.

All around him were desperate and distraught faces. Some of them panted like he did. Keith held on near the tail of the board, but at the front, a woman was lying on top of it, her breathing laboured.

"What's wrong with her?" Keith quietly asked the man beside him.

"Not sure. Think she took a hit that broke a rib."

Keith recalled the blow that had knocked the wind out of him and nodded.

The man who'd brought him over wasn't the only one in a lifejacket. A handful of people bobbed like corks nearby. When they had the energy, they swam out to grab people and bring them to something buoyant. There were other floating objects in the water besides the windsurfer board, and little groups of people were huddled around whatever they could grab without sinking it.

Once he was able to let go with one arm, Keith reached beneath the water to peel off his socks and stuff them into the pockets of his shorts. Floating there, he was finally able to start thinking again. He wished he hadn't.

Searching the faces he could see, all he found were strangers. Once he thought he spotted his mom, but when the woman turned, it wasn't her.

"How old are you, kid?" the retiree asked him.

"Sixteen." Normally he'd dispute being called a kid, but at the moment, he didn't care.

"Who'd you come here with?" He must have noticed Keith searching.

"My parents, my friend Russell and his mom, and Mandy and Aisling, some classmates."

The man patted Keith's back. "I hope you find them."

"Thanks." It was strange that he found that comforting. The man hadn't tried to tell him that everything was going to be okay, or that he was sure they were fine. He told the truth, and it was simple: he hoped Keith found his people.

It must have taken half an hour, but a boat finally approached their little group. It was a small ski boat, but its inboard motor was shut down. A single person was carefully paddling it over.

"She hurt?" the paddler called out, gesturing with his chin to the woman on the windsurfer.

"Yes!" several people replied.

The ski boat pilot lowered the ladder at the back of the boat, and let people on one by one. He didn't think they should move the injured woman, but he thought he could tow the windsurfer with her still on it. Some people instantly set to work disconnecting the sail.

The boat rode low in the water by the time Keith clambered aboard. Only three more people were allowed on before the owner said no more, and raised the ladder. There weren't many who remained in the water, and they all agreed they were going to try holding on to the windsurfer while it was towed.

I should do that, Keith thought, shivering where he stood at the back of the boat. *I'm young and healthy, I should be one of the ones hanging on.* But he couldn't bring himself to say the words out loud, to actually volunteer and give up his spot. All he did was stand there and watch. Watch as people huddled awkwardly on and around the board, trying to refrain from touching the wounded woman too often, but also doing their best to keep her from slipping. The ski boat driver kept their speed low, just putting along, but it still looked like a challenge for the people on the windsurfer to keep it balanced, while helping those along the sides keep from slipping.

"Fucking idiots," someone near Keith grumbled.

He assumed she was talking about the people on the windsurfer and frowned, because he thought they were doing a pretty good job considering the circumstances. But when he turned to find the speaker, he saw everyone looking off to one side. He followed their eyes, only now discovering just how much more he could see thanks to the boat's elevation.

There were so many people in the water. A huge band of them traced the shore. The densest clot was where it remained shallow enough to stand, the swimmers having spread out and mostly having made their way to boats or something else that floated. The beach and nearest docks no longer had anyone standing on them that Keith could see, although he averted his eyes pretty quickly. Luggage and clothing littered the ground, but between them, the sand was a deep red. Before he turned away he spotted some movement. It could have just been a dirt devil, but he didn't think so. He thought some people had been left injured on the beach. Isn't that what snipers did in a war? Merely injure a soldier in order to lure out others hoping to save him? Keith shuddered to think those things were that intelligent.

He finally located the idiots the woman had referred to. It was another boat, fairly far to the east, but big enough that he could see why they were idiots. Instead of waiting for smaller boats to bring people to it, a huge craft was attempting to load up on its own, and was moving much too fast. As far as Keith could tell, the craft hadn't hit anybody, but it kept kicking up an enormous wake. Swimmers struggled over the waves, and even those standing in the shallows must have been getting pissed off as the deepest were raised up off their feet and pushed toward shore. Everyone was lucky that the lake was relatively calm, but it wouldn't stay that way if boats kept pulling bone-headed maneuvers like that one.

Their ski boat approached one of the super yachts. Those on the windsurfer got to board first as eager volunteers worked to help the injured woman. When it was finally Keith's turn, he stumbled his way from the ski boat onto the yacht's swim platform. Climbing up the ladder at the back, he readily accepted the many hands that reached down to aid him. His muscles continued to tremble from his time in the water.

"Keith!"

He whipped around, searching, nearly in tears just from hearing the sound of his own name.

"Keith! Over here!"

It was Aisling. Not the most friendly of faces, but still one that he knew. In that moment, he didn't care about what he looked like, or what she might think of him; he pushed his way over to her and wrapped his arms around her lanky form. Based on the tightness of the hug she gave him in return, he knew that his was the first familiar face she'd seen. No one else had made it to this yacht. He still had no idea if anyone else had made it, period.

29:
NOW

KEITH STOOD IN water that just reached the bottom of his swim trunks and thought through his options. What he wanted to do was to swim over to his kayak, but he resisted the urge. It was tied up too snugly to the dock. If he tried to put his pot of supplies in it, the dirt devil would take a swipe at him, and it was all too easy to picture those claws carving through his plastic boat like butter. To protect his kayak, he had to keep his distance.

Option two was to make use of the pot. He considered this one long and hard, but as he paced back and forth in the shallows, he saw the challenges there. Namely, what to do with the supplies currently in the pot. He didn't like the idea of just dumping them out into the water, but there weren't any convenient rocks to put the things down on.

Maybe the next dock over? Keith studied the distance. It wasn't what he would call close, but it wasn't very far either. From what he could see of the shallows, he should be able to walk over there. Well, it wasn't like he had anything better to do just then, so he started walking.

It was more of a challenge than he had anticipated. Sometimes the ground beneath his feet was sandy, sometimes it was slippery rocks, and sometimes it was sucking mud. He could rarely tell before he put his foot down, making every step a surprise. Seaweed tangled about his legs and feet, threatening to trip him as their caresses made him shudder.

He lurched along, clinging tightly to the pot. Not only was the terrain inconsistent in terms of solidity, it was uneven. Keith found himself sunk down to his hips one moment, and then trying not to slide off a rock at ankle depth the next. He made progress, but grumbled the whole way. It wouldn't have been so bad if he could use his arms to help him balance, but they were both needed to cradle the big pot.

The dock was finally close. The last little bit was dense sand and easy going. As he approached, he moved a little deeper instinctively, knowing he could still reach that dock with the water up to his armpits. That little bit of distance saved him.

From the corner of his eye, Keith spotted movement as the dirt devil rushed out of the soil. He pushed back from the dock, half-swimming with the poncho floating up around him. By the time he got his feet steady beneath him, the dirt devil was standing in the exact spot he had planned to put his things.

"Fuck you!" Keith shouted at the beast.

It was the same size as the one he had left behind. Looking over his shoulder, he saw that that one was gone, meaning it was probably this one. It must have found a dry enough path through the soil to rush over and get here ahead of him.

"Seriously, fuck you!" he shouted again. It made him feel a tiny bit better, but didn't solve his problem.

The dirt devil snipped its claws. Keith had never seen one do that before. Was it frustrated that it had missed again? Or was it laughing at Keith?

"Why did you have to come here, huh?" Keith demanded. "And I don't just mean this cottage, but here. Earth. Why did you have to come to *my* planet? Why couldn't you have gone to Mars, or something? There's no water there, you would have loved it."

The dirt devil ripped off the end of a board. Just a small piece, but it threw it at Keith.

"What the fuck!" Keith startled, shifting farther away. He'd never seen one of these things throw something like that. It was an awkward movement for the dirt devil, its front legs not built for throwing. Not only was the piece of wood small, but its aim was terrible and the throw was weak. Even if Keith hadn't moved, he wasn't sure it would have hit him, and if it had, it wouldn't have done any damage. But it was deeply unsettling. Keith knew these things could plan ambushes, but this was akin to tool usage. What if it kept advancing? Would the dirt devils eventually learn to wear boots and carry umbrellas when it rained? Would they figure out how boats worked?

The second dock had proven to be a dead end, so Keith began to make his way back to where his other supplies were. He knew the dirt devil could beat him there, making him a runner caught between two bases, but the journey should give him some more time to think up a new plan.

It was a little easier heading back since he now had a rough mental map of the terrain in his head, but his mood was darker. By the time he reached the spot where he'd jumped in, he had given up on finding a clever solution. The dirt devil was waiting for him on the dock, not even bothering to try to surprise him again. It was lying there, looking for all the world like it hadn't just rushed back and forth. Keith felt it was mocking him. He felt laughed at.

Keith placed what he could in the water. Anything that sank was carefully lowered among some rocks that would hopefully keep everything in place. The things that floated, he jammed into his pockets and into the hood of his poncho. The towel he wrapped around his neck, hoping to keep it dry in order to use it on the sunken supplies. The knife set he especially wanted to dry off afterward, not wanting any of the blades to rust.

"You're going down," Keith told the dirt devil.

It watched him placidly, unconcerned with whatever the foolish human was doing. And Keith felt foolish. He should have done this from the start. He should have been more careful after entering the cottage and not have wasted any time. He probably shouldn't talk to the creature, it wasn't like it could understand him anyway. Still, he continued, muttering curses at it as he tested what a good amount was to fill the pot. Full was too much, too heavy to fling far, but he wanted as much water in the pot as he could manage.

"Okay, are you ready to burn, bitch?" Keith approached the dock with his partially filled pot.

Casually, the dirt devil got up and walked off the dock, like a dog that had gotten too hot in the sun. Keith didn't get a chance to soak it.

"Oh, come on!" he screamed, wanting to have hurt it at least a little.

Furious, he threw the water at the patch of dirt where it had disappeared. He then filled the pot, over and over, emptying it out on the dock and splashing the stone path, making sure everything was thoroughly soaked. Clouds moved in to hide the sun, so at least it wouldn't burn off as quickly as the rain had.

"Could have used you earlier!" Keith shouted at the sky.

Satisfied with his soaking, Keith hauled himself up onto the dock, the pot filled with the best amount of water for flinging, just in case. He moved fast. Removing the sodden towel from over the kayak opening, he saw that it had barely done its job. There was water in his boat, but not enough to cause concern. He took his bundle from the tool shed and jammed everything in. There was no space for him, but at the moment, that didn't matter. He untied the kayak from the dock, emptied his pot in order to drop it on top of everything else, and then slipped back into the lake. The dry towel he held overhead with one hand, while the other clung to the nose of his boat. Kicking his feet, he made his way back to the shallows, hoping that nothing escaped his pockets or the poncho hood.

Standing in the shallows, he organized his stuff. He had a lot more now, and had to pay attention to where everything could fit. Up in the nose, he stuck the lifejacket, stubby flippers, and the swim mask he'd removed from the dry bag. The toothpaste, spices, taco mix, salt, food tins, and knife set then went into the dry bag, which in turn sat inside the big pot on the floor in front of his seat. There wasn't going to be a lot of room for his legs, but there'd be enough. The bumper he tied to the rear handle using the boat rope, and the emergency kit he left hanging over the side. The hammer, pry bar, and hatchet, Keith bundled up in the paint tarp and tucked under the rear bungee cord. Under the front bungee cord, he tucked the plastic tarp, and the sodden towel. The dry towel, which was no longer dry after wiping down a lot of his stuff, he placed on his seat. The broken fishing rod he decided to deal with later, thrusting all its pieces under the seat, making sure to keep at least one part within reach. The ski rope he half tucked under there as well, its coils bunched up between one of the pillars and the side of the boat.

The balance of his kayak was different, but from the shallow water, he managed to climb in fairly smoothly. As his bare shins rose out of the water, he noticed a couple of fat leeches clinging to him and shuddered. At least he now had salt to make removing them easy. He peeled off his water shoes to let his feet dry out, and pulled the poncho off, finding spaces for them around his seat. Utterly exhausted, he wasn't up for much paddling, and so mostly just drifted.

He didn't get to do this for long. The clouds opened up again, sending more rain crashing down upon him.

"Seriously?!"

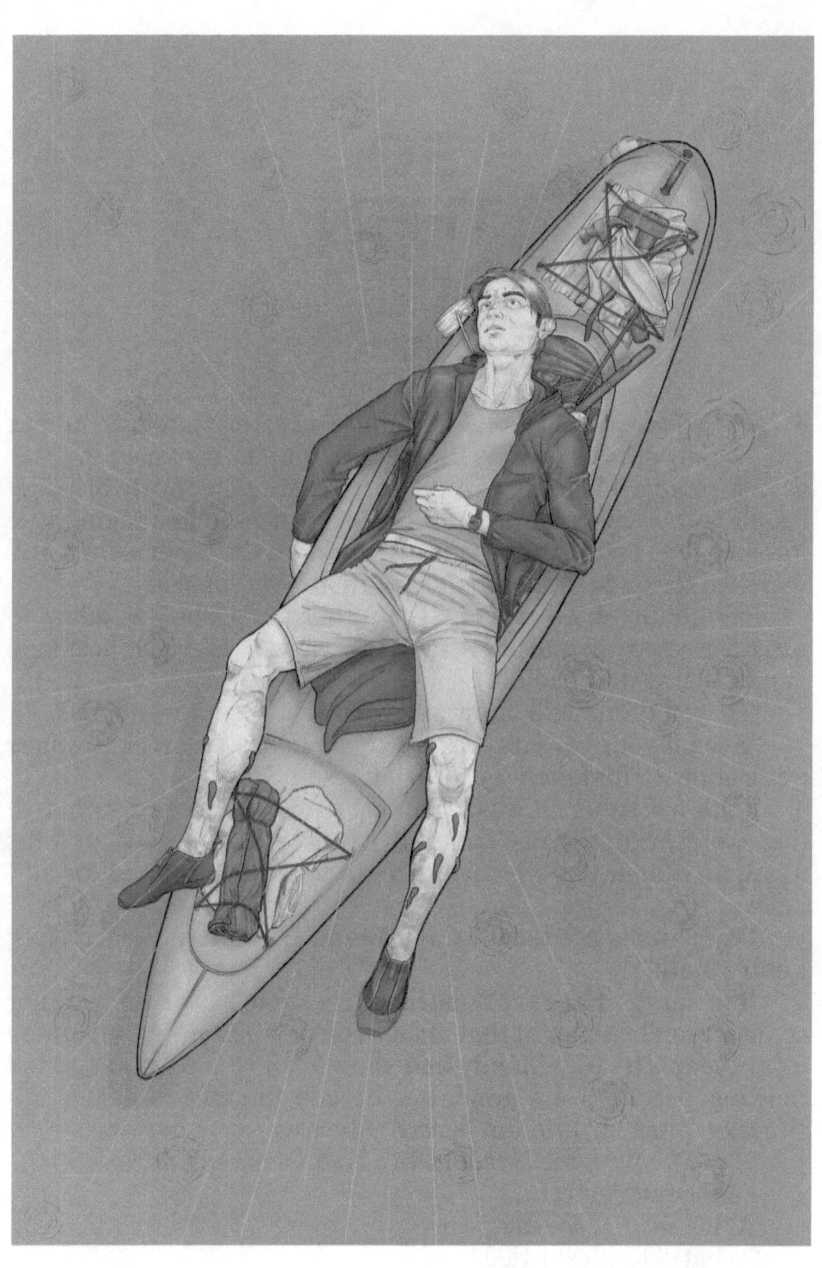

30:
THEN

KEITH AND AISLING stuck together on the yacht, but they didn't say or do much. They found a spot near the rear railing, where they could watch the smaller boats bringing people to the swim platform. Sitting on the deck, legs hanging over the side, they rested their arms and chins on the lower railing and searched for faces they recognized. There were none.

Eventually, word reached them that the yacht was going to carry everybody to one of the even bigger ships after the next load of people was dropped off.

"Do you think we'll know anyone there?" Keith wondered.

"Even if your parents are already on board, I don't know how we're going to find them on such a big ship."

Keith felt stung. "I wasn't talking about just them." Although they were primarily on his mind. "There's also Russell and his mom, and Mandy. Hell, your parents could be on board for all I know."

"My parents are dead." Cold. Blunt. Like she was correcting Keith's math.

"I'm sorry." His cheeks burned. He should have known. For some reason he thought that maybe she had just gotten separated from them. The way Mandy had shut down in the car suggested that her parents were gone, but he had thought that Aisling's situation must be different because she was acting normal.

Mrs. Phelps' hand. Mr. Blatty's body being unearthed.

Keith shuddered.

"Who did you see die?"

"What?" Keith startled.

"You just went away somewhere. Who did you see die? It had to be someone."

"Oh. My neighbour, Mrs. Phelps. And Russell's dad."

"Do you want to talk about it?"

"Do you?"

Aisling sighed. "Not really. But this feels like the sort of thing my therapist might tell me not to hold in."

"You have a therapist?"

Aisling stiffened, realizing she had let something slip that maybe she shouldn't have. "Yeah? What of it?" Her tough voice was back, the defensive walls reconstructed.

"Nothing. I just didn't know is all." Keith couldn't risk pushing her away. "Does it help? Having a therapist?"

Aisling shrugged. "Sometimes, I guess. I don't know. We're probably all going to need one after this."

"Yeah." Keith swung his feet. "One of the dirt devils brought back Mr. Blatty's body," he blurted out.

"What?"

"It had sucked him into the ground. He was badly injured, but he'd still been alive when it did it." His words came out in a rush. "This was over at Russell's house. Later, when we were at my house grabbing some stuff, the dirt devil came back. Russell splashed water on it, I think he hurt it. Like, *really* hurt it. I swear it knew who we were, and dragged Mr. Blatty back out of the ground as a way to retaliate."

"Did Russell see this?"

"No, he doesn't know. It happened right before we left."

"Jesus."

"Do you think it's possible? That it was that smart?"

"Yes, I do."

Keith was hoping she wouldn't. What he wanted was for her to tell him he was crazy, that he hadn't seen what he thought he had seen, or that it was just a coincidence. He didn't want them to be intelligent.

"What did you see one do?" Keith figured she must have seen something to make her believe so readily.

"I didn't *see* anything," she corrected. "I don't know for sure what happened, but it's the only explanation that makes sense."

"What?"

"We were using the hose on the back patio. There was one that kept popping up like whack-a-mole, but we were managing to keep it at bay. I think it was testing us. It never came at us the same way twice. But then . . . I swear—*I swear*—that I heard a sound like tortured metal come from underground. Next thing we know, the water pressure is gone. No more garden hose. I'm pretty sure the dirt devil figured out where the water was coming from, maybe how it worked, and destroyed our intake line or something."

"I'm sorry." He assumed that would have been when she lost her parents.

"Yeah, well . . . " She stared at her hands, which she had clasped together and were now squeezing until her knuckles turned white. Keith decided not to tell her about how he thought they had laid traps like snipers on the beach.

"What do we do if we don't find anyone?"

"There's gotta be someone in charge aboard that thing," Aisling gestured with her head vaguely in the direction the yacht was heading. "We just do whatever they tell us. They'll have a radio and are probably in contact with some sort of government guy. Maybe even the military."

Keith picked at a hangnail. "How many do you think there are?"

"Dirt devils? No idea. It seems like a lot, but they can move extremely fast underground, so it's hard to say. They don't need many to feel like a lot."

"I didn't mean the dirt devils." Keith gestured toward the receding shore.

"Oh."

There were still so many people clustered in the shallows. The farther they got, the less detail Keith could make out, but the more shoreline he could see. On, and on, and on, people waited for rescue. The whole lake was probably surrounded by a ring of people, Canadians on one side, Americans on the other. Dirt devils wouldn't give a shit about borders.

"I bet a lot of people who live downtown survived," Keith decided to try his hand at positivity. "Not a lot of dirt there."

"That's true," Aisling nodded. "And a lot of people would have most of a condo building between them and the ground. There's probably a bunch of rich folk still just sitting up there, watching the news."

"Probably worried about their boat being stolen."

"Yeah. Like this one." Aisling patted the railing.

"You think this boat was stolen?"

"Don't you? I mean, what are the odds the owner beat everyone else here?"

"I guess." Keith found himself suddenly uncomfortable. He didn't like the idea that they were on a stolen yacht. It made him think of the woman who'd stuck a gun against his guts. Sure, the yacht thief was saving lives instead of threatening them, but both were people deciding that the rule of law no longer applied. How many others would think that way, and what were they going to do?

"Do you think they'll have anything to eat where we're going?" Aisling wondered.

"How can you think about food?" Keith's stomach alternated between feeling like a shrivelled up raisin, and being a loose wad of acid. The idea of eating anything made him queasy.

"I haven't eaten since last night," Aisling told him. "I'm starving."

The ship they were brought to was massive. Any bigger, and it would be oversized for the Great Lakes. Boarding it took a long time. They had to wait on the yacht as small groups were chosen to climb up what looked like a cargo net. The injured were going to stay where they were, but a doctor was with them. Maybe Dr. Kimiko was on board another yacht somewhere, performing the same duties.

Aisling grabbed Keith's hand to make sure they were chosen together. Her grip was like a cage of bone. Keith wished it was Mandy holding his hand instead, and not out of desperation. She probably had soft hands.

"Keith," Aisling hissed at him with a sharp tug on his arm. It was their turn and he'd been daydreaming.

With two others, they started to climb. They limited how many could go at once, because of the difficulty. While the waves were low today, they were still waves, and they affected the two ships differently. As they rocked unevenly over the crests, the net stretched and slackened. Keith could also feel the motion of the other climbers.

Looking down between his hands, he saw he was over water.

The two boats couldn't snug right up to one another, and so there was a gap. Not a large gap, but big enough to fall through and become trapped between the hulls. Keith's mouth went dry.

"Don't look down," Aisling told him too late, shaking the net a little to get his attention. "Keep climbing."

Keith just kept reminding himself that he couldn't fit through the gaps in the net.

They had no warning. Somehow the bottom of the net became disconnected from the yacht. All Keith knew was that he was suddenly swinging toward the side of the cargo ship. With a shout, he hooked his elbows through the net and awaited impact. It never came. The hull of the ship wasn't straight from the deck to the keel, but at an inward slant, that was sloped just enough for their swing to miss colliding with it. All the climbers managed to hold on, but they had all stopped moving out of fear.

With his eyes squeezed shut, Keith hoped to block out the world. It no longer mattered that he couldn't fit through the net, that gap between the boats was now a straight drop down. His bare feet started to ache where the straps that made up the net were digging in. The net kept moving, which didn't help with his fear.

"Okay, you're secure again!" someone bellowed from below, cutting through the frightened shouts of others. "Keep climbing!"

"Come on, Keith!" Aisling had been lower than him, but now was high enough to tap his foot. "Keep going!"

Keith squinted down toward the yacht. They had secured the bottom of the net again, hopefully better this time. Closer was Aisling's scowling face. The net was wide enough that she could go around him, but it looked like she would pry Keith off and toss him into the water if she had to do that. He resumed climbing.

At the top, he was met by a pair of burly men. They reached over the railing and hauled Keith the rest of the way up. They gave him no warning that they were going to do it, he just suddenly found himself plucked off the net like a kitten off of curtains. When he was planted on his feet on the deck, his limbs kept shivering, partly from the effort of the climb and partly from fear.

"Welcome aboard!" A strange man slapped his shoulder, just about knocking Keith off his feet. He hoped he wouldn't have to stay here long.

31:
NOW

KEITH HAD PUT his poncho back on, but had also unfolded the blue tarp over most of the kayak's opening and rear end. In order to see, he had to trade places with his pot and food bag. Sitting down in front of the seat wasn't the most comfortable position, but it was the only way he could keep the kayak's opening entirely covered, while still having a sort of hooded gap to peer out of. It was a good thing he hadn't planned to do much paddling. He ended up disconnecting his paddle in the middle, and tucking one end under the forward bungee cord, now that the tarp was no longer there. With just the one paddle blade, it was easier to stick it out to either the left or right in order to steer. It was all he was really capable of at the moment.

It wasn't raining as hard as it had been earlier, and there were no signs of lightning. Keith debated picking another cottage to raid, but after what had happened last time, he just wasn't up for it. Besides, he was running out of room in the kayak. There was no guarantee that the place he selected would have food, and other than that, the only thing he thought he could use was a sponge to help soak up the water in his boat.

Having to use his headlamp to see beneath the tarp, Keith pulled the emergency kit inside. He emptied the contents onto the seat, and used the bucket to start bailing. He wouldn't be able to get all the water out, but the fact that there was enough to use the bailing bucket could turn into a problem if left unaddressed.

Once that task was completed, Keith figured he might as well deal with the broken fishing pole, while continuing to periodically stick his paddle out to adjust his position. He thought he had probably already used his headlamp too much, and so turned it off to spare whatever batteries remained. He put the broken rod on the nose of the kayak making it visible in the grey, rainy light, and set to work. Using one of the fish knives, he cut the line as close to the weight as possible. He nearly pierced his hand with the hook in his desire not to lose it. Hook and weight were then carefully placed on his dry bag, in a sort of divot he created out of folds in the rubber. Untangling the line from the broken bits was tedious, but he took his time to do it right. When he finished, he had a reel attached to a reel seat, and enough rod to reach the hook keeper, which he turned into a guide. There was no way to cast the thing—it didn't even have much of a handle off the bottom—but he could play out the line and trawl with it. Getting a fish to bite and then reeling it in would be a whole other problem, but that could wait for another day. If he actually managed to catch a fish now, it would have to be sushi.

The day was abandoning him. Keith ate a can of cold mushroom soup for dinner and searched for a rock. He couldn't find one. He searched for a tree hanging over the shore, but couldn't find one of those either. With his rain tarp limiting his mobility, he couldn't paddle very far in search of a safe place. It continued to grow darker and darker, until Keith wondered if he should turn on his headlamp. He could have missed something, but did he want to spend his batteries that way?

When the sun sank beneath the horizon, it was practically pitch black out on the water. It was still raining, and the clouds hid the stars and moon. The only obvious thing he could see, were the solar lights some people had attached to their docks or placed along paths. They gave Keith a rough idea of where the shore was, but that was it.

Paddling awkwardly, Keith continued his slow way forward. He hoped to come across a shallow water marker, something anchored that he could tie up to. For a few seconds at a time, he'd turn on his headlamp and sweep the area ahead of him. He'd memorize what he saw, and then turn the light back off until he thought he had reached the edge of that section. Several long minutes passed between those quick seconds of light.

He came across a place to stop quite accidentally. When something bumped against the kayak, Keith startled, fearing he had hit the shoreline. In his attempt to find a shallow rock, he had been paddling closer to it than he had when the sun was up.

But the object he'd hit, now bouncing along the side of the kayak, was small and floating. Keith turned on his light, and lifted the tarp away from that side.

A duck decoy. Keith grabbed its head before he could drift past it. These plastic ducks were sometimes used to mark rocks, or just as decoration. Maybe they actually worked at luring in real ducks for hunting, but Keith had never known one to be successful. This one had a rope tied to the bottom, so it was anchored in place, not just floating free. By tugging on it, Keith found he could lift whatever the weight was on the bottom, so its anchor wasn't very heavy, but he thought it would do. There wasn't a strong current here.

Plucking out the ski rope, Keith wrapped a few coils tightly around the duck's neck. He then tied one knot near the duck, and a second to the straps on the side of his seat. He was secure.

He was also exhausted. It had been a long, stressful day. Tugging the tarp a little, he completely closed himself in. There was no way to properly lie down in the kayak, especially not with all his new gear, but Keith shifted himself and his things around until he was as close to comfortable as he could get. Sleep came quickly, and was full of dreams.

The one he remembered most was of that first night, standing in Russell's pool. He saw Mrs. Phelps being eaten, but more slowly this time. She stretched her hands out to Keith, begging for him to help her. No shrieking, just a pitiful pleading. Keith wanted to help. He tried to splash the dirt devil, but he could never get close enough. Mrs. Phelps blamed him as she was swallowed, leaving nothing but her hand behind, still reaching for him. When Keith turned around to find his parents, she was there, in the pool. It was her, but not her. She had no arms, but her disembodied hand moved as if there was one still attaching it to her shoulder. In that hand was a revolver. Mrs. Phelps raised the gun and fired.

Keith jolted awake. His feet bounced around inside the kayak, kicking at his confinement, while his hands scratched at the tarp covering him.

A grave! I'm in a grave! He was not, but it took his mind a couple of dreadful seconds to realize this. He forced himself into stillness, breathing hard through his nose. It was dark, but not pitch black. He clung to the small amount of light that managed to get through the tarp. It was daylight, bright sunshine beaming down on his shelter. The fact that he wasn't roasting yet meant it must have still been early. Once the sun started to climb, his shelter would heat up, but for the moment, he was okay.

Carefully shifting, his sense of alarm returned. He was not okay. He remembered going to sleep tied to a duck decoy away from shore or any rocks. So why was part of the kayak now grounded?

32: THEN

ABOARD THE HUGE cargo ship, Keith and Aisling had their names taken down, as well as their ages. They were assigned a place on top of a stack of shipping containers—Keith did not enjoy having to climb another cargo net—being trusted not to do something foolish, like fall off. It was brutally hot up there as the sun climbed into a cloudless sky, but they had been provided sunscreen, and an umbrella to share, which cast a smaller shadow than they needed. They'd also been provided with some sail fabric that was spread over the metal to keep it from burning them. Water was also offered whenever they wanted, and Aisling was happy to devour the weak curry and rice that had been distributed. Keith only picked at his. He'd had a sandwich earlier in the day, but that wasn't why he had no appetite. Eventually, Aisling ate his helping as well.

There wasn't much to do on the ship but wait. People huddled all over the containers, clumping under whatever random object they had been given for shade. Inside the tower and below decks, people were gathered cheek by jowl. Anyone young and healthy and not in a large group had been banished to the tops of the containers, but they were also beginning to get crowded. Soon, the ship wouldn't be able to take on any more passengers. What would happen then? There were lots of theories, but no one near them knew for certain.

"Do you think Russell or Mandy are here somewhere?" Keith asked.

Aisling just shrugged. Keith felt the movement. Trying to share the shade, meant they often had their arms brushing up against one another. Keith was uncomfortable with the contact. Partly because his parents and Russell were the only people he could remember sitting this close to him before, and partly because the contact produced more heat. He suspected Aisling felt the same, since she kept trying to shift slightly away, only to end up close again as the sun caught her skin. At least the umbrella was easy to hold. Others on the containers had towels, blankets, foam boogie boards, even large chunks of cardboard. Whatever items made it to the ship that could be used for shade, eventually found their way to the top of a stack.

They sat and watched the boats. It was much easier to gaze at the shoreline when this far away from it. There was no detail from here, just a dwindling population as the boats continued to fetch the remaining survivors in batches. Keith was pretty sure all the swimmers had been picked up, and it was now only those shallow enough to stand still waiting to be retrieved. The number of small boats tendering had been reduced, however. People were running out of gas, and being forced to use their paddles. Some appeared to have given up, and had dropped anchor near a yacht with their last full load.

"Why do you think they anchor near the yachts?" Keith asked.

"Contact," Aisling answered as if it should have been obvious.

"Huh?"

"Those yachts probably have radios on board. They and the big freighters can communicate with one another. How do you think they managed to organize all this?"

"I didn't really think about it."

"Yeah, well, it's the radios. There might be a few cell phones involved, but I'm betting a lot of people's got ruined. Those small boats won't have radios, and so they're staying near the yachts in case there's news. They're probably also hoping for a tow, in case we end up moving."

"Moving? Where would we move to?"

Aisling only shrugged again.

Hours went by. Both Keith and Aisling took a turn leaving the containers to find a bathroom, with the other guarding the umbrella during their absence. Climbing the cargo net was stressful, and the bathroom situation was disgusting with so many people having to share, but the worst part was actually being separated from Aisling. Keith didn't like her, but he knew her. When he was alone on top of the containers while she was using the facilities, he spent the whole time watching the top of the net, waiting for her to reappear. He'd lost everyone else, he didn't want to lose her, too.

"Did you ever have Mrs. Berkley?" Aisling asked him once she was back.

"No, I took art instead of music."

"I think I saw her."

"Here? On board?"

"Yeah. I didn't go over though, so I'm not sure."

"Think anyone else from school is here?"

"Could be. I mean, anyone from our neighbourhood would have come to this same beach, right?"

"Yeah. Unless they have a pool they stayed in."

"Or found someone else's pool."

"Or went to a river."

"Or tried to go north to the lakes up there."

"So they could be anywhere." *Even underground.*

"But if they came to this lake, they'd be somewhere on these boats." Aisling waved at the nearest flotilla. "If you found out a teacher was on board, which one would you want it to be?"

"Hmm," it was an unexpected question, forcing him to think about it. "Mr. Doyle. He's my favourite art teacher. He's pretty cool. What about you?"

"Mrs. Scott, my grade three teacher." Aisling had gone to a different elementary school so Keith didn't know who that was, and Aisling gave him no clues as to why she would pick her.

"What about the teacher you'd most hate to see?"

"Oh, easy, Ms. McGil. She's one of the girls' gym teachers. She's *the worst.*"

"Yeah?"

"Oh yeah. Last year I had her for gym. It was during the first lunch period so most of us were starving. She would just sit on a bench off to one side eating a sandwich while we ran laps."

"Seriously?"

"Seriously! And this one time, during health class, we were given this worksheet to do. I finished it quickly because it was super easy, and took out a book to read. She comes around and is all like 'why aren't you doing your work?' and I'm like 'I finished.' She then told me I should do some homework I got from another class, but I didn't have any, at least not with me. This woman hated the fact that I was reading. *Reading*! What kind of teacher tries to discourage that?"

"Jesus."

"Right? What about you? Who was your worst teacher?"

"Mr. Baba."

"The science teacher? I thought he was kind of cool."

"I had him for math. Maybe he's a better science teacher, because he's a terrible math teacher. You'd ask him how he got a certain number while going through an equation on the board, and he would just go through it again the exact same way, so we still had no idea how he got that number."

Aisling laughed. "Oh man."

"Yeah. And while it's not as bad as getting into trouble for reading, he *hated* it when I'd draw in class. I'd get little notes back on my tests about studying more and doodling less. I mean, I know I wasn't an A-plus student or whatever, but it wasn't like I was even close to failing. Also, he almost never got my name right."

"Oh yeah! Poor guy. English was definitely not his first language. He tried his best."

"Sure, but you'd think that correcting him *every* class would eventually get the name to sink in."

"He kept calling André *Andrew*, and there was another Andrew in my class. By the end of the year, when he called on Andrew, we would just ask which one."

"I'm pretty sure he would have given me detention if it didn't mean he'd also have to stay late after school."

"Yeah, whatever happened to detention? It always seems like they go straight to suspension these days."

"I know a kid who got suspended for skipping class. Like, how is that a punishment? He doesn't want to attend school, so they give him a reason not to come? Stupid."

"Yeah."

It was nice talking about school. Normal. They continued to discuss their teachers, and stupid things they had seen or heard about other students. It was a way to pass the time. Around noon, a platter of cucumber sandwiches made its way up to the top of the containers and was passed around. This time Keith ate, although the sandwiches definitely could have used some more cream cheese, as well as some dill. The fact that he and Aisling got only one sandwich apiece concerned him. How much food was on this ship?

"Keith?"

He wheeled around and leapt to his feet. It wasn't one of the voices he had been hoping for, but it was a familiar one nevertheless.

"Keith!"

"Renly!"

The two teenagers ran toward each other, and stopped just shy of hugging. Keith could feel a need for the connection, but at the same time, he wasn't close enough with Renly for that sort of contact.

"You made it!" was the first thing Keith could think to say.

"Fucking yeah, I did! As soon as that message came through, my mom was waking me up and jamming a helmet on my head. We were on her bike before I even knew what was going on." Renly's mom had always been very proud of her motorcycle. It was an oddity, given her anxious nature about everything else. "We got to the docks before this big fucker even left port. They must have got the same alert, because they let us and a bunch of other people on right there."

"Nice jammies," Aisling commented, joining them.

Renly flushed. "Goddamnit, why'd *you* have to survive?"

"I've been called a cockroach before," Aisling shrugged.

"Well you look like one."

"Okay, take it easy." Keith placed himself somewhat between the two, although it didn't look like it would come to violence. "We all survived, and we're all here. I think that's pretty awesome. Have you seen anyone else, Renly?"

"Not yet, but then that's why I'm looking."

"Where were you and your mom placed?"

"In that big tower, near the bridge."

"It's called the superstructure," Aisling told him.

"Yeah, I know, I just didn't know if Keith did."

Keith had not, and he admitted as much. Renly went on to tell them that he had heard Keith's name being said by the radio operator, and that's why he came looking for him. The crew had a list of everyone on board, and were now reading it out over the airwaves, letting all the other ships and boats know who they had. At least one other ship had already completed their reading as far as Renly knew. They were compiling a huge master list that they were going to use to try to bring divided families back together. Since they were going alphabetically by last name, Keith was fairly close to the top of their ship's manifest. It was going to take awhile to get through everyone on their ship, especially since they often had to read out the spellings of people's names.

"Still, that's pretty cool." Keith's spirits had lifted.

"Yeah. I'm glad I found you, too," Renly went on. "I came here first since it's the most open area and got lucky."

If you can call me being up here because I lost everyone lucky, Keith thought bitterly, but he tried to push that aside. There was a chance of being reunited with his parents and he had to hold on to that.

"I was going to walk around the ship and see if I could find anyone else. Want to come?"

"Yeah."

"I'll come, too," Aisling added.

"You weren't invited," Renly scowled.

"She can come," Keith insisted. "Just . . . try not to kill each other, okay?"

"I can't promise anything," Renly muttered.

33:
NOW

OKAY, SO HIS kayak had bumped up against something. The shoreline? A shallow rock he had missed last night? Keith carefully shifted, testing the kayak's balance. It seemed there was shallow water to his right, but when he pushed left, that whole side ground against rock. His keel was definitely hung up on the bottom. The sound it made whenever he shifted caused him to grit his teeth. A hole in his boat would be serious trouble.

Keith sat still after his brief experiments. If it was land out there, he didn't want to draw the attention of a dirt devil. He may have already done that, and so he was determined to stay perfectly still for several minutes. If a devil thought someone was in here, it would have attacked already, but it hadn't, so that was a positive. But it was also possible that one may have only taken a vague interest, and in that case, it could be watching. Keith lay still and hoped that his previous movements might be taken for the waves he could hear slapping against the plastic to his right, or maybe a small animal that wasn't worth hunting.

Or it could be that there was nothing out there at all, and Keith had gotten himself pointlessly worked up. Better safe than sorry.

Once he counted to three hundred, Keith knew he had to do something. Not only was just sitting there not improving the situation, but he had to pee and would rather not do that in the kayak.

Tweezing the tarp with his fingers, he slowly inched up the side toward whatever he was hung up on. Whenever the tarp crinkled—which was often—he paused for a few seconds and waited for a death that never came. He wondered how close he was to the end of the tarp, when it suddenly stopped moving. Keith froze, fully believing that a beast had grabbed it, before his logical mind could catch up. The tarp hung over the sides of the kayak into the water. When he'd been beached, it must have gotten trapped under the kayak. It wasn't a dirt devil pinning it, it was his own boat.

Keith needed to move. He could maybe pull up the water side of the tarp from where he was, but that wouldn't help him since he needed to see what he was caught on. If he only wanted to peer out, the closest edge of the tarp to the kayak's opening was at the front.

Picturing a snake in his head, Keith eased his body forward. He thought of a snake's slow, deliberate movements and tried to emulate them. Unfortunately, snakes had a much better musculature for that than Keith did. He was neither a dancer nor a gymnast, he didn't even do yoga, and so his core was not prepared to hold certain positions for extended periods of time. The tarp whisked along his body and head when he slipped.

This time he counted only to one hundred and fifty. It was also possible he had counted faster than before, because his bladder was getting more insistent. When he remained alive, he thought *fuck it*, and pulled the tarp quickly back over his head.

For a few seconds, the sunlight blinded him. He squinted about, checking for movement, prepared to leap into the water. As the world came into focus, he saw his caution was unneeded, as he was completely alone. It wasn't a rock that he had been beached on, but a cement boat launch with a very gentle slope. Not far from the kayak's nose was a low dock. Past that, on top of a small hill, was a cottage with smashed windows and a door hanging off one hinge. A good place for dirt devils to hide from the rain. A few patches of grass glistened, and a couple of muddy puddles clung to some shadowy divots, but that was all that remained of yesterday's rain. The dirt devils were probably underground if they were anywhere, but the sight of the damaged cottage made the hairs on the back of Keith's neck stand up.

Unable to wait a second more, Keith peed over the side of his boat. His urine stank as it splashed against the boat ramp, and trickled down to the underside of the kayak's bow. He could have gone directly in the water, but wasn't about to turn his back to shore.

Something moved among the trees, but even the jolt of fear couldn't get Keith to stop midstream. The movement had been brief, but large. Nothing large lived on land anymore, nothing but the dirt devils.

Hurry up, hurry up, hurry up, Keith urged his bladder. His eyes kept darting between the trees, searching for any sign. Was that really a bush, or one of their brambly backs? How much time would he have if a monster leapt out of that patch of dirt? Keith didn't want to piss on his stuff, but his legs tightened, ready to spring backward. In his mind, he could see himself jumping away, getting his foot caught on the edge of the kayak and in the tarp, tumbling over backward, and cracking his head on a shallow rock. Yet that was still better than the alternative. He thought of Mrs. Phelps' hand, but more than that, the screams of Diego echoed through his mind.

His bladder finally emptied. Keith stumbled out of the boat and into the lake. He grabbed his kayak and hauled it off the boat ramp, wading deeper with his shorts still partly pulled down. He didn't stop until he was waist deep, and only then was he able to breathe. Turning back to face the shore, he might have pissed again if he hadn't just completely drained the tank.

A dirt devil was at the top of the boat ramp. It was just sitting there, perfectly calm, watching Keith. He hadn't heard the thing charge at him. Maybe it hadn't? Maybe it hadn't appeared until he was in the water?

Keith's mouth was dry. He folded up his tarp, trying to shake the water off the ends as he did. Half his attention was on this task, the other half watching every twitch the dirt devil made. Not that it twitched. It just sat there, watching Keith. Studying him, it felt like. Was this one that Keith had come across before? Was he being stalked, or was he just unlucky? He studied the features of the dirt devil, trying to memorize them. He hoped for a distinctive scar, but there was nothing like that. He'd never seen a devil with a scar before. He'd never seen one with any lasting injury.

The decoy duck was still being strangled by the rope Keith had tied to it, but whatever it had had as an anchor was gone. Probably a rock that had slipped free while being dragged by the kayak. Keith untied the plastic, traitorous duck to leave it behind.

With his kayak reconfigured for paddling once more, Keith hopped in with a slosh of water off his shorts. He was tired of being damp all the time. As he paddled away from the boat ramp, he couldn't help but glance over his shoulder several times. The dirt devil was always just sitting there, watching him. It didn't disappear until Keith was so far away that it was only a dark smudge on the shore. Only after it was gone did he feel safe enough to eat some breakfast and take a drink of water.

His water intake was low. He knew he should be drinking more, but with every sip, he risked getting a bad bacteria, or a parasite, or something. He missed having filtered water. He missed a lot of things.

Fed, he removed his swim shorts and wrapped his lower half in a towel. It was time to get back to his search.

The day passed as others had, with Keith sitting in his kayak. When he found good rocks for it, he would climb out to stretch his legs and use one of his towels as a sponge in the hopes of getting more water out of his boat. He paid less and less attention to the shore as constant disappointment dragged at him. He wasn't going to find a winter house here. The one he'd been forced to flee was special, probably one of a kind. This lake was a graveyard.

He paddled down a long channel and didn't notice that the spacing between the cottages was growing until they disappeared altogether. Nothing but forest lined either side of the waterway. Horseflies buzzed about Keith, and he cheered every time he managed to take one down. It was just him and nature. It was the sort of idyllic place where you might spy a deer pausing for a drink. But there weren't any deer anymore. Nothing that large could survive the dirt devil invasion. Humanity was finding a way, but so many other species would be gone from this Earth, never to return. Keith thought about the prairies. So much flat land, so much soil. How long would it take for the native plants to make a comeback there? It was too depressing, so he thought of the rainforest instead. They were a vertical world, and while the dirt devils could probably figure out how to climb trees, it wasn't their element. He didn't think they liked to be away from the ground, away from their shelter. Also it was called *rain*forest for a reason. Maybe the orangutans would be okay.

Keith had travelled down the winding channel—a river, he now thought—for a couple of hours without seeing a single sign of human incursion. But one finally arrived and his heart sank.

Spanning the river ahead was a dam.

34: THEN

L IVING ON THE ship was hell. The sun was unrelenting, and to escape it meant going inside the structure, where people were packed so tightly together that the heat ended up being the same, plus the air was stale. Keith, along with Aisling and Renly, explored every corner of the ship that they were allowed. They had spotted a few familiar faces, but no one they'd talk to.

When night came, it brought the relief of darkness. Keith and Aisling lay on top of their shipping container, not sleeping despite the day's insane events. There was no such thing as comfort up there, the sailcloth a poor barrier against the uneven hardness of the metal beneath it. Some people had been hurt. Nets and more sailcloth had been laid over the gaps between the stacks so no one had fallen off, but there had been some serious stumbles, and legs that had plunged through gaps in the netting. There had been complaints, but no action from the crew. They had done all they could, and there was no other space to place people.

"I wish they would turn off the lights," Aisling groused. The ship was ablaze with light, helping those who needed it to get to the bathroom, while also making it obvious where they were on the lake. Smaller boats had anchored as close as they dared, trying to make use of the ship's lights so that they wouldn't have to drain their own, smaller batteries. Keith imagined that, from above, they were laid out like a dead caterpillar with a bunch of ants preparing to cart it off.

"I don't think it would help me sleep," Keith admitted.

"It wouldn't help me sleep, I just wish I could see the stars."

The light was bright enough to obliterate their view of the galaxy.

Keith did his best to sleep. He nodded off a couple of times, but then his body would hurt and he'd have to shift into a new position. Nearby, some guys in their twenties were using the blanket they'd been given as a long pillow. It made Keith jealous. The umbrella he and Aisling had was just more hard surface. Aisling eventually had the idea of using the umbrella to block some of the ship's lighting. Keith tried not to let it annoy him that he hadn't come up with it.

He was useless, unable to do anything helpful or productive. He was just another mouth the poor crew had to find a way to feed.

The sun came far too soon. Keith was sore everywhere, and exhaustion weighed down every part of his being. He appeared to be the same size as usual, but if asked, he'd have sworn he was twice as heavy. Even his eyelids were difficult to lift.

"Fuck off," Aisling grumbled at the sky.

When Keith tried to go to the bathroom, he was redirected. The plumbing had taken a pounding, and so the washrooms were now reserved for women, and for shits. Guys who just had to pee were sent to one of several points around the ship, where they could piss into a funnel that had been rigged up to guide the urine down to the lake without touching the ship or splashing onto one of the nearby boats. Keith took a full minute to get the works going despite feeling like he was about to burst. The piss points—as they were almost immediately named—didn't offer much in the way of privacy.

"Be glad," Aisling muttered when he told her about the situation. "The bathrooms are foul beyond description."

Breakfast was a slice of toast with a single egg on top. People who had broken the ship's rules got nothing. Fear and paranoia had found a home in everyone's hearts. Panic couldn't be far off.

As they were eating, Keith watched a crew member making his way along the top of the containers. He was stopping at every small group and individual, and spent a few minutes with each, poking away at a tablet in his hands. Maybe he was taking a more thorough census, or maybe he was listening to complaints and suggestions to improve their situation. Just knowing someone appeared to be doing something made Keith feel more at ease, so maybe that was the point. Although some people ended up hugging the crewman; what was that about?

Finally it was their turn.

"Name?" he asked Keith first. So much for remembering who was in their assigned spots.

"Keith."

The crewmember sighed. "*Full* name."

"Oh right."

After Keith gave him the information he needed, the man poked at his tablet. Keith wanted to lean over and see what was on the screen, but thought that might be rude.

"Okay, we have a couple of Benchleys," he eventually said. "Tell me if you recognize any of them." He started reading off names and ages, all of them Benchleys. They were trying to find his relatives! There were more than Keith had expected, and they were listed by age. They passed his mom's age and Keith thought there must have been a mistake, but then the man read the name Douglas Benchley.

"My dad! That's my dad!" He practically jumped up with excitement.

"Okay, great. We're not sure exactly where he is."

Keith's mood sunk.

"But we have an idea."

It buoyed up again.

"He was reported by a yacht. He might be there, or he might be on one of the smaller boats around it."

"Great! That's great! What about my mom? Her name is Sigrid."

The crewmember tapped away but ended up shaking his head. "I'm not seeing a Sigrid Benchley, or any name close enough for a typo. That doesn't mean she's not here. Lots of people haven't been counted yet, especially on the smaller craft."

She hasn't been counted yet. Keith clung to that.

"What about Russell Blatty? And Kimiko Blatty?" he blurted out.

"Sorry, kid, we're looking up immediate family only right now. It'll take too long to get to everyone if we look up every name they can think of."

"Look them up for me," Aisling said.

"What's your name?"

"O'Connor. I'll bet you have a bunch of O'Connors listed there, but not one of them will be someone I know. My parents are gone, and my extended family's in Alberta. Look up the Blattys for me. And Mandy Follett, I think I might be the closest thing to family she has left."

Keith saw Aisling bristle at the pitying look the crew member gave her, but it was that pity that made him sigh and search for the names.

"Mandy Follett is registered at the same yacht as his dad," he told Aisling. "And the Blattys are registered together at a different one."

Keith felt a weight shift off of his heart that he hadn't even been aware was there. A small lump remained for his mom, but it was easier to breathe.

"Can you get us all together on the same boat?" Keith asked.

"Getting you to your dad should be easy," he answered. "It might take longer for the others."

"I'm not leaving without Aisling." Keith hadn't realized he was going to say it until it was out of his mouth. He nearly jumped when Aisling reached over and briefly squeezed his hand.

"Sure, since she admits to having no one else, we'll count you together as a family. Aisling, you're now a Benchley if anyone asks." He tapped at his screen, adding a note or maybe changing her name altogether.

"Thank you." She was still a little stiff with the crewman.

When he moved on, Keith tried to keep from exploding with giddy excitement. It was like someone had told him he was going to Disney World, instead of just a smaller boat.

"I gotta tell Renly," he realized. "Maybe he'll want to come with us."

"I don't know. I got the impression that they were being very particular about who got to move where."

"They can't just keep people here if they want to leave."

"Keith, I don't know if you realize this, but we're in the middle of a crisis."

"I realize," he flushed, not happy to be reminded of what Aisling was normally like.

"They can't just let people go wherever. They need to keep track of everyone so that they can move supplies to where they're needed. And there are space considerations. Some of those smaller boats will literally sink if you try to fill them with people as densely as this ship has."

"Okay, I get it. But there's no harm in asking if Renly and his mom want to see if they can come with us." Why couldn't he be stuck here with Russell?

"Do what you want," she dismissed him.

Keith regretted making sure that she got to come with him.

35:
NOW

IF HE WERE to turn around, Keith figured he wouldn't find another route to take before nightfall. It would be a lot of wasted hours. But how could he continue?

Needing to know just what he was facing, Keith paddled up to the dam. The water was high on this side, less than three feet down from the top of the cement barrier. There was a metal grate covering a hole in the middle of the waterline, which had its own little dam of sticks and seaweed piled up against it. He could tell by the current that water was still getting through, but not so much that he would struggle against its pull.

The dam was a span of concrete, a hundred feet across at a guess. He should be able to approach it without having to worry too much about dirt devils, so long as he kept an eye on both ends. The structure was narrow, not like the road he'd expected, but maybe a golf cart could drive across it, if it were careful. If a cart could even get there; there didn't appear to be any adjacent roads on either end, not even a break in the undergrowth to suggest a footpath. A sign stood on a short metal pole, but the sun and seasons had had a lot of time to work on it, bleaching out the letters until it was nothing more than a white, metal rectangle. This dam was old, and hadn't been checked on in years.

By kneeling in the kayak, Keith was able to peer over to the far side. He had anticipated the water there to be lower, but not to the degree that it was. Instead of five or six feet down, the drop appeared to be half as long as the bridge was across.

"Yeah, fuck that," Keith muttered.

He was about to punt himself away from the dam when his

eyes travelled farther along that low river. Just before it curved out of sight, there was a cottage. It wasn't the cottage itself that gave him pause, but what floated a short distance off the dock: a raft. The colour suggested it was the plastic kind, durable and well balanced, but also unlikely to shelter dirt like the wooden kind. Not only would it make a great place to stop for the night, but if he could haul up or disconnect the anchor, he could bring the raft with him. More space and a better place to sleep every night was a boon too good to pass up.

But how could he get down there? How could he get his kayak down there?

Keith studied the shore. On one side, it was all forest, just dirt and trees in a big scoop that sloped gently down to the river below. If dirt devils weren't an issue, he imagined he could portage his way down with only a bit of difficulty. But dirt devils were an issue. On the other side, there was a jumble of rocks and a series of sharp cliffs. If it were just Keith, he thought he could scale his way along them to get down to the river, but there was no way he could do it with a kayak in tow. So how could he get his kayak down?

"What would you do, Russell?" Keith asked himself.

What would happen if he just threw the kayak over the side? His supplies would fall out. The boat would likely land wrong, either sideways or upside down so that it filled with water, or maybe it would shoot down like a spear, plunging beneath the surface nose first. There was a high chance he'd sink his craft if he did that. He needed a way to make sure it landed on its hull. The best way to do that was to somehow drop it from lower down.

The ropes. He had both a ski rope and a tow rope.

Keith climbed out of his kayak onto the dam, keeping one foot hooked under a seat strap so it wouldn't float away. He felt like a small rodent that had decided to cross a barren field. Instead of watching the sky for birds however, he kept scanning either end of the dam for movement. He was exposed, but not completely, currently able to dive back into the water behind him at a moment's notice.

He checked one rope and then the other for length by hanging them over the side of the dam. The tow rope was just shy of the water, and the ski rope was longer, actually coiling on the surface since it floated. They would do nicely.

"Maybe I should have taken physics," Keith grumbled as he prepared his craft, hoping his plan would work. It seemed fine when he pictured it in his head—while tutoring him through some worded math problems, his dad had played to his strength and taught him to visualize everything—but he knew from experience that that wasn't always how things would go. It didn't help that it wasn't as easy to visualize with his eyes open, but he couldn't close them. They were too busy ticking back and forth from one shore to the other.

He took all his supplies and crammed them into the middle—disconnecting his paddle as well—hoping to make everything snug enough that they'd hold each other in place through any jostling. The plastic tarp went last, its sides jammed down into any gaps. The boat rope wasn't long enough to help him with the lowering, but it was long enough to tie from one seat strap to the other, and help hold the tarp down over top of everything. He debated with himself whether spreading the tarp over the opening and wrapping it all up in rope would allow him to safely toss the kayak like a bad burrito, but decided against it. He had already started one plan, and could all too easily picture the ropes coming free, or the tarp failing to keep the water out.

Check the forest: clear. Check the rocks: clear.

Using whatever handholds he could find, Keith dragged the kayak up out of the water, onto the dam with him.

Check the rocks: clear. Check the forest: clear.

If he had to dive into the water now, everything he had would be left behind at the mercy of the dirt devils. The end of the tow rope with the clip easily snapped around the rear handle of the kayak. The ski rope, which actually didn't have a handle for water skiing, ended in a loop, so he threaded it through itself around the front handle.

Check the forest: clear. Check the rocks: clear.

Unable to reach both ends of the kayak at the same time, Keith had to hold the ropes in either hand and eyeball it to get an equal length. He didn't want to start with one side already lower than the other. Should he wrap the ropes around his arms? That meant taking off his dad's watch, and he didn't want to do that.

Check the forest: clear. Check the rocks: clear.

Now came the hard part. Feeding out a little slack and then

gripping the ropes as tightly as he could, he then used his feet to push the craft over the edge.

"Son of a bitch," he hissed as he took on the weight. The kayak wobbled dangerously, and Keith gave it some more rope to balance it out. The ropes bit into his hands and he hadn't considered just how slick they were, how much they wanted to just slide through his grip. It was too late to change anything, he had already begun. It was all he could do to prevent the ropes from burning through his fingers, to lower the boat at a steady, even pace. He wished he could see the kayak as it lowered, but he had to brace his feet against a small lip at the edge of the dam, and there was no way he could lift his butt up without getting pulled over.

He could hear the kayak scrape and grind against the side of the dam. If he wasn't careful, the whole thing might snag on that side, and flip the boat sideways. Could it be flipped all the way over? Keith couldn't think straight as the pain ate into his fingers.

Don't let go! Don't let go! Keith shook that dark memory aside, picking an older one to focus on.

Mr. Kass, a gym teacher he'd had, used to take the class on field trips to try out sports like curling, golf, and—the one Keith now thought of—rock climbing. Keith had learned to belay there. Lowering the kayak, he desperately wished he could bring the ropes together, to wrap them around his back and make his weight work for him. He knew though, that if he tried to change anything, he'd drop the boat for sure.

Check the rocks: clear. Check the forest . . .

"Fuck!"

Not clear!

Keith released the ropes and shot to his feet. The lines whipped past him, the tow rope's float clipping his calf, as the kayak dropped unaided from an unknown height. But Keith didn't think about that: the dirt devil was coming for him, running across the cement dam like an oncoming freight train.

There was no way Keith could outrun it to the rocks and manage to hide. After three long strides that he hoped had taken him past where the kayak had plummeted, he launched himself out into space.

36: THEN

KEITH HAD TO spend another night on the ship before being allowed to join his dad. At least the food situation had improved. Several huge helicopters had come with big nets of supplies hanging from their bellies. The supplies were dropped off on the large ships, and some of those boxes were slated for dispersal to the smaller boats. It was during that dispersal when separated families would be allowed to get back together. It wasn't a smooth process, but it was progress.

There was a lineup of people leaving the ship. Keith stood shoulder to shoulder with Aisling, while Renly and his mom crowded up behind them. Mrs. Harris didn't like the ship at all, and had been willing to claim to be Keith's aunt in order to disembark. Most people wanted to transfer *to* the big ship, and so no one really argued with those who wanted off.

"Benchley party!" a crew member boomed.

Everyone was in a line, but they didn't get off the ship in that order. Keith hurried forward with his little cluster, eager to see his dad, but also not wanting to hold up the works. The crew members had become increasingly harried and agitated. They snapped at everyone, and put them on the 'skipped meal' list for even tiny infractions. Mrs. Harris had muttered a few times about this place being a kettle ready to blow. Renly said it was more like a hand grenade with a pin slipping loose.

The way off the ship was the same way he got on. Keith was not enthusiastic about climbing the cargo net again, even though he now had quite a bit of practice. Looking down at the water so far below made him queazy.

"Hurry up, kid," a crew member growled at him.

Aisling, Renly, and Mrs. Harris had already gone over the railing, making their slow way down. Keith followed after them with sweaty palms and a dry throat. He'd have felt a lot better if it were his hands that were dry, and every few steps down, he paused to wipe one and then the other on his T-shirt. His shirt had gotten pretty grubby during his time on the ship, as had the rest of him. The crew members reserved the showers for themselves and a few select others; Keith was not one of them. He didn't even have any deodorant, and with all the baking in the hot sun, he had spent most of his time sweating. Miraculously, Aisling hadn't commented on the stink he must be giving off, but Keith guessed that was only because she herself didn't smell like fresh flowers in spring and would rather not be reminded.

Keith checked how far he had to go. His thoughts on stink had only managed to distract him a third of the way down. He was still up high enough that he regretted checking.

"Keith, hurry the fuck up!" Renly shouted up at him. "Shouldn't you be good at this?"

Yes, I should be, he thought to himself. *Just think of the net up to the containers.* Foot, foot, hand, hand. Foot, foot, hand, hand. Foot, foot, hand, hand. The motion of his body was the same as when climbing the container's net, but the motion of the net was not. The waves were higher today than they had been at any previous time. The ship had stabilizers, but the yacht down below did not—or at least not ones as effective. It rocked over the waves, which rocked the bottom of the net, the movement travelling up its whole length. Keith could feel it, and wanted to believe it made him sea sick, but he knew it was just fear that soured his stomach.

"Keith!" Renly huffed, exasperated.

"Shut up, he's doing fine," Aisling snapped at him, then shouted upward. "You're almost at the bottom, Keith. Just a little farther."

"I'm right beneath you," Mrs. Harris added. "You're almost within reach."

Keith hated that everyone else knew he was afraid, but when he felt Mrs. Harris' hands tap his feet and start guiding him down, it was such a relief. He still wanted to throw up a little when he stepped onto the solid deck of the yacht, but he could breathe much easier.

"You did it," Mrs. Harris praised him with a pat on his back. She hadn't done the same for her son, since he had had no trouble climbing down the net. In her eyes, Keith was weaker. And maybe he was.

The yacht was being used as a staging ground, and was not their final destination. They were guided inside by a man who was much more friendly than any of the ship's crew members had been lately, and were given a place to sit while they waited for the transport that would take them to where Keith's dad was waiting with Mandy. They had no idea if the Blattys had been moved yet. Keith still didn't know if his mom was alive, but didn't like to think about that. He believed that she was. She was waiting with Dad, and would be so excited to see him unharmed.

Sitting in the yacht, Keith felt even grosser than he had aboard the freighter. He was no more dirty or stinky, but the cleanliness and the wealth surrounding him provided a sharper contrast. Even the table was too good for him; his fingernails had so much dirt under them that he didn't want to place his hands on the shiny hardwood. Renly kept shifting, also uncomfortable, but Aisling was looking around in disgust. This was clearly a millionaire's yacht—maybe even a billionaire's—and the wealth was on full display. Crystal chandeliers and gold-trimmed panelling. Plush rugs and ornately carved furniture. Keith would bet that there was also some seriously expensive tech hidden in the walls. And now it was just a service entrance for the container ship.

"How often do you think this was used?" Aisling muttered to him.

"Huh?"

"This boat. How many hours do you think it spent away from the dock before this?"

Keith shrugged. He got the sense that Aisling's family had never had much in the way of money, and didn't want her disgust to boil over into full-on anger.

"This place is worth more than my house," she grumbled. "And it was used probably once a year, maybe twice. Most likely to host clients. I could live on this thing and be better off than I've ever been."

"It's probably worth more than all our houses," Mrs. Harris told her.

Keith shifted uncomfortably. He had no idea how much his house was worth, but he doubted it was cheap. His family wasn't loaded like this, but they were well off. He didn't think he was spoiled, but he also never really wanted for anything he needed.

"If it makes you feel better, the owner's probably dead," Renly added.

"Renly!" his mother hissed at him.

"Well, he probably is!"

"That does make me feel better." Aisling actually smiled at him. Keith was pretty sure it was the first time they had agreed on anything.

When their party was called again, they were brought to the swim platform where a big woman in a canoe was waiting for them.

"I'm going to need one of you to help paddle," she said without greeting.

"I'll do it." After his failure on the cargo net, Keith felt he needed to redeem himself.

"Ever paddled before?"

"A little bit."

Mrs. Phelps had owned a cottage. She spent long stretches of her summers up there, and since Keith's and Russell's fathers helped her open and close each year, as well as with various maintenance projects, she let the two families vacation with her. It usually ended up being two week-long stays, in which Keith and Russell had to share a pullout couch. Sometimes the families rented a canoe, but Keith was rarely the one paddling it.

Mrs. Phelps' hand.

"You all right?" Aisling had noticed him shiver. He'd probably paled, too.

"I'm fine." Keith climbed into the front of the canoe and grabbed the second paddle.

"You just paddle however you like, I'll take care of everything else," the big woman called to him. "The rest of you, cluster in the middle there. Try to keep your center of balance at the center of the canoe. Think like luggage."

Actual luggage was tightly packed around them. Keith didn't know what was in the bags and boxes, but he assumed food, maybe some solar blankets, and first-aid supplies. He was happy to just face forward and paddle. Surprisingly happy, actually. Not only was he heading toward his father, but he was *doing* something. He was using his body for more than just climbing a cargo net, and could actually see the forward progress the canoe made.

That boy's going places. Where had he heard that? From a TV show or movie, or had one of his grandparents said it? He had no idea whether his grandparents were alive. One set lived in an apartment building with its own pool, and the other was out in the country, near a stream that was large enough to protect them, but would they have gotten the warning in time? None were very tech savvy, and although they all owned cell phones, they tended to turn them off at night, and not all of them were great at remembering to turn them back on as soon as they woke up. Best not to think about them, or anyone else in his extended family, or really anyone outside of his immediate group. That was a dark place best left alone. He thought of *The Lion King*, and the shadowy place that Simba was warned never to go. In that movie, it was an elephant graveyard full of hyenas; Keith's shadowy place felt more dangerous than that.

To avoid the shadowy place, Keith studied the boats they passed. Most of them were tied together in little clusters, sharing their anchors. Those that had rain covers had pulled them out and half covered the vessels, providing protection from the sun. Those without covers either shared with those that did, or else built tiny sun shields out of paddles, oars, lifejackets, blankets, towels, umbrellas, shirts, whatever they could. From these pockets of shade, faces peered out, watching the canoe. Were they hoping it was coming to them, or that it wasn't? The canoe carried supplies, but also more people. In the gaps between the anchored boats, both big and small, more canoes, as well as kayaks, rowboats, paddleboats, and stand up paddleboards moved about, ferrying more people and supplies. At one point, Keith spotted a paddleboat shaped like a big swan, the kind of thing that should be on a small lake or pond, that boyfriends and girlfriends giggled about taking out on the water. He had once dreamed of riding in one of those things with Mandy.

Finally, they seemed to be heading toward a particular cluster of vessels. In the middle of it was a pontoon boat, with a large cover over the front and back, giving it a somewhat tortoise-like appearance. A shell, at any rate. Lashed to either side were a pair of wake boats that had propped up their rain covers on the arches in the middle of the crafts. It was nice to see that where they were going had plenty of shade. Next to the port side wake boat, a low and expensive-looking fishing boat had no shade at all, but a man sat there with a line in the water, seemingly unconcerned about everything going on around him. Opposite him, attached to the other wake boat, were a small aluminum fishing boat, and a very tiny sailboat meant for one or two people. The sail was currently rolled down; no one had yet taken the fabric for anything.

They pulled up to the back of one of the wake boats that had a tiny version of the yacht's swim platform. Two women met them there, and Keith forgot their names almost as soon as they had been given them. He had spotted his dad waiting for him in the pontoon boat.

"Dad!"

"Keith!"

Keith scrambled out of the canoe, leaving the big woman to cry out in indignation as he set it rocking. Stumbling across the wake boat, he reached the front of the pontoon, and the platform it had there outside of its surrounding railing. Dad opened the little door in the railing, and didn't even let Keith inside before wrapping his arms around him. He knew Mandy was supposed to be nearby, but Keith didn't care, didn't even think of her as a long held sob bubbled up out of his mouth.

"Mom?" he finally asked when he felt in control of himself.

"I don't know." Dad held him even tighter. "I don't know."

37: NOW

SHOULD HAVE *dived off the other side*, Keith thought as his body flew through the air.

Gravity took hold, and he plummeted. He had no idea how deep the water was below.

His dad had taken him cliff jumping once. Just the once, because when they'd come back, and Keith admitted to where they had been, Mom ripped Dad a new one. Russell hadn't come on that little excursion—he had caught a pretty bad summer cold that year—and so it had been a bonding day for Keith and his father. They were supposed to be fishing, but when they came across some other kids jumping from the cliffs, Dad asked Keith if he wanted to try, and he did. Dad had jumped too, even before Keith. He'd jumped more times and from higher ledges. The other kids thought it was great, watching this old man jumping off, hooting and hollering on his way down, as if he were a teenager like them. Keith loved watching him, too. Jumping, on the other hand, had scared the shit out of him. It didn't look high from the water, but once he was up there, suddenly the distance seemed two or three times greater. Keith had only jumped off the one ledge that seemed safest. It was a little less than a storey high, wide enough to fit more than one person, and jutted out far over the water. Even after the first jump had gone successfully, Keith's knees knocked together every time he climbed back up there, and he had to spend several minutes working himself up to go again.

There'd been no hesitation this time. The dam was way taller than that rock ledge had been, and there had been no one to go first and promise Keith that it was safe. He had just jumped.

Mid drop, Keith remembered what his dad had taught him. He pinched his nose shut as hard as he could, and locked his other arm around himself. Legs straight, knees squeezed together, feet pointed and hooked at the ankles. He had to make himself a spear. He had to pull everything in to keep from slapping the surface of the water, because it would slap back and hard.

Should have worn my lifejacket, he thought as he took his last, deep breath.

Keith punched through the water, managing to miss the kayak. The force of the impact almost pried his legs apart, but he held firm, protecting his crotch from what would be a devastating kick. It still hurt, but it could've been worse.

When he'd cliff jumped with his dad, they had both worn lifejackets, which buoyed them back to the surface. Not wearing one now, Keith arrowed into the water, quickly feeling the cold and the pressure of the depths. Better than breaking on a shallow rock.

But then he *did* find a rock. Just as he released his limbs in order to stop his descent, his right leg grazed a boulder, twisting and scraping along it. Keith screamed in pain, all his breath releasing in a flurry of bubbles racing up to the surface. Clawing with his arms, Keith dragged himself up after them. His right leg was on fire, drowning out the pain of the impact to his feet, crotch, ass, hips, and elbows. It threatened to drown him as well, his right leg useless in the struggle to reach air.

His fingers hit an obstruction, and then his head, and he panicked. He needed to breathe!

It was only the kayak, easily shoved aside. Keith breached the surface with a mighty gasp, his leg aflame, but everything else shivering with the cold. His first lungful of air was expelled with another scream, the one he hadn't released on the way down. The third contained some triumph when he realized his kayak was upright, and appeared unharmed. The victory didn't last long, because the moment he moved his right leg, he was gasping in pain again.

Grabbing hold of the tow rope, Keith wrapped it around his body. It allowed him to swim with his arms and one good leg while also bringing the kayak along. The raft was too far to swim to, so he headed for the side of the river with all the rocks. Part of the jumble poked up above the surface, making little islands. He figured he'd be able to find a safe spot to stop for a minute. If he'd looked at that jumble before jumping, he never would have been able to.

Before reaching one of the islands, he found a rock about a foot beneath the surface and sat there. He had to will himself to look at his leg.

Blood drifted out of his body, the current carrying it away.

"Good thing there are no sharks here," Keith told himself, feeling lightheaded as he located the multiple lacerations that were producing the blood. As far he could tell, none of the cuts and scrapes were deep enough or wide enough to warrant stitches. His leg looked straight, but both his knee, and even more so his ankle, were already swelling, and trying to move them left him gasping. Had he broken something? He had no way of knowing. He'd need an x-ray machine, on the water, that came with easy to follow instructions, and it didn't seem likely that one of those was just going to appear.

Keith gazed up at the top of the dam. The dirt devil wasn't there, so he had nothing to curse at and flip off.

"Can't keep sitting here," he grumbled to himself.

Pulling the kayak over to his left side, he started to undo the ropes and reorganize his gear, moving his right leg as little as possible. Why hadn't he prioritized finding a first-aid kit at either of the cottages he'd entered? Stupid!

Some splashes drew Keith's attention away from his self-chastisement. Twisting around, he spotted small stones and pebbles clattering down the rocks to plink and plop into the river. They had fallen because the dirt devil was there. Its head moved back and forth, studying the terrain lower down.

"You can't reach me," Keith told it. He quickly double-checked, and no, even the closest little island was at least eight feet away. "I'm surrounded by water." He splashed for emphasis.

The dirt devil crept closer, still searching for a way.

"This will not hold you!" Keith shook and rocked his kayak, the thought of it trying to land on his boat making his mouth taste like pennies.

The beast jumped down onto the largest of the islands, close to shore.

Keith had been reeling in his ropes. Now he just jammed the

bundle into his kayak and scrambled to follow after it. He couldn't scramble very fast; his right leg shrieked every time he tried to move the ankle or knee.

The dirt devil came closer, delicately picking its way across the rocks toward him. It was a determined monster, standing on its hind legs on the smaller rocks, its shoulders hideously hunched. At least it wasn't throwing anything.

Biting back a scream when he thumped into the kayak, Keith fought his own terror and pain as he fumbled to get his paddle back into one piece. When he did, he was in an awkward position for paddling, but was ready to resort to using his hands for propulsion. He punted off the submerged hump he'd been sitting on, just as the dirt devil hopped over to the nearest dry rock.

His injured leg hung awkwardly across the kayak's nose. His healthy leg was inside, helping to bear the weight sitting on his hip. With his torso twisted, Keith could paddle, just not comfortably. Comfort was not required, just more water between him and the beast. With frantic energy, he made his way to the middle of the river before looking back.

The dirt devil flicked its forepaws at Keith, then turned around and made its way back to shore. Had the flick been a gesture? Was that its way of flipping off Keith, or was he giving it too much intelligence? Either way, Keith found himself repeating the gesture at the devil's back, hoping it was an insult.

By the time Keith reached the raft, his body was aching from the awkward position he had been sitting in. The nose of his kayak had streaks of blood running down it. He pulled up alongside the floating hunk of plastic and quickly tied the boat rope between his seat strap and the ladder. He then painfully hauled himself out, flopping onto his back and lying flat.

"You better be worth it," he growled at his new acquisition.

38:
THEN

JUST BECAUSE MOM wasn't with Dad, that didn't mean that she was dead. There was still hope that she was among the uncounted somewhere. Both Keith and his father clung to that hope, but Keith knew every time it came up around Aisling and Mandy that they didn't believe the same. Mandy's looks were pitying, while Aisling would sigh like he was naive. Now that the two girls were back together, Aisling seemed to forget that she and Keith had gotten along so well on the ship. He felt that even Renly was getting more respect from her than he was.

When they'd arrived at the flotilla, other people had left it. There was a lot of shuffling around going on, so Keith didn't really bother to get to know anyone, except for one man. Mr. Sidebottom—a name Renly laughed at until his mom, Aisling, Mandy, and Keith's dad all gave him the most withering of scowls— had been fishing when their canoe had arrived. It seemed he was the leader of this little group, and had no intention of leaving the flotilla. The fancy fishing boat was actually his. He'd already been awake and packing up when the alert came through. The boat had been on a trailer, and because he was ready to go, he got out ahead of most people and was able to launch it without too much difficulty. Keith wondered if he behaved like a sea captain all the time, or whether it was just an act for their current situation.

"We'll find your mum, boy-o," he would tell Keith while patting his shoulder. To Mr. Sidebottom, everyone was either boy-o or girlie, regardless of age, and even if they told him they hated being called that. Criticism just rolled right off him, which might be why he was good at taking charge. Didn't mean he was good at *being* in charge, but Keith didn't know him well enough to determine that.

That first night on the flotilla was infinitely better than being on the cargo ship. There were four padded benches around the pontoon boat and a padded spot over the rear hold that were good for sleeping. They'd been given to Keith and his group, and even though there were six of them, Dad stayed up most of the night keeping watch from the driver's seat. He said he could nap the next day. Keith slept on the bench across from him, and didn't wake up once until morning.

On the second day, Russell and his mom arrived. Mr. Sidebottom was, at first, enthusiastic about having a doctor on board, despite Dr. Kimiko taking an instant dislike to him. His thoughts on the matter eventually darkened when he learned that patients would be brought to her. They were all just minor injuries from what Keith could see, people who managed to hurt themselves while aboard their boats. He watched a lot of fishhooks get removed from skin.

It also rained that day. Not for long, but long enough. A fearful excitement could be felt in the air, as everyone hoped that this would be their salvation. Some boats put to shore to grab what they could, and not one person was attacked, which encouraged other boatloads of people to follow suit. The rest watched, waiting. The shower lasted maybe twenty minutes. When it stopped, about half of the people fled back to their boats on the water. A large number of those who'd put to shore thought for sure that they were now all safe, and everyone wanted them to be right. The sun dried the sand, and they were proven wrong. Those on the water, watching, screamed when they saw the dirt devils had survived the rain, but the noises they made were nothing compared to the terror of the people on the beach. Keith had a small panic attack, but no one noticed as they dealt with their own surge of horror and despair. Besides, his reaction was mostly internal. He just stood there, locked in place, feeling like a rat trapped inside his own skull, frantically scrabbling against a smooth enclosure with no way out. To survive the heartbreak, he latched onto the hope that his mom was alive even more desperately than before. He didn't dare think about the alternative.

By the third day, their crew had settled. Along with Mr.

Sidebottom, their flotilla housed a young Black couple, a nineteen-year-old from India who was still working on his English, a retiree who needed batteries for his hearing aids, and a woman who used to be the CEO—or CFO? CCO?—for some company Keith had never heard of. *Used to be* was the operative term. She bemoaned the fact that she fully believed they wouldn't survive this. Not *they* as in people, but *they* as in her company. Keith didn't care enough to listen to her, but had understood that much.

There were fourteen of them on those boats. They rotated who got to sleep on the pontoon benches, while the others tried to get comfortable in the wake boats. All except Mr. Sidebottom, who spent the nights alone on his fishing boat. He let people board it only when they needed to grab the supplies they stored there.

"He wants to maintain his captain status," Aisling theorized.

The teenagers had taken to hanging out in the aluminum boat and the small sailboat, as far away as they could get from the adults and their endless worry. Not that they themselves weren't worried, there was just a different quality to the parents' concern, that sometimes involved too much staring at the teenagers. Even Saksham, the teenager from India, hung out with them, despite the difficulty he sometimes faced in following their conversations.

"He was never a captain to begin with," Renly huffed. "He's got no fucking crew. Driving a boat doesn't make you captain. I'll give him boat pilot, but that's it."

"You don't have to be an actual captain to see yourself as one," Aisling retorted.

"I think he's hiding something." The way Russell said this, he didn't really believe it, he just wanted the conversation to find safer ground. "We don't actually know what he has stored in those cubbies around his boat."

"Yeah," Mandy added, trying to help. It was a theme of their conversations: trying to guide it to a place where Aisling and Renly wouldn't argue. "Like, what if he's got a little kid stashed away in one of those big fish holds?"

"Creepy." Keith shivered, hoping it looked faked. The idea of a man keeping a child like that was sickening, but the shiver actually came from imagining himself *as* that child.

"What is creepy?" Saksham asked Keith.

"Spooky. Scary. Unsettling." Sometimes it was a challenge to figure out a way to describe what something meant using words Saksham already knew.

"When something makes you feel uncomfortable in a scary sort of way, then it's creepy." Mandy was usually pretty good at it.

Saksham nodded as if he understood. They had yet to find out if he really did, or if he just nodded to move the attention off himself.

"He's got food in there." Renly never tried to explain words to Saksham. "I've seen it."

"Food?" Aisling raised her eyebrow in that way she had. The one that said she was ready to fight the moment anyone slipped up.

"Yeah, like, protein bars and shit. I've seen him. He sneaks them out in the middle of the night when he thinks everyone's asleep."

"Someone's always awake in the pontoon seat," Keith pointed out before Aisling could in a more antagonistic way. The adults rotated staying awake and on guard. Guarding against what, Keith had no clue, but he liked knowing someone was up.

"Yeah, but they're too far to see. He's *very* sneaky about it. You have to be in the wake boat beside him." Renly *had* been in that wake boat the previous night.

"You didn't see anything," Aisling scoffed.

"Yeah," Mandy sided with her. "You would have had to be awake to see something."

"I *was* awake!" Renly scowled.

"Dude, you snore," Russell told him. "We could all hear you."

"I *was* asleep, but I woke up in the middle of the night." He crossed his arms, pissed that no one believed him. "You weren't awake the whole fucking night. You wouldn't know."

"He was snoring when I peed," Saksham shrugged. "But maybe awake a different time."

Everyone shifted awkwardly, not enamoured with the bathroom situation being brought up. A tarp sat near the pontoon boat's swim ladder, providing the only privacy anyone got, and it risked falling if you didn't drape it over yourself correctly. Depending on what you were doing, touching the water was almost entirely unavoidable if you wanted to make sure you didn't miss, but knowing how many other people were using that lake as a toilet made even brief contact repulsive. Everyone was glad that Mr. Sidebottom had yet to catch a single fish. If he ever did, no one had any interest in trying that sushi.

"How long do you think we have to stay here?" Today Mandy asked the question that came up daily. "I would *really* like a change of clothes."

There was agreement all around. Some suitcases were occasionally fished out of the lake by paddlers willing to get near the shore—the dirt devils hid in the sand, one or two always popping up in response to their approach—but they actually tried to find and return the bags to their original owners. Since a number of people had grabbed their important documents, they were able to identify a lot of owners, and thanks to the database, could determine fairly quickly if they were alive. The database had expanded to include immediate family of the missing, so only if none of them showed up, would a bag's contents be added to the general pool of supplies. At least, that was the word that reached their flotilla. They were radio-less and reliant on the grapevine.

"Holy Moly!" Russell shot up onto his feet, dangerously rocking the little sailboat in which he and Keith were sitting.

Everyone wheeled around to look. One of the container ships was on fire. Not theirs, but the next one down the line had billowing black clouds pouring out of it.

"Dad?" Keith called over his shoulder.

"I see it!" he called back.

Everyone scrambled over to the pontoon boat, since it rode the highest out of the water. It didn't offer much more of a vantage point, but there seemed to be a consensus that standing near one another was a good idea.

"Dr. Blatty, you might be called over there," Mr. Sidebottom said, forced to use her name because she wasn't looking at him, and there were too many 'girlies' nearby.

"I certainly hope not. Unless they're prepared to give me a lot of equipment and supplies that I currently do not have, there isn't much I can do. Burns require a lot of attention."

Keith watched as Russell's hand found his mom's. He had admitted to Keith about being anxious his mom would be called away.

Into the night, the ship burned. There were no explosions, but flames were occasionally seen. Smaller boats swarmed underneath, collecting all the evacuees. Thankfully they weren't downwind, because the few times the smoke did reach them, it was vile. Dr. Kimiko advised them to breathe through their shirts as much as possible.

The next morning, some patients with minor injuries were brought to their flotilla. Dr. Kimiko assessed them and then sent them off with instructions for care, which was pretty much all she could do. It was through them that they had learned what had happened.

A riot. It had started out as a simple protest. People had become fed up with the way things were being done, and had organized a march around the deck. It had gotten out of hand as they collided with anti-protesters, and then it turned to violence. No one Dr. Kimiko saw knew how the fire had gotten started, but they knew how they had gotten their blackened eyes and skinned knuckles. Always in self-defence, they claimed. Dr. Kimiko didn't judge, but Mr. Sidebottom sure did.

"Did it to themselves, the idiot bastards," he grumbled with a shake of his head. "Those ships are too large, too crowded. We need to stay in small pods like this one. Much easier to maintain discipline and order. Much easier to see and solve a problem before it blows up like that."

It made a sort of sense, but Keith kept silent about what he'd been thinking. Their supplies came from the larger ships. That was where the helicopters were able to drop off their big nets. Mr. Sidebottom was in control of their flotilla, setting the watch, and always rationing out what they got in a fair way, but there was very little for him to actually do. They spent their days waiting for word from higher up the literal food chain. But Dad liked Mr. Sidebottom, said he'd been doing a good job from the start.

"What did Mr. Sidebottom do exactly?" Keith finally got the guts to ask Mandy. "You guys have a lot of respect for him, but I haven't seen him do much."

She shifted in her seat, and Aisling glared at Keith. Not for long though. Aisling was curious, too.

"Russell, did you guys have trouble that first day?" Mandy asked him.

"Yeah. The first night was especially bad, but we were okay. We were in a bunch of aluminiums like this one, tied to a big sailboat. When the sailboat saw it might be a target, they attached their anchor to us and then separated. They kept on the move all night, only coming back once the sun was up. Our defence was to look like a target that wasn't worth it."

Keith looked from Russell to Mandy and back, wondering what the hell they were talking about.

"You guys were on a big ship, so you don't know," Mandy explained. "We didn't have any supplies down here. People got hungry, got desperate. There were attacks, raids against any flotilla that looked like it might hold something the pirates wanted."

"Pirates," Renly scoffed.

"Guys in boats taking what they want from other people in boats, through violence? Sounds like pirates to me," Russell backed up Mandy's word choice.

"Anyway, Mr. Sidebottom kept us safe," Mandy continued. "He organized us, had us arm ourselves with oars and paddles. Told us where we were likely to be attacked, and what to do if that happened. We didn't have much, but hid most of it. He left a little in an easy to find spot, just in case we had to surrender. He figured that if they found that small cache, they would stop there and not go looking for the rest."

Keith thought it sounded like a good plan on paper, but there was no way to know if they would stop the search at just the one cache. And if they thought they'd been tricked, that couldn't end well.

"Anyway, we got lucky. This one boat went by, eyeing us like the men inside meant to do something. We followed Mr. Sidebottom's orders, and stood firm. Didn't say anything, just looked them in the eye. We're lucky that no guns made it out here, at least not near us. I didn't hear any gunfire that night. I think anyone who managed to hold on to a firearm had wet bullets to deal with, or else wanted to save them for something even more dire. Anyway, the next morning things got better. There was more organization, more radio communication, and supplies were evened out."

Being reminded of the gun that had been stuck in his gut made Keith feel queasy.

That evening, word travelled through the grapevine. There was finally a plan. They were all going to leave Lake Ontario, and make their way to the ocean along the St. Lawrence Seaway. Military ships from both Canada and America were waiting there for them. Rescue, at last.

39: NOW

EVERYTHING HURT. Keith stayed on the raft for the rest of the day, and all of that night. He pulled the blue tarp over himself for protection from the sun and the biting insects. The paint tarp he had folded into a long rectangle for some padding, and one of the towels he wadded up as a pillow, but sleep wasn't enough. His body ached, his right leg in particular. He'd wrapped the second towel around it to help stop the bleeding, but the swelling persisted, the skin around his knee and ankle stretched tight and painful.

The raft had some helpful functions. There were two pieces that could be popped out of the surface to form slanted backrests, like deck chairs. Between them, a round table could also be popped up. Keith used these to hold the blue tarp above him like a low tent. So far he'd yet to find another use, but for now, that was enough.

Pulling the tarp aside, Keith greeted the morning sun with a grimace. Half crawling, half slithering, he made his way to the ladder. The kayak had remained tied there all night. Grabbing the arched handrails, he manoeuvred himself around so that he could back his legs out between them. After using his good leg to kick the kayak aside to the end of its rope, he used that same leg to bear his weight as he hobbled down into the water, one ladder rung at a time, hissing through his teeth the whole way. He hoped the cool depths would help to bring the swelling down, and lowered his leg as far as he could and still breathe. Some of the dried blood would wash off, but Keith avoided scrubbing, not wanting to remove any of the scabs that had formed. He'd taken off his shirt under the tarp, but his swim trunks remained. He'd have taken them off too, if he thought he could manage it without screaming. Removing the towel from around his leg had been bad enough.

The water helped reduce his other bodily aches. His hands, especially. He kept himself in place with one arm hooked around a ladder rung, allowing all his fingers to flex and relax. Flex and relax. He'd lost a few layers of skin to the rope while lowering the kayak, and they'd stiffened into claws overnight.

The kayak kept bumping into him, pinning his head between its side and the raft. It made it difficult to relax, and kept reminding Keith that he couldn't just stay there all day.

Actually, I could, he thought as he pushed the boat away from him again. He didn't *need* to keep moving. He could take a day off, rest, heal up.

Be bored.

Keith got to work. Since he was in the water already, he first studied the raft from that angle. The top of it, he guessed, was a little over a foot above the surface of the water. The ladder would be easier to climb, but in an emergency, he could probably scramble up without it. At least he could have if his leg were working. The platform floated on two squat plastic pontoons that flanked the ladder. Peering between the rungs of the ladder, he could make out the far side, but it was so low under there, he'd be practically kissing the underside of the raft in order to breathe. Much closer to him was an anchor attachment. Next to each squared off pontoon, a thickly moulded chunk of plastic had a metal U bolted through it, and a chain that ran down into the water. Based on the slant of the chains, Keith guessed they attached to the same anchor.

Pulling himself through the water along the side, Keith winced whenever his right leg tried to twist, but it was a lot better than crawling across the raft had been. At the corners of the raft were reflectors, and underneath the edges he could feel moulded handholds, but these were both utterly useless to him. In the center of the back end, he found a second set of anchor attachment points, both chains disappearing at a slant similar to those in front. So two anchors held this thing in place. That meant two heavy weights to lift up if he wanted to bring the raft with him.

Back at the ladder, he hauled himself out. Sitting on the raft, his injured leg stuck out in the slightly bent position it preferred, he ate a breakfast of tuna with some of the taco mix stirred in. It didn't taste as good as he had hoped. While he ate, he contemplated the anchors. The first step would probably be to get a look at them.

"I knew you'd come in handy eventually," Keith commented as he retrieved the swim mask from his supplies. It hadn't been an intentional get, but he was now glad it had been in the dry bag.

After adjusting the size and spitting onto the lens to try to prevent it from fogging up, Keith put the mask on and slipped back into the water. The river wasn't very clear. It was still early in the year, when pollen and other such natural pollutants made everything a hazy brown. It wasn't terribly deep though, maybe only seven feet, and Keith could make out the bright yellow of the raft anchors fairly easily between the strands of seaweed. Diving down, he used his arms to pull himself as close as he could, but his injured leg protested. The increase in pressure squeezed his torso and pressed the mask harder against his face. The depths were also much colder. He couldn't stay down long, but he thought that one dive might have shown him all he needed to see.

The anchors were plastic, like the raft, and in the shape of half globes. They were probably filled with sand, but with a bit of luck, they hadn't been completely filled. Keith had been able to see cinder blocks down there with them, attached using a whole bunch of cable ties. He hoped this meant the anchors would be light enough for him to haul up on his own once he detached those cinder blocks.

The chains were an issue. They weren't thick, but they were coated in slime, and housed thousands of razor sharp zebra mussels. If Keith had had gloves, it wouldn't have been much of a problem, but then if he'd had gloves, his hands wouldn't hurt as much as they did.

Climbing back onto the raft, he sprawled out to warm and dry in the sun while he thought. The cable ties wouldn't be too difficult; he could probably cut them with one of the fish knives. Getting down to them was more challenging. Again, if he just had gloves, he could pull himself down there via the chain. He really needed gloves.

Would his water shoes work as gloves? No, they'd be too clunky, especially working the knife. He could wrap his hands in his towels, but that seemed like a good way to destroy them. Same for his poncho. The tarps were too big, and the ropes were too long for wrapping.

Sitting up, Keith gazed at the cottage the raft belonged to. Definitely not. It was set well back into the trees, and he could see the signs of a dirt devil attack. Even the mini-van sinking into the mud just beyond it had its windows smashed out and distinctive slices cut through its metal skin. There were no sheds near the shore, not even a boat he could poke around in. The lack of a boat made Keith hopeful that someone had escaped, but he definitely wasn't going to get a pair of gloves from this place.

He had sacrificed his leg for this raft, he wasn't about to leave it now. At least not permanently. After rinsing his blood-spotted towel and preparing his kayak, he planned to find a place with a shed near the water, and hope it had work gloves inside. He'd search boats too, in case a pair had been stored by a fisherman. He told himself he'd only go out as far as half a day would take him. If he couldn't find gloves, then he'd find something easier, like a lifejacket, and carve that up to make something that could protect his fingers.

Paddling was suffering. There was no comfortable position for his leg, only varying degrees of pain. His hands also ached around the shaft of the paddle. The current was with him, which helped for the moment, but he knew he'd have to fight it to get back. But he'd made a plan, and he was going to stick to it.

The river bent and then forked not far from where he'd left the raft waiting for him. He chose the right, just because it was closer. It took him along a winding course, with very few cottages, and none of them promising. He didn't even spy any boats to investigate.

After hours of agony, a boathouse eventually appeared, lifting Keith's spirits. He told himself he'd check that out, then take a break by floating in the lake, and then head back to the raft even if he'd found nothing. He could follow the other river course tomorrow.

Before reaching the boathouse, the river revealed more of itself, bringing Keith to a halt. There was a boat on the water, anchored about a third of the way into the river. It was a pontoon boat, with a big cover like some sort of shell. He could vividly recall the pontoon boat he'd lived on for a while, and this one was similar, but its top had been covered. Animal pelts and bright tarps formed a haphazard quilt, adding several extra layers over the top of the whole thing. Someone had sealed it up, made it warmer inside.

Winter house?

Keith paddled toward the thing. He could only see the front end, an anchor line clipped to a ring in the middle of the platform there.

"Hello!" he called out as he approached, not wanting to startle anyone who might be inside. "Anyone there?"

Conflicting emotions battled inside of him. He'd been searching for a winter house, but he didn't want this to be it. This was a small house, one that wasn't likely to be home to very many people.

"Hello?" His voice was too loud, making him wince, but silence was the only answer he got. Was the person who'd set up this place dead? If so, maybe he'd be able to find himself a pair of gloves inside. The boat was too big to take, but he could stay there for a bit to rest, and take his time choosing what he wanted to bring with him. Those pelts must be warm.

A gunshot sliced through the air at the same time the water jumped in front of him. Someone was shooting at him! Keith was a sitting duck out in the open. Even if he were in good condition, there was nowhere he could quickly paddle to for safety, especially given that he had no idea where the shot had come from. He did the only thing he could do, and that was to raise his hands, still holding the paddle between them.

"You stay right there, boy-o!" a man bellowed. Keith knew that voice.

"Mr. Sidebottom?"

40:
THEN

"**W**E'RE NOT GOING with them," Mr. Sidebottom declared as he handed out everyone's breakfast ration.

"What?" more than one person asked.

"It's a foolish risk to go."

"The military is waiting for us," said the CEO lady. "They have a plan to take care of us."

Mr. Sidebottom shook his head. "That may be, but getting there? This plan for the big ships to tow the little ships won't go well, you mark my words. I don't care how long they make the ropes, or how slow they go. Besides, there are a lot of locks between here and the ocean. Getting through those won't be easy."

"Locks?" Saksham whispered to Mandy, making a gesture with his fingers to suggest a padlock.

"I'll explain later," she whispered back.

"And where do you suggest we go?" asked the young woman.

"North. To the smaller lakes. There're lots of islands up there, and there's no way these bastards can inhabit all of them. We can find ourselves a safe place up there."

"That's stupid." The CEO crossed her arms. "What would we do for food? And this sunshine isn't going to last forever."

"We can handle a bit of rain. And we can grow our own food. Those dirt devil things don't like the water, but our animals have no problem with it. They'll find the safe islands, and then we can hunt them."

"Keith, go sit in the aluminium."

Keith frowned at his dad. "Why?"

"Just go, please."

"I should get to be a part of this conversation." His dad always let him be involved, why had that changed?

"Now, please!"

Everyone was staring at them.

"This is such bullshit," Keith muttered and turned toward the other boats. He made a show of stomping across the pontoon boat, and wishing he had a door bigger than the railing gate to slam. Dad had been acting strange ever since they got separated from Mom, but this time it didn't make sense. They were just talking about an idea, a plan that would affect Keith just as much as everyone else. He should get to participate.

He sat down in the aluminum boat in a huff, but he wasn't alone. Russell climbed in shortly after.

"If you didn't get sent away, too, I don't want to talk to you," Keith grumbled.

"No, my mom told me to go as well."

"Why? They're just talking, why aren't we even allowed to listen?" Keith glared at the pontoon boat, but the conversation was no longer happening there. They must have moved to the wake boat on the far side, or even Mr. Sidebottom's fishing boat.

"I don't know. They're probably going to bring up stuff they don't want us to hear."

"Like what? What aren't we allowed to know about?"

Russell shrugged.

"Mandy and Aisling are still over there. So is Renly."

"Mrs. Harris must not care about what Renly hears, and the girls don't have any parents in the group."

Although no sooner had they brought it up, than they spotted the others coming toward them. Aisling was ready to blow, her face bright red and her fists clenched as she scrambled across the flotilla.

"Fucking adults," she huffed, taking up residence with Mandy in the little sailboat. "Think they know so much more than us. What the fuck was that?"

"They are like a government," Saksham said. Even he had been sent away, and he'd be twenty before the year was over. "We are the people."

"Well the people didn't vote for them, and the people don't like being uninformed," Aisling snapped. "This is exactly the kind of bullshit that led to that ship being burned. We should protest. We should go over there and refuse to let them talk without us."

"Why are they icing us out?" Even frowning, Mandy was beautiful. "I don't understand it. There's nothing they could be talking about that we're not old enough to hear. We're all well aware of the danger."

"They just want to be in control." Renly shifted uncomfortably when all eyes turned to him. "Look, you all know how my mom can get . . . weird, sometimes. Every August, she takes me to the mall to buy new clothes for the start of the school year. It's embarrassing as hell, but I don't get a say. If I fight it, she just gets more stubborn, and ends up picking out all my clothes for me. When I co-operate, I'm more likely to get what *I* want."

Aisling was nodding. "I get it. My therapist talked about this kind of thing once. She said something like, when someone feels they're in a situation they can't control, they'll take charge of what they can. Usually that means commanding a space, like cleaning or whatever, but in this case, I guess maybe it's being able to tell us what to do." She spoke while looking at her feet. The way her head then shot up, with her eyes startled, she hadn't really meant to say all of that out loud. She hadn't meant to tell everyone that she had a therapist. They all received a glower as though being challenged to comment on it, but all the teenagers kept their mouths shut on the subject.

"My parents used to send me out of the room if they were going to fight," Mandy admitted. "We all knew that I knew they were fighting, and yet they would send me to my room anyway. I overheard my mom talking to my grandma about it once. They didn't want me to know the details, so that whatever they decided on, they could present a united front. There's going to be an argument about this, and they don't want us to know who's taking what side."

"It's still messed up," Keith huffed, although he was a little less angry now that he wasn't in this boat alone. "We're sixteen. Saksham is nineteen! We're not little kids. We should get to have a say in what we do, where we go."

"You're right," Aisling agreed. "So if it were up to us, what would you guys want to do?"

Keith hadn't thought that far ahead. He didn't know what he wanted to do, he just wanted a seat at the table. He wanted to know what was going on.

"Obviously we should go to the military," Renly sneered.

"I don't think it's that obvious," Aisling bit back.

"Why wouldn't we go? They're the ones who've been feeding us. They'll have the firepower to blast those bitches back into space, and then we can get back to normal."

"The locks will be dangerous," Russell reminded him.

"So will trying to survive on our own," Renly countered.

"What are locks?" Saksham asked again.

"They're a part of waterways," Russell told him. "They allow boats and ships to move between two bodies of water that aren't at the same level."

Mandy mimed him a quick example with her hands in case he didn't understand all of Russell's words.

"The lock controls will be on shore somewhere," Russell continued. "And only so many boats can fit in one at a time. These big ships probably have to use them solo. Filling and emptying, and filling and emptying, that's going to take a long time."

"And growing our own crops won't?" Renly fired back.

"Someone's going to have to go on land no matter which option we choose." Mandy wasn't saying this to anyone in particular, her eyes directed toward the beach.

"Yeah, and I'd rather the guys with firepower be the ones to do that."

"We all know where Renly stands," Russell said. "What about everyone else?"

"I think we should go north," Aisling voted.

"I like that plan," Saksham agreed. "I do not like soldiers."

"Why not?" Renly snapped. "Soldiers are going to be the ones to eradicate these fuckers."

"Renly, let everyone say what's on their mind," Russell tried to calm him down. "Keith? What do you think?"

"I don't know," Keith told them, but that wasn't exactly true. What he wanted to do was stay put. He wanted to hold on to the chance that his mom would be found, and felt that leaving would destroy that. He also didn't want to leave his city, the only place he'd ever lived. "What about you, Russell?"

"Right now, I'm leaning toward the ocean. I see the advantages of going north," he quickly added under Aisling's glare. "But to me, the ocean sounds better. We have people to help feed us."

"We don't have enough information," Mandy growled. "We don't know *where* the food being helicoptered in comes from. We don't know if they have more of it, and if they have the fuel needed to keep getting it to us. Most likely, it comes from a storage centre on land somewhere, which means people could've already died for it, and if more do, maybe they'll stop sending people to retrieve it. When the food gets low, I don't think I want to be near a bunch of people who've already proven they'll turn to violence when they get hungry. On the other hand, we have no idea what's north. We don't know what the waterways are like. We don't know that we can find somewhere safe. We just don't know *anything!*"

Everyone stared at Mandy, who was red-faced and shaking with fury. Keith hadn't realized just how angry she was. He didn't think anyone had, considering the surprise on their faces. Not even Aisling.

Mandy got up and gave the impression that she wanted to storm off, but there was nowhere to storm off to. This only made her more furious, as all she could do was huff back down facing away from everyone. Aisling reached out a tentative hand, and then withdrew it again before touching Mandy's shoulder.

Discussion over.

41:
NOW

KEITH COULDN'T BELIEVE IT. It *was* Mr. Sidebottom. Not quite as he remembered him, but definitely him.

He still held his paddle over his head as the man stepped out of the forest—the *forest!* He was on land!—holding a rifle pointed at Keith's head.

"Mr. Sidebottom, it's me. Keith." He swallowed a dry lump in his throat.

"Keith." Mr. Sidebottom said the word like he'd never heard it before. Was he suffering brain damage? The hideous scars criss-crossing his face, leaving bare patches through his wild hair and beard, certainly indicated he'd been through even more shit since Keith had last seen him.

"Yeah. Keith. We met on Lake Ontario?"

"I remember who you are, boy-o."

"Can you lower the gun, please?"

"No." He had walked out of the woods and now stood in the shallows in hip-waders. Over his clothes, he wore a sort of netting made of animal skins. The straps were wide, and bulbous. Along with the real rifle he carried in his hands, a Super Soaker hung from a belt on one side, and a simple water pistol on the other.

"Can I lower my arms?" Keith asked.

"No."

"Please? I messed up my leg pretty badly and this is getting extremely uncomfortable."

Mr. Sidebottom's eyes darted along the entirety of his kayak. "Fine. Keep your hands where I can see them. Paddle over this way."

Keith did as he was commanded, taking much broader, more sweeping strokes than normal to make sure Mr. Sidebottom saw his hands weren't going anywhere else. He kept his eyes locked on the barrel of the rifle.

"Get out." Mr. Sidebottom flicked his rifle to indicate where Keith should do that.

His leg screamed in protest. Keith stifled his own scream, letting it out in a series of gasps and grunts. Better to hurt his leg than get shot.

"Where did you come from?" Mr. Sidebottom asked, giving no indication he saw Keith's struggle.

"Up the river. Over the dam." Keith had to speak through gritted teeth. He splashed into the water, accidentally booting his kayak away from him.

"Over the dam?" Mr. Sidebottom caught the boat with one hand, the other still holding the rifle steady on Keith.

"Yeah," Keith spluttered. "That way." The water was a little deeper than his waist. Between that and the paddle he still held onto as a leaning post, he could stand while taking his weight off his bad leg.

"That how you messed up your leg?"

Keith nodded.

Finally taking his eyes off Keith, Mr. Sidebottom rummaged through the kayak. "Why'd you do that?"

"I saw a raft I want on the other side. I need gloves to get it though. I was looking for some when I spotted your boat."

"You're alone?"

"Yes. The winter house . . . " He didn't want to explain.

"Winter house?"

"Where we lived through the winter."

Mr. Sidebottom shook his head. "You kids with your naming shit. What did you call those beasts again?"

"Dirt devils."

Mr. Sidebottom snorted. "That's right. Devils. Accurate."

"Are you alone?" Keith asked.

He grunted. "You don't have much here." He stopped looking through the kayak but kept it at his side.

"It's been a few days." Keith had already lost track. "I haven't been able to find much."

Mr. Sidebottom looked Keith up and down, but more importantly, he shouldered his rifle. "Come with me. I'll help you fix your leg."

"Thank you, Mr. Sidebottom."

Keith struggled to pick his way through the shallows with only his paddle for support. He wished he had his kayak to lean on, but Mr. Sidebottom held on to that, walking it through the water.

Next to the pontoon boat, a long shelf of submerged rock allowed Mr. Sidebottom to walk up beside it without ever getting deeper than his knees. He pushed Keith's kayak between the pontoons, using a spare rope there to tie it up.

"Come on." Mr. Sidebottom headed for the back of the boat that dwarfed Keith's own. He hesitated to follow. His kayak looked trapped—it definitely wasn't easily accessible—and after all his close calls, that made him nervous.

Mr. Sidebottom pulled on some cords hanging among the furs and tarps covering the boat. The sides lifted up like crude blinds, uncovering the boat's original top, which still had its screen inserts in the windows. Keith noticed that all the gaps between the boat's siding and floor had been stuffed with blankets, or some other fabric.

At the rear, the ladder was down. Keith wasn't surprised by that, but he was surprised to discover that the motor was gone. The whole engine had been removed, and instead of a tank of gas strapped down on the opposite side of the rear ledge, there was a cooler missing its lid and drainage plug.

Mr. Sidebottom climbed the ladder easily, and pulled off his waders, which went into the cooler. He then started to undo some ties that held together the pelts covering the rear door. Keith waited until the man had gotten the door open and had stepped inside before attempting the ladder himself. With only one good leg, he struggled immensely.

"Leave the paddle along the back," Mr. Sidebottom grumbled at him. "And take that wet shirt off. I don't want you dripping everywhere."

Keith did as he was told, grateful he wasn't being asked to remove his shorts. He was uncomfortable enough already, and still wasn't sure he'd even be able to. He didn't toss his shirt into the cooler though; instead he left it spread flat on the ledge in the hopes it would dry before he put it back on.

When he finally got upright on the ledge, Mr. Sidebottom tossed a couple of towels at him before he could step through the entryway. Keith wrapped one around his shorts, and the other around his shoulders.

"Those are both for your shorts," Mr. Sidebottom corrected him. "Try to keep the water from seeping through them."

Keith felt weird hobbling into this man's home bare-chested. And it clearly was his home. The longest bench was made up as a bed. One of the forward benches had some plywood placed overtop, turning it into a table. The actual table that used to be in the boat had been removed, as had the captain's chair, in order to free up some floor space. The sides were lined with more insulating material, while useful items decorated the remaining surfaces, and most likely filled the holds under the bench seats. Keith hadn't been positive before, but now he was certain that this was the same pontoon boat he had lived in on Lake Ontario. He had put those strips of duct tape along the canvas ceiling himself.

Mr. Sidebottom removed that strange harness he had and draped it over the remaining console. Keith heard the water slosh inside of it. It probably wouldn't save Mr. Sidebottom, but it would certainly wound any dirt devil that attacked him.

"Lay down on the floor there," Mr. Sidebottom grunted.

Keith did as he was told, easing himself down. The only light came in through the screens Mr. Sidebottom had uncovered, which was not much. The shadows around the boat made Keith nervous, and he was glad he got to remain relatively close to the exit.

"Ow!" Keith yelped as Mr. Sidebottom manhandled his injured leg.

"I'm trying to see if you dislocated anything."

"Have I?" Keith gasped.

"Don't think so. Except for maybe this toe."

Keith screamed as Mr. Sidebottom wiggled it. He'd thought that pain had just been an extension of what had happened to his ankle.

"I think I can get it back in place."

"You *think*?"

"Let's hope you haven't broken any bones." Without warning, Mr. Sidebottom grabbed Keith's toe again.

Keith had no idea whether the man fixed it or not. He only knew sudden, sharp pain before being folded up in wings of darkness. He passed out.

42:
THEN

THEY WERE GOING with Mr. Sidebottom. Not everyone was, but Keith and his dad were. The Blattys were coming too, and so were Mandy and Aisling, but Renly and his mom were not. They had arranged for someone to take them to a boat that was going to travel with the ships. The CEO lady and the old man were also leaving, but the Black couple and Saksham were staying with the flotilla. Keith had expected more to leave. Mr. Sidebottom must have been really convincing.

"You should tell your dad you want to come with us," Renly practically begged Keith the morning he was set to change boats.

"I don't think that would work." A lame excuse. If he really tried, he could change his dad's mind. But he wasn't sure he wanted to. He didn't like either option, and so was content to let his dad decide what they were going to do.

Renly was angry when he left. His goodbyes were terse and had to be forced out by his mother. Mrs. Harris made one last attempt to get everyone to join them.

"I have to do what I think is right, just like you do," Dad told her.

The last Keith saw of Renly was the back of his head, down among hunched shoulders, as the canoe carrying him disappeared behind a yacht.

By the time the sun sank below the horizon, the fleet was gone. The huge ships, with long lines cast behind them for towing, left one at a time. Each ship that left appeared to abandon dozens of boats in its wake. When the one that Keith and Aisling had briefly lived on departed, Keith saw why. Some had decided, like them, not to go, while other boats had been abandoned. Watching that ship leave, Keith felt they had made a huge mistake. He almost shouted at everyone that they needed to follow, that if they hurried, they could join the towlines. He almost did that, but the shouting in his head never found his lips.

They spent the day moving all their supplies onto the pontoon boat. Anything that could be useful, they found space for, either under the bench seats, along the front and rear platforms, or even hung over railings. The large compartment at the back of the boat, between the rear ledge and back bench seat, they mostly reserved for gas tanks. The boats without removable tanks, Dad siphoned as best he could, topping up the tanks that could be moved. Mr. Sidebottom told everyone that they didn't need all the other boats, that they would just slow them down. Janet and Markus, the couple, convinced him to keep the little sailboat. It wouldn't be very difficult to tow, and they could use it as a sort of tender boat. The sails were first removed, however, and added to the pontoon boat's supplies.

"We're going to give them a generous head start," Mr. Sidebottom declared several times. "We're not leaving tomorrow, but the day after that." He never explained his reasoning for this, but then, no one asked.

The wake boats and aluminum were cast off the day after the ships departed. Mr. Sidebottom's fishing boat wasn't going to be cut loose until they left, giving them some space to move around until then. At least, that's what he said his reasoning was for not setting it free with the others.

"We should check the shallows for more supplies," Dad mentioned. "I can see there's still some bags floating around, and some boats over there aren't too close to shore."

"Send the boy-os," Mr. Sidebottom said. "I need you to help me snare these boats here."

The abandoned vessels floated freely, some of them getting close enough to grab and search. Others came directly toward them on a collision course, and needed to be caught in order to prevent damage.

"I can do it, Dad," Keith said before Dad could protest. "Russell and I won't get within ten feet of the edge of the water."

"If you're sure."

"I'm sure."

"Mom?" Russell looked to Dr. Kimiko. She nodded her consent.

Keith would have loved to go with Mandy, but there was only room for two in the little sailboat, and Russell was just as good. It was nice to get away from everyone else, to be able to talk about whatever they wanted without the risk of being overheard. Sitting side by side, they quickly found a rhythm for their paddles.

"I think I'm gonna die if I don't figure out how to talk to Mandy," Keith admitted once they were far enough away.

"Still got a mad crush on her, huh?"

"I think it's worse now."

Russell laughed. "Just talk normally, man. Be yourself."

"I don't know how to do that when she's around. I feel like I'm constantly putting my foot in my mouth."

"You'd have to open your mouth to do that. Have you talked to her directly *at all*?"

Keith flushed. "Not really. How am I supposed to do that when Aisling is always right there, ready to rip my head off?"

"She's not going to rip your head off."

"You only say that because she's actually nice to you. Not all of us are so fortunate."

"Whatever, man. This is a *you* problem, not a *we* problem."

Keith huffed.

Russell fidgeted with the end of his paddle, missing a stroke. "Do you still think your mom is out there, somewhere?"

The question hit Keith like a sack of bricks, causing him to miss more than one stroke. "I don't know," he finally squeaked out. He wanted to say yes. He wanted to be confident that his mother was still alive. But this wasn't like the comics he read, the ones where the hero could *feel* that their loved one was alive after the villain had taken them. Keith felt nothing, one way or the other. There was only a hope, and that hope was being whittled away more and more with every hour that passed. It was getting to the point where Keith wasn't even sure he *wanted* his mother to be alive, because if she was, what did that mean had happened to her? Why hadn't she found him yet?

Russell awkwardly patted Keith's shoulder. "I'd hug you, but you stink," he added.

The remark caught Keith off guard, forcing a laugh out of him. "You're pretty rank yourself," Keith fired back.

They paddled toward shore, tossing insults, trying to come up with the best one. Their voices dried up as they neared the beach. No matter what they said the other smelled like, it was nothing compared to the throat-clawing reek they were paddling into. The source was obvious.

Corpses rotted on the sand. There were bodies that had spent days out in the sun, some of them partly submerged in the lake. Gulls occasionally swooped down to grab a bite, but any that stayed too long, were snatched up by the beasts waiting below.

"We shouldn't have volunteered," Russell said, his voice a dry whisper.

"We don't have to go close to the sand. Just to those boats." Keith did his best to inject a confidence into his words that he didn't feel.

A lot of boats they decided to ignore the moment they looked at them. Some vessels had made it all the way to the water's edge. Others bumped up into the backs of those, creating a chain the beasts would be able to hop across if they were so inclined. Based on some of the shredded metal they saw, at least one had been before they'd gotten here.

"There are bags underwater," Russell noticed.

"Shallow enough for us to reach?" Keith found it difficult to tear his eyes away from the sand. Despite the scattering of corpses, the beach was so empty, it was hard to believe the morning of crushing chaos he had endured.

"I'm pretty sure I can stand here," Russell told him.

Because Keith hadn't been paying much attention to him, his thoughts were slow in forming a response. By the time he was ready to speak, Russell had hopped out of the boat with a splash.

"Hoo! That's chilly!" Russell had sunk up to his armpits.

"Should I get in?" Based on his friend's reaction, he didn't really want to.

"It would go a lot faster if you did."

Touching the water with his hand, it didn't feel so bad, but when Keith sank deeper, he found the same chill Russell had.

"We're both good swimmers. We should fill up this sailboat as much as we can, and then swim it back out there."

"Okay."

They trawled along the beach, using their bare feet to find the submerged bags. Some bags Keith needed to dive in order to retrieve, but most of the time, he just needed to locate a strap or handle, and then he could lift the bag high enough with his foot to grab it with his hands. In the water, the bags felt lighter than they were out of the water. With the bigger suitcases, both Keith and Russell needed to work together in order to hoist them high enough to dump them into the boat. The rare time their route took them near a boat that wasn't part of a chain to shore, they picked through it.

"Hey, I think this might be my mom's bag," Russell reported as he brought a suitcase to the surface.

"How can you tell?" All the bags looked generic to Keith's eyes. A few times he thought he might have found his own backpack, but couldn't be sure without rooting through the contents.

"This green thing next to the strap. Sometimes my mom goes to medical conferences, and she added this to make it easier for her to identify at the airport."

"Well, we'll find out when we get back to the pontoon boat. Let's toss it in."

Eventually, the little sailboat got to the point where it threatened to sink on them if they added much more, and so they decided that they were done.

"We should check out that yacht," Russell suggested as they pushed into water deep enough that they could no longer stand.

"We don't have room for anything else."

"We'll check, and if there's anything good, then we'll take a second trip for it."

"Why don't we just drop this stuff off and then come back anyway?"

"Trust me, this'll save time."

"Fine." Keith didn't want to admit that the boat frightened him a little. Unlike the others they'd checked, this one floated offshore, secured by an anchor. They'd been watching it since yesterday, and no one had seen any signs of life on board. Why had *this* yacht been abandoned when all the others remained in use?

They tied the little sailboat to the swim platform, where it looked like a toy next to the mighty yacht.

"What do you think a ship like this costs?" Russell pondered once they had climbed out of the water and were wringing out their clothes.

Keith shrugged. "Millions."

"More, I'd say. Tens of millions. Maybe even hundreds."

"More than we'd ever make. I don't think astronauts get a huge paycheck."

"Maybe you'll make a comic that sells to everybody, and then the big movie production houses will have a bidding war for the rights. You'll get to be a producer or whatever though, so you'll also make a shit ton off the ticket sales. Maybe you'll make enough to buy one of these for each of us."

Normally Keith would laugh when Russell made these sorts of claims, but now he could only force out a smile. Dreams of the future felt more ephemeral than ever with the dirt devils running around. He was also still nervous about checking out this boat, or ship, or whatever the hell it was classed. Renly could've told him.

They made their way inside and were greeted by a stink not all that dissimilar from the beach.

"Russell," Keith hissed, not needing to say more to convey to his friend that he didn't like this.

"Maybe it's just the toilet tank overflowing," Russell suggested. But he also whispered, which sounded like he thought something else.

They didn't get far before they found the first body. It was a boy, maybe a little younger than Keith and Russell. He was sprawled on the floor in a puddle of dried blood with a deep wound in his back.

"We should go." Keith grabbed Russell's shoulder and attempted to pull him away toward the swim platform. To the outside. To an escape.

Russell shrugged him off and went deeper. "It's fine."

"*That's not fine!*" Keith was caught between a scream and a whisper, a place that felt very close to hysteria.

Russell ignored him and kept going.

"Russell!" Keith didn't like his friend going off alone, or being left behind. "Russell!" He scurried after him, trying not to look at the body, but also feeling compelled to. "Where are you going?"

"I have to see."

"See what? We should leave!"

"I want to know if it was a dirt devil."

"*What?* Are you nuts? If it was a dirt devil, then it's probably still on board. Come on, let's go. *Please.*"

But Russell ignored him. Keith had no idea where his friend's grim determination was coming from, but nothing he said seemed to stop him. All he could do was follow.

Every door that was opened sent Keith cringing back from it. Not because there could be a dirt devil inside, but because some of those doors hid more corpses. Five of them were older men and women, but once they came across a kid, and Keith puked on the carpet.

"You're right, we should go," Russell whispered, although he made no move to leave. His eyes were locked on the child's blank, grey stare, so white above the crimson slash across her throat. Someone had nearly taken the girl's head off.

Keith finally pulled Russell back to the hallway. He almost got him to turn toward the exit when a sound deeper in the ship made them both jump.

"Russell, no!" Keith seethed. He tried to physically restrain him, but Russell wasn't about to let him. Keith ended up getting pushed hard enough into the wall that a piece of artwork fell off it. The glass frame shattered, nearly drawing out a yelp from both of the boys.

It did draw a yelp out of whoever they had heard deeper inside.

"That wasn't a dirt devil," Russell whispered, quickly heading off to find the source.

"No, it was probably just a mass murderer!" Keith whispered back, forced to follow. He couldn't just abandon Russell. To his shame, he realized he would have if it was Renly, but he couldn't leave behind his best friend.

"Or it could be someone who's hurt."

As they approached the half-open door where the sound had come from, Keith wished he had thought to grab some of the broken glass. Anything would be better than his bare hands should they be attacked. He tried to console himself that at least he didn't notice any bullet holes. That didn't mean there hadn't been any, just that he hadn't seen them on this ship of horrors.

Russell led the way through, boldly throwing the door open

with a bang. Keith was right at his back, close enough to see the woman on the far side of the bed jump. She started moaning softly, "no, no, no, no," but even without the voice, even though she hid her face in a crumpled heap with matted hair, he knew who she was in an instant.

"Mom!"

43: NOW

KEITH WAS AN INVALID, and didn't have much of a choice but to stay with Mr. Sidebottom for days, a week, more. He lost track. Every day Mr. Sidebottom would leave the boat to hunt and fish and gather. When he'd go, he'd leave Keith with a list of instructions to follow, including when to nap. Keith tried to follow them, although they weren't written down, and easily forgotten. It was especially easy to forget the exercises when he hurt too much to do them. The only one he liked, was when he got to hobble down the swim ladder and float around in the lake. It got hot inside Mr. Sidebottom's boat.

Of course, when Mr. Sidebottom got back, he'd have more exercises for Keith to do, which he'd 'help' him with.

"How do you know this is the right thing to do?" Keith asked through gritted teeth when he was being pushed particularly hard.

"Because before all this I was a physiotherapist."

"What? You never said that before."

"No one ever asked."

"So when all those people came to see Dr. Blatty with their sprained wrists and twisted ankles, you probably could've given better advice than she did."

Mr. Sidebottom shrugged. "I had more important things to do."

Keith had tried asking more things about Mr. Sidebottom, but didn't always get answers. He wanted to know what had happened to the man since he'd last seen him, and especially what had happened to Saksham. Sidebottom said that he got picked up by another group, but it wasn't a very satisfying answer, as well as being one that was easy to lie about. Other than that, though, Mr. Sidebottom told him nothing.

When Keith got to rest, he lay on a mat on the boat's floor with his leg raised. Mr. Sidebottom had made a sort of sling for him that hung from the steering wheel. Lying there, Keith could feel the metal bracket that used to hold the pilot's seat in place, and his head nearly brushed the rear door, but it was better than the exercises.

Day by day, his joints improved. His list of exercises expanded to include a few chores to do around the boat, although there weren't many of those. Not that Keith couldn't do more chores, it was just that Mr. Sidebottom had everything a certain way, and he followed a certain routine that Keith was already disrupting. When he wasn't directly helping Keith, he ignored the teenager.

Keith could tell that most of the food he ate came from his own stores in the kayak. Once he was well enough, he pulled his boat out from between the pontoons, and, after brushing away a bunch of spiders, checked his supplies. All the food was gone. Mr. Sidebottom had taken it and put it somewhere else. He'd left the waterproof bag, and all his other gear, it was just the food that was gone, spices and taco mix included. Even the salt. If Keith decided he needed to sneak away, he was going to have to do it without anything edible. Not unless he stole from Mr. Sidebottom's stash. For now, there was no need to do that, but Keith liked to keep his options open.

"Next time you need something from your kayak, just ask me to get it," Mr. Sidebottom said when he returned that evening.

Keith was startled, wondering how the hell Mr. Sidebottom knew he had looked through his kayak. Did the man check every day? Did he keep track of the spiders down there? Since Keith hadn't taken anything out of his boat, he couldn't think up a good lie, and so said nothing. He couldn't exactly accuse Mr. Sidebottom of stealing, not when all his food seemed to be fed to him. He once tried to tell Mr. Sidebottom to feed him less, that two meals a day was plenty, but he was ignored, and Keith wasn't about to pass on a prepared meal. Mr. Sidebottom had built a fire pit on the water by building a cairn out of a bunch of rocks that held a burn barrel above any waves. Every hot meal was a godsend for Keith. Even the meals that weren't hot, that were left in a container for Keith to eat while Mr. Sidebottom was out, were so much better because they had been cooked at some point, and were often flavoured from Mr. Sidebottom's own supply.

One day, Keith stopped recognizing the food from his stash. He'd eaten it all, and was now being fed entirely by Mr. Sidebottom. Surprisingly, the meal sizes didn't change, and the flavour improved. The meat may have been from squirrels, and the fish from the lake, but it was fresh and not carrying the taste of tin.

While Keith had lost track of the specific days, he knew it had to have been at least two weeks, maybe closer to three. The scrapes on his leg had healed, and his knee and ankle seemed to be better. He continued to do Mr. Sidebottom's exercises, but it was only his toe that complained during them. It was a lot easier to keep his toe from bending than it had been his knee and ankle, especially with the weird splint Mr. Sidebottom had made.

Having less to do, Keith made up his own chores. He'd noticed that Mr. Sidebottom had built reinforcements for the frame that held up the boat's top. His additions were inelegant and haphazard. Using the knowledge he had gained from his dad, Keith set to making improvements. When Mr. Sidebottom noticed, he gave a grunt, but didn't tell him to stop. It was difficult to work on while keeping the roof up, but that added challenge meant it took more time out of Keith's day.

"So what's the plan?" Keith asked one evening over dinner. He'd have asked earlier, but Mr. Sidebottom only ever stopped moving when he was eating or sleeping, and he got up so early that dinner was the only real chance Keith had to talk to him.

"What do you mean, boy-o?"

"Well, if I'm going to stay here, I'm going to need a better bed, for instance."

"You're not staying."

Keith wasn't surprised by this. "Okay. So how long am I to stay?"

"A few more days."

"And then I just go? Do I get any food to bring with me?"

"No, you do not just go, boy-o."

Keith frowned, not understanding what Mr. Sidebottom meant.

"I have a job for you."

"What kind of job?" Did he want Keith to deliver something when he went? Did he want him to pull the pontoon boat somewhere?

"Finish your dinner."

"What kind of job?" Keith tried again. Mr. Sidebottom gave him nothing.

During his last few days, Keith pondered what it could be that Mr. Sidebottom wanted him to do. He couldn't imagine it was anything good, not if Mr. Sidebottom wouldn't tell him what it was. One morning, he woke and decided to leave. It was a cowardly choice—especially since he decided to take some of the man's food—but it felt like the right choice. When he got into the water to check on his kayak, however, he discovered it wasn't there. Only the ropes that held Mr. Sidebottom's sunken coolers occupied the space between the pontoons. He could steal the food, but not get anywhere with it.

"Where's my boat?" he demanded of Mr. Sidebottom, confronting the man in the shallows the moment he returned.

"Safe."

"Where is it?" Keith stepped up close, furious.

He hadn't expected Mr. Sidebottom to sweep his legs out from underneath him. He landed in some thigh deep water with a splash and a splutter, only getting angrier.

"Safe," Mr. Sidebottom repeated with a growl. "Why? You thinking of going somewhere, boy-o? Before you repay your debt?"

"Debt?" Keith got upright and shook the water from his hands, when what he wanted to do was slug the man in the face. If he did that, though, he bet that the rifle butt would make a sudden collision with his skull. He had to be smarter.

"Yeah, boy-o, debt. You think my administrations come for free? You think I fed you for nothing? Debt, boy-o. I need you to do a job, not slip away while my back is turned."

"*What* job?"

"You'll do it tomorrow if the weather's right."

That made Keith's spine tingle. A job that required the right weather? It had been sunny the last few days, so that could only mean going ashore when it rained. But Mr. Sidebottom seemed to go ashore everyday—Keith had begun to suspect the land on one side of the river was an island—so what could he need Keith to do?

Maybe there was something heavy Mr. Sidebottom wanted, something he couldn't carry on his own. He probably decided to wait for rain so that Keith would feel safer. Or because he didn't have another one of those water-filled harnesses for Keith to wear. That made sense, didn't it?

Keith spent the night unable to sleep, and not because of the chair bracket in the floor beneath him. Or not entirely because of it. What could Mr. Sidebottom want him to do? He kept thinking of innocuous tasks, things that Mr. Sidebottom might just need a second pair of hands for. He kept telling himself it wasn't going to be bad. Simultaneously, he kept praying that it wouldn't rain.

44:
THEN

MOM WOULDN'T TALK about what had happened. On the yacht, when Russell and Keith found her, she'd latched onto her son and cried. Keith stayed there, trying to comfort her, but not actually knowing how. He was left alone with his distraught mother and the reek of rotting corpses, while Russell rushed out of the ship to get help. Time had no meaning while Keith waited, his mother unable to form words or even really hear him. The relief he felt when he got to pass her off to his father and Dr. Kimiko came with a heaping of guilt.

Since then, they had departed Lake Ontario. They moved slowly, saving the gas for emergencies, like when they had brought the pontoon boat over to the yacht of death. Every day, the eleven of them took turns paddling. Two sat on the front ledge, and one sat on the starboard side of the back ledge. The back ledge was not only wider on that side behind the angled door, but opposite it held a gas tank, leaving no room for a person. The fourth paddler sat at the port side door in the middle of the boat. That's where Keith was sitting when he overheard his dad trying to get his mom to talk about what had happened.

"Can you please just tell me?" he whispered, but not quietly enough. They were on the front ledge, and Dad must have thought Keith was at the very back. "I promise, my thoughts and feelings won't change whatever it is. I can't help you if I don't know anything. Could you at least tell me if it's something they did to you, or if it's something you had to do?"

The little hairs on the back of Keith's neck stood up. He hadn't thought of the fact that Mom might have been the one who hurt those people on that ship. How could she have? One of them was a little girl. No, Mom definitely didn't kill her. In fact, Keith refused to believe she had killed any of them, even if one of them was the actual murderer. He couldn't picture his mom doing that. He didn't want to.

He didn't want to think of the corpses he'd seen either, but those were always just below the surface of his thoughts. Keith liked to paddle because it gave him something to focus on. When he was forced to take a break, he helped with the other chores around the pontoon boat, which really only consisted of going through the bags he and Russell had found, and laying out the clothing to dry on top of the cover that was their roof. Not exactly a job to keep the hands busy, but balancing on the railing was sometimes a bit of a feat.

One of the backpacks he had grabbed turned out to be his own. The zipper had been opened so a bunch of stuff was missing, and his laptop was destroyed, but some of his clothes had made it. The most important item was a pair of underwear that was entirely his. Other than Dr. Kimiko—Russell had been right about having found her bag—everyone else wore clothes that had once belonged to a stranger. This included underwear for those who found the idea of going commando somehow even worse.

They left the lake, following what Mr. Sidebottom called the Trent-Severn Waterway. He said they could take it all the way up to Georgian Bay if they didn't find a place they liked en route. They passed under some bridges, and then came to a barricade.

"I thought we were going this way because there wouldn't be any locks?" Keith asked his dad.

"No matter which way we went, we'd come across locks," Dad sighed. "I was hoping we'd get farther than this though."

The rest of the day was spent in discussion. Essentially, it boiled down to whether they should wait for rain or not. It had only rained the once so far, but they had seen that people had been safe on the beach during the downpour, and so figured they would be safe going ashore if it rained again. But that meant waiting, and not knowing how long a wait it would be meant worrying about their food supply. Already they didn't have much left.

"I suggest we risk it," Mr. Sidebottom pushed. "When it rains, we'll want to use those times to raid wherever we can for supplies. If we wait for rain at every lock, we'll barely get anywhere."

Back and forth they went, all the while paddling against a strong current. They hadn't even reached the actual lock yet, which was in a chute to one side of the river. Keith was sitting in the middle of the pontoon's forward ledge, awkwardly paddling between his legs, while his dad hauled away on one side, and Russell the other. They had enough paddles for everybody, just not enough good spots to make use of those paddles. Still, he was in a better position than those kneeling on the bench seats and leaning awkwardly over the railing, barely able to reach the water.

The lock was open on their side, allowing them to go right in. Mr. Sidebottom taught them how to tie off. Keith was strangely comforted and terrified by the high sides all around them, a strange mix that left his body confused about how it should be reacting.

"Does anyone even know how to make the lock work?" Mom asked. She'd been silent during the whole discussion about whether to wait for rain or not. Keith hadn't thought she'd even been listening until then.

No one confessed to knowing, not even Mr. Sidebottom who'd gone through this exact lock before. Nevertheless, he got his way, and they were going to try without waiting for rain.

"Locks like this aren't terribly complex," Mr. Sidebottom told the party that was heading off the boat. "To go up, you just close both doors and fill the middle with water. Going the other way is the same process but with draining. They shouldn't need a lot of switches and levers for that."

The fact that Mr. Sidebottom wasn't going and his mom was, made Keith's shoulders tense up. The adults had drawn straws to see who would be leaving the pontoon, and Mom had lost, along with Markus.

"I can go in your place," Dad insisted in a hushed tone.

"No. We agreed. I'm going." There was a hardness to Mom that Keith hadn't really seen before. He didn't like it, there was too much coldness in it.

Janet also didn't like the idea of her husband going, but at least he got to carry the one Super Soaker they'd managed to find in the water. Mom was just given a bucket.

"The controls should be just up there," Mr. Sidebottom pointed. "There'll be a set of stairs you can walk up. *Cement* stairs."

Knowing they wouldn't be directly on dirt was little comfort.

Keith had figured out why the walls frightened him: a dirt devil could easily drop on their heads. The same way one could emerge near the stairs and bound up them after Mom.

"We should have gotten to draw straws, too," Aisling muttered to Mandy in a voice not meant to carry. It was impossible to have complete privacy on the boat, however, and Keith happened to be closest to the pair.

"You *want* to go up there?" Mandy hissed.

"I want to not be treated like a little kid who needs protecting. We're not invalids."

Keith thought that Mr. Sidebottom had overheard as well, because he got a sort of gleam in his eye that hadn't been there before. If the teenagers were part of the drawing, it bettered his odds at not being chosen.

"I'll be back before you know it," Mom told Keith, her tone straining to sound like it had before the yacht of horror, but not quite getting there. She and Markus slipped into the water barefoot, and swam for a spot where they could climb out. Dropping them off had been discussed as well, but both Mom and Markus liked the idea of wearing sodden clothes, like they'd be any sort of armour against those scissor-claws.

Keith hated feeling helpless. Watching his mom head into danger, he suddenly understood Aisling to a degree. Perhaps it was better to go and face the monster yourself than it was to watch a loved one do it for you. Mr. Sidebottom would be so happy to hear he wanted to be part of the next drawing.

45:
NOW

THE RAIN WAS COMING. It hadn't reached them yet, but the storm clouds were close enough to be seen between the tops of the trees. It was headed their way, and both Keith and Mr. Sidebottom knew it.

"Put on those shoes of yours," Mr. Sidebottom ordered, after barely giving Keith enough time to eat a rather measly breakfast.

Keith followed Mr. Sidebottom off the pontoon, wondering if he'd ever see it again. It had found its way back into his life once already. He watched Mr. Sidebottom lower the tarps and pelts, closing it off from the elements, and thought about running. Maybe he could find another boat, something to replace the kayak. If he was fast, he might even be able to use the storm to grab more supplies. But Mr. Sidebottom still carried his rifle and looked ready to use it on Keith if he bolted.

"What's your first name?" Keith asked as they walked through knee-deep water, following the shoreline. He was leading, and felt a prickle along the skin of his back, wondering if the gun was pointed at it. He wasn't about to look over his shoulder to find out.

"Doesn't matter," the man answered.

Keith decided to drop the mister. Now he was just Sidebottom, undeserving of any titles. Keith wished he had done it sooner. Maybe then he would have thought to escape in time, but instead, he had addressed the man the same way he would a teacher or the parent of a friend. It conveyed a degree of respect the man had never earned, not in Keith's eyes. Would he feel different if he had spent that long-ago night with him on the pontoon boat instead of the cargo ship, like Dad and Mandy had? Maybe, although he doubted that this moment would be any different. Sidebottom had found a body to use, and he was going to use it, damn any history between them. Had he used Saksham the same way? Or had he really been picked up by another group like Sidebottom said he'd been?

They followed the river to a point that got shallow, where rocks poked up above the surface every few feet. Markers bobbed in place on either side, warning boats that would no longer come.

"Cross," Sidebottom ordered.

Keith had to step carefully. The rocks were jumbled and slick, and he wasn't looking to sprain his knee or ankle again. Although if he did, maybe he could get out of this.

"Faster," Sidebottom growled, jabbing him in the back with the rifle. Keith nearly yelped, and he did slip, but managed to catch himself before falling over.

"I'm going as fast as I can. You've obviously crossed here before, why don't you lead the way to show me how?"

"Just keep walking, boy-o."

"My name is Keith," he grumbled as he pressed on.

Near the middle of the river were two flasher markers with about twelve feet between them. Keith sank up to his neck through that section. He imagined small boats could make their way through the gap so long as they went slowly. Keith wished he could go slower, but even here, Sidebottom urged him onward. A glance over his shoulder revealed to Keith that the man carried the rifle above the waterline, held awkwardly so as to keep it pointed at him. If he fired like that, he'd probably hurt himself, but unless he missed, Keith would come out far worse in that exchange.

On the other side, they continued to follow the river. It opened up until Keith was pretty sure it was a lake again. Sometimes the shoreline became difficult to follow, especially when it was solid rock at a steep angle. One of the times Keith slipped, it was bad enough to skin his elbow, but the joints in his legs remained perfectly fine. His toe constantly complained, but there wasn't anything he could do about it. Sidebottom didn't fall, didn't even slip.

All the while, the rain held off, and Keith cursed it for doing so. He had hoped the storm would hit them hard, and hit them fast, the shower lasting only a couple of minutes before drying up again.

Without the rain, Sidebottom wasn't going to force him to do whatever it was, and so he needed it gone. Right now, his hope was that it would pass by, missing them completely. With the gun at his back, Keith had no more illusions that he was being *asked* to do something innocuous. There was danger ahead and danger behind, and he wasn't sure which was worse.

They kept coming across docks, and Sidebottom insisted that Keith climb over them as opposed to swimming around. Maybe he knew what Keith was thinking. If he'd been able to swim, he could have ducked down and hidden in an air pocket under one of the floating docks. Sidebottom could still shoot him, but he'd have to find him first, and would waste bullets in the attempt. As long as Keith was smart, he could stay underwater most of the time where the bullets' speed would be dampened, and only come up for air where he was hidden under the wood. But wherever they travelled, the water was either too shallow for Keith to be able to dive under, or else there was nothing to hide beneath so he'd have his head blown off the first time he surfaced to breathe. At least he was able to scramble over the docks quickly. Sidebottom had clearly been through here plenty of times before and had placed flat rocks and other sunken junk to form handy steps.

Keith couldn't help but notice the dirt devil scarring on the wood. There had been a lot of activity in this area, and some of it seemed pretty fresh.

"That dock there," Sidebottom eventually commanded. "We'll wait beside it for the rain."

A plastic chair had been sunk into the shallows, held down and upright by some rocks. Sidebottom settled himself into it, the water just reaching his ribcage. A body surfing board that had been tied to the chair became a floating shelf for him to rest his rifle on.

Keith studied the property. There was a twelve-foot wide flat section lining the water's edge, the grass growing long and green upon it, although a few trees and weeds were already starting to invade. Waiting for them, watching them, was a dirt devil. It seemed more interested in Keith than Sidebottom, but then maybe it had seen Sidebottom sitting here before. Strange that it hadn't appeared and tracked them sooner, where it might have been able to snatch them as they crossed a dock.

Beyond the grassy strip, the land rose sharply. It was peppered with ancient deciduous trees, and the occasional conifers, whose roots kept the soil from washing away. At times the winding path up to the cottage was so steep, that the owners had built rock steps through sections. The structure was at least two hundred feet back from the water, but with the height and the winding path, more than that distance needed to be travelled to reach it. In a few spots, the path could be shortened by leaping over bushes, but not in the sections of near vertical rock. Two more dirt devils lingered on this hill, lounging amongst the trees in a way Keith had never seen them do before. He also hadn't seen so many in one place since the beaches of Lake Ontario.

At the top of the hill, the cottage loomed. Keith couldn't make out much of it. A large, wide deck thrust out over the edge, hiding just about everything from where Keith stood below. A big beam stuck out even farther to form a swing set on the only flat spot Keith could see beyond the grassy verge. Latticework hung down from the deck, reaching just shy of some small, prefabricated sheds along the same tier as the swings. Other than that, everything up there remained a mystery.

"So what is it you want me to do?" Keith tried asking again.

This time he was given the answer, and it made his blood run cold.

46:
THEN

ETTING THROUGH THE lock actually proved to be not so bad. Keith was a nervous wreck until the doors started to close behind them. This was then followed by the water level rising up. When the opposing doors opened, they waited for Mom and Markus to get back before continuing along the waterway. They returned unscathed.

As the paddling resumed, Markus explained what had happened. No dirt devils had made an appearance; that was the first and most obvious thing. More importantly, however, were the instructions. Someone must have been through there before them, because the controls were all labelled in a way that even someone who didn't know how locks work, would be able to figure it out. Mr. Sidebottom wondered if the lock master had done that before abandoning his post, but there was no evidence one way or the other. Mom doubted it though, because the locks didn't run at night, meaning no one would have been there when the alert announced the start of all this. She guessed it was someone who had taken this route before them—likely in the other direction given the way the lock was open—and that they had figured it out through trial and error.

"That could cause one hell of an error." Dad hadn't stopped smiling in relief since Mom returned.

"They probably tied up their boat outside the lock while they experimented," Mom replied. "It would be the smart thing to do, unlike what we did."

Mr. Sidebottom seemed to get a little huffy about that, although it wasn't like anyone had suggested they stay out of the lock until they figured it out. They had gotten lucky is all.

So they paddled and slept, and paddled and slept. Every time they came to a lock, everyone who hadn't yet gone drew straws to see who would open it this time. Keith got paired with his dad on the third one. He got to hold the Super Soaker, and his hands shook the whole time, but they made it back to the pontoon boat without any issues.

"We should get ready, it looks like rain is coming," Mr. Sidebottom commented one day after everyone had taken a turn operating a lock, and they had started the drawing anew. There were a lot more locks than Keith had thought there'd be.

"Maybe we should move into a larger boat," Janet suggested. She suggested this frequently. They were all on top of one another all the time, and it was getting on everyone's nerves. There weren't enough comfortable places to sleep when they anchored at night, leaving some to try to get comfortable on the floor, the only cushioning being the small pile of clothes that didn't fit any of them. Despite the deodorant they'd found in some bags, and the fact that most of them tried to wash themselves at the start and end of each day, between the sun and the exertion of paddling, everything still stank of sweat. They needed soap, especially for their clothes.

"No, we should stick with what we know," Mr. Sidebottom insisted. His usual winning argument, was that all the other boats were tied alongside the shoreline, and that only the locks were important enough to risk leaving the water for. "Besides, a larger boat would be even harder to paddle."

"We could grab a sailboat." Janet pointed one out. They were approaching a large series of docks that were adjacent to what they guessed was a town. As soon as it started raining, they were going to raid it for supplies.

"Does anyone here know how to sail?" Mr. Sidebottom asked in a rather challenging tone.

None of them did.

"We could learn," Janet insisted. "I had never paddled anything before now either."

"Sailing is much more difficult than paddling, girlie. A lot more can go seriously wrong. You want to risk your boy-o getting conked on the head? Falling unconscious into the water? Or if you lose control we end up smashed on the rocks against the shore. Do you want that?"

Janet could see that she wasn't going to change Mr. Sidebottom's mind, but it was obvious that her mind wasn't changed either.

"We need to prioritize food," Dad spoke up, changing the subject to a less divisive one. "Grocery stores, convenience stores, even restaurants should still have things that haven't gone bad."

"We should split up," Markus suggested. "We can cover more ground that way."

"We'll make five teams of two," Mom agreed. She and Markus had become friends since their outing to the first lock. It had helped her become more like herself again. "One of us should stay behind to take care of the boat. You know, untie it and push away from the dock if anything dangerous shows up."

"Saksham, think you can handle that?" Dad asked him before Mr. Sidebottom could volunteer for the job.

"Yes, I can do it," he nodded firmly. Keith was happy that Saksham wasn't going to be paired up with Mandy. The two of them whispered together at the back of the boat more often than Keith liked. He knew that Mandy was free to choose whoever she wanted to spend time with, but he couldn't prevent the jealously that spoiled his thoughts.

Keith was paired with his mom, and Mandy was going to accompany his dad. Russell and his mom made another team, as did Markus and Janet, leaving Aisling and Mr. Sidebottom together.

"Maybe Aisling should stay behind and Saksham should go with him," Mom whispered quietly to Dad, within range of Keith.

"He has no patience for Saksham's learning, you know that," Dad replied.

"I just don't like that he's going to be alone with a teenage girl."

"Why? He's never done anything to suggest he might do something bad to her. He treats the girls the same way he does the boys."

Mom scoffed, seeing things differently from Dad.

"Aisling will be fine." Keith didn't like letting them know he had heard them, but he didn't want this to turn into a fight and so injected himself into the conversation. "If anything happened, she could just beat up Mr. Sidebottom. I'd be more worried for him than her."

"I still don't like it." Mom used that tone she had to say she didn't want to hear any more on the subject. Her mind wasn't going to be changed, but it also meant that she wasn't going to bring up her concerns where Mr. Sidebottom could hear them and become offended. Though Keith hated confrontation, he almost found himself wishing she *would* offend him, just to see how he would react. There were times he felt that he noticed things about Mr. Sidebottom the others didn't. Maybe Mom saw even more things than he did, and that's why she was worried about Aisling.

Dad seemed on the verge of saying something anyway, when Mandy interrupted.

"Excuse me, sorry, I don't mean to break up the Benchleys, but I was hoping I could talk to Doug about our search plan."

"Sure thing, Mandy."

With everyone knowing what was expected of them, the pontoon waited about twenty feet away from an empty slip at the docks. Everyone was ready with a paddle, prepared to bring them in as fast as they could the moment the rain started.

"There it is! Go! Go! Go!" Mr. Sidebottom shouted the moment it started spitting.

Keith was in the middle of the front platform again, where he usually ended up when it was all hands on paddles. He had developed a sort of forward dragging technique that he thought was helping, but couldn't say for certain. The moment they reached the dock, everyone sprang up and off the boat. All except for Saksham, who remained behind alone, clutching his paddle to his chest, the boat key dangling from his fingers. He was given permission to start the engine if it was needed to save the pontoon.

"We have to hurry. We don't know how long the rain is going to last." Despite what Keith thought about Mr. Sidebottom's reluctance to go ashore and operate the locks, he was now leading the way at a brisk pace. Aisling followed hot on his heels, carrying a water bucket. They had only four buckets plus the water gun, and Mandy had won the draw for the Super Soaker.

Keith was concerned that the spitting wasn't enough, but he followed his mom, keeping his bucket at the ready. By the time they reached the end of the dock, however, the rain picked up, coming down in gentle sheets.

"Refreshing, isn't it?" Mom smiled at him over her shoulder, but it failed to hide the fear in her eyes.

"Yeah," Keith replied, trying to hold his own fright in check.

There were only three directions to go when they left the dock, yet Keith and his mom happened to choose the way no one else had. At a brisk pace that threatened to turn into a jog, they followed a boardwalk, and studied the storefronts. Tchotchkes were useless, and while the clothing was tempting, it wasn't what they really needed. The first place they passed that sold food, was an ice cream parlour. All of it would be melted by now, and so they reluctantly passed it by.

"If we had containers, I'd suggest we stop to try to collect the syrup," Mom commented. "It might not be as good, but Rocky Road is still Rocky Road." She was trying to make light of the situation. Had she done the same for that little girl on the yacht of horrors? Keith lifted his face and let the rain wash his cheeks to hide the tears that prickled in his eyes.

You have to be harder than this, he told himself. *You have to be stronger.* Why would Mandy ever take an interest in him, if he cried at the drop of a hat?

Glass shattered elsewhere in town, making them both nearly jump out of their skin. One of the other teams must have found a place.

"Here." Mom led the way to a coffee shop on a corner. It was at the end of where the docks crowded the shore. Across the connecting street, the buildings became less dense, allowing for more trees. Keith eyed the trees warily. Or rather, he eyed the soil they grew from.

The door to the coffee place was locked. Neither Keith nor his mom were surprised by that, given the time the alert had reached people. There was a conspicuous lack of boats at the docks, which, while allowing them to find a good slip, made Keith wonder where they had all gone. Maybe to Lake Ontario where they'd joined the shipping freighters and left. It would explain why all the locks were open in that direction, and contained instructions like the first one.

"We'll need to break the glass," Mom decided when furiously rattling the door did nothing.

"With what?"

"I don't know. I've never broken something on purpose before."

"You've broken eggs on purpose."

"Touché. Look around for something we can use."

It didn't take long. Where the docks stopped was a quaint little garden, lined with rocks. Keith hesitated about approaching the dirt, but then reminded himself again about being harder. Most of the rocks were too big for him to lift, but he managed to find a smaller one he could hoist up with both hands.

"Look out!" he shouted, to make sure Mom stayed well away from the door. She now held on to the bucket.

The glass shattered with a mighty crash. Keith had expected an alarm to go off, but once the tinkling stopped, it was silent but for the rain.

"We have to hurry. We can't trust the rain to last." Mom used the bucket to knock out a few hanging pieces, and then entered the shop, having to crouch to get under the push bar bolted to the metal frame. Keith followed right behind her, the glass breaking even more beneath his ill-fitting shoes that they'd found in a suitcase.

They didn't find much. The meat and produce in the fridge had been without power for too long, and had rotted on the shelves. All the doughnuts and bagels were riddled with mould. Still, Keith and his mom picked out the bits that hadn't turned green or grey, and ate the tiny morsels. They were so hungry that even those ultra stale crumbs were worth the effort it took to extract them from the bad parts.

They didn't leave the coffee shop empty-handed. Keith filled his backpack with bags of flour and sugar. Mom had a backpack of her own that she loaded down with condensed soup, and a tin of coffee beans.

"I'm not sure we can eat those," Keith said referring to the beans.

"Who said anything about eating them? I'm going to find a way to make us some coffee. Even you can have some."

Keith was startled by the suggestion. Mom was always saying that he wasn't allowed to have coffee until he was eighteen, claiming it would stunt his growth. Even when he got taller than her, she said no, thinking the caffeine would warp his still developing mind. If she knew how much pop he drank when he was at his friends' houses, she would have murdered him. At his own house, the rule was only one a weekend.

They checked over the equipment, but it all looked too big, too complicated, or definitely needed more than a boat battery as a power source to run. Some knives went into their bags, though, and Mom grabbed a stack of cups, plastic cutlery, and a few plates and bowls. Keith never would have considered taking any of these. Following his mom's lead, he picked up some plastic trays. He couldn't think of an immediate use for them, but Mom didn't question his decision. Maybe they could use them to create more shade.

Back outside, the rain still held, but neither of them thought they should risk searching for another place. Keith was quite happy to retreat.

They were the first team to return, where they found the pontoon boat still in place, but Saksham was nearly in a panic.

"Saksham? What's wrong?" Mom asked.

Flustered, he spouted off something in Hindi.

Mom looked at Keith to make sure she hadn't just misunderstood, but she hadn't.

"Take a breath," Keith advised. "Slow down."

Saksham took a breath. "They go. They take boat and go." His English was more broken up than usual, a sure sign of distress.

"Who?" Keith and his mom asked at the same time.

"Markus and Janet. They take a boat."

"What boat?" Keith moved to the back of the pontoon, but the little sailboat they used for storage was still tied up behind them.

To answer, Saksham pointed down river. A sailboat, much larger than the one they towed, was making its way through the rain.

"They just left us?" Keith was stunned.

"I try to call for someone, but no one hear." Saksham was finally starting to settle down. "I call for them to stop, but they would not. They ignore me."

"How long ago was this?" Mom asked.

"Not long."

Keith could have guessed that based on the distance. Long enough that he and his mom must have still been in the coffee shop to not have heard Saksham, but not so long that they had gotten very far.

"Were their bags full?" Mom asked next.

"I don't know. I think so. Hard to see. They took the boat from over there." Plenty of empty docks lay in the direction Saksham pointed, but it was easy enough to assume they had taken one from a distance.

"Well, they can make their own decisions. They're not our concern anymore." Mom seemed ready to forget about the fact that Markus was her friend. She turned to Keith to get the supplies from him and place them together with hers.

"Mom?"

"Yes, dear?"

"Are you okay?"

"Of course, I am. Why wouldn't I be?"

There are dirt devils, and you were on the yacht of horrors, and now your new friend has abandoned you, Keith thought

"Where are they going?" Saksham wondered aloud. "We've been going upstream. They have chosen down."

"Maybe back to the lake?" Keith shrugged. "Could be they decided to follow the others after all. Or decided to try a different place."

"Maybe they don't want us to catch up to them," Saksham supposed. "Mr. Sidebottom will be very annoyed when he finds out."

"Fuck Mr. Sidebottom," Mom grumbled.

She must not have realized that she had said that aloud until she saw the shock on Keith's face, her own expression quickly mirroring his.

"I'm sorry," she blurted out next. "I don't know where that came from. Keith, don't use that kind of language."

As if he were six instead of sixteen. "I know, Mom."

She focused more on her work, trying to make the little shelter perfect. Keith and Saksham decided not to talk about Markus and Janet again, although Saksham continued to watch their boat. Keith watched the shore instead, waiting for his dad and Mandy and Russell.

Mr. Sidebottom and Aisling returned next. She carried their water bucket in one hand, and a small, red jerry can in the other. It looked like a balanced load, but she moved slowly to keep pace with Mr. Sidebottom. His walk was more of a waddle, as he carried an oversized gas can between his knees, struggling with both hands. Keith jogged out to help them.

"We should be able to use the motor now," Aisling told him. "Along with the other tanks, we should have enough gas to get us to the next place with fuel pumps."

"Great. Markus and Janet have left us. They took one of the sailboats." Best get it out of the way now, like ripping off a Band-Aid.

Mr. Sidebottom muttered something under his breath, too tired from hauling the fuel to really get his ire up. Aisling kept her mouth shut on the subject.

Russell and Dr. Kimiko were the next to return. They had both brought big, wheeled suitcases with them, which were now stuffed. When leaving the pontoon boat, they were the only team given a specific target to search for: a pharmacy. They'd found one, and Dr. Kimiko had gone through all the medical supplies, while Russell used her guidelines to sort through whatever food they had there. Russell was a little bummed to learn of Markus and Janet's departure—Janet had an interest in the Mars rovers, which they'd talk about while paddling—and Dr. Kimiko talked her way into feeling neutral about it. Even though there were fewer bodies to help with the work, there were also fewer bodies to feed.

Dad and Mandy were taking their time. The rain started to slacken off, and they still weren't back yet. Everyone grew anxious. When the rain stopped all together, Mr. Sidebottom began to gather together their buckets.

"We should find them."

Keith wondered if he'd be as interested in the search if they hadn't already lost two crewmembers.

Just as they were prepared to depart, Dad and Mandy appeared. They were jogging due to the rain stoppage, but had big smiles on their faces. Each of them pushed a shopping cart stuffed to the gills with goods. It seemed they had found a grocery store.

"Well, I can confirm that they have supplies," Dad said when he learned about Markus and Janet. "We were headed down the same way for awhile. We came across a Bulk Barn, and they agreed to search it while we went farther."

Mandy said she refused to let the couple spoil her good mood as they worked to get the shopping carts aboard. They could sort and store everything later; right now they all just wanted to get away from the dock before the dirt devils decided it was dry enough to come after them.

Having not been used for a long time, the motor struggled for a moment to start, but once it caught, it roared to life. Keith hadn't realized just how accustomed he'd become to the quiet until it was shattered like that. It made his skin crawl, as if there was now a sound it was hiding. Even the smell irritated him.

With the engine running, they could probably have caught up to Markus and Janet. Instead, they continued on upstream, leaving the couple to fend for themselves. Keith couldn't help watching their boat until it was out of sight. He wondered whether it was them, or his own group who were making the bigger mistake.

47:
NOW

THUNDER HAMMERED FROM the sky before a single drop of rain fell. The dirt devils knew what it meant. One of them ran up the hill to the cottage, while another sank into the soil. The third, the one closet to the water's edge, remained. It had lowered its body beneath the ground, but its head stayed above, watching them. Watching Keith.

"Why don't you shoot it?" Keith grumbled.

"Have you ever dug one up?"

"No." *Yes*, but he couldn't think about that right now. It was too awful. The screams . . .

"So you don't know about the seeds."

"I know about them."

"Good. Well, when they're out like this, it's behind an eye. Not only is that a small target, but there's no way to know *which* eye it's currently hiding behind. I fire a shot—even if I don't miss—I might not have been aiming at the right target. Waste of a bullet, really."

Keith remembered the dirt devil behind his house, the one Russell had splashed in the face. It had been dragging its head around in the soil. Russell had probably gotten some water in its eyes, badly wounding the only part of the dirt devil that really mattered. They weren't really seeds, but they were the same general shape, and weren't much smaller than a human eyeball. The top and bottom were rigid, as solid and speckled as grey stone, but along a slit in the sides were hundreds, thousands, maybe even hundreds of thousands of legs. Maybe they weren't really legs, but frills of a sort. Keith hadn't liked looking at it, even though it was dead. They assumed those many "legs" were how it moved so fast through the soil. How it created the massive body of a dirt devil around itself was another matter all together, one that Keith still couldn't quite wrap his head around. As Russell was fond of pointing out: alien.

"This is a waste of my life," Keith grumbled.

"You'll get it," Sidebottom snapped. "You'll get it, and we'll be able to save humanity."

"You don't even know what it is!"

"Doesn't matter. They think it's important."

"This isn't some movie! They're not all going to drop dead just because I stole something of theirs." Because that's what he was being asked to do. Go up there, find out what the dirt devils were protecting, and steal it.

"You don't know that! They're aliens, it could be anything! It *could* be some sort of master mind."

Keith shook his head. "If that were the case, why would they hide it here, huh? Why not somewhere you couldn't see, and figure out that they were even protecting anything? Why this close to water? If it were vital, they'd move that thing to the prairies, or to the middle of some desert, where we'd never be able to get to it."

Sidebottom rose up out of his seat, pointing the rifle at Keith. "You're going to go up there," he growled. "You're going to find out what it is. You're going to take it and bring it to me."

Keith wished he had a map. He wanted to know where the nearest body of water was in relation to the cottage, other than the one in which he stood. Once he was up the hill, he could flee into the woods, but go where? If the storm lasted, maybe he could put a lot of distance between himself and Sidebottom and start again, but if it was just a cloud burst, he'd be dead.

"Did you ever think it could be a trap?" Keith thought aloud, doing his best to ignore the rifle. "That they figured out this would be the best way to get at you?" Dirt devils could be smart.

"Of course. That's why *you're* going."

"Have you ever sent anyone else up there?"

The silence made Keith think he had. Others had been ordered up the hill before him, and they hadn't come back. Or if they had, it wasn't in a way that satisfied Sidebottom. Had he shot them then? Probably he had. It was looking less and less like Saksham had been picked up by others.

"Any advice?" Keith asked.

"Don't get caught."

"Can I least have your water gun?"

"You can take this." Instead of the Super Soaker, Sidebottom tossed over the little water pistol. Keith tested its range: better than he expected for such a cheap thing. He could get six feet reliably, and more unreliably. The problem was how fast it used up the water inside. He'd maybe get a dozen shots. Maybe. Popping the plastic cork out of the back, he dunked it underwater, making sure it was as full as it could get. If he had to use it, he was probably dead anyway, but at least he could hurt the thing that killed him. Too bad he couldn't hurt Sidebottom the same way.

The clouds started to spit.

"Get ready, boy-o."

"*Keith*. My *name* is *Keith*. Keith Benchley. If I'm going to do this for you, the least you could do is use my fucking name."

"All right, *Keith*. Get ready to run."

The sky broke open and the heavens rained down.

48:
THEN

NOW THAT THEY were using the motor, they made better time along the waterway. Even when they took a few wrong turns, they got back on track before running out of gas. A series of storms kept sweeping through the area, enough for them to make plenty of stops. So many storms, in fact, they had to put up the sides of the pontoon boat's top. When the sun was out, it got hot inside that turtle shell cover, but everyone was tired of being wet, even if the rain did keep them safe. Saksham got sick because of the damp, but Dr. Kimiko took care of him, and it only lasted a few days. It rained so much that they even used the cover it provided to work some of the locks, which was especially helpful when they came across one that was actually a set of two locks back to back. They spent a few days after that studying some islands, but couldn't determine that they were safe, and so moved on. When they reached another set of double locks, they found people.

"Hello! Hey!" They were flagged down by the strangers on a pair of small sailing yachts that were anchored together. Keith glanced over at Mr. Sidebottom—who always drove the boat—and saw a dour expression twisting his face. He got the impression that the man wouldn't have stopped had the other boats not been in their way.

"Hi!" Dad called out, friendly as ever. The sun had come back, but the humidity forced them to lower the front of the boat's cover. When it was up, they couldn't reach the bow platform, but now Dad stood there, waving back to the small collection of people gathered at the railings of the other boats.

When they got close enough, Keith noticed that they all

appeared to be kids and teenagers, except for one woman older than his Dad and wearing a leg brace. Unlike the others, she didn't wave; she just stood there with a ramrod-straight back, assessing their approach. Keith thought of the woman who'd jammed a pistol into his gut and shuddered.

"Keith? Are you all right?" Mom had noticed his reaction. It would have been impossible for her not to have. She had gotten nervous the moment they knew people were on those boats, and stood at the back where she could keep her eyes on both the strangers and her son at the same time.

"I'm fine." Keith tried not to flush with embarrassment. His mom had drawn Mandy's attention to him. She was assessing him to try to see what his mom had. What faults might she decide she saw instead?

When they reached the yachts, Mr. Sidebottom stopped their boat close enough to talk, but not close enough that one of them could jump aboard. Saksham dropped the anchor over the side at his order. This close to the locks, the current would sweep them away if they didn't.

"Do you guys need help?" Dad asked.

"Yes," came the immediate response, from more than one person.

"What's wrong?" It was Dr. Kimiko who asked this time, wearing her professionally calm face.

"We've been stuck here for weeks." A girl younger than Keith whined.

"We don't know how the locks work," the older woman explained. It had been a long time since they'd left behind those that had had instructions. "We've been able to survive off what we've found in the town back there, but walking that far has already proven deadly, and someone either sank or stole the boats on the other side of the lock."

Dad nodded. Last night, they had anchored near the town, and had gone through a lock just a short while ago. Getting around the lock on foot to reach the town would have been arduous and fraught with danger.

"I take it there are no boats above, either," Dad commented.

"No, we tried there as well. We've been stranded. You obviously know how to work the locks, would you mind helping us? We don't need anything else."

Keith almost expected Mr. Sidebottom to ask what was in it for them, but their captain kept his mouth shut. It made Keith feel guilty for always thinking so poorly of him. Everything he disliked about the man was based on assumptions he'd made about reactions he'd seen. Or thought he'd seen.

"Yes, we can help you with that," Dad told the woman. "Pick some people and I can teach them while moving through."

"Dad, it's mine and Mandy's turn to work the locks," Keith reminded him. While they always split into the same teams when checking out towns, they continued to draw straws for locks when it wasn't raining. This was the first time Keith had drawn a lot at the same time as Mandy.

"Maybe I should go instead," Dad mused.

"Dad. We agreed on the drawing. I can teach them just as well as you could." Although having those strangers tag along meant not getting to be alone with Mandy. Maybe he could impress her with how well he could teach them? That was weak.

"Don't worry, Doug. I'll take care of him." Mandy grinned as she patted Keith on the shoulder. Keith did his best to act casual about her touching him, to not stiffen or startle.

"We agreed on the drawing." Surprisingly, it was Keith's mom who backed him up. She fretted whenever he left the boat without her, but she had never tried to stop him. "Keith and Mandy can do this." Was that more for Dad or for herself?

Dad gave a resigned sigh. Keith was glad he wasn't going to have to argue with him. He was prepared to leap off the boat and swim to shore right then if that was what it took. Well, he told himself he was ready to do that. *Courage*, he reminded himself.

Four teenagers from the yachts were picked to come with them. Keith was disappointed to see that two of them were guys, and one of those two guys was a Spanish Adonis. The other guy was at least average looking, but Keith couldn't help but compare himself and feel like he came up short. The two girls carried themselves with confidence, and one was quite pretty, but she couldn't hold a candle to Mandy's beauty.

"Do you have anything to protect yourselves with?" Keith asked them, lying on the front ledge of the pontoon boat, fully filling his water gun. They had several after so many raids.

"We're covered." It was the normal looking guy who answered, but his tone was haughty, making it sound like Keith was an idiot just for asking. It made Keith angry, but he hid it well, mostly because he could glower down at the water. Mandy made him feel a little better by handing down her Super Soaker, trusting him to fill it for her.

The four teens who were going to learn transferred over to the pontoon boat and introduced themselves. The pontoon was the quickest way to drop them off and retreat, since the yachts were lashed together. The first lock was currently filled, meaning they'd have to empty it before the boats could move in, requiring them to stay back.

"Stay behind us, and keep your eyes sharp," Mandy ordered as they stepped off onto the large block of cement at the base of a long staircase. "If one of those dirt devils shows up, get to the water as fast as you can."

The pretty girl—Pauline—glanced nervously at the water, and then up the stairs. Keith understood. The stairs weren't adjacent to the water. If you had to leap from them, you had to jump far enough to clear several feet of cement if you hoped to hit the river. On the other side of the stairs, foliage grew, meaning dirt, meaning the dirt devils could appear rather suddenly. Until they were at the top, where they could dive into the lock, they would be incredibly vulnerable. So far, they had gotten lucky that only Saksham and Dr. Kimiko had once had to leap away from dirt devils, but that had been as the pontoon boat had been leaving the lock, and they'd been able to jump into water not far down from where they stood. Based on how much of a chicken he'd been while cliff jumping with his dad, Keith didn't think he'd be able to jump into a lock that wasn't already full.

Mandy led the way up the stairs, her shoulders hunched and water gun at the ready. She side-stepped her way up, keeping the plastic muzzle pointed at the bushes. Keith kept as close to her as he dared, his own weapon aimed forward, over her shoulder. He wasn't sure whether his heart beat more from the danger, or from her close proximity. He had to resist the temptation to pay more attention to her than to the threat that could show up at any moment.

Not knowing if dirt devils were drawn by sound, they kept quiet as they rushed up the steps as fast as they dared. Pauline was behind Keith, and when they reached a landing, she bumped into him. Keith just about jumped out of his skin.

"Sorry," she whispered. She was also watching the bushes more than the way forward.

"It's fine," he hissed back.

A few steps past the landing, he felt her free hand take hold of the back of his shirt, using him to set the pace. He wished Mandy would do something like that, would see him as a protector.

No! Focus, you asshole, Keith chastised himself. Now was definitely not the time.

When they made it to the top of the stairs, everyone instinctively clustered by the filled lock.

"We can't all fit in the booth," Mandy said, pointing to the little building that housed the controls. "Keith, why don't you take two of them in to show them how it works, while the rest of us watch your back. Then we'll switch places for the second lock."

"All right." It's why they always chose two people to go: one to work the controls, and the other to keep an eye out. The dirt devils had only gotten dangerously close the one time, but they were regularly spotted in the distance.

Pauline stuck to Keith, and Shawn followed Pauline. That left Tully with Mandy, but also Diego, the guy with the perfect teeth who should be staring in a rom-com. Hopefully he was more comedy than romance.

While Keith worked the controls to drain the lock, Pauline stood right at his shoulder. Shawn kept glaring. It left Keith with the distinct impression that he was being used as a pawn in a problematic relationship between the two. Literally between them. At least draining the lock gave him something to focus on, something that wasn't the arm touching his on the left, or the eyes filled with murder on the right.

Once the lock was empty and open, everyone huddled over by the railing, periodically glancing over to watch the boats make their way inside.

"No problems?" Mandy quietly asked Keith.

"I'm pretty sure those two were paying more attention to each other than to what I was trying to teach them," Keith whispered back.

"No, I meant with the controls."

"Oh. No, they're fine."

"Good. I keep worrying that we'll find one that's broken. Or that we'll come across a place without power. You gotta imagine it'll go out eventually."

Keith hadn't thought about that. Now that Mandy had put the idea in his head, he found himself tensing up. What would they do if the power to the locks went out before they found a safe place? They would be trapped, like the two yachts had been.

"Clear!" Mr. Sidebottom bellowed from inside the lock.

Keith scurried back to the control booth, not really caring if Pauline and Shawn kept up. As he closed the lock doors and got it filling, he wondered what would happen if the power went out in the middle. What if they got trapped *inside* one of the locks? The thought made him queasy, and he no longer gave a shit about how Shawn felt, or whether Mandy found Diego attractive.

But the power didn't go out. The lock filled fine; the boats were fine.

"I just noticed how weird that is," Mandy commented as they hurried alongside the lock to the second set of stairs.

"What?"

"The first lock was in the up position, but this next one is already in the down position. Why would someone use only one lock?"

"That is weird."

They found out upon reaching the top. The second control booth no longer had a door, and old blood marred the interior, as well as over near some sort of building where the rain hadn't been able to get at it. Whoever had been using these locks hadn't gotten a chance to finish.

"Do you want me to work the controls?" Keith asked when he saw how pale Mandy turned.

"No. I'm fine." Her voice and expression hardened. "Just watch my back."

"Of course."

"Clear!" came Mr. Sidebottom's bellow as the boats readied themselves in the second lock.

Keith stood at the door to the control booth, his water gun primed. Pauline no longer stood against him, and Shawn had stopped his glaring. Well, he stopped glaring at Keith anyway; those furious eyes were now directed at their surroundings.

"Where's their boat?" Shawn grumbled.

"What?" Keith wasn't sure he'd heard right.

"The dead person. Where's their boat? Shouldn't it have been tied up in a lock if they were caught part-way?"

Keith begrudgingly admitted that he had a point. "Maybe it sank. Might not have been large, and the locks can get pretty deep for boats with deep drafts."

"But what would have made the boat sink?" Pauline wondered.

That was when the dirt devils showed up.

49: NOW

THE MOMENT THE last dirt devil disappeared, Keith hauled himself up onto the scarred dock. Sidebottom told him to run, and so he ran. He'd have liked to run away, but had failed to find an exit route before this moment came, and so he had to go up the hill. Maybe there'd be a lot of windows he could look through, determine there was nothing, and return to the lake without having to go inside.

His toe complained every time his foot landed, but his terror kept him from stopping. Whenever either foot came down, he kept expecting to lose it. If a dirt devil was willing to risk a little pain, it could easily reach up and lop off a lower appendage, no problem.

His thighs burned as he scrambled up the hill. Adrenaline propped him up. The rain kept coming down harder and harder, turning sections of the path into mud slicks. He slipped and banged his knee, but it wasn't the one he'd hurt before, and it didn't get knocked out of place, so he was up and moving again in a heartbeat. The sections of rock weren't much better, just more dangerous if he fell.

When he reached the swings, Keith thought it had both taken him forever to get there, and no time at all. He didn't want to be there. He didn't want to be near the cottage, where dirt devils could take shelter in the ground beneath it, or in the actual structure itself. To get away from the ground, he ascended the wooden steps up to the deck, his breathing ragged from sprinting uphill.

All the windows and a pair of sliding glass doors had shattered glass beneath them. Drapes hung over the openings, some inside, some sucked outside, and all of them mouldy and ripped from long exposure to the weather. They were sodden with the current downpour, the wind strong enough to shift them in lazy flopping motions. Beyond the curtains was darkness, not easily penetrated from where Keith stood. He didn't want to approach the windows. He didn't want to get within snatching distance. Sidebottom shouldn't be able to see him right now. He could lie, say he checked and found nothing. But he didn't know what Sidebottom knew about this place. It seemed unlikely that he wouldn't have come up here himself at least once.

Not wanting to try the windows yet, Keith followed the deck around the side of the cottage. It didn't wrap all the way around the back, but met with level ground there. All he found were more broken windows. Even the back door had had its window smashed. The dirt devils, or Sidebottom's handywork? If he had time and tools, Keith could chop a hole through the roof, really let the rain in, make the whole place a no-go zone for the dirt devils. But he had no tools and no time.

There'd been no upkeep at this cottage since maybe last year's spring, leaving fallen branches scattered about. Keith picked up one that was fairly long and fairly straight, and broke off all the bits that protruded from it. Using this branch he pushed aside curtains so he could look inside while still standing in the rain.

Bedrooms, kitchen, and a living room. All were in deep shadow, but he could make out that much. He spotted nothing strange, nothing that Sidebottom would be interested in. He figured he could leave until he realized he hadn't seen a bathroom.

"Fuck," he hissed to himself. If Sidebottom had done at least as much as him, he'd ask about the bathroom.

Keith was going to have to go in.

He picked one of the sliding glass doors on the lake side of the cottage. The frame was clear of glass shards, and the larger opening would make for a much better escape route than a window. Pushing the curtains to either side, he kept his lame squirt pistol pointed ahead of him. And then he stepped into the building.

There wasn't much light, but he could see well enough. Despite the storm and the curtains, light still got through the windows, and all the interior doors were open. Every stick of furniture bore damage from the dirt devils' scissor-claws. It had been pushed about, no longer sitting true with any of the walls. Elements of the décor were scattered about, yet some pieces sitting on upper shelves or hanging high on a wall managed to remain in place. Keith stepped carefully, trying not to crunch anything.

He had mapped out the place based on what he'd seen through the windows. He knew where the bathroom should be. Instead of a regular window to the outside, it had had metal slats high up on the outer wall to act as ventilation. The bathroom was going to be dark, but he hoped it wouldn't be pitch black.

Keith approached the hallway at the back. The bathroom would be on his left, down at the far end. He found he had no spit, his mouth totally dry. Instead, he had to pee. Well, if his water gun ran out of ammunition, maybe he could create his own.

He rounded the corner just as a flash of lightning highlighted the world. Two things appeared in the brightness. The first, was that there *was* something in the bathroom, something strange. The second, was the dirt devil standing between it and Keith.

No thoughts, only a blind dash back to the deck. The dirt devil pounded after him, hammering the floor in time with Keith's heart. In a pure panic, he didn't flee for the door where he'd pushed the curtains aside, but to the other door that felt closer. The sodden drapes slapped at him as he fought for the gap between them. Knowing the devil was too close, he fired his pathetic gun, not even aiming. He got lucky: the thing howled in pain and rage as it staggered back a step.

Keith pushed through, got outside, scrambled for the railing.

The dirt devil was furious. It leapt after him despite the storm. The curtains tore, wrapping around the beast. If it had howled before, it was really screaming now. The wet curtains had wrapped around its head, and only became more tangled the more it thrashed. Add in the rain, and the creature was in agony. Only there wasn't as much rain as before. Maybe it was a just a break in the storm, but maybe it was already passing. There wasn't much time.

Keith wanted to run back to the lake, but he didn't. He ran back inside the cottage instead. He had seen *something* in the bathroom, and needed to know what it was. Not just for Sidebottom, but for himself.

An egg. Or maybe a plant. Something vaguely ball-shaped, with sticky tendrils holding it to the floor. Still not thinking clearly,

Keith grabbed it with his bare hand and yelped. It was hot. Scorching, even. If the floor hadn't been laid with ceramic tile, it would have eventually burned.

Not knowing if the wet would damage it, Keith peeled off his shirt and wrapped it around the ball that was only a little larger than his fist. He had to plant his feet to either side and haul with all his might to get the sticky stuff to let go, but let go it did.

He had it. He had what Sidebottom wanted.

With the bundle wrapped up and hanging from one hand, he dashed back into the living room. The dirt devil was still crying in pain out on the deck, no longer thrashing, but still breathing. Sobbing, actually.

An unholy shriek wheeled Keith around just before he reached the door. A second dirt devil had come, had singed itself to pop through a back window. Keith could see its eyes. There was nothing there but rage.

50:
THEN

PAULINE SCREAMED, the first to spot one. She just kept screaming as she fired at it, furiously pumping her water gun. Shawn joined her, but Keith turned around to shout through the opening to the lock house.

"Mandy! We gotta go!"

"The lock's still closing!"

"There's no time!"

He glanced over his shoulder. The dirt devil was dancing and weaving, trying to find a way past the two streams of water. Pauline and Shawn were going to run out of ammo soon at this rate. Keith had to join them.

"There's a second one!" Shawn shrieked as it started charging up the steps.

"Tully! Diego!" Pauline screamed, her voice rising higher with every syllable. "We need you!"

The two others burst out of the control booth, water guns firing. Pauline was out of ammunition. She kept working the pump, but no water was coming out.

"Lock's filling!" Mandy shouted as she left the little building. She was just in time to witness Pauline's leg get snipped in two. There was so much blood.

"Pauline!" Shawn bellowed, charging at the beast and firing for all he was worth while it grabbed Pauline's torso and started dragging her away.

"The face!" Diego roared. "Aim for the face! They react more to that!"

It was too late for Pauline. She was dragged beneath the

ground, leaving behind only a well-toned calf and a sneakered foot.

Shawn went next. He'd chased the dirt devil, trying to rescue someone who couldn't be saved. Rage had blinded him, and he stood on the dirt, emptying his water gun into the soil. Keith watched as he got sucked down into the ground, only able to gasp with widened eyes before disappearing.

"Mandy!" Keith turned to look for her, but she was already gone. She had run to the upper lock door and leapt over the railing. He just caught her splash as she landed in the water on the lake side of the door.

"I'm out!" Tully cried, stepping back behind Diego.

Keith took her place, firing at the remaining dirt devil. It kept at a distance, dodging their shots that were less concentrated the farther the water had to go.

"Get to the lake!" Keith ordered, pushing Tully and then tugging on Diego's shirt between shots.

They backed up together, Keith and the supermodel boy, alternating their shots to keep the dirt devil at bay.

"Jump!" Mandy shouted from the water as they reached the area past the lock.

Their co-ordination left them. Teamwork flew out the window as they all tried to get into the water at the same time. That horrible clacking of scissor-claws on concrete came rushing up behind them.

Tully was the first into the water. Keith was about to jump when Diego cried out, only halfway over the railing. Instinctively, Keith dropped his Super Soaker to grab Diego's hand.

"Don't let go!" Diego cried, his eyes filled with pain and tears and raw terror. "Don't let go!"

Keith didn't let go. He planted his feet on the edge of the cement, his knees locked on either side of a vertical bar, his belly being crushed into the top rail that his other hand clung desperately to. He roared, pulling with all his might, pulling against the dirt devil that wanted to drag Diego away like Pauline had been.

"Don't let go!" Diego kept screaming, the words so garbled with pain he might not even have known he was screaming them, over and over and over.

Keith never let go, but Diego's arm did. The dirt devil reached over his shoulder, and with a snip, cut right through his perfect bicep, and even the humerus bone beneath. A clean slice, which sent Keith flying backward now that the resistance was gone. His fall into the water felt like it was in slow motion. He saw Diego's pleading eyes as he was pulled backward. He saw the disconnected arm trailing away, streaming blood, the hand on the end still clasped in Keith's. And then he splashed into the water, back first.

"I've got you! I've got you!" It was Mandy, pulling Keith through the water, away from the cement block.

Keith realized he'd been flailing instead of swimming. He also realized he was still holding Diego's arm and released it with a startled yelp. It blessedly sank out of sight.

"Are you okay? Are you hurt?" Mandy was still shouting, even though he had calmed down. When Keith got a look at her face, he saw that it was because she was still terrified.

"I'm not hurt." But he was definitely shaken.

Tully squawked and splashed, and Keith feared the arm had resurfaced, but wheeling around to her, he found that she was awkwardly trying to fire her reloaded water gun.

The dirt devil was back. It sliced through parts of the railing, the metal clattering and splashing as it fell. Tully shot it right in the face, and the beast went down howling. They watched with horrid fascination as it writhed around on the pavement at the water's edge. There was no dirt for it to drag its face through like the one behind Keith's house had.

"You got it good," Mandy whispered in awe.

"I shot it in the face like Diego suggested." Tully threw up, a difficult thing to do while swimming, and it half drowned her. "Oh fuck, there's the other one," she groaned after she'd stopped spluttering.

Keith had found his water gun and was preparing it for use, but never got the chance. The dirt devil looked at them, looked at its fallen companion now pathetically pulling itself away, and then turned toward the still filling lock. All three swimmers had been fighting a current trying to pull them toward the opening that let in the water.

"*No!*" Keith shrieked as the dirt devil leapt over the side. The boats were trapped down there. "*Mom! Dad!*" He started to swim for the lock doors, but Mandy practically jumped on top of him.

"You can't help them that way!"

Oh God, the screaming! They're screaming! "I have to try!"

"No! I can't lose you, too! There's a better way to help them! Come on!"

Mandy headed for the spot where the downed dirt devil had snipped through the railing, pulling on Keith's shirt to make sure he followed. Tully reluctantly trailed behind them, her face so pale it looked grey.

"Help me up," Mandy ordered. The edge of the cement was fairly high above them.

Keith tried to lift her, the water working against him as he sank down, not having any leverage. Tully held him up as best she could. By stepping on his head, Mandy finally lunged high enough to grab the edge of the cement. When she pulled herself up, Keith tossed his water gun up beside her, hoping like hell that the injured beast was still down. Then Mandy was gone, not waiting for him and Tully to follow. They failed to, unable to get high enough on their first attempt, but Mandy's plan became clear after that.

Suddenly they were fighting a much stronger current. The lock doors opened wide, letting a torrent of water rush inside. The boats would be in danger of sinking, but it would fill the lock much faster. The rush might also damage the dirt devil. Keith hoped it killed the thing, but he had more pressing concerns at the moment. The water was powerful, trying to suck him and Tully around the still-opening doors. They were metal, the slick siding not offering much to grab onto. Lunging upward, Keith managed to snag a vertical bar in the door's overflow opening.

"Keith!" Tully screamed. She wasn't right up against the door like he was.

Just before she could sweep past, Keith reached out with his free hand. She caught it and gripped it tightly in both of hers. Diego's last words flashed through Keith's mind. He wasn't going to let go. Tully was going to make it.

"Shit!"

Keith hadn't noticed that Mandy was back in the water until she was being sucked toward them. Before they could think of making a chain, the torrent slowed. The doors kept opening, but the water beyond them levelled out. Keith continued to hold on, letting the door push him and Tully toward Mandy. The only sounds were the motor works and the pained whines of the dirt devil Tully had shot. The silence from inside the lock was devastating.

When the lock doors finally thumped into their open position, Keith let go and dropped back fully into the water. His arms ached, but he had to keep swimming. He had to find out what had happened.

With the machinery no longer running, the weeping could be heard. There was at least one person still alive. Keith swam faster.

"Mom!" he shouted as he neared the edge of the door. "Dad! Russell!"

"Keith!"

His dad, thank God! One of them had survived!

"Keith, stay out there!"

But it was too late, he'd already swum around the edge of the door, Tully and Mandy right on his heels.

The lock was awash with blood. Both yachts had had holes sliced through their hulls and were filling with water. No one moved aboard either of them. The pontoon boat was in much better condition, but dark crimson sloshed and dripped over the sides.

Off the front of the boat, Keith's dad dove into the water so fast that Keith wasn't able to get a good look at him. Not until he was up close, swimming alongside Keith and trying to pull him away.

"Dad? Dad, what happened?"

"I'm sorry, Keith."

"Dad?" Alarm pounded in his veins.

"Your mom didn't make it."

51:
NOW

ALL KEITH COULD do was run. He bolted through the shattered glass and sprinted across the deck. That cruel sound of a dirt devil's claws pursued him. It even came right outside into the drizzle, and this time there was no sodden curtain for it to get tangled up in. But still it flinched when struck by the rain, and that extra second allowed Keith to leap over the railing.

A part of him felt like a passenger in his own body. He was screaming, believing every move would lead to his painful death. His arms and legs worked on autopilot, not caring if they could actually do what he needed them to do, they were just doing it.

When he vaulted the railing, he should have fallen and broken his legs. Instead, his feet miraculously planted themselves on the beam that supported the swings. Any other time, Keith would have walked such a beam slowly, if he walked it at all, but now he ran. The railing cracked behind him as he reached the end and threw his body out into space.

This time. This time, I'll fall and will probably break more than just my legs.

He fell, but not a great distance. He smacked into an evergreen, branches whipping his limbs before he managed to catch one under his knee and another under his armpit. He hung there awkwardly, painfully, but alive. He expected dirt devil claws to make ribbons out of his back any second, but at least ten of those seconds passed without bringing any additional pain.

A loud thump behind Keith got him moving. He hauled himself up, getting his feet on some branches to stand, his body twisting around others. Sap stuck to him everywhere.

Behind him, the dirt devil had attempted to follow and failed. Its bulk was too much, and it had slid sideways. Based on the vicious gouges in the wooden beam, it had attempted to keep holding on before falling to the ground below. That had been the thump. Keith couldn't see it anymore and guessed that the beast had sunk under the soil. He took that moment to catch his breath. Between gasps, a wheezing sort of laugh came out of him. His terror was replaced by the delirious euphoria at still being alive. It didn't last long.

The whole tree quivered. Keith felt dizzy looking down, but there was the dirt devil. Or maybe it was the third creature. It pounced, trying to grab a low branch, but its weight and the extreme sharpness of its claws hindered it. The branch snipped off like it was nothing. The dirt devil even tried to scale the trunk, and only succeeded in making gouges, and peeling off ribbons of bark and wood.

"Ha!" Keith shouted down at the thing. "Fuck you!"

The dirt devil became incensed. It stopped trying to climb the tree, and instead used its razor claws to deliberately rip chunks out of the trunk. Keith had to cling tighter as the whole thing shook.

It began to tilt, leaving Keith no time to think. As it started going down, he jumped, this time for a nearby oak. The wind slammed out of him as his torso caught in a high fork. He was barely able to control his arms enough to keep from sliding back out. It was miraculous that the egg thing was still bundled in his shirt, and that his shirt was still gripped tightly in one hand.

The pine went down with a thunderous crash, and a mighty snapping of branches. There was also a splash. The very top of it had managed to reach the water.

He was halfway to the water now. The oak was stronger than the evergreen, and in seconds, the dirt devil was making another attempt at climbing. It had a little more success, but not enough that it would keep trying for long.

Keith searched for another tree closer to the water. There was nothing he thought he could jump to. Maybe if he could get out farther from the trunk, but the only limb thick enough was practically vertical and grew in the wrong direction. Scrabbling awkwardly with the toes of his water shoes, he got up onto his feet, his free arm fiercely hugging the trunk. He kept searching frantically for somewhere, anywhere, he could get to.

The tree shook. The dirt devil was tearing it apart again. It wouldn't be long before the whole thing went down. Keith didn't have enough time to make a decision, not that any choices had presented themselves. The tree tilted, and all he could do was hold on tight and hope he didn't get flattened.

Branches snapped, raining bits of leaves and wood down around Keith's head while he squeezed his eyes shut. He thought it would be the last thing he ever felt, but then the tree came to such an early and sudden stop, that he was nearly thrown from his perch. Opening his eyes, Keith found he wasn't on the ground. The oak had been caught by another tree!

Just as Keith was starting to feel relieved, the oak rolled and settled a little deeper against the catch tree. It probably wasn't done falling yet, but Keith looked down to the base anyway, figuring it was the dirt devil. The beast was down there, using the angle of the tree to help it climb unsteadily.

"Shit!" Keith scrambled upward, the angle helping him get higher as well. He fought his way through a tangle of branches, the bouncing of the tree beneath him making him nauseous with terror. It could still let go at any moment. It could continue its fall to the forest floor, bringing Keith down with it.

He reached the catch tree, and climbed his way into it. It was smaller than the fallen oak. Between him and the dirt devil moving around, it jostled and bent beneath the shifting weight. Keith spotted another pine he thought he could get to, but before he could try, the catch tree gave way. With a horrible popping and crackling, it broke. Keith was falling again and he didn't think there was anything to save him this time.

Eyes shut, wind streaming past, Keith clung to the trunk and waited for the end. Unlike when the oak went down, he was now on the wrong side, the down side. Impact was going to squash him flat.

Instead, impact knocked him flying. The tree stopped abruptly, flinging Keith down like a burning marshmallow off a stick. His back burned as it slapped through branches, smacked by the larger ones and whipped by the smaller. He stopped with a splash.

A splash! Keith floundered upright, getting to his feet in waist-deep water. He was in the lake, although not by much. The tree trunk had gotten hung up on a rock and smacked him loose, but its branches still flared around his head like a cage. The splintering crackle of wood suggested that the dirt devil was still coming, he just couldn't see it.

Keith fought his way through the branches, not sure where he was going, just hoping it was away from both the tree and the shoreline. He broke free of the leaves, and jumped when a sharp crack, louder than the falling timber had been, shocked his ears. Behind him, a dirt devil yowled and then fell from the branches it had been using to pursue Keith. It slipped, landing in the shallow water where its pain and screaming were amplified. Keith stumbled back, away from its thrashing. He watched it flail, trying to grab something, anything, that it could use to pull itself out, but its claws just kept slicing through the wood and bristles, creating a green flurry.

"Ho. Ly. SHIT!"

Keith wheeled back around, slipping on the rock and nearly falling on his ass again. Sidebottom was standing there with his rifle. He had shot the dirt devil before it could grab Keith. He hadn't hit the proper eye, but it had been effective enough.

"Not the route I would've taken down, let me tell you this about that, boy-o!" he bellowed and laughed. "That sure was something! I've never—" He cut himself off as he zeroed in on the bundled T-shirt, still locked in Keith's hand. "Is that it?" His eyes glowed brightly with a manic delight. "Is that it!?"

"It is." Keith pulled it up to his chest.

"Give it to me, boy-o. Hand it here." Sidebottom reached with a grabby hand, but Keith waded backward, keeping it out of reach.

"No."

"Give it here." Sidebottom raised his rifle again, although it wasn't pointed at a dirt devil this time.

Keith held the bundle out sideways. "You shoot me, and I drop it. It hasn't touched much water yet. Do you want to risk it dissolving?" It actually got dunked when he'd been thrown off the final tree, but Sidebottom didn't know that.

Sidebottom hesitated. His eyes darted from Keith, to the dying, moaning dirt devil, and then to the bundle.

"Here's what's going to happen." Keith's body ached all over. He just wanted to sink into the cool water, to bathe the many scratches that adorned his torso, but he needed to strike while the iron was hot, while the advantage was all his. "We're going to walk back to your boat. You first. I'll follow with the . . . the object, let's say." He didn't want to give Sidebottom any clue about what it was. "Once we're back to the pontoon, you're going to get my kayak, and you're going to load it up with food. Oh, and throw in a new shirt as well. Only then, once everything is ready to go, will I hand over the object."

Sidebottom considered his options.

"Think fast," Keith told him. "The rain could come back any minute." Even the drizzle had stopped during Keith's treetop adventure.

"Fine. Come on." Sidebottom lowered his gun and wheeled around to lead the way.

Keith breathed a sigh of relief. He had to bite back the moan of pain it wanted to turn into. He clutched the weird thing to his chest. It was still warm. Not as hot as it had been, but still quite warm. Parts of his shirt were already drying around it.

The last surviving dirt devil followed them along the shoreline. One of its buddies had died in the lake, and the other was probably resigned to death, still trapped in the curtains. This third one, though, Keith was fairly certain had been the one that had chased him out of the cottage. It winced as often as he did, droplets falling upon it from the trees, and grass and brush still holding onto moisture whisking around its legs and feet. It stood on the docks when they swam around them. Its eyes stayed locked on Keith, and transmitted fury.

At one point, Keith held the bundle out from his body, dangling it over the water he'd taken pains to keep it above when circling the docks. The dirt devil froze mid-step, the brambles on its back rising like hackles. Whatever this thing was, the devil didn't want it dunked. Good to know his threat to Sidebottom wasn't toothless.

Sidebottom could still kill him. Once he had the whatever-it-was, he could just shoot Keith. It was a risk Keith had to take. He didn't think Sidebottom would kill him. The man only did what benefited him, and killing Keith wouldn't do that. Or would it? He wouldn't have to give Keith any food, and he could keep the kayak for himself.

No, Keith shook his head. Sidebottom was crazy, but he wouldn't kill Keith like that. Not after he'd gotten what the man wanted. Still, he remained nervous the whole way back.

The dirt devil made angry sounds when they crossed the

shallow section, not liking that its . . . thing . . . was getting farther away. Still, it continued to pursue them as closely as it could. Keith hoped that when he handed off the object, the dirt devil would keep its focus on Sidebottom, and not hold the kind of grudge against Keith that had it pursuing him until death.

At the pontoon, Keith waited in the shallows while Sidebottom went to get his kayak. It was somewhere on land. The dirt devil across the way seemed extra irritated that it couldn't cross when it saw Sidebottom step into the woods. It bellowed, and, fearing it was trying to summon other dirt devils, Keith held out the bundle over the water. The dirt devil shut right up. Keith pulled the bundle back to his chest.

The kayak was unharmed as Sidebottom slid it into the lake. It appeared that all of Keith's gear was in it. He was so relieved to see its shade of bright green, that his legs nearly gave out.

"Now the food," he instructed Sidebottom.

Grumbling, the man did as commanded. He filled Keith's waterproof bag with provisions, some of it canned goods, some of it dried meat and fish. He even threw in a few foraged nuts and berries that were still fresh. He made a show of holding out a T-shirt for Keith to see before tossing it into the kayak.

"Gloves," Keith remembered. "I want you to throw in a pair of work gloves as well."

Sidebottom shook his head as he retrieved a pair to toss in. "Anything else, boy-o?"

"Remove the bullets from your rifle. All of them. Place them on the back of the pontoon."

Sidebottom raised an eyebrow, but removed the magazine and opened the slide to take out the one in the chamber.

"Good. Now drop the gun."

"What?"

"In the water." Keith wished he could toss all the bullets in the lake. The wet powder would make them useless. He wasn't sure a wet gun would stop Sidebottom from being able to fire it, but he hoped the man wouldn't take the risk. He never would have agreed to dunk his bullets, but this he might do. "Now!" Keith barked, holding the bundle away from him.

Sidebottom sighed and dropped his gun. It disappeared beneath the water with a plop.

"Walk away from the boat. I'll leave this on the back, next to your bullets."

Sidebottom sloshed away, giving Keith plenty of room.

Keith put the bundle where he said he would. He then used the back of the pontoon to help him get into his kayak. He was surprised to find he had missed sitting in that moulded seat. The paddle felt intimately familiar in his hands.

"Goodbye, Sidebotttom," he called out as he pushed away from the pontoon boat. "I hope I never see you again."

52:
THEN

MOM WAS DEAD. She wasn't the only one. She'd died alongside Dr. Kimiko, Russell's mom. Both Russel's parents were gone now. The woman from the yachts had died, along with a dozen of the kids and teenagers that had been with her. Saksham had made it, but his leg bore a long gash that had everyone worried. They'd cleaned and bandaged it as well as they were able, but without Dr. Kimiko, they weren't sure if there was more they should, or even could do. Russell had a massive bruise along the side of his head, making half his face swell up. He'd been smashed into the wall of the lock, slapped away by the dirt devil. Aisling had jumped in and saved his life, swimming for both of them in a fight against the rushing water. Russell had been unconscious when his mother had died, the one saving grace of his injury.

The pontoon boat was still functional, and they motored away from the grisly scene. Keith helped Mandy and Aisling use duct tape to repair rips in the canvas top. They also scooped up buckets of water while they drove, sloshing them over the deck and seats, rinsing away all the blood. Keith tried to think of anything but the fact that some of that blood was his mother's.

Along with Tully, two other teenagers from the yachts had survived, as well as two younger kids. The five of them sat in a tight huddle, their faces drawn and pale. Some of them had been injured as well, but none as badly as Saksham.

"We didn't even get to bury them," Russell whispered one night, when he and Keith were lying beside each other on the floor.

"I know."

"We just left them there in the lock."

"I know." *Please stop talking about it,* was what Keith wanted to say. His mom was dead. There'd be no finding her again. This time she was gone for good, and Keith didn't know how to process that information.

After getting lost on a lake for a short while, they finally reached the next lock, and nobody wanted to get out of the boat. It was too sunny, too dry. No one needed to suggest that they wait, they all just did. It took two days before rain came. Two days of boredom, and heat, and cramped quarters. The rain came at night, but no one slept well anyway. Mr. Sidebottom and Dad left the pontoon to work the lock controls. There was no drawing of straws, no debate. While the lock filled, they stood at the top, water guns ready despite the rain. A teenager named Frankie drove the pontoon, having grown up around small watercraft. He was the only one with a job to do, something to focus on. Keith got to listen to the panicked breathing of the others, those suffering PTSD from the previous attack. Although maybe it was just TSD, maybe not enough time had passed for the P for post to be added. Anxiety attacks all around.

It was a long way to the next lock, especially when they got lost a few times. It was in a very populated area, and when they got there, they found they finally had no power to run the thing.

"We can figure this out," Mr. Sidebottom insisted. "We just need to find ourselves the right tools, and I'm certain we could work it by hand."

"What would be the point? We should just go back to where we spotted all those canoes along the bank," Dad insisted.

"And do what with them?"

"Next time it rains, we can portage."

"And every time it rains, your little boats will be flooded."

"We'll use bailing buckets."

The argument between the two men went around and around and around. Sometimes Keith would try to interject with a comment or two, but he was ignored, just like everyone else. Dad and Mr. Sidebottom were going to work this out between them, and that was it. They didn't seem to care what the majority wanted.

Not until the majority got together and overwhelmed them.

"We'd rather risk the canoes." Aisling was their front person, her natural anger allowing her to steamroll over anyone. "What are we going to do when the next lock is out of power? And the next one? And the one after that? Are we really going to keep trying to work the doors manually? No. We don't want to do that. We'd rather carry canoes. We want to risk the canoes."

Mr. Sidebottom had been overridden, despite having some valid points. The pontoon boat may have been crowded, but it still let people lie down, and had all those holds in which to stash their supplies safely away from the elements. It never needed bailing, and the cover provided them with protection from the sun. And there was the motor, of course. While the canoes would be easier to paddle, they would *always* need to be paddled. Still, they were the better option if they wished to keep climbing up the waterway.

The canoes were all sitting up on a bank, with their tail ends just touching the water. They weren't tied up, and all that was inside were lifejackets, paddles, and collected rainwater. It was easy to stand in the shallows and pull them deeper, and then continue standing there while they bailed them out with buckets. No one knew why the canoes were there. It certainly didn't look like a campground. It also didn't look like they had been there since the beginning, which meant whoever had been in charge of this small flotilla had deliberately put to shore despite the danger. No one could think of a reason why someone would do that, and there was no way the canoes had just drifted to where they found them, not all together like that, and not as high out of the water as they were.

"Maybe they had just had enough," Mandy suggested while they bailed.

"All of them?" Aisling scoffed.

"We don't know that this is all of them. There could have been more canoes."

"They probably needed supplies," Russell suggested. His tone was always dour these days. "With all these buildings around, they probably thought they'd be safe and could get things quickly."

Keith shuddered at the suggestion. They put ashore for supplies fairly regularly, and always trusted that the rain would protect them. If this group had made a mistake, they could just as easily make the same one.

"At least we know this isn't an island," Tully said. "So we don't need to check whether they found some safe place."

"If they had planned to come back, wouldn't their supplies still be here?" Carol pointed out. It was the loudest Keith had heard her speak. She said she was fifteen, but she was a little mouse of a person, and acted like one, too. It was easy to forget she was there, even on the crowded pontoon. Aisling called her Mrs. Frisby. All Keith could remember about the story, was that the mouse, Mrs. Frisby, was very brave while trying to save her family. He couldn't tell if Aisling had meant to insult or compliment Carol with the name.

"They didn't have any supplies, that's why they stopped," Russell restated.

"Or someone came through here before us, and saw that they were easy for the taking," Aisling added. "They left the lifejackets and paddles behind because they didn't need any."

Many theories circled the canoes, but none of them mattered. The canoes were theirs now, and they were going to make use of them.

"I can't! I can't!" Saksham gasped when they tried to move him. He spent most of his time lying on one of the bench seats. They tried to bathe his wound every day, and gave him antibiotics from the supplies Dr. Kimiko had gathered, but it still looked hideous. And it smelled. Maybe it was just the bandages they had to keep washing and reusing, but there was a smell. Maybe the antibiotics weren't working.

"There's no way Saksham should be in a canoe," Mr. Sidebottom finally put his foot down. "We can't move him."

"Well we can't leave him," Dad insisted.

"This is why we should stay on the pontoon boat," Mr. Sidebottom grumbled. "Look, why don't the boy-o and I stay here? I'll look after him, and if it rains, I'll see if I can find those tools to work the lock. You keep going, and find us that island. We'll catch up when we can."

"Saksham?" Dad turned to him. "What do you want to do?"

Saksham spent a whole minute thinking about it.

"I will stay," he eventually told everyone.

"He must be in a lot of pain," Keith whispered to Russell, who nodded in agreement. It was clear to everyone that Saksham didn't like Mr. Sidebottom and that Mr. Sidebottom didn't like Saksham. For the nineteen-year-old to agree to stay with the man, he must have been desperate.

No one liked the decision, but then no one liked the other choices they had either. The remaining supplies were split between the two groups, but they agreed to stay together until it rained. It came the next day, and they said their hurried goodbyes.

"I'll miss you." Mandy cried as she hugged Saksham, and Keith felt a flair of jealously. It quickly turned to guilt when he looked at his leg and the pain on his face. Still, the way he touched Mandy's hair when she let him go made Keith want to punch him. Instead, he shook his hand and wished him luck. He said the same to Mr. Sidebottom.

As they carried the canoes and their supplies up the stairs, Keith glanced back only once. He was pretty sure he'd never see either of them ever again.

53: NOW

KEITH PADDLED HARD. He returned up river, fighting the current, trying to put as much distance as he could between himself and Sidebottom as fast as possible.

It was tempting to take the other fork in the river, to turn and let the current aid him once more, but he continued back toward the dam. He had taken a hell of a detour, but he still intended to get that swim raft.

Upon reaching his destination, he took a break. He sat on the raft with his feet in the water, finally dealing with the terrible ache in his toe. It had not enjoyed the tree hopping at all. As he lay back, he couldn't believe that had actually happened. He couldn't believe that he was alive. Maybe he wasn't. Maybe these were his dying thoughts, a last-ditch effort at comfort before he suffocated from being sucked underground by a dirt devil. No, he wouldn't imagine his foot being in so much pain if that were the case.

He didn't let himself rest for long. Once he'd processed all that had happened, he got to work. The first thing he did was check his supplies. They were all there. He also sorted all the food Sidebottom had given him. He'd been given a lot and thought he could make a whopping sixty meals out of it all, so long as he made them small. He could get a full month out of the food if he went back to two meals a day, but Keith didn't want to do that. Twenty days was plenty and so, by God, he was going to have lunch.

Sitting there, feet in the water, eating his lunch, he felt . . . good. Surprisingly good. Confident. He was alone again, but after staying with Sidebottom, it's what he wanted. Looking from one shoreline to the other, he didn't see any dirt devils. For the time being, he wasn't stalked. It was a good feeling, no longer being prey.

Meal complete, he got back to work. He first donned his mask and gloves. He wished he had a safe way to carry the knife he'd chosen, but he didn't, so keeping it in his hand would have to do. After a deep breath, he slipped off the raft next to one of the chains, and pulled himself down. Cutting through the cable ties was more of a challenge than he'd bargained for, but after what he'd just gone through, it seemed downright easy. Several breaths and several follow-up dives later, the cement blocks were cut loose from the anchors. Keith sprawled on the raft afterward, taking in great lungfuls of air and warming himself in the sun that had found a hole in the cloud cover. He'd have been tempted to lie there for the rest of the afternoon if he hadn't remembered that he wasn't wearing any sunscreen.

The towels in his kayak were dry—Sidebottom must have had everything under a tarp—but the shirt he'd been given was a little too large. Still, it was better than nothing.

The anchors weren't difficult to lift now that they were separated from the blocks. Kneeling by first one chain and then the other, he was able to haul them up onto the raft, and balance the yellow half-orbs on opposite corners. The chains were covered in algae and invasive zebra mussels. Keith thought he'd scrape them off once they'd dried out.

Untethered from the bottom of the river, he immediately started to drift.

"Shit." Keith wasn't expecting to move toward shore so fast. He scrambled into his kayak, hastily tying a short length of the tow rope between the rear handle and the raft's ladder. It turned out that the raft was towable, just not in the nice, smooth way Keith had been imagining. With every stroke, he moved forward, the rope between him and the raft tightened, and then the raft tugged forward. Between strokes, the raft continued to move forward, bumping into the back of the kayak.

Whoosh, bump. Whoosh, bump. Whoosh, bump.

A couple of times, he got the second stroke in before the bump, but that didn't make matters any better. The constant change in tension kept throwing off his rhythm. It was ridiculous and annoying. And there was no way he was going to cut the raft loose.

As he approached the fork in the river, he slowed—*bump*—and searched for any sign of Sidebottom. He had told the man about the raft. He'd know where Keith had gone.

The cloud cover had returned, and thunder rumbled far in the distance. Insects were kicking up a racket, but otherwise the air was still. Keith searched for movement, for any shape that didn't fit among the trees. For any shape that was human—or more specifically, a human man with a rifle. There was nothing. As Keith drifted toward the other fork, the world felt peaceful.

It didn't take long for that to change. The wind picked up with a vengeance only twenty minutes later. Keith would have liked to have been farther away from Sidebottom's place before stopping, but he had no choice. The howling wind rushed at his face, stronger than the current. If he didn't stop, he'd just go backwards.

Throwing himself back onto the raft, he shoved the anchors off the corners. He would have liked to use only one, but he wasn't sure just one would cut it with this weather. For a terrifying moment he continued to drift, the bottom of the river too deep for his anchors to reach. Eventually they touched, though, and after a bit of sliding, settled into position a comfortable distance from shore.

Keith grabbed all his supplies and brought them onto the raft. Popping up the table and lounge chair backs, he used them and the ladder handholds to prop up his plastic tarp. With the ski rope crisscrossing his space, he tied down the tarp as much as he could, leaving a little opening at the ladder so he could peer out and keep an eye on the kayak. The paint tarp he folded into a sort of mattress shape, while anything else with weight went toward helping hold down the edges of the tarp. It was incredibly cramped inside his makeshift tent, but it was dry. As the rain came down in a torrent, Keith tried to tighten the areas that sagged, scrambling around in the dark. If he had had enough forethought, he would have prepared this whole setup before heading out, but he'd wanted so badly to get away from Sidebottom.

Through his opening, Keith could see the rain pattering down into his kayak. He would have to bail it out in the morning. Hopefully that didn't first involve hauling it up from the bottom of the lake.

Lightning lit up the world, and thunder tore open the sky

overhead. Keith instinctively tried to lie flatter than he already was. Just how close to shore was he again? Did he need to worry about being struck by lightning, or were the trees close enough to protect him? And were the anchors truly good enough to hold him in place against this wind? Luckily, it had pushed him around so that the opening of his little tent faced the way he had come. As well as keeping an eye on his kayak, Keith could keep an eye up river, should Sidebottom try using the cover of the storm for something.

When the lightning and the rain lessened, Keith was able to relax more. It didn't stop raining, so he remained in his shelter, but he no longer thought it was about to fall down on his head at any given moment.

He ate some dinner lying on his side, the world outside growing darker and darker as the sun left it. Using his poncho and a towel as a pillow, and his other towel as a small blanket, he was able to get somewhat comfortable in the close confines of his tent. As least as comfortable as he had been on Sidebottom's boat, maybe even a little more since there was no seat bracket to contend with.

Keith wanted to continue keeping an eye on the river, but the day caught up with him. He only meant to blink, but even with some thunder still grumbling in the distance, his eyes failed to reopen, and he fell asleep.

54: THEN

KEITH'S ARMS ACHED all the time. On sunny days, they suffered a gruelling amount of paddling as everyone moved from one lock to the next, or else explored the area for anything they could scavenge. Rainy days were always saved as much as possible for portaging, and so sometimes the small towns they came across ended up being raided when it was dry. It seemed to Keith that he always carried more water in the form of ammo onto the shore than he did supplies back to the canoes, running all the while. The raids were quick, just smash and grab affairs, with one supply picker and three water-gunners to watch their back. Keith couldn't decide which role was worse.

When it did rain, they hauled ass. Out of the water, and up the stairs with all their canoes and supplies. They were too heavy for a simple two-person portage, and so multiple trips had to be made. Some days, the rain held out long enough, and the locks were close enough together, that they paddled as hard as they could in order to climb more than one lock. Those were the days no one had the energy to even talk, even after all the locks started to go the other way, and they found themselves carrying their loads down the steps instead of up.

Between them, they had four canoes and eight paddlers, along with two small kids who sat among the supplies. Dad had taught the kids to fish, and so they spent most of the day monitoring the lines in the water, or scanning the area for anything the others might miss. When they did catch fish, they were cooked when everyone anchored for the night. They had one anchor which a canoe dropped, and everyone else tied up to them. Lashing a board between two canoes, they set up a sort of table, where the fish caught that day were prepared and fried on a small propane stove. It didn't take long for everyone to start hating fish, but it allowed their other supplies to last longer. They had begun to notice that they weren't the first to hit the small towns they raided.

Some days, they came across other people living on the water. They would stop and talk, but never stay with them. These others would comment that they liked their idea of finding an island, but never joined them. They were all living on boats too large to carry up the locks. Instead, they decided to make their own island out of whatever they found floating. Keith and his friends would wish them luck and continue on.

Dad was determined to find an island. He spoke of one in particular, on the lake where Mrs. Phelps had her cottage. He was certain that was the place for them, that they would be safe there, that they could ride this out, to the point where he barely looked at the other islands they passed. Ever since Keith's mom had died, Dad had had this single-minded focus. He clung to his thoughts of the island, using them to drive himself and the others forward.

Every morning before they started out, they drew lots to determine who was in what position in what canoe. None of them were truly skilled, and the canoes all bore different loads, so they always changed it up. Some canoes were also easier to sleep in than others, although no one would call any of them comfortable. In this way, everyone paddled with everyone else. And while paddling, there was nothing else to do but talk.

Tully told her story first, about getting to the water when the alert came. She had lost her folks after the first rain, when they thought it would be safe. Frankie's story was similar, although his dad had survived long enough to be killed trying to get to and from the nearest town when they'd been on the yachts. It was why so many kids and teenagers had ended up parentless on the water: either their parents had gone to see if it was safe, and learned the hard way that it was not, or they didn't survive a supply run. Some hadn't died right away when attacked, but suffered injuries that no one knew what to do about. A handful bled to death, while others died slowly of infection. Only Gillian, the one adult who had been found with them, had gotten away clean. At least she had until the lock attack that had also killed Keith's mom.

Carol had joined the yachts later. She had lived farther away from the water system, and had ended up standing around in a pond, never completely dry even when climbing onto a muddy hump. For days, she'd been trapped there with her father—her mother had left years before—until it finally rained. They ran for it, but neither was strong, having had little to eat. When they reached the water, they were picked up by a small group who took them in. Travelling down the Trent-Severn Waterway, that group ran into bandits. They had nothing to give, and in the ensuing fight, only Carol had escaped. She kept going down the system, swimming all the way to the next lock, her only flotation device a torn lifejacket. After running down those steps during a fortuitous rainstorm, she met and fell in with the others. She had no idea what happened to the bandits, since no one had seen any further sign of them. Aisling stopped calling Carol Mrs. Frisby after hearing her story.

The two kids, Chris and Mike, were brothers. They didn't seem to know exactly what happened the night the dirt devils came. The older, Chris, remembered his dad throwing them off a high cliff into the water, and that was the last he saw of him. Neither could recall what happened to their mom, only that they were alone for days, until the others found them living off of a suitcase stuffed with snack food on a raft.

Russell told their story, about his parents and him scrambling to the pool, and how Keith's family had joined them. He shared the horror of watching his father get sucked underground, and Mrs. Phelps get eaten. He talked about the dirt devil that had broken into Keith's house, and finding Mandy and Aisling on the road. He even brought up the old woman with the gun, so Keith didn't have to. His story differed from Keith's own for a bit when they reached Lake Ontario, but not by much. Aisling filled in the bit about being on the ship. Keith had even less to share than Frankie, his story having been lived alongside others.

"I was asleep at home when the message came," Mandy said one afternoon when she was at the front of Keith's canoe. "I'm not allowed to have my phone in my room at night, and my parents didn't believe the alert when it woke them up. They didn't wake me. Not then, anyway. I was woken by their screaming. A dirt devil had gotten inside. It had ripped through the screen door we'd left open in the back, since there was no A/C. My little brother reacted to the shrieking first and ran to my room. I didn't know what to do. Neither of us knew what was happening, and it was dark, and . . . " She took a shuddering breath and focused on her paddle for a few strokes. "We went to see what was going on. Nick—my brother—grabbed a flashlight out of the hallway. The dirt devil was in my parents' room. It had torn them to pieces. I ran. I ran downstairs and was out the door before I realized that Nick wasn't with me. I screamed for him, but couldn't bring myself to go back inside. We have a pool, but I didn't know to get in it. I just stood there until the dirt devil came back out. I got lucky. It was carrying Nick and so it didn't have time for me. The thing body-checked me as it ran past, and I just happened to land in the pool. Nick disappeared beneath the ground, just like Russell's dad. I could have saved him, and I didn't. I let my little brother die."

"It's not your fault," Aisling interjected, paddling at the front of a neighbouring canoe. "I've told you a hundred times that it's not your fault. What were you supposed to do? Even if you grabbed him, you wouldn't have known what to do. You'd probably both be dead if you hadn't done what you did. If you want to blame anyone, blame your parents for not listening to the warning."

"I could have saved him," Mandy mumbled, almost too quietly for Keith to hear. He didn't think he was supposed to. "Anyway, Aisling eventually showed up. It was her idea to use the Super Soakers and to get away on the bike. I would have died if she hadn't come. She saved me. Although we weren't really sure where we were going until Doug picked us up."

"And I'm glad we stopped," Dad said from the front of the farthest canoe, which wasn't really far. They tended to stick close together. "Both of you have been a great help."

"I'm really sorry about your parents and your brother." Keith could only offer limp sympathy.

"Thanks. I'm sorry about your mom."

That was the way every story ended. Someone would offer condolences for those lost, and the storyteller would respond with condolences for their own bereavement. No one had gotten out of this unscathed.

Keith's gut was roiling. He still had his dad. Somehow that made him feel guilty. Everyone else had lost so much more than he had. At the same time, the pain of losing his mother struck deep. He was torn between two conflicting pains.

Russell had lost his mother at the same time as he had, but to Keith, he was handling it much better. More than once, Keith had broken down in the middle of paddling, trying to keep his hitching sobs as quiet as he could, hoping that the times he sat in the front, the person in back somehow didn't notice. He didn't stop paddling, though. The physical exertion was what got him through, every time.

Not everything they talked about was serious. Keith was delighted to learn that Tully was as into comics as he was. Whenever they shared a canoe, they discussed their favourite issues and runs, theorized about how certain superheroes would handle the dirt devils—because once everything was normal again, dirt devils would definitely show up in the storylines—and told each other about comics the other hadn't read.

"Just so you know," Tully whispered one night, "I'm not attracted to you. We can be friends, but that's all."

Keith snorted, enjoying her blunt honesty. "Well I'm not attracted to you either, so we're good."

"Yeah, you've got quite the thing for Mandy. I noticed."

"Has *everyone* noticed?"

"Probably."

"Even Mandy?"

"Even Mandy." Keith was glad it was dark, so that Tully couldn't see how red his face must have turned.

"Do . . . Do you know what she thinks of me?"

"No idea."

"So I still have a chance?"

"I don't know. I guess. As much as anyone has a chance with anyone right now."

"Do you have a crush on anyone?"

"No one here." Which meant no one at all, because the previous crush was likely dead. Maybe it had been Diego.

Whenever Keith shared a boat with Mandy, he did his best to have an actual, honest to God conversation with her. Finding something they shared a mutual interest in was proving more difficult than he had expected. On Tully's advice, he tried mostly to ask questions, but he struggled to think them up, and certain topics she didn't want to talk about at all. After learning about what had happened to her family, he knew to avoid that subject like a dirt devil. The problem was that he didn't know her parents or little brother, and anything that reminded her of them was also taboo. How many times did he stumble into one of her painful memories? Even once was too often, but how could he talk to her without knowing the boundaries?

They travelled along the Trent-Severn Waterway, talking, and fishing, and paddling. Sometimes the locks they traversed were different from the ones they were used to. Twice, the locks were huge ponds that counter balanced one another to lift up and down. More complex, but probably quicker than those that had to fill and drain. At least, Keith assumed they'd be quicker; with the power out, they had no way of knowing. A handful of the locks were apparently hand driven. They could have moved the things manually if they wanted, but climbing the stairs was faster, and faster was safer. A lock right near the end was called Big Chute, and was like one of those pond things, except there was just the one and it climbed a marine railway.

"I've heard of Big Chute," Mandy commented as they waited for rain. "A friend of mine has a cottage near here. She told me her family comes here once a year to watch the boats."

"Which friend is that?" Aisling asked.

"Nicole."

"Isn't she the one—" Russell started before realizing he shouldn't finish that sentence.

"Go on," Mandy challenged him, sitting in the back of his canoe. "Isn't she the one, what?"

"Who wears too much makeup?" Russell skated into the lie. And they all knew it was a lie. He was going to say that she was the one who was caught giving the captain of the boy's hockey team a hand job in the handicap washroom.

Aisling had no such need for niceties, for lies. "Is it true?" she asked Mandy. "Did the handicap handy actually happen?"

"It's not like she's a slut," Mandy defended her friend. "They'd been dating for months."

"What's this about?" Dad asked.

"Nothing," Keith, Russell, Mandy, and Aisling all replied simultaneously, which obviously made it not nothing.

The rain came, and they climbed the lock. There was only one more after Big Chute, and then they were there: Georgian Bay. They had made it all the way along the Trent-Severn Waterway.

"Look, there's an island right there," Frankie pointed. "A couple of them, even. We should check them out."

"We're going to the one I know about," Dad insisted.

"Dad, these are a lot closer." Keith would like to stop. He had suggested stopping at previous islands, but had never won the argument.

"They might not be big enough. And they're very exposed out here. Rough weather coming in off the bay would hit them hard. We keep going."

"Is there even a way to get from here to there?" Carol whispered to Keith.

"I don't know," Keith whispered back. "I didn't study the lake we visited like Dad did."

There was a way to get to the lake, but it wasn't as easy as climbing a set of stairs beside a lock. A torrent of water rushed down a set of rapids under a trio of bridges. Dad said they needed to go up them.

The first two bridges were close together, and they could pass them both in a single portage. Just beyond them was a somewhat calmer section, with a safety rope spanning the waterway. It was barely raining as they hauled their canoes up, tying them one by one to the safety line so that they wouldn't float away. The portage was a challenge, taking them along a narrow path beneath the bridges. The rock ledge under there was slick, and they had to move single file, which was not the usual way they carried their canoes.

"You kids take a break. I'm going to go scout the way ahead." Dad handed Keith his watch, like he always did when they separated.

They moved the canoes a little farther from shore and huddled beneath the collection of umbrellas they'd gathered along the way. Keith decided to sponge out the bottom of his canoe while they waited.

"Doug?" Mandy called out.

Keith's head shot up from the concern in her voice.

"Dad?" he shouted louder when he failed to see the man. "Where'd he go?"

"I don't know," Mandy answered. "I wasn't watching."

"Dad! Did anyone see what happened to him?"

Everyone shook their heads, some with guilty faces. They were all exhausted and had taken the opportunity to rest.

It stopped raining, and Keith really began to panic. The last bridge was wooden, a walking path for people. The water frothed and roared out from underneath it, a small but raging waterfall. Sheer cliffs flanked that section. They would need to leave the water's edge to get to the other side, which would mean that Dad had left the water's edge to scout ahead. Where was he now? Trapped on the far side of the bridge, or still on land?

Everyone was anxiously searching, and so they all saw the body as it came over the short falls.

"Dad!"

55:
NOW

IT TOOK SOME experimentation, but Keith found a way to make pulling the raft easier. Using the boat rope, he tied the bumper lengthwise between the back of his kayak and the raft. With the line as tight as he could make it, the joint was mostly solid, and the bumper eased any collision still happening between the two. The raft could still jack knife on Keith, but that just made it easier to reach the thing whenever he stopped. While his food was still stashed down between his knees, along with the poncho in case of sudden rain, everything else remained on his water trailer.

After his first stormy night sleeping on the raft, Keith paddled hard the next day, travelling as far as he could to make sure he was well away from Sidebottom. Not only did he not want to get shot or roped into some other horrid scheme, he also didn't want to be anywhere near that pontoon boat whenever Sidebottom decided to do whatever experiments he had planned for that thing he'd grabbed. Keith guessed it was an egg, and given the size of the creatures in seed form, it could probably hold more than one, even hundreds, maybe thousands, if they were dust sized like the ones from the meteorite. The thought of a bunch of baby dirt devils, of any size, spilling out all over the deck of the boat gave strength to his arms.

By the next morning, he decided he was far enough away that he could take his time, take proper breaks throughout the day. He set up the raft better. Rebuilding his tent, he made it take up only the back half of the raft. One corner was pinned down by the rear anchor, while the sides were folded under and held by all his nonfood gear. Along the back edge, he carefully folded the paint tarp for sleeping, with the lifejacket laid down as a pillow and his towels for blankets. It was a tight fit, but he liked having the front half of the raft free. It gave him a place to stand up and pace little circuits when he needed to stretch his legs, especially when he dropped the forward anchor off its corner. If it rained, he could unfold a section of the tarp to reach the ladder and increase his sheltered space.

One windy day, Keith reached a huge bay. There was no way to fight against the wind, and so he sat on his raft and let it carry him. As long as he didn't get too close to shore, he wasn't picky about where he went.

With his broken rod, he experimented with fishing. He couldn't cast, but he could do some trolling.

The loneliness started to creep back in. He was still glad to be away from Sidebottom, but he began to want company again. Fishing made him remember his time in the canoes last year. He had had lots of company then. He missed their conversations.

He also missed the little propane burner. Keith was shocked to actually catch a fish, and not a tiny one. It wasn't a monster, nothing a sport fisherman would write home about, but it was large enough to consider eating. Keith had the knives and the knowledge to use them, but he had no way of cooking the fish. He'd have to find an island, and wood, and something to start a fire with. In the end, he decided he had enough food for the time being and let the fish go.

The big bay he was being blown across had a few islands dotted about. Keith considered stopping at one to raid a cottage, but always just drifted by. There were things he could use that they might have, like blankets, a proper tent, an air mattress, a propane stove, matches, and so forth, but he couldn't bring himself to stop. The idea of going ashore sent a shudder through his whole body. He still bore the scratches from the last time he'd been on solid ground, and found himself getting queasy whenever he looked up at the tops of trees. He wasn't ready to leave the water.

All day, the wind pushed him across the long bay. Keith knew that if he wanted to stay in one place while he slept, he would need to find somewhere sheltered, and shallower than this. He climbed back into his kayak and fought the wind to move sideways toward a different part of the lake before the wind could shove him up on the far shore he'd been approaching all day. It was hard going, and he kept getting splashed by waves, but once he got land between him and the wind, the water was much calmer.

He soon found out that the land was an island. He didn't find out because he went around it, or saw where the bay connected on the far side, he learned it was an island because of the moose.

There was a moose on shore.

Keith sat in his kayak with his mouth hanging open. How long had it been since he'd seen an animal larger than his hand? And he'd *never* seen a moose before, not unless you counted the one way at the back of the Toronto Zoo. Never a wild moose. But here one was, walking along the water's edge. Keith wanted to warn the animal, to shout, to tell it to get into the water. A dry rasp that couldn't compete with the waves lapping the rocks was all that came out.

A mother fucking moose, kept repeating in Keith's mind.

The only way that moose could have survived was if it were on an island free of dirt devils, and that it knew better than to walk on the main land. Keith couldn't see how big the island was, but he didn't think it was large enough to support a moose. Maybe the other islands he'd passed by were safe, and the moose knew it could swim to them. Moose could swim rather well if Keith remembered right.

The moose didn't stay in sight very long. It seemed to notice that Keith was watching, and so turned to disappear into the trees.

Keith found a good spot to throw down his anchor near a dock. It was tempting to explore the island, specifically the cottage, but even the presence of the moose couldn't make him get past his all too recent fear. Besides, moose could also be dangerous, and Keith didn't want it thinking he was trying to take away what little land it had managed to claim for itself. The island, and everything on it, belonged to the moose.

The next day, Keith was reluctant to leave, hoping he'd spot the moose again. He didn't. Maybe that was for the best. If the moose decided it didn't like him, it wasn't like a dirt devil. It could come out into the lake and was more than big enough to smash the hell out of Keith's craft. As he paddled away, he kept checking over his shoulder, but the moose never reappeared. Seeing it already felt like a dream.

Two days later, Keith was starting to regain his confidence when it came to the shore. He was beginning to think that the next time it rained, he was definitely going to raid a cottage. The thought of a softer mattress egged him on. It was still sunny though, so he kept paddling, hoping to find other people.

He didn't find other people, but he found a place that was like spotting the Holy Grail of supply depots emerging around a corner. He crossed open water to get to it, grateful that the wind wasn't too strong that day, but still getting splashed a little.

He'd found a marina.

56:
THEN

KEITH LEAPT FROM the canoe, sinking into water that reached his ribs and shocked him with its cold. The current was surprisingly strong, and he nearly had his feet swept out from under him. There was a large, flat, shallow rock just ahead that he lunged for, taking long, precarious strides until he could reach it. Someone else jumped into the water behind him, but he didn't turn to see who it was. His eyes were locked on his Dad's body.

"Dad!" he called out again, getting onto the slippery rock and crawling as often as he ran upright across it. "Dad!"

"Keith!" His dad was alive!

"I'm coming, Dad!"

His father was swirling around in an eddy that would spit him out any second now. He was floundering, barely keeping his head above water. He had to be injured.

Keith reached the edge of the rock, where the water was deep and rushing. He couldn't reach the eddy. He didn't have time to, anyway. Dad got trapped in the outflow and was yanked free.

"I got you!" Keith screamed, throwing his arms out.

Dad grabbed a hand, slipped, grabbed the other hand. Keith was nearly pulled off his knees, off his perch. Water was flowing over Dad's head. He couldn't breathe! Shouting, Keith tried to haul him back, but found he couldn't move. The water was too strong, and he didn't have much leverage. It was taking everything he had just to keep from being pulled in himself.

"Dad!" Keith shouted, refusing to let go. "Dad!" He didn't even know if the man could hear him.

Suddenly. arms were wrapped around Keith's middle. They hauled back, adding their strength to Keith's, and together they pulled Dad out of the water and onto the rock. Dad coughed and spluttered, but he was alive and conscious. For now. Red blood flowed in ribbons from injuries he had sustained to his legs.

"We need a tourniquet!" Aisling. Aisling had come, and was now shouting for more help. "Bring two of them!"

Frankie came with a pair of belts that they strapped around Dad's thighs. They couldn't do anything else to try to stop the bleeding until they had him out of the water.

"Help me get him into a canoe," Keith grunted, hauling on his dad's shoulders.

"What do you think I'm doing?" Aisling snapped. She and Frankie locked arms, making a seat to hold Keith's dad by the waist.

Tully and Carol had moved all the supplies from one canoe into another, and had then slid it down the rope line until it was against the shallow rock. Getting Dad in under the thwarts was a challenge, but once they did, he was lying basically flat.

"Move." Mandy pushed Keith aside so that she could reach his legs. She had grabbed all their first aid supplies and placed them on the bow seat.

"Do you know what you're doing?" Keith asked.

"No, but I have a book." She also had gritted teeth, and a sharpness to her eyes. "Aisling, come stand here and read the book with me. Frankie, get on the other side of the canoe in case I need a pair of hands over there."

"What about me?" Keith tried to find space for himself.

"Keep out of the way."

"I want to help." It was the first time Keith could recall ever getting angry with Mandy.

"Come on," Tully tugged on his arm. "Unless you've been hiding the fact that you're a trained doctor, I don't think there's anything you can help with. Besides, this isn't a job you should have to help with."

"I want to help," he growled. "Where's Russell?" His mom had been a doctor, surely he must have picked up something over the years.

He spotted Russell at the far side of the rock, soaking wet and dragging something dark out of the water. Oh hell, was there another body?

"Russell?" Keith sloshed through the shallow water, his feet slipping on the rock.

"It's dead!" Russell called to him.

"What's dead?"

Instead of telling him, Russell just held it up. Keith fell back on his ass, startled. He clenched his jaw as pain shot up his spine, the water not deep enough to completely buffer the impact.

"Holy shit!" Tully shouted, having followed behind Keith. She managed to keep her feet under her, though.

What Russell had pulled from the water was a dirt devil. It was one of the smaller ones, the size of a large dog, and its limbs and jaw hung slack.

"Help me," Russell said as he dragged it along behind him.

"What the hell are you doing?" Keith gasped. Tully offered him a hand to help him get back on his feet.

"I want to know more about these things. I'm going to cut it open. Help me."

Keith was still angry and the thought of slicing into a dirt devil really appealed to him just then. He and Tully gathered a pair of canoes and strapped the table between them. They then heaved the dirt devil up onto the table.

"What do you think you'll learn?" Keith asked.

"Don't know. Hopefully how to kill them faster."

They set upon the dirt devil with knives usually reserved for the fish they caught. Every time a pained cry came from the boat his dad was in, Keith cut deeper. Tully watched but didn't participate, while Carol kept Chris and Mike away from both operations. The boys were crying.

"What is all this shit?" Russell muttered.

"Doesn't look like organs," Keith agreed.

When they'd cut into the thing, all they kept finding was long, white, ropy stuff. It ran all through the torso and down the limbs.

"There's no blood," Russell observed. "Unless this yellowy stuff is blood, but it's so thin." Cutting the hide of the dirt devil did nothing but reveal the white things. When they sliced through one of the white things, a small amount of mostly clear liquid dribbled out.

"We should probably be wearing gloves," Keith commented.

"Too late now. Look, there's no bones."

"Must make it easier for them to sink into the ground."

"I have no idea how it maintains its structure. How the hell do its joints work? Is this all muscle? Could it move like an octopus if it wanted to?"

"As you always say: alien."

"True. Oh. Oh, shit." Russell turned away, his face pale. He'd been digging around in the torso and discovered that the dirt devil had fed.

"It's a cat," Keith sighed with relief. "It's just a cat, dude." He pulled it out from between the ropes. He was going to chuck it when Tully stopped him.

"Hey man, come on, that was probably someone's pet. Give it here, I'll lay him gently in the current."

"It's got no stomach," Russell commented, composing himself. He still looked like he was about to empty his own. "How does it digest? It just shoves the food in, and what? And what happens to the cat when it goes underground?"

"Those are questions for someone smarter than me."

"Have you noticed all the lines go up to the head? Let's try there next."

Keith stared at the teeth. Gingerly, he pried them apart with the tips of two knives in order to stare down the beast's gullet. He trembled, thinking it was going to suddenly snap at him, despite having been carved up. Past the teeth and the tongue, he got a good look at that white throat. It was white because it was those ropy things. However it made its outer skin, it did the same inside the mouth but only for a limited distance.

While Russell followed the ropes up through the back of the head, Keith poked the beast in the eye. His belly twisted as it came out of the socket with a squelching pop. To make the outer skin, the ropes connected to the surface with a fair amount of space between them, the ends flaring out to form the flesh and brambles. With the eye, several of those ropes, smaller than the others, formed a bundle, the ends of them creating the eye itself.

"Hey, they're not symmetrical anymore," Russell noted. "They're heading more toward the left side."

"So are the ones that make up this eye," Keith reported.

Russell cut through the face, following the lines. There, behind an eye they found the seed.

"This is it!" Russell carefully excavated the little thing from the corpse, keeping most of the ropes attached. "This is the bastard!"

It didn't look like much.

"Wait, so all this white stuff comes out of that little guy?" Keith struggled to believe it. He could see all the ropes branching out every which way from just under its many legs, but he couldn't imagine how they could fit back inside.

"Alien," Russell mumbled, peering closely at what they thought of as its back. "No eyes. No nothing that I can see other than this armour and these appendage things. Did you know that some ducks have a dick as long as their body?"

"I didn't, and I didn't need to know that either."

"It's true. When it's time to get down to business, it shoots out of them so fast, you need a slow-mo camera to see it. I bet these guys are like a hyper-extreme version of that. When they need a big body, *pow*, out these white things come."

Keith could see it happening, he just couldn't understand *how*. All he could do was remind himself that it was alien. He was likely never going to learn the how of it.

"Keith?" Mandy called over to him. "Your dad wants you."

The partly-dissected dirt devil was forgotten in an instant. Keith hurried over to the other canoe, bending over awkwardly to wash his hands along the way. The clear stuff from the dirt devil came off incredibly easily, practically dissolving as soon as it got wet.

"Dad?" Keith was shocked to stillness when he looked down over the side of the canoe. His father was very pale.

"Keith, hey." Dad reached up a weak and trembling arm. Keith grabbed his hand more to keep it from falling back down on Dad's face, than to hold it.

"You look . . ."

"Terrible, I know."

I was going to say like you're dying. "What happened, Dad?"

"I got greedy. There are some stores up that way. Thought I could get some supplies, but then the rain stopped, and a dirt devil came after me. I got to the water, but swam past a boat. Too close. It managed to jump onto it. It actually reached into the water trying to get me. Well, it did. Sank itself, but it got me." His voice trailed off into a whisper.

"Okay, Dad. You need to sleep."

"That's what Aisling keeps telling me."

"You should listen to her. She's smart."

"She is. She'll get you out of this."

"You, too. You're coming with us."

"Of course. I just . . ." His eyes drifted shut. They looked worse that way. When his hand went slack, Keith placed his own on his father's chest, making sure the man was still breathing. He was.

"What's wrong with him?" Keith demanded of Mandy, Aisling, and Frankie.

"I'm not a doctor," Mandy scowled.

"We think it's blood loss," Aisling shrugged.

"Will he be okay?" Keith's eyes darted down to Dad's legs. Someone had covered them with a blanket so that he couldn't see what they had done. His hands twitched to pull it back, but he resisted. Better if he didn't know.

"Dude, we did what we could," Frankie answered. "But like Mandy said, none of us are doctors. We're pretty sure we stopped the bleeding though."

"He just needs rest," Mandy insisted, although her confidence felt false.

"A canoe is not a place to rest. We need to reach the island."

"And how do you propose we do that, Keith? Huh?" Aisling scoffed. "Doesn't look like it's going to rain again today." The sun had emerged. The rain clouds were moving away, and leaving blue skies in their wake.

"We'll wait," Mandy shrugged. "We always wait."

"We can't wait this time!" Keith didn't know why they couldn't understand. "My dad can't wait!"

"Okay, then you find a way to get us out of here without the rain." Aisling flipped her hair at him as she walked away.

Keith wanted to be the one to find a way to get them moving again, but all he did was angrily stomp around on the rock. There was no way forward without leaving the water.

"I got it," Russell said after about an hour. Earlier, he had dumped the dirt devil corpse into the water and let it wash away. "How much rope do we have?"

Turned out to be a lot. They had grabbed a bunch during their shore raids.

"Okay, this should be plenty." Russell had tied several into one long rope.

"What's the plan?" Aisling asked.

"Someone is still going to have to leave the water, unfortunately. I'm thinking they'll run around the bridge and get back into the water as soon as its safe. If they have these safety lines crossing the river down here, then they *must* have one up there as well. Using that to secure themselves in place, they let the rope float down the river to here. Tying the line around our waists, we can be pulled up, one by one."

"What about the canoes? What about my *dad*?" Keith knew he didn't need to remind his friend that way, but he was compelled to.

"One of us will stay down here. When the rope comes back, they'll tie up the canoes, one at a time. With everyone else up there, we should be strong enough to haul the canoes up."

"Up the waterfall?" Tully raised an eyebrow.

"Yes, up the waterfall. Look at it, it's not sheer. The rock is angled. There might be some scraping, and our stuff will get wet, but I think we can do it."

"Let's tie everything down. We don't want to lose anything if the canoe tips." Mandy instantly set to work.

"I'll carry the rope over to the other side," Keith volunteered.

"Not a chance." Aisling took the rope from Russell. "No offence, but you're all pretty weeny in the muscle department. I'm the strongest of us, so I'll go first." She allowed no room for objections, just started moving through the water toward the safety line, which she could use to pull herself to shore.

"I'll stay here then, and tie up the canoes," Keith made another offer.

"I should do that," Carol spoke up. "I'm lighter than all of you, other than Chris and Mike. I should go last. That way, I can ride in the canoe with Mr. Benchley and make sure he's okay, without adding too much weight." No matter how many times Dad told her she could call him Doug, she stuck with Mr. Benchley.

By the time Keith thought to help organize the supply canoes, Mandy, Tully, and Frankie, with some help from the kids, had already gotten it done. Aisling had reached the shore—Super Soaker in hand, rope slung across her body like a bandolier—and was already climbing out, ready to go. They were going to try Russell's plan without a second thought. And Keith fumed, having done nothing to help his father.

57:
Now

THE MARINA HAD a boat launch, and Keith found he could safely anchor near it without being too close to land. Then he began his wait.

Next to the water were a boat mechanic's shop and some gas pumps. Keith planned to ignore those, as well as the scattering of craft moored at the many docks. Might one of those boats be better than his kayak and raft combination? Maybe, but he wasn't about to switch. He knew this kayak. It was *his*, and he wasn't about to give it up.

Past the boat mechanic shop was the place Keith really wanted to check out: the general store. It was a fairly large-looking place, and he knew he'd be able to find some things he wanted. He couldn't say for certain from where he sat, but it didn't appear damaged, which was a good indicator that it hadn't been looted. It was possible that the door was unlocked, and so there wouldn't be any damage, but Keith doubted it. Since all of this had kicked off in the middle of the night, anywhere that wasn't open twenty-four hours remained locked until someone broke a window. Keith could see the exact window he intended to break. There was a grouping of nine panes in the upper half of the door, and he was going to punch a hole through the one nearest the lock. Not literally punch a hole, his hammer was going to do the breaking. He'd also bring his pry bar up there in case there was some unforeseen difficulty in getting the door open. Or maybe he should bring his hatchet? He had time to think about it.

Waiting for the rain was boring, but restful. Most of the time was passed lying in the shade of his tarp to protect him from the sun. When it was early morning or late in the afternoon, when the sun was weaker, he'd emerge to get a bit of exercise and feel like he actually did something. He used one of his towels like a sponge, getting all the water out of the kayak. There was a cautionary sticker stuck to the inside that he read and reread while doing it. The first warning was to never paddle alone: far too late for that. He practised fishing with the broken rod, even though he couldn't keep anything he caught. He even went swimming a few times, just to swim. With his mask and flippers on—his toe feeling well enough to wear them—he studied the bottom of the lake, finding little bits of humanity that had fallen from boats and docks, that were then left down there to decay. Some of it he dove down for, but none of it proved useful. The pocketknife was rusted completely shut, the sunglasses were missing a lens, and what use was there for the money in the wallet? Also, who lost their wallet and didn't go diving for it themselves? Maybe they had shown up last year. Three vehicles with empty boat trailers clustered together, just out of the way of the boat ramp. Not official parking spots, so at least three people had managed to get their boats, get them here, and then get them into the water. Impressive. A fourth trailer holding an old ski boat was ready to back down, but it was never going to get any closer to the water than where it was. The front end of the truck it was hooked up to was a ruin.

The rain didn't want to come. It was glorious weather for someone living in the past. For Keith, it was a nightmare. He was just so bored. Sometimes he slept through part of the day, but that only made it more difficult to sleep at night. On shore, at the bottom of the stairs to the general store, there was a little free library. Keith could see books through the glass in its little door, donations from people who needed more shelf space, or perhaps didn't like what they had read. Keith wished he had one in his hands, any one. He'd even settle for reading a cookbook at this point. But the little library was at least twenty feet from the edge of the water, across loose gravel and dirt, and Keith wasn't about to risk it. Still, he felt like the box was taunting him.

When the rain finally came, it was at night. Keith slept lightly, and was woken by the soft patter on the tarp. In a fumbling hurry, he pulled on his headlamp, shoes, gloves, and poncho. Tools in hand, he shot out of his tent and splashed into the water to begin wading up the boat ramp. The rain had picked up force during that short time. Keith prayed it lasted long enough, but planned to retreat the *moment* it stopped. He could always wait longer for more rain.

He grabbed a novel at random on his way past the little library, just in case that scenario came about.

The door was locked, sending a small thrill through Keith. He smashed out the pane just like he'd imagined doing a hundred times while waiting, making sure to clear the whole frame. He then reached in and fumbled around until he found the latch for the deadbolt. The door still didn't open, but only because there was a button lock in the handle. As he gained entry, Keith was grateful that he hadn't needed to use either the hatchet or the pry bar. He had ended up bringing both, just in case. Stripping off his poncho, he placed it on the ground, wrapping it around his tools and the book. It was the only reason he'd brought it, knowing he'd be soaked no matter what from wading through the water.

Keith clicked on his headlamp and shone it around the store, feeling like a kid in a candy shop. Literally, there was a shelf full of candy off to one side. His first stop, however, was behind the register counter. From there, he grabbed a bundle of shopping bags, intending to fill as many as he could.

"Time to shop," he whispered to himself.

He raided the side of the store filled with food first. Sidebottom had given him a lot, but more was always better. It wasn't a robust collection, but it was mostly shelf stable, and had survived being here since last year. Every time Keith filled a bag—including one of candy—he placed it by the door. He checked on the rain at the same time.

The cooler of ice cream was a vile, melted mess, and most of the things in the stand up fridges and freezers were ripe with rot, but not everything. Keith grabbed cases of water and bottles of Gatorade, beaming about the fact that he wouldn't have to drink raw lake water for a while.

Past the food were cleaning products. Keith took some paper towels and an all-purpose cleaner just in case some bird eventually shit on his stuff. There was soap and shampoo, and a full tube of toothpaste to replace his partial one. Better yet, was the new toothbrush to finally go with his toothpaste.

The other side of the store held items for people to have fun with on the lake. He bypassed the water skis and towable tubes and inflatable pool toys. At the sand toys he paused, and then selected the largest bucket, a bright yellow one.

He almost missed the tents. There were a bunch of boxes containing different types of hammocks, and Keith almost mistook the tents for more hammocks. There were two kinds of tents. One was small, just large enough for Keith to lie down in, and tall enough to sit up in. That one would definitely fit on the raft. The other was larger, with a square base, and enough height that he might be able to stand up in the middle. That base might have been too large for the raft though. Keith grabbed one of each, figuring he could experiment.

A collapsible emergency paddle, a second waterproof bag, a new ski rope, a few packets of short boat rope, a loaded tackle box, and a complete fishing rod got piled next to the door. He finally located what he wanted most: a portable propane stove. He'd have to be careful, there were only three little tanks he could take to go with it, but now he'd have the ability to cook any fish he caught. It'd be a challenge without a frying pan, but he thought he could make the big pot work.

There were no Super Soakers, but a vast collection of small squirt guns were moved to the door, so that Keith could try them out and select the best of them. He began to worry about space, and so returned to the inflatable toys. He selected a towable tube, one of the smaller ones, and picked up a hand pump to go along with it. The final items he pilfered from the back of the store were some clothing: pajama pants, sweatshirt, and a baseball hat he liked better than the floppy one he'd found. Strangely there were no swimsuits. At the last minute, he remembered to locate the sunscreen, and then spotted some laminated maps of the lake just before he headed out the door. Finally, he would know where he was and could plan where he wanted to go next.

It was still raining, so Keith hustled his goods down the stairs. He piled up his bags just underneath them, planning to move everything in stages. His legs were soon aching from repeatedly running up and down. At least the second section was easier, when he started bringing his stuff from under the stairs to the dock beside the boat launch. He didn't make very many trips before the rain petered off.

Keith snatched up the tents and ran into the lake, abandoning everything else for the time being. He tossed the heavy, awkward boxes into the kayak, and then climbed back up onto the raft and crawled into his tarp tent. As he lay down, the whole excursion felt like a dream. It had gone so well.

He thought for sure something terrible must happen in the morning.

58:
THEN

"IF I START screaming, it means I'm dying."

Those were the last words Aisling had shouted to them from shore before running off. All they could do now was wait. Keith kept sloshing back and forth through the water. At one end of his route, he stood as close to the bridge as the flat rock would allow, where he could peer up through the opening underneath it. At the other end, his father slept in the canoe, where Keith was useless, only able to look in on him. Pacing and staring and waiting. Keith was helpless and he hated it.

"She'll make it," Mandy told herself.

"What if we can't hear her scream over the sound of the rapids?" Mike asked her.

"She'll make it," Mandy repeated directly to him, with a biting tone.

Keith tried to think of something they could do if she didn't. Aisling had the majority of the rope with her, and if they lost her, they lost it as well. The rest of the rope was being used to tie down their supplies, but even if they used all of that, they might not be able to make another rope long enough. A voice in the back of Keith's head wanted to ask aloud what the back-up plan was, but he kept squashing it. He wasn't going to ask. Not just to keep from upsetting Mandy, but because he didn't want to rely on anyone else to come up with anything.

He didn't want Russell always being the hero.

"Look! Look!" Chris shouted, jumping up and down. "The rope! She made it!"

The colourful line came streaming down the white water,

following a similar route to Dad's unfortunate path. Tully was ready with a paddle, reaching out and hooking the line to bring it over to them. There was a moment when they all feared the whole line would come washing down, but it eventually stopped.

"Mandy, you should go first," Russell took charge. "I think you have the best strength to weight ratio."

"Okay." She picked up the slack and wrapped it around her body. "How do I let Aisling know I'm ready?"

"Tug on the line," Frankie said before Keith could. "We'll make that our signal once you're up there. Five rapid tugs means it's time to pull."

"Why five?" Keith wondered.

"Because we might pull on the line while tying up the canoes, so we should pick a number that can't happen accidentally. Five seemed good."

"Five it is." Mandy pulled rapidly on the rope, and everyone hoped that Aisling understood. She did. "*Whoop!*" Mandy was swiftly pulled off the edge of the rock and into the rushing water.

"That looks hard," Mike said nervously as they watched.

Mandy clung to the rope as the water pushed and shoved her about. She spun onto her back and then her front again, twirling this way and that. Several times she got a face full of water, or got dunked completely for several frightful seconds.

"You'll be okay," Tully comforted Mike. "It'll actually be easier for you and Chris, since you've got your lifejackets on."

"We should have kept all the lifejackets we found in the canoes," Keith muttered as he watched Mandy slip backward a bit. Aisling must have lost her hold, but she had it again, and resumed pulling.

"Yeah, we should have," Tully agreed.

Dad had found a pair that fit the boys during one of their raids, but everyone else was so confident in their ability to swim, that they got rid of the others, feeling they were a useless waste of space. Now the joke was on them.

"Keith, you should go next," Russell suggested.

"Fine."

Mandy was out of sight, so Keith went to check on Dad again. He looked the same as before, which was to say awful.

"We're going to get you to your island, Dad," Keith promised. "Just hold on, and we'll get you there."

"Rope's back!" Frankie called out.

Keith prepared himself the same way Mandy had, by wrapping the slack around his chest. He wished Mandy could give him some advice about how this would go. There was nothing for it but to do it, so he gave the rope five sharp tugs, and then jumped into the deeper water so that he wouldn't be yanked off his feet like Mandy had been.

Drowning, that's what it was like. Keith coughed and spluttered, never knowing when his face was going to be in the air, and when it was going to be underwater. He figured that this was what it was like to be water boarded. No wonder people were so against it. Keith would definitely say anything to make this stop.

The rocks made it even worse. Whenever the water pushed him down, he was dragged along the stone. It had been worn smooth by the years of rushing water, but he still got scraped up. At one point, while he was twisting and turning, he got his feet under him. He hadn't realized he'd flipped completely backward until the pulling of the rope yanked him upright. Good, clear air! Keith took a mighty breath that filled him with hope. He thought he might be able to walk up the rock. But as soon as he raised a foot, his other leg got kicked out from beneath him, and he plunged back into the water. He had also seen just how far he had to go and despaired.

It was impossible to tell how long it lasted. Forever, was what it felt like. The rope tugged in fits and starts, sometimes taking long enough between the pulls to make Keith believe he was being left to die. He finally found a technique that sort of worked. He kept his face upward, and clung to the rope over his shoulder. With his chin tucked, his shoulders took the brunt of the water, often leaving an air gap for him. His legs he splayed out, trying to use them like rudders to keep from rolling one way or the other, sometimes kicking off the rock bottom to do so. By the time he got good at it, he didn't need to do it anymore.

"Keith! Start swimming!" Aisling shouted at him.

Keith rolled over onto his stomach and began kicking and pulling with long sweeps of his arms. There was still a strong current he had to fight, but the surface of the water was a lot calmer. The pulling of the rope hurt less, and his head didn't go back under.

"Here! Grab my hand!" Mandy reached for him over the side

of an aluminum fishing boat. It was secured broadside, both front and back, to the safety line running across the river. Getting it there and tying it up must have been what had taken Aisling so long, but it was a great idea, giving them a stationary point to pull from.

Climbing into the boat was a challenge, but less so than being dragged up the falls had been. Mandy helped him up while Aisling counterbalanced the boat to keep it from flipping.

"How . . . the hell . . . are we . . . going to keep . . . the canoes from flipping?" Keith panted.

"Not sure." Mandy looked as bruised and battered as he felt. "I have a feeling we're going to need to send someone back down there to sit in them for balance."

"Back down? That?"

"I know."

"It's the best plan we got." Aisling also panted. Sweat poured off her in rivulets, and she wore red welts on her shins and arms. He didn't know why, she hadn't had to come up the falls.

"We should send the rope back down." Keith realized he was still wrapped up in it and began untangling himself.

"Can I catch my breath first? Christ," Aisling growled. "You're not exactly light, you know."

"This boat's too small," Mandy frowned at it. "Aisling, we should turn it. If we point the nose toward the bridge, we'll be able to line up."

"Damn, you're right. Come on, let's move it."

"What are we doing?" Keith got the rope off himself and started to send one end down the river. It was tied to the far side of the middle of the fishing boat so he could have just tossed it in the water, but he wanted to make sure it went down without any knots.

"To pull together, we need to stand one behind the other," Mandy briefly explained while she untied the front of the boat. Aisling leaned over the back, pulling the untied corner up against the safety line to secure it there.

"This is less stable," Aisling commented when she'd finished, the boat wiggling in place from the rush of water.

"It'll have to do."

"The rope's almost played out," Keith told them.

Aisling groaned. "Seriously? You couldn't give us a second to take a break?"

"My dad's dying!" Keith snapped.

Aisling didn't have a response for that. No response existed.

"Well . . . next time, give us a minute to move this end of the rope, okay?" Mandy said. "It would be better tied to the back than the side now."

"We have no time to prepare you, Keith, so you'll be in the middle. Mandy, you're up front again." Aisling took charge, barking orders. "Have they tugged on it yet?"

"Not yet," Mandy reported.

"Hopefully we can grab back some slack. This idiot gave them the whole line."

They were able to get a bit of slack, but not much. The first few pulls, Mandy had to do alone. She braced her feet on the front bench and hauled. Once there was enough extra rope, Keith grabbed on.

"We pull together!" Mandy needlessly shouted. "One, two, pull! One, two, pull!"

Keith leaned back on the rope when she did. He wouldn't trade places with whoever was on the other end of the line for anything, but this job had its own painful challenges. Gripping the slick line with his bare hands was the worst of them, but he also learned why Aisling had bruised legs when his footing slipped, and his shins bashed into the middle seat. Behind him, Aisling looped the rope around her waist once she had the slack, leaning her whole body back against it every time they pulled. She then acted as an anchor and gathered the slack whenever Keith and Mandy reset their hands. She was acting like a belayer.

"Did you have Mr. Kass for gym, too?" Keith asked quickly between hauls.

"What?" Aisling snapped.

"Mr. Kass. For gym. He take you rock climbing?"

"No. Mrs. Ryan did."

"Shut up and haul!" Mandy snapped. "We have to keep time! One, two, pull! One, two, pull!"

Keith was soon out of breath, but Mandy kept up the rhythm. One of their friends was at the end of that line. They were going through a hell that Keith had so recently left, and it was up to the three of them to get their friend out of it as quickly as possible.

"Frankie!" Mandy shouted as he emerged from the rushing water. "Swim, Frankie!"

For a moment, Keith thought the guy was dead, but then he started flailing his way toward the fishing boat. They still had to pull on the line, but it was easier now that Frankie was helping.

"Keith, untie the rope from the side of the boat," Aisling ordered. "We're going to retie it back here so that when we start, we can all grip it."

The boat wobbled back and forth as Mandy helped Frankie scramble into it. He fell to the floor with a bang of the aluminum and sat there gasping like a caught fish.

"Keith, since you've been rock climbing, I want you at the back," Aisling told him next. "If I had known you already know how to belay, I would have stuck you back there last time." She sounded extremely bitter.

They took a bit more time to rest up, despite Keith's urgency to get this done. Mandy had taken charge of the end of the rope, and she wasn't going to let it back down until she thought everyone was ready, Frankie included.

It was crowded with the four of them in the boat, but hauling was easier for everyone. Aisling had taken over the front position, and Keith worked as the anchor. Frankie started singing some dumb song, but it kept them in time, and was better than Mandy shouting at them.

Tully emerged from the water next. When she got into the boat, she leaned over the side and vomited lake water.

"At least it was in my stomach and not my lungs," she commented.

The boat could barely fit the five of them in a line, and every move they made rocked it precariously back and forth. Together, they hauled Russell up the falls.

"I made a mistake," he groaned. "This was a terrible idea."

"No way to change plans now," Aisling laughed, her eyes shining as much as her sweaty skin. "Mandy, we can't all pull in a line anymore, there's too many of us. You take a break and hang off the back of the boat."

"You've been pulling the longest, you should be the one to take a break," Mandy fired back.

"Nah, I can go longer. Although maybe Frankie should take over the front for a little while."

"I can do that."

They banged around in the aluminum some more as they changed places. Mandy went over the side instead of the back. She held on to one of the bumpers there, the current sweeping her legs toward the bridge, but she was able to help stabilize them a little.

Mike was the first of the kids to come up. He seemed to be fine. His light weight allowed them to pull him much faster, and his lifejacket did its job, keeping his head above the surface and holding him away from the rocks. He took hold of a bumper on the opposite side from Mandy.

Once Chris was up and holding on to the side of the boat, he started taking off his lifejacket.

"Chris! Put that back on!" Tully yelled at him.

"But Carol wants it. We found out it fits her." His brows pinched, not sure which of the teenagers he should be listening to.

"Send it down," Russell agreed. "Mandy? Can you hold on to Chris, just in case?"

"Sure, but doesn't anyone else want to take a break?"

No one did, even though Mandy was eager to help with the pulling again.

Mike remained where he was, but Chris was manhandled, passed around the sides of the boat until he was next to Mandy, where she could keep an eye on him. His lifejacket was tied to the end of the line and sent back down over the falls.

The canoe was easier to pull in some regards, and more difficult to pull in others. It floated, so less water pulled against it, but because it floated, it was more likely to swing from one side to the other.

"Carol?" Frankie huffed, the sudden break in his song throwing everyone temporarily off rhythm.

"Carol!" Keith leaned to one side and shouted as she rose into view. In the middle of the canoe, she balanced on the edges with her hands and feet like some deranged spider protecting the goods within. They heaved her all the way up to the fishing boat. "Carol, my dad," Keith gasped, not knowing how to properly phrase the question burning inside him.

"He's fine," Carol said. "I didn't think the canoes were going to be able to stay upright without anyone helping them balance. I'm going back down for the next one."

"Are you crazy?" Tully coughed in surprise. "You're going *down* the falls?"

"I have a lifejacket, and the rope will be tied to me." She had already untied the line from the canoe and was securing it to the lifejacket. "Someone has to do it and I'm the best one for the job." She was so confident, so sure. Quiet Carol, taking on a dangerous task like it was nothing. The courage of Mrs. Frisby for sure.

Lowering her was a bit of a challenge. They didn't want her going too fast if she hit rocks, but slowing her when the rope wanted to rip through their hands was painful. With the line running around his hips, Keith was in the best position to control her speed, so the others ended up leaving it to him. Some of them took the canoe and paddled it out to where an abandoned ski boat was anchored, and used some of the ropes there to tie it up—foolishly they hadn't sent up the canoe with their own anchor first. The kids remained on the boat with Tully, after Mandy convinced her to let her take her place. Those who swam back grabbed the safety line across the water and pulled themselves over to the aluminum boat.

Everyone worried about what condition Carol would be in when she returned, but she was fine. Sodden, but she didn't complain once about any injuries, or about nearly drowning. Keith didn't care whether she was hiding her hurts, he just wanted to know that his dad was still breathing.

Again, Carol was lowered while the canoe was paddled over to the anchored boat. The third came up just as easily as the previous two. Keith was anxious after Carol went down again. The final canoe was to be the one his dad was lying in. An insidious voice inside him whispered that they had gotten lucky bringing up the other boats, that they had wasted their luck on the supplies, and now his dad was going to pay the price for it. Carol's theory made sense, about saving that canoe for last so that she had the most practice, but at the same time, she and everyone else would be the most tired.

Carol rose up in spider pose once more. Her face was pointed down this time, monitoring Dad, but otherwise she appeared the exact same.

"He's fine!" Carol called to Keith once the canoe was on steady water. "Even woke up!"

Keith had to wait for the canoe to be pulled up alongside to see for himself. Dad was clearly still exhausted, but he had enough energy to tell everyone he was proud of them.

They were all eager to get underway. The canoes were brought together and paddlers assigned. Chris would have to take over Dad's empty seat, but he seemed fine with that. He said if he got tired, he and Mike could trade off for a bit.

Keith always sat in the back of Dad's canoe. His father had been propped up a little so that he could see over the sides of the boat. With his head near Keith, he could easily speak to him when he needed to. He guided their little flotilla with weak gestures, and words spoken through gritted teeth. His legs were in constant pain. They only had some over-the-counter stuff to help him with it, and even taking more than the recommended dosage removed only a bit of the bite. Dad tried not to let Keith know how much pain he was in, but failed miserably at it. Keith knew, but pretended to be blind to it for his dad's sake.

The sun sank, and they had to anchor. Keith wanted to travel through the night, but everyone else outvoted him. They believed that they would only end up getting lost in the dark, and wasting more time than they could gain. Sleeping was more difficult than usual, having lost some space to Dad's sickbed, not to mention all the body aches.

The next morning was beautiful. The lake was calm, a pristine sheet of glass. Dad was already awake, so Keith didn't have to worry about disturbing him as he settled into his seat.

"A perfect morning," Dad told him. He looked worse than he had at sunset. "I'm glad I get to share it with you."

"We'll share a lot more perfect mornings, Dad."

"Hmm, yeah. Lots more."

Everyone ate quickly that morning. They were all excited to get going, knowing that they could reach the island today, provided they didn't get lost. Their canoes cut V shapes in the water as they headed out, the ripples travelling far, like they'd last forever.

Reaching a bay, they found the island. It might not have been the actual island, but the moment they saw it, everyone decided that it was. The island they'd found already had people on it, people who waved excitedly when they spotted the canoes, joyful at encountering more life that had managed to survive.

"Dad, look, we made it! There are other people here! It's safe! Dad! . . . Dad?"

But Dad was gone.

59:
NOW

KEITH WOKE UP to overcast skies, a raft that was still floating, and supplies awaiting him. He didn't trust it. When he emerged from his dreams, he thought for sure that last night's raid hadn't actually happened, yet there was the booty. The now-soggy tent boxes still stuck out of the kayak, and some grocery bags sat on the dock where he'd be able to reach them without getting out of the water.

Breakfast was eaten with a close eye kept on the shore. The gravel near the stairs in particular. Keith thought for sure that a dirt devil was going to emerge, that it was going to tear up everything he had left over there. Then it would bound over to the dock, and ruin what was in those bags as well. Afterward, it would turn its attention to Keith, and maybe it would think that the raft looked like an island it could reach with one powerful jump. And it would reach it. Keith wouldn't die, not right then, but he'd be cut up badly enough that he'd bleed to death in the water, slowly and painfully.

But there were no signs of any dirt devils by the time he finished eating, so he decided he might as well get to work.

He took the tent boxes out of the kayak and placed them on the raft. There was rainwater in his boat from the night before, so he bailed it out as best he could, using a towel for a sponge again. Looking over to the boat mechanic's shop, Keith wondered if there could be a giant sponge somewhere in there that he could use in the future. Provided he had a future.

Everything from inside his makeshift tent was placed in the kayak. The wet tarp he draped over top. Once the raft's built-in chair backs and table were lowered, Keith returned his attentions to the tent boxes.

The big one was too big. Keith had to fight the thing to get its ground sheet unfurled across the raft, and it turned out that he was right when he thought it wouldn't fit. There was no way he was going to get that thing back into its box, so he dragged it through the water to the launch dock and threw it on the end. The part of him that still thought of the world as not being full of dirt devils told him that he was littering. He told that part to shut up.

The small tent did fit. He fussed about where to place it, only able to pin down one corner with the rear raft anchor. Since he had grabbed a new ski rope, and could easily get more if he wanted to, he used the old ski rope and tow rope to secure the tent. He bound all the corners together with the ropes wrapping underneath the raft. Every time he dove under, he half expected to pop up to scissor-claws in his face. A bigger problem was catching his breath between dives. The tent had a lot of corners to pin down. It wasn't just a rectangle, but had a sort of hood that extended off the front, over the door, creating a little sheltered cove at the entrance. That, combined with the anchor points in the middle of its long edges, had Keith diving and tying so much, he almost ended up needing a third rope.

Stripped naked and dried off with his second towel, Keith climbed into the tent to try it out. The ceiling was low, but it was definitely higher than his makeshift tarp-roof, and he could sit up inside. He filled most of it when he lay down with his head near one end, but there was still space down past his feet where he could store a few supplies. The floor remained as hard as ever.

Keith had a growing list in his head. He wanted to find either a big sponge, or maybe a whole pile of those little scrubbing sponges he'd seen in the store, as well as pilfer another rope, and now he also planned to return to the inflatables section for one of those pseudo-air mattresses. It wouldn't be as good as a proper air mattress meant for sleeping instead of floating, but it would do.

After having some lunch, Keith donned his damp swimsuit again. He moved everything back over from the kayak, but returned the tarp to its position over the opening, so that if it rained, he wouldn't need to bail again. He retrieved the bags from the dock and started to sort them. The heaviest was entirely

Gatorade, and another was stuffed with candy. He tried some of the candy. Anything that had been exposed to the air was vile, but the packaged stuff still seemed to be good. He tossed the bad candy into the water, figuring the fish might like some of it, and if not, it would just eventually dissolve.

Litter bug.

By the time he had brought everything over, he had more food than his dry bag could hold, so Keith decided to split it up. He'd keep a loaded dry bag in the kayak for emergencies, but store the rest on the raft. Decision made, he then had to wait. He needed the rain to come back to get everything else.

Keith spent a further four days outside the marina. It would have been only two, but after he'd gotten everything to his raft, he realized he hadn't grabbed any matches or lighters for the little grill, and the built-in starter wasn't very reliable. Most of his time waiting for rain involved him inflating the towing tube. Using the hand pump was exhausting, so he needed to take frequent breaks. Still, it gave him a lot more space to store things once he'd tied it to the back of the raft. Mostly it held his overflow of food and drinks, and he draped the paint tarp over it to reduce the amount of water that would get in there during storms.

With all the added weight, it was harder to paddle than it had been before, but Keith didn't mind. He could go slower and pause whenever he wanted, without having to worry too much. With his wealth of food and over a month of summer still remaining, he wasn't in so much of a rush to find a new winter house. Part of him believed that he wouldn't find one at all—he didn't deserve to find one. It was a disparaging thought, but Keith accepted it, and began mental preparations for what he would do if he had to spend the winter alone. His life was worth living, just maybe not around other people. He imagined he'd go crazy like Sidebottom, but so long as he didn't threaten travellers passing through, he figured he'd be doing okay. The dark hole in his mind could become a home if he let it.

Now that he had a map, he had a plotted course. There was no particular destination in mind for any particular reason, but he followed the randomly chosen route anyway. It took a few days to really get the rhythm of paddling with such a load, and he had to reorganize some of his supplies due to a weight imbalance.

Sleeping, however, was vastly improved with the air mat, and the fact that he could change out of his swim trunks. It was still too hot for the sweater, but it made a decent pillow when wrapped around the life jacket.

One afternoon, Keith found himself paddling into a mini forest of tall grasses. It wasn't labelled on the map, but the map indicated that there was more lake on the far side, and so he should be able to push through.

The kayak, raft, and tube all hissed as they slid through and over the grasses. Every stroke of his paddle was a struggle. Normally it was only like this when he got started after a stop and had to rebuild his momentum. The grass ate every ounce of momentum, forcing him to dig in for every inch.

Mosquitoes buzzed around his head. Small flies, some possibly the biting kind, kept landing on the nose of his kayak. Strange beetles were also drawn to the brightly coloured craft invading their home. There were spiders here, their webs delicately strung up between blades of grass. Keith felt like he spent as much time defensively swinging his paddle around him as he did paddling.

Something made a significant plop in the water nearby and Keith startled. Could've been a turtle, or muskrat, or even just a fish jumping, but it also could've been a snake. There were rattlers in these parts, and even though they could get big enough for a dirt devil to consider snatching, they started off small enough to be ignored. Besides, snakes were wily, able to hide in the small cracks of rocks. And they were capable of swimming.

"This was a mistake," Keith told himself as he slapped another mosquito.

He raised himself up in the kayak to look over his flotilla, debating going back. There was a swatch of flattened grass behind him, but even farther it was already standing back up. He couldn't see where he had entered, so he couldn't see how far it would be to return. Redirecting his gaze forward, he tried to spy how far he had to go, but even kneeling wasn't enough to see over the top. He could stand, but decided against it. He needed to commit to the direction he had chosen. Besides, he wasn't sure he could actually get his floating train to turn around.

A pair of ducks exploded up out of the grass, making Keith scream. Yes, this was definitely a mistake.

Dinner time came and went, and the sun was getting low. Keith kept going. The bugs got worse, but there was no way he was going to camp out here in this hellish place. If he did, he'd wake up to all his stuff draped in webs, and he was certain there'd be a big snake just lying in wait for him outside his tent.

He pulled on his poncho, tucking the hood under his hat so at least the back of his neck was safe.

The sun left him, but the moon provided enough light to see by. Keith was starting to think he was somehow going in circles. His arms quivered and ached, every inch forward a battle. He seriously contemplated disconnecting the tube.

And then, just like that, he was free. The grass suddenly fell away, and Keith was out in open water. He wanted to cheer, but his lungs protested. Instead, he paddled out, farther away from that green nightmare, where the bugs might leave him alone. When he finally stopped, he splashed water over the nose, sides, and back of his boat to get rid of the hitchhikers, and then threw the tarp over it. He also washed away the bugs from the raft and tent, but was too tired to do the same for the tube. He was too tired to even bother with dinner, and instead, zipped himself away in his tent as soon as the anchor had taken hold.

He slept and dreamed of being in a green maze stalked by a dirt devil.

60:
THEN

"**M**Y PARENTS USEd to dance in the kitchen." The words hurt to say. The past tense, *used to*, were daggers. Worse was the imagery that those words summoned. Mom and Dad, happy and alive, dancing poorly to rock music in the kitchen that was now as ruined by dirt devils as they were. Whenever Keith had found them dancing, he'd felt embarrassed, and knowing that only made the memory ache more.

"Thank you for sharing that, Keith. Frankie, would you like to share next?"

Keith stood up, knocking over the plastic lawn chair he'd been sitting in, and stormed off. He couldn't stand this shit. All of them sitting in a circle "honouring" their loved ones? No. Keith had shared, three times a week, just like Jan wanted them to. He understood that Jan thought it would help them with their collective grief, that it would promote healing, but it wasn't working. It was doing the opposite. Every time Keith had to share a memory of his parents, or of other family members and friends he didn't know the fate of, it just ripped the wounds open all over again. It was picking at a scab before it was ready to come off, and Keith just kept bleeding.

"Keith, are you all right?" Mr. Steel asked, his hair as grey as his name. This was his island, and as such, he got to exclude himself from the sharing circle whenever he wanted.

"I'm fine," Keith snapped, obviously not.

"Why don't you come over here and help me then."

When Keith and the others had joined the island community, the population went up to twenty, nearly doubling the number of residents they had found there. Space inside the solo cottage was always at a premium, forcing most people out of doors. Keith had seen why his dad wanted to come to this place. Solar panels on the roof collected enough energy to run the water system, a fridge, a freezer, and a hot plate. Mr. Steel worried all the time about the battery hooked up to the solar panels, and whether they would be able to keep everything running through the winter, when there was less sunlight. Already they had worked out a method for getting safely up onto the roof in order to clean the panels, and brush off future snowfall.

"What are you doing?" Keith asked.

"Working on the garden."

"I thought all the seeds we have were already planted?" This was also not the garden where the vegetables were growing.

"And you're right. But I'm hoping we'll find some more seeds before spring, and then we'll need a bigger plot, won't we? Might as well do it now so that we're ready."

The current garden was woefully small. Not a lot of people had thought long-term and taken seeds when they had raided stores on their way here, and those that had, lost most of them along the way. Keith didn't think long-term was worth thinking about. No one knew what was going to happen when winter came and the water froze. Would the dirt devils cross over to them?

"What do you need me to do?" Keith asked.

"Stab the ground, mostly. We need to turn all this over, get rid of the grass, remove rocks. Make it good planting soil."

It was harder work than Mr. Steel had made it sound, but Keith went at it with a will. It was better than remembering.

"Hey, Keith!" Russell called over to him after he'd worked up a sweat. "We're going fishing, want to come?"

"No!" Keith called back. "I'm just going to stay here and help Mr. Steel!"

"You sure?"

"Yeah!"

Russell didn't push any harder than that. He never did anymore. Keith was starting to get the impression that his friend didn't really want to spend time with him.

"Fishing would be easier work than this," Mr. Steel commented.

"I'm fine," Keith grunted.

That's what life on the island was like. Bursts of hard work, between too much time to think.

Everyone had a place to sleep indoors, either a bed or a couch or an air mattress, but at night there was always someone crying. And if the tears were quiet, then there was the snoring. Some people had retreated to tents outside, but as the temperature dropped, they were being forced back in. Keith hated it here, but there was nowhere else to go. At least these people were, for the most part, smart and proactive. They intended to survive, no matter what winter brought them. Food had already been stuffed into every cupboard and onto every shelf, and even piled in the corners. So much that they thought they could make it to spring, but after that, they'd have to start surviving on what they could produce. This didn't stop them from continuing to rob nearby cottages every time it rained, especially for clothing.

Autumn arrived, cold and brightly dressed. Thanksgiving was barely observed. There was a definite air of tension among everyone on the island. Would the snow be as effective as the rain? Would they be able to keep from murdering one another as they were continually forced indoors for warmth?

Keith always busied himself with one project or another. Taking down trees was his favourite task to do. Mr. Steel had to approve every tree that went down, but then Keith did all the labour. He used an axe in order to save on gas, and learned the best angles at which to chop. Cutting a tree down took hours, sometimes spilling over from one day into the next. After it was down, he then set to work turning the branches into kindling and the trunk into firewood. He'd then dig, removing the stump and cutting up roots. While they'd need the firewood for the winter, Mr. Steel mostly approved their removal for garden space. Big trees meant there had to be soil beneath them, and the island was covered in more rocks than dirt. People regularly offered to help Keith, but he always claimed not to need it. He didn't even like them hanging around just to talk while he worked, not if they were going to bring up the past.

The first snowfall came in November. It was a light flurry, and had been preceded by plenty of frosty mornings. No one who went out fishing saw any dirt devils while the snow had been falling, but then they didn't see the monsters all that often even during the dry spells.

The lake started to freeze. Russell had helped Jack steal what they needed to redo the water system so that it was heated all the way through, and the pipes wouldn't burst. Everyone complained on the days the water had to be shut off for this job, but praised them when they were finished. Keeping the lines heated meant more energy usage, and so the hot plate was removed from the system, and all their food got cooked on an old fashioned, wood-fed iron stove, or a bonfire outside. They even used the barbecue on special occasions, when they thought there was a meal worth the propane usage. Aisling had spotted another cottage nearby with solar panels, and there were plans to figure out how to take them and safely attach them to their system on the island.

The worst time was when the lake was covered in a layer of ice that was too thick in parts to push the canoes and kayaks through, but too thin in others to walk on. Not only was everyone confined more to the island, but the number of fish brought in was reduced. Keith despised the taste of fish, so he didn't mind so much about the latter.

One morning, they awoke to find the lake frozen completely solid. It was carefully tested, and found stable enough to walk on. This was when everyone worried most about the dirt devils, until Mandy spotted a pair, off in the distance, checking out this winter feature. No one had noticed that dirt devils run hot. As one of the things stepped gingerly onto the ice, its clawed feet started to melt it, the resulting water causing it enough pain for it to retreat. The second devil ran a short distance out onto the ice, and then wheeled around to return to land. So they could probably cross short distances if they were angry, but hopefully not long ones. Mandy had watched them experiment through a pair of binoculars and reported her findings, sending up a general cheer.

When the snow came down in a thick layer that stayed, that's when everyone started calling the place a winter house. Not *the* winter house, but *a* winter house: a place that could be safely lived in during the winter. There were some who hoped to move back out into tents in the summer, perhaps even onto other small islands where they could spend a week at a time fishing before bringing their catches back.

The thick snow hadn't come before Christmas, making the holiday a limp affair filled with more depression than joy, but when it had fallen in early January, their spirits soared. The dirt devils would melt the snow just as easily as the ice, so they were trapped beneath the protective blanket. There was a sense of freedom, despite the blasting gusts of icy temperatures. Snowmobiles, along with snowshoes and skis, were eventually found, and they really opened up a lot of the lake. Cottages all over the place were now accessible so long as a dirt devil wasn't in residence; the raiding no longer needed to wait for bad weather. As long as there was snow on the ground, they could go out. The gas for the snowmobiles was limited, but with them, they could even steal beds to replace the couches and air mattresses people were sleeping on. Mr. Steel told everyone to keep an eye out for milled wood, because he had books on construction that would allow them to expand the cottage and make more bedrooms.

Keith kept making firewood. He'd walk over to the mainland in his snowshoes, where a tree had fallen, and hack it up. Because he had to walk there, and then walk back with the logs on a sled behind him, he didn't get nearly as much done as on the island. But he was alone while he chopped, and that was worth the effort.

Then spring came and Keith ruined everything.

61:
NOW

KEITH'S DREAMS LED him into some sort of factory. He assumed that's what it must be because of the sound. It was repetitive, and layered. A squeak, and a clunk, and a whoosh of water. Over and over again as he ran through the building, trying to find a place to hide. Not from a dirt devil, like at the start of his dream, no. This time he ran from himself.

The sound kept growing louder, approaching, filling the world.

Keith woke with a start, realizing that the sound wasn't from his dream, but was in reality. Something was coming toward him, was practically right outside.

After snatching up his hatchet, he unzipped the tent flap and threw himself out. He landed in the area he considered the tent's porch, where he kept the little propane tanks secure. With a single bound, he was out from under the overhang, and standing on the raft, the hatchet held high over his head.

A woman screamed, startled by his sudden appearance.

Keith took a second to make sense of what he was looking at. The sound he had heard was the woman's paddleboat. The squeak and clunk had been the turning of the pedals and wheel, the whoosh the water being pushed underneath it. The woman was old, older than Keith's mother, but not as old as Mr. Steel.

"I'm sorry, I didn't mean to frighten you!" the woman shouted, still frightened herself.

Keith realized he was still brandishing the hatchet. He lowered it and himself. It was easier to see her that way; she was shaded by a plastic roof attached to the paddleboat. As he sat on his raft, he got low enough to see that the port side seat beside her, along with the back storage wells, were filled with supplies. He put his hatchet down, feeling a little embarrassed. What on earth had he thought was outside that he'd be able to use a hatchet on? Well, there was always Sidebottom.

"I'm sorry," Keith mumbled. "You startled me."

"I figured." The woman sat with a hand on her rather pronounced bosom, trying to slow her heart rate. "Catch you sleeping, did I?"

"Yes." He rubbed at his eyes as if to prove it.

"Are you all alone?" She searched around the area, where no other boats were to be seen.

"I am." Keith felt his hackles rise again. Was this woman a bandit? She looked nothing like what he imagined one to look like, but then he also never thought an old biddy would stick a revolver into his belly either, until it had happened. His eyes quickly darted about her boat, searching for a gun.

"You poor dear. How long have you been on your own?"

Keith shrugged, not wanting to answer.

"Do you have a place to go?"

"What do you mean?"

"Somewhere on land that you're going to. An island."

"Not right now."

She nodded briskly. "Right then, you should come with me."

"I don't know you."

"Oh, of course, how silly of me." She'd drifted broadside, and now reached over the gap of water between them, holding out her hand. "My name is May."

"Keith." He found himself thinking of Aunt May from Spider-Man, even though this woman carried a lot more weight on her bones. It made him lower his guard some, despite a person's name saying nothing about their personality or motives.

A strange expression seemed to flutter across May's face when she heard Keith's name. When she didn't comment on it, he chalked it up to her having once known someone with the same name. He'd had an odd reaction to meeting a man named Wyatt back at the winter house, because he'd had a close cousin with the same name. That cousin was likely dead now, just as this May's Keith was.

"Well, Keith, I think you should come with me."

"Come where?" He reminded himself that Sidebottom had been helpful until he hadn't been.

"I come from a community. We have several islands free of monsters, and are expanding to more all the time. You don't have to be alone."

Several islands. Keith tried to resist gaping. "How many people are in this community?"

"I don't rightly know. Dozens. We're probably over a hundred now."

That time Keith's jaw did drop. "Over a hundred?" he spluttered.

May's smile made her eyes glitter. "That's right. And that's just our community. We're in contact with others over the radio."

Keith struggled to take in this revelation. Multiple communities, and just one had over a hundred people by itself. If he hadn't already been sitting down, he'd have fallen over.

"I know, it's a lot to take in, especially if you've been alone for a long time," May chuckled. Then she noticed the pallor of Keith's face. "Are you alright, Keith? You're starting to look a little green."

Keith nodded, but he was actually having a bit of a panic attack and trying not to throw up.

"I can see you've done quite nicely for yourself," May chattered on, praising his heap of supplies. "But humans are a social species. It's obviously your decision, but I really think you should come with me. There's always work in need of more hands."

Keith lost the fight. He got himself to the other side of the raft in time, so at least May didn't have to watch him vomit.

"A meal disagreeing with you?" May asked hopefully. "It happens to the best of us."

Keith muttered.

"What was that?"

He splashed water both in and around his mouth before turning back to face May. "I don't deserve it," he admitted again, this time loud enough that she could hear.

"Well, no one deserves a tummy ache, but they happen."

"No. I don't deserve to come with you. I don't deserve to be around people." *Other than Sidebottom.*

"Nonsense."

"I did something terrible, May!"

Her mouth flattened into a line, and her brows pinched, but she wasn't looking at Keith in anger, she was staring off to one side, thinking. "Lots of us have done terrible things." She said each word very carefully, before facing Keith again. "You at least seem to feel guilt over whatever it is you believe you did. Do you want to pay for that guilt? Then it's not up to you to set the punishment. Come with me. We have a sort of court system in place, and they deal with this kind of thing all the time. You can sit before them, explain everything in detail, and they will decide the appropriate punishment. Maybe it'll be hard labour, maybe it'll just be bland rations. Maybe it'll even be banishment. But they would decide, not you. It'll give you a chance to apologize as well."

"I don't think there's anyone left to apologize to." Keith felt his stomach churn again.

"If there's no one specific, then you can apologize to humanity as a whole. But you might be surprised. We've had plenty of new people show up since the spring. It's possible you know at least one of them."

"I doubt it."

"Come with me. I insist."

Having someone else cast judgement on his actions did have a certain sort of appeal.

"Come on. Do what you need to do to get ready, and follow me." Her voice held a note of command, and Keith intended to obey.

In his tent, Keith changed into his swimsuit. May was polite, and turned her whole paddleboat to face the other way while Keith slipped off the far side of the raft to give his body a quick scrub and to pee. He chose a Gatorade for that day's drink, plunking the tall bottle into the kayak's cup holder after removing the tarp. Despite skipping dinner, he wasn't hungry yet, but he had food with him that he could eat without preparation for when he was. After he slathered on the sunscreen and donned his hat and T-shirt, he was ready.

"Do you want me to tow that tube for you?" May asked, having to raise her voice a little to be heard over the sound of her noisy paddleboat.

"I'll keep holding on to it for now."

"All right. Makes it easier for me to keep pace anyway." Even at full speed, her craft wasn't very fast, and if Keith hadn't been towing so much weight, he'd easily outpace her.

Most of the journey was silent, other than the rhythmic clunking of May's boat, but a few times they spoke. Keith told May how he had gotten to where he was, about his journey through the rushes. She was very interested in the marina he told her about, and downright excited by the map he'd taken.

"We're always looking for places with useful items," she explained. "Also islands we could add to our expansion process."

"I saw a moose living on an island."

"A moose!"

"I don't know its exact location but I think it's on that map. If I told you where it is, would you promise not to hunt it?"

"Yes, I promise. Everyone would promise. We're very careful about large animals we find on islands. There's this one island, near where I live, where a pair of.swans have made their nesting ground. I'm not kidding when I say they have an armed guard. We're pretty much all vegetarians these days. Well, except for the fish. A moose! Wow! That must have been something."

"It was."

It was going to take a few days to reach the community, but since they were following May's route home, she knew all the best places to stop for the night. Keith told her that he didn't need an island, just shallow water to anchor in, but she stopped at small islands anyway.

"I *can* sleep in the boat, but I always wake up with all sorts of pains," she explained while setting up her tent on a long stretch of dirt-free rock. "If I can get out, I do. Probably good for my back as well, getting to stand up for a bit and stretch. That's very clever of you to tow that raft along. Your own personal island." May did a lot more of the talking than Keith, and he liked it that way. He liked her enthusiasm about everything, and he especially enjoyed whenever she told him some story that involved the community. She really seemed to love it there, but also explained that she needed time to herself on occasion. It's why she volunteered to go out in her paddleboat to search for people and expansion opportunities. She said that being alone for a couple of weeks would make her appreciate the company again. Keith liked the idea that if he didn't want to be around people, he could disappear for a while and still be useful to the community.

That night, after he'd drifted off to sleep in his tent, he dreamed of the worst thing he had ever done.

62: THEN

SPRING CAME AND BROUGHT mixed feelings. The warming air and the chance to plant were reasons to rejoice, but the unfrozen lake was not. There was no more walking anywhere. If you wanted some time alone, you had to take one of the canoes or kayaks.

Russell had stopped inviting Keith to come fishing. Keith still had zero interest in fishing, but he missed the invites. He missed even the illusion of his friend wanting to hang out with him. One morning, when the day was very hot and humid, he watched Russell paddle off in one of the canoes with Mandy. It looked like rain was coming in, so they probably weren't planning on fishing, but instead were going to raid a cottage for supplies. Keith would have gone raiding with them if he'd been asked, but he hadn't been. Instead, he stayed on the island and helped Mr. Steel with the garden expansion.

"We need more dirt again," Mr. Steel huffed.

"Well it is supposed to rain soon. I can go get more."

Mr. Steel nodded, since that was his intention in bringing it up.

Keith thought about asking Tully to come with him, but he found her hanging laundry. She looked busy, so he didn't bother her. He gathered the tools he needed and headed out in a canoe on his own.

He followed the direction that he'd seen Russell and Mandy take, thinking that maybe he could gather his dirt from whatever cottage they planned to raid. They hadn't gone as far as he had expected. Rounding a corner, he spotted their canoe anchored a little way offshore, waiting for the rain. They were both sitting in the middle of the boat. They were kissing.

Keith was confused at first, feeling that he must be mistaken, but he was not. His emotions quickly plunged into rage. He dug deep with his paddle to turn around, to leave them, but he was spotted.

"Keith! Keith, wait!" Russell called. Based on the tone of his voice, he knew Keith was angry.

Keith didn't wait. He paddled onward, searching for a place where he could gather some dirt. Where he could do his job. It started raining.

"Keith!" Russell had managed to pull up the anchor and follow after him. His shouting chased Keith across the water, but Keith ignored him. Pretended he wasn't there. Disrespected him, as he had felt disrespected. He found a spot to put to shore and gathered his tools.

Russell followed. His canoe pushed up alongside his, and he sprang out after Keith. Mandy remained in the boat, her expression one of sour annoyance.

"Keith, stop, man!" Russell finally caught up to him and grabbed his shoulder.

"Fuck you!" Keith's voice squeaked, not the manly bellow he had wanted it to be.

"Dude, come on."

"No, you come on! You know I was half in love with her!"

"You were in love with the idea of her," Russell stated calmly. "You barely know her."

Keith dropped the shovels and buckets and pushed his friend. His former friend. "Like you know her at all?"

"Well, yeah." Russell gave him a look that called him stupid.

"You never hang out with her!"

"How would you know?" Russell was finally starting to get angry. "We haven't hung out in *months*."

"We're together all the time."

Russell snorted. "That's a lie, and you know it. When do we even occupy the same space? When we're sleeping in the same room? The handful of times we bump into each other over meals? Those don't count as hanging out. I can't remember the last time we even exchanged this many words with one another."

"That doesn't give you the right."

"The *right*? The right to what? Wait, Mandy!? Are you fucking shitting me right now?" For him to start cursing, he must be truly furious. "You think that just because you had a crush on her in school gives you some sort of claim? Dude, you haven't even talked to her in forever. That's one of the things *we* talk about! You're a fucking mess! Mandy and I hang out all the time, which you'd know if you came fishing with us even *once*."

"You stopped inviting me." Keith hated knowing that he sounded like a petulant child.

"Because you always said no! Even worse, you seemed annoyed that I was asking, so I stopped asking. It *hurt*, every time you refused, so I stopped giving you the chance to wound me. I figured if you wanted to come one day, you'd let me know."

On the inside, Keith was a hurricane. Negative emotions raged in a swirl through his head and heart. He hated Russell so much right then he wanted to actually punch him, but at the same time, he wanted to hit himself just as much.

"I thought you and Aisling were going to be a thing." Keith didn't know what words were going to come out of his mouth until they did.

"Aisling's not interested in me like that. We're just friends. Speaking of which, *Mandy* has a say in all of this too, you know."

"I know that!"

"Do you? Because she came onto *me*, not *you*. She's attracted to *me*, not *you*. Maybe things could've worked out differently, maybe she'd have ended up seeing you differently, but ever since your dad died—"

The frayed thread of control snapped, and Keith threw his fist into his best friend's face. His former friend.

"Fuck!" Russell cried out, muffled by the hands that had gone up to hold his nose. When he removed them to look, they were covered in blood. More poured down over his mouth and chin and stained his shirt.

Keith was stunned by the amount of blood, and in that moment, Russell struck back. He grabbed Keith's shoulders, pulled him over, and drove his knee up into his gut. The air whooshed out of Keith. He fell to his knees gasping for air.

"No wonder Tully doesn't even want to hang out with you anymore, and she's the nicest person I've ever met." Russell stormed off, and by the time Keith managed to get a foot under himself, Russell had gotten back into his canoe and explained everything to Mandy.

"Fuck you, Keith!" Mandy shouted, unseen between the trees.

Keith finally managed to get up. He stumbled toward the lake, but Russell and Mandy were already gone. What would he have said, anyway? That he was sorry? Because he wasn't. Maybe for a brief window he had been, but he was in that deep pit of his mind now, the one that tried to deflect all the blame onto others.

I have a job to do, Keith reminded himself.

But he was furious. Gathering dirt was a process that took time. To make sure what he gathered was good and safe, he'd normally dig up a shovelful, and dump it on a large metal tray he'd dragged up there with him. He'd then sift through it with his hands to remove the rocks, and to search for any dirt devils in small form. It was too finicky a routine for his current state of rage. Instead, he just hauled up the dirt and dumped it into the buckets as it was.

The greatest mistake of his life.

Keith had filled all the buckets, and the rain kept falling. He placed them in his canoe, and paddled back to the island. He saw Russell and Mandy's canoe already there. He didn't want to see either of them. He didn't want to see anyone, but that was kind of impossible.

Keeping his mind focused on work, Keith picked up one bucket at a time, and brought them over to the garden site. Mr. Steel would tell him where they should go, but he was inside right now. The rain was bad for the old man, even a warm shower like this one, which didn't last long. As Keith moved his buckets, he caught people staring at him. So Russell had told everyone. Good, let them know what had happened, maybe then they'd leave Keith alone.

That's what Keith had been thinking all through autumn and winter: *leave me alone*. Despite those words, what he really wanted was someone to understand. To say and do the right things, to comfort him the way he needed. But no one did, because anyone who made the attempt got pushed away. They did what he told them to do instead of what he needed them to do. It angered Keith, and the subconscious knowledge that the anger wasn't fair to anyone only fed his self-hatred.

It rained all night, and no one talked to Keith. They looked at him like they thought about it, but his scowl repelled them all. The expressions he hated seeing most were the ones of pity.

Early the next morning, Keith was walking down to where they kept the boats, intending to bail out the canoe he had left upright. The sharp pierce of a sudden scream had him dropping into a crouch, his eyes widening.

"*Dirt devil!*" someone shouted, just as Keith spotted it smashing Mr. Steel into a tree.

I did this.

Keith stopped thinking at that point. He was closer to the kayaks than he was the canoes. He flipped over the nearest of them, snatched up the paddle beside it, and pushed out into the water. It's what everyone was told, again and again: what to do if a dirt devil ever found its way onto the island. Surely they would all be right behind him.

Digging his paddle deep, his mind on fire with guilt and fright, Keith headed out over the water. He paddled and paddled and paddled, until he had what he thought he wanted. He was completely alone.

63:
NOW

THERE WAS NO recovery from that. Keith continued to follow May, but what drove him on was justice. People had to know what he had done. They had to know that he was responsible for the deaths of probably everyone on that island. He needed to be punished for it. He accepted his guilt, wholly and completely, and was finally ready to face the consequences.

It took two more days to reach the community May had spoken of. Keith had the same dream each night along the way. All that blood on Russell's hands and face. Mr. Steel hitting a tree. They were added to the collection of other horrible images he had in his mind, but these were the ones that were his fault.

"We'll head to the main island first," May explained as people appeared on a shoreline ahead. "You'll stay there while our organizers decide where to place you."

"And the judges?"

"They'll talk to you there, too. It's part of the process."

Keith couldn't believe how many islands they passed. Some people looked at them because of Keith's haul, but most ignored them, used to seeing small boats moving about. Canoes, kayaks, paddleboats, paddleboards, and every other type of human-propelled vessel were travelling the water between the islands.

"So many," Keith gasped. "All these islands are safe? No dirt devils? Err, no monsters, I mean?" While dirt devils was a pretty self-explanatory name, he wasn't sure if May would understand right away.

"That's right. We have a pretty effective way of testing for them. You call them dirt devils?"

"Yeah. A friend of mine came up with it." *She's probably dead now.* "How do you test for them?"

"Electricity. We have a ton of boat batteries, that we hook up to these big metal rods that we then shove into the ground. The little buggers hate it. They come straight to the surface, faster than worms. We do it when it's raining, because then they don't want to get big. They pop around like a kernel of corn in a hot pan, trapped between two things they hate. Makes them easy to find. We gotta be real careful though. A few people have been electrocuted, and those little guys will still hurt you badly if you grab them. We wear steel mesh gloves as a precaution, but once they're popping, you just gotta slap them into a bucket of water. Bingo, bango, no more monster."

"Wow. Who came up with the idea?"

"Some military scientists."

"The military?"

"Scientists, yeah, they set up this whole operation. Here, and a bunch of other places. Came swooping in on helicopters. I'm one of the few people who was already here at the time, and it was quite the sight, let me tell you. They plan to take back all the habitable islands first, and the hope is that once the civilian population is stable enough, they can then scale up their efforts to work on the mainland. That'll be much harder given the size of the mainland, of course."

"Of course." Keith could barely believe it. Take back the mainland? That was within the realm of possibility? Really?

"Here we are." May guided Keith to a large dock, where a bunch of watercraft bristled along every inch of it. She headed for the nearby beach instead, where more small boats were waiting, but there was still room for both of them. The island was big enough that Keith wouldn't have known it was an island if it weren't for the people on it. The place had several cottages that he could see; he assumed there were more that he couldn't.

"Now, you go on up there and introduce yourself," May said, pointing to the closest A-frame cottage after they'd secured their craft on the beach. "Just tell them that I collected you."

"Wait, you're not coming with me?" Keith had grown to like May's presence, and was nervous about meeting new people whom he'd have to spill his guts to.

"There's some people I want to find first. Actually, wait a minute." May peered through the trees at a cottage next door where a few people were on the deck. "There's one of them now. Hey, Aisling!"

Keith jumped from the name, startled. This woman knew someone named Aisling? And she had known someone named Keith? His brain was spinning in the attempt to make sense, giving the Aisling who had been called over enough time to emerge from the tress.

And it was Aisling. *The* Aisling, the one Keith knew, the one he had abandoned to the dirt devil he had brought to their island. Her mouth dropped as she saw him, but she kept on coming.

"I *knew* I knew the name Keith," May chuckled. "When they came, they told us about the kid they lost. I *knew* it had to be you, especially when you called them things dirt devils."

Keith was barely listening. Aisling had started running over, multiple emotions fighting for dominance on her face.

She punched Keith. No slapping from her, just a solid fist connecting with the side of his head. Keith had no instinct to strike back, knowing he deserved it. Besides, he couldn't, the blow was so fierce and surprising, that he collapsed. Or he would have, had Aisling not followed up her strike with an equally fierce hug that threatened to crush him. It had been so long since anyone had hugged Keith. The tears were squeezed right out of him.

"I'm sorry," Keith sobbed into her shoulder. "I'm so sorry. I . . . I'm so fucking sorry."

"You better be," Aisling gasped. Was she also crying? *Aisling?* "You had us so fucking scared, you idiot. Where did you go? What happened to you?" She pushed him away, held him at arm's length. Her eyes glistened, and she didn't wipe the tears away.

"It's my fault. The dirt devil. It's all my fault."

"Yeah, I know. Where did you go?"

"In a kayak, like we were told."

"You weren't told to fuck off to nowhere. You were supposed to stay in the bay."

"I . . . I couldn't stay there. Everyone . . . Did anyone else survive?"

"Yeah, pretty much all of us. Jack turned the hose on the thing and managed to get it right in the face. Got that seed thing, I guess.

We watered it down until it stopped moving. Mr. Steel didn't make it though."

Keith dry-heaved, guilt and relief fighting for dominance.

"Keith . . . Did you think we were all dead? All this time?"

He nodded. "I thought I'd killed you all," he hiccuped.

Aisling hugged him again. "Christ. We thought you'd killed yourself, if I'm being honest. After your depression, and then your fight with Russell . . . We should have tried harder to help you."

Keith sobbed. He couldn't form words that made sense. Aisling blamed herself? That was far from right.

"Aisling? Who is . . . Holy shit, it's Keith!"

Aisling pushed Keith away, quickly wiping at her eyes, embarrassed to be caught hugging him.

"*Renly*?" Keith's knees wavered. "What are you . . . ? How . . . ?"

"Who do you think told the military to come here?"

"The generals who have maps and knew this was a spot full of freshwater islands, and was a good, strategic place to set up a community," Aisling snapped at him.

"Fuck off, Aisling. Keith, man, it's great to see you. You should have come with us. It was mad crazy! Getting those big-ass ships through those locks was like a war every time. And the fucking military ships! So badass!" Renly continued to spout on in his curse-filled way about living with the fleet, and learning about the dirt devils' weaknesses—he learned through the fleet's civilian grapevine—and how he and his mom volunteered to join this place since the military needed to get rid of the civilians around them. He had just started describing the helicopter ride when more people Keith knew showed up.

Tully. Carol. Frankie. They were all staying on the main island, and word had spread fast, especially since May had gone off specifically to spread it. Even Mandy came.

"Markus and Janet are here," she told Keith. "Do you remember them?"

"Of course." The couple who had gone their own way. They'd survived.

"I also saw Saksham the other day. He's not on this island right now, but he'll want to say hi. We can go see him later."

So Sidebottom had been telling the truth. He hadn't killed Saksham after all.

When Russell showed up, he came at a run. Keith stiffened, preparing himself for another blow like Aisling's. But Russell wasn't that kind of person. He reached Keith out of breath and, still puffing, drew him into a warm embrace.

With so many people around, Keith didn't want to start sobbing again, but it was a hard fight. Aisling, ever astute, managed to convince the others to leave them alone, and guided them toward the cottage, even Renly who admitted to her that he was "confused as fuck."

"I'm so sorry," Keith told Russell.

Russell held him away like Aisling had and looked him right in the eye. Keith expected anger, but as usual, he was wrong.

"Dude," Russell said. "We're brothers. Sometimes brothers fight."

Keith couldn't remember the last time he had laughed, even chuckled, and the sound made a wide smile spread across Russell's face.

Keith suddenly sobered again. "I killed Mr. Steel."

"He was dying anyway. He had cancer, you know?"

"I didn't." How many more times was Keith going to be shocked today?

"I kind of guessed. You spent all that time with him, but I figured you weren't really talking."

"Still, cancer or not, I killed him. It's my fault."

"I know. You'll have to face the judges here."

"I'm ready."

"They already know the whole story from us. Well, pretty much the whole story; obviously we don't know your exact part of it. Just tell me one thing: did you know you had dug up a dirt devil? Did you *know*?"

Keith shook his head. "I didn't. But I didn't take the precautions we were supposed to."

Russell sighed like a weight had been taken off of him. "I knew there was no way you would have brought that thing back on purpose, but . . . you were so angry."

"I know. And I'm sorry."

"I'm still dating Mandy, by the way." Russell smiled.

"Good. I'm glad." And he was.

"Now straighten yourself out. There are lots of girls here that you haven't met yet, and some of them are celebrity hot."

Keith laughed again, and it felt good. Horrible, because of the guilt and shame still in him, but also good.

"How did you get here?" Keith asked Russell as they walked slowly toward the A-frame.

"The day after you left, a group of Indigenous people showed up. They told us all about this place, and we agreed to join them. You should have been there. When we headed out in the morning, there was this whole celebration about it."

"Was there singing?"

"Yeah."

"I heard the singing, but it was so far away, I started to think I had dreamt it. I couldn't get to you guys. I took a wrong turn and went down some rapids."

"You'll have to tell me all about it."

"I will. Especially since I ran into Sidebottom."

"Mr. Sidebottom? Pontoon boat guy?"

"The same. Had the same pontoon boat, too. I guess he found a way up the lock, or somehow got around it. And get this, he kidnapped me for a bit so that I'd steal this weird thing from the dirt devils. I think it was an egg."

"An egg? Think you can draw it?"

"Yeah."

"Make sure to tell them that." He pointed to the building they now stood in front of. "They want to know everything they can about the dirt devils. All information like that gets passed on to the eggheads."

"Yeah, I figured." Keith glanced through the windows. They were being watched by a group of adults. They looked official, and were waiting for Keith. Aisling stood awkwardly near them. She must have told them he was here. That was okay. Keith was ready to face whatever came.

"Hey, Keith?" Russell grabbed his wrist before he could reach the door.

"Yeah?"

"I'm really glad to have you back."

"I'm glad to be here."

"No, I mean . . . I'm really glad to have *you* back."

Keith nodded. "I know what you meant. And I'm really glad to be here."

Russell returned his nod. "I can't come in, but I'll be waiting right here for the news. I'm sure you'll be fine. Trust me when I say that some people have done a lot worse, and they're still around. They get the shitty jobs and are closely watched, but they're still around."

Keith looked past his friend to the bright green kayak on the shore, the raft and tube still hitched to the back, all his supplies still loaded. It was ready to go. He could leave, right now. The little craft had never looked so small before.

"Russell, I don't plan to go anywhere for a long time. I'm staying with you, brother."

Russell patted his shoulder, and Keith opened the door. Aisling gave him an encouraging smile and a thumbs up as she was ushered out through the back.

"Mr. Benchley, I'm sure your friends warned you about the judgement that will take place here today. Are you ready to proceed?"

Had this happened a month ago, he would not have been.

Keith pulled back the chair he'd been gestured toward and sat down. "I'm ready."

ABOUT THE CONTRIBUTORS

All her life, **Kristal Stittle** has split her time between the city of Toronto and the woods of Muskoka. Trained in 3D animation, she continues to create images when not writing. You can find all of her works, along with her internet dwelling, by visiting [kristalstittle] [dot] [com].

Kerisson Wemerson (@kerissonlp) is an illustrator, designer and visual artist passionate about storytelling. He is known for his work on book covers, advertising, music and for his personal project, MusicComics, in which he creates sequential art through excerpts of songs, giving images and stories to the melodies and lyrics that often inspire his linework.

Blacky Shepherd is a Pacific Northwest-based artist and writer, best known for his Horror collaborations with Cullen Bunn. He's also done work on *G.I. Joe* and *Transformers* for IDW Comics, and is currently working on a boutique toy line based on his original characters.

GRAB ANOTHER TENEBROUS TITLE!

Grab another Tenebrous title!

Home of New Weird Horror, New Weird Dark Fiction, Oddities, Abnormalities and All Manner of Eccentricities You Never Knew You Needed More Than Oxygen

FIND OUT MORE:

www.tenebrouspress.com

@TenebrousPress on social media

HAIL THE TENEBROUS CULT